Dear Ana,

I.I.E

For me,

and for anyone else who wants their story to count

too.

The heart beating in my chest belonged to the girl buried six feet under where I was standing.

ten years earlier

Dear Ana,

Hospital food sucks.

I've been staring at what looks like chicken and vegetables on the plate in front of me for twenty minutes now, but it still hasn't transformed into a juicy burger. Maybe the nurse will feel bad and give me two puddings for dessert.

If you were thinking that I'm talking about food as a stall tactic, you thought correctly. I don't know why I'm doing this. The psychiatrist that's been visiting me every day since I've been admitted suggested I start writing in a journal as a way of coping with my accident. I thought it was useless at first—I still do. But then I heard them mention you the other night when they thought I was sleeping and your name has been consuming my mind ever since.

You don't know me and I don't know you, but we're connected in a way most people will never understand. You gave me a part of yourself. A huge *part. The single most essential part of all living things. Now every breath I take feels . . . stolen. I can hear your heart beating your name in my ears, and pumping blood that isn't mine through my veins.*

You saved my life, and I know I should be thankful, but all I feel is guilt. A heavy, suffocating feeling of guilt that's made its bed right on my chest and doesn't want to leave. It works its way uninvited into every thought that crosses my mind and I can't push it out. I don't know how to live with the burden that someone had to die in order for me to be alive.

Ana. *Who knew one word could hold so much meaning? Before last night you were just an organ, but now you're a person. A* girl, *with a family and friends who loved you, and are probably broken right now because I snatched you away from them.*

I should be thankful, but I'm not. I should be relieved and happy to be alive, but I'm not. Because the truth is, Ana, as guilty as I am, I'm also angry. I'm filled with an intense rage that's burning a trail through my body and scorching every part of me your blood touches.

Yes, you saved my life. But you saved my life when I didn't want it to be saved.

NOW

I pressed my hand on my chest in a failed attempt at calming down the thumps beating erratically against my ribcage. It *knew*. Her heart knew where I was, and it was desperately trying to claw through my chest cavity and escape back to its rightful owner.

Ana Williams
Beloved Daughter, Sister, and Friend
Your Heart Will Live Forever
1992-2010

I still couldn't believe it had already been ten years. Ten fucking years since the worst day of my life. I always assumed Ana was my age, but according to her gravestone, she was three years older than me. Or *would* be, if she was still alive. At least she was frozen at the ripe age of eighteen. At least she never had to worry about getting old and wrinkly.

At least she was dead.

"Your heart will live *forever*," I repeated under my breath, and a strangled laugh tumbled from my lips. Did her family put that there because they knew I would visit her one day? Did they mean it metaphorically? Religiously? Or were they just stating facts because they knew someone else had her heart? Either way, it felt like a slap in the face. A slap I unequivocally deserved.

None of that mattered, though. I wasn't here to analyze her gravestone or pretend to weep over her oh, *so* tragic death. I was here because I needed my last moment on this earth to mean something. My lungs' last breath needed to be significant enough that it would make up for the weak and pathetic act I was about to submit to. So far the only thing this place was doing for me, was ripping open the hole in my soul even wider than it was before.

It wasn't guilt tearing me apart. It wasn't grief, or sadness, or shame. Those feelings were consistent and steady and I barely noticed their presence anymore. This was something else. Something bigger and deeper that I recognized instantaneously, like an old friend—no, not a friend—an *acquaintance* that I knew since birth but kept my distance because I saw how they treated the people close to me. I saw how quickly they tainted your innocence with toxicity and turned you into a monster and I didn't want to be a monster, but sometimes I couldn't resist saying hello just to see how it felt. *This* was one of those sometimes as I stood here, glowering at a fancy stone inscribed with ironic metaphors and that new but old anger rising up into my lungs, chest, throat, and begging to come out in a wave of dreadful vengeance.

The scene played out behind my eyes and suddenly a shovel appeared and I was vigorously digging away at the snow and wet dirt standing between me and the forever eighteen-year-old girl resting peacefully beneath my feet. The shovel wasn't enough so I dropped onto my hands and knees and desperately started scooping out the oozy mud with my nails. Her coffin flung open and I was finally face to face with the person who stole my eternity of solitude in this silent field of wilderness and dead people. I grabbed her rotting corpse and shook her out of her relaxing slumber to show her what she caused, and what had become of me over the last ten miserable years—

I blinked. Her coffin disappeared, the dirt was back in its place and my nonexistent shovel vanished into thin air. As satisfying as my vivid imagination made it seem, I didn't *do* messy and loud. I was going to take back the future she snatched away from me quietly. *Softly*. And no one could fucking stop me.

Ana couldn't stop me.

I took a deep and shuddering breath to steady her frantic heart. Death . . . the word was sugar marinating on my tongue and tainting my saliva with all of its sweetness. It filled my mind with a delightful explosion of liberation and freedom. I was scared—*of course* I was. My skeleton was quivering with anticipation and fear, but no afterlife could be more agonizing than having to live another day on this damned earth. Getting myself to do it was the hard part, but I knew the pleasurable thrill of relief would follow soon after. I couldn't wait to feel her heart thump its last cursed beat in my chest. I couldn't wait to feel nothing forever.

Don't worry, I reassured her frazzled organ, *you'll be reunited with your suitable owner soon.*

As would I.

I reached my trembling hand into my pocket and slowly pulled out my gracious savior—

"Excuse me."

My head whipped up at the sound of his voice, the contents of my pocket slipping through my fingertips and disappearing in the wet snow. The mix of rain and flurries were falling too heavily for me to see anything except for a silhouette looming over me, but his voice hit me clear and precise, almost like his lips spoke the words directly into my ear. They didn't stop there. I felt his velvet speech flow smoothly into every part of my body without consent. I stood up quickly, my foot discreetly moving to further conceal the tiny pills, and pushed back my hood to get a better view.

Piercing green and blue eyes were glaring at me. I blinked a few times to adjust my vision, but the mismatched gaze only belonged to one person . . . like his eye color gene couldn't decide which parent to give him so instead he got one of each. I met his glare with curiosity but quickly looked away once I noticed the red rims.

The glassy veil of previously shed tears.

The flowers fisted in his grip, withering under the weather.

"I'm sorry," I whispered without thinking, desperately racking my brain for something to say. But what could I possibly say? He was here, which meant he knew Ana, and would most likely know that *I* didn't. God, how could I be so *stupid*?! Why did I think coming here was a good idea? I should've just done it in my bathroom and called it a fucking day.

"Who are you?" he asked warily, taking a step closer. I immediately took two steps back, my fight or flight reflexes on high alert at his sudden proximity. He lifted his large hand— probably to push the wet hair out of his face, or to adjust his hood that had fallen too far down his forehead—but it didn't matter because I was already gone.

"Wait!" I heard him call out to me, but I didn't look back. I sprinted through the rows of gravestones, disrupting the dead as I sloshed noisily in the rain and silently prayed he wasn't following behind me.

After what felt like hours, I finally saw my car in the distance. I grabbed my keys and quickly unlocked the door, jumping into the driver's seat without bothering to put my seat belt on before starting the ignition and roughly speeding away.

But where was I supposed to go? What was I supposed to do? I had no plan B. I spent five years idealizing my symbolic goodbye to the world—*twenty-five-year-old nobody kills herself at the foot of her heart donor's grave*—yet I never spared a moment to prepare for the possibility of someone intervening.

It wasn't over. I was driving in a storm. If I sped up, crashing would be inevitable . . .

Twenty-five-year-old car crash survivor dies in a car crash on the tenth anniversary of the previously mentioned car crash.

A giggle slipped through my lips at the thought. It wasn't just symbolic—it was poetic.

I fixed my determined, unrelenting, *unwavering* gaze on the busy intersection flashing red, tightened my gloved fingers around the wheel, and pressed my foot deeper into the gas pedal . . .

. . . and then drove straight into an abandoned parking lot.

I turned my car off and threw the keys in the passenger seat with a frustrated shriek.

Look at me.

"No," I snapped.

Only a second passed before I reluctantly glanced at my rearview mirror.

Coward.

I had specifically booked time off from both my jobs so I could get the deed done at her grave. *What a waste*, I thought bitterly. I knew deep down nothing good would come out of visiting her, but I was desperate. Desperate for a solution.

Desperate for an escape. Desperate for a way out of the shackles of misery my life had me confined in. That's why, despite all logic, I broke multiple rules at work and illegally used my login information to search up my medical records to figure out her full name. It wasn't my fault. I'd asked a million questions over the years—*How old was she? How did she die? Did you see her family? Did her family see me?*

No one ever gave me any answers.

Ana Williams. Such a plain and ordinary name for the plain and ordinary girl who just happened to be the center of my universe. I was always imagining a faceless girl in my mind when I pictured her, but now I had all the pieces to complete the puzzle. Except it wasn't the beautiful, smiling girl I saw online. No, my sick and twisted brain automatically altered her face to what I assumed it would look like today.

Expired. Lifeless. *Deceased.*

Not only did this trip fail to provide me with even a *hint* of closure, it somehow managed to make me feel worse, which I didn't think was possible. To make matters even more lovely, my bottle of opioids prescribed ten years ago was now deteriorating in the precious dirt that hugged Ana's grave. That bitch took what should've been my coffin, and because that obviously wasn't enough for her, she also took the only thing I had in my possession that would successfully stop her heart. I mean sure, shoving a kitchen knife through my chest would also do the job just fine, but could I not leave this earth with even a shred of dignity?

Overdosing was clean. *Simple.* No one would even know at first. They would only find out the truth days later, and I knew my parents wouldn't expose me. Not because they cared about me or my reputation, but because it would make *them* look bad. How shameful . . . to have a daughter who killed herself. What a disgraceful fucking *sin*.

I continued to stare through the windshield, my brown eyes reflecting back at me. Except the longer I stared, the more those eyes started to change color as my thoughts drifted to the man at her grave. I knew I wouldn't be the only person visiting Ana on the anniversary of her death, but I thought I was clear after I spent *hours* watching her family and friends come and go from afar like the creepy stalker I was. I watched them mourn over her, cry over her, completely break down over her. I even waited an hour after everyone was gone just to be certain, but of course her line of loved ones wasn't over. It made sense that her boyfriend would want to visit her alone—why didn't I expect that? If I had just *waited* a little longer . . .

I wondered what he would think if he knew he'd just come face to face with the girl who got her heart. Who stole it from the hundreds of people waiting. Maybe he would've thought twice before barging in. Maybe he would've fed me the pills himself.

My phone beeped in my pocket.

where are you? -Mama

I flickered my gaze back up to the window and scowled at those stupid eyes.

The metal cuff around my ankle started to tug roughly.

It was time to go home.

After driving under the speed limit and stopping double the time required at every stop sign, I eventually turned the corner onto my street. The weather was making my vision worse than usual, and I almost didn't notice the car parked in my spot.

A black sedan—Dodge Dart Limited—with red seats and an indent in the bumper.

My blood immediately started pounding roughly in my ears at the sight. I carefully parked in front of my house and cut off the engine before they could see my headlights through the blinds.

I clutched the steering wheel hard, my hands wrapped so tightly around the rubber my nails were digging into my gloved palms. All the air in my car was slipping through the cracks and I suddenly couldn't get enough. I couldn't breathe, and I couldn't move, and I couldn't go *inside*—

But I had to. The sooner I got inside, the faster I could escape into the confines of my room unscathed.

There were exactly 52 steps between the curb and the front porch. I knew this because counting the steps toward my demise was a comforting and distracting act, but it couldn't distract me forever.

I hesitated slightly. I could hear his voice, followed by my parent's laughter. I held back the bile in my throat before pushing open the door.

"Salam Mama, Baba," I said without looking in their direction. I quickly leaned down to remove my sneakers and shoved them into the closet.

"I put your dinner in the microwave, do you want me to heat it—?"

"Not hungry, goodnight," I interrupted, heading for the stairs to make my escape.

"Hi Maya, how are you?"

His voice cut through me like glass, threatening to trigger all the horrific memories floating behind my eyes. I took the stairs two at a time without giving any indication that I heard him, but my mother's words drifted up behind me and jerked my metal cuff, stopping my legs from going any further.

"Don't worry about her, Mikhail," she said soothingly. "You know how Maya is . . ."

But she never finished her sentence. *How am I, Mama?* Nobody knew, least of all her.

I stepped into my room and closed the door, but I could still hear them talking and laughing, making my ears bleed acid. I stripped out of my damp clothes robotically before grabbing my headphones and sitting inside my cramped closet.

My body knew me so well that it immediately started to fold in on itself, making me smaller and letting me hide. It bent at the waist, and then again at the knees as I clutched my abdomen and tried not to let my insides come tumbling out. I knew I was in my room, but I wasn't. Not really. I was trapped in my mind, frantically swimming around and searching through the murky depths of my brain for *something*, but never fucking finding it. I kept searching until eventually I just got lost in the excruciating feeling of hopelessness that was constantly washing over me, and lingering stagnantly in the air I was submerged in.

Just breathe, I reminded myself. *You're safe, Maya. He can't hurt you anymore.*

The tight space in my closet slowly started to cocoon me into a bubble of darkness, and my thoughts once again strayed to the man at Ana's grave. The man who *interrupted* me. I was finally going to do it. I was finally going to jump out of the cycle of detrimental survival I'd been imprisoned in day after day. I was finally ready to sculpt my own future . . . God, who was I kidding? It was so much easier to blame some stranger than admit to myself that I was never going to go through with it.

And in the end, it didn't matter. It didn't matter that my plans got ruined. It didn't matter that I threw in the towel at the last second and surrendered to my fear instead of giving in to my pain. Whether I was buried under the ground or living in this house, they would always be a complete family without me.

Besides, I already died thirteen years ago but nobody noticed because the person that killed me was my brother. He killed me over and over again, but nobody noticed because the blood oozing from my wounds was invisible. It ran clear, camouflaging into my surroundings to remain eternally concealed. Only I could see the bright red puddle of agony I was endlessly immersed in. It was my only constant in this bleak world . . . *he* was my only constant.

I dug my fingers deep into the buds in my ears to forcefully block out all the horrible noise coming from my brain until it was quiet and all I could hear was my shuttered breath. My nerves were still anxiously tingling, but after a few minutes, the silence initiated my body into a state of numbness, protecting me from feeling the full weight of my parent's betrayal and shielding me from the crushing realization that I was completely and unconditionally alone.

THEN

Dear Ana,

We were siblings for twelve years before he started to hit me.

I don't know why I was so surprised when it happened. All the signs were there, in plain fucking sight. It's a straightforward concept, Ana— angry people always start by hitting things around you before ultimately hitting you—and Mikhail was exactly that. Angry. *From the moment my brain was developed enough to understand my surroundings, the first thing I noticed was his rage. It was deep and it was destructive. The second thing I noticed was that it was random. He would be fine for hours, days, weeks, and then . . . boom. An explosion would go off in his soul, obliterating everything and everyone in his path. The problem was that I could never figure out what the trigger was. There was no pattern to follow or routine to memorize so I was constantly on my toes, waiting. Always wary. Always scared.*

And the third thing I noticed about my big brother was that he hated me. It was obvious, Ana. The only thing not obvious was whether his hatred was warranted.

He chose my birthday for the initiation. That was typical for Mikhail. He loved to turn everything into a fucking spectacle. Every breath he took was a theatrical production and I always got a front-row seat, free of charge.

He didn't start right away, for dramatic effect of course. He let me enjoy my chocolate chip pancakes without interruption. Money was tight so I wasn't expecting any presents, but just as I was digging into my second plate my dad told me to come outside with him. I remember squealing with joy at the sight of my new green bike. I could tell from the paint scratches on the sides that it was probably used, but I didn't mind. It was more than I could ever ask for.

That part of my birthday all seems like a fever dream, looking back at it. The one thing that stands out to me now is my brother. At the time, I didn't think much when he never wished me a happy birthday. I never questioned the way he stood beside my smiling parents, watching silently as I rode my new—well, new to me—bike up and down the street. I was too excited to notice how, unlike my parents who were watching me enjoy my gift with delight, he was watching me with disgust.

Which led right into Act I—Mikhail repeatedly plunging a pocket knife into the tires of my bike.

I caught him right after I came back from the bathroom, but he didn't look surprised to see me. He planned it, Ana. Every move was perfectly calculated in his fucked up brain.

"What are you doing, Mikhail?" I demanded, swallowing the sob growing in my throat. I was trying to sound firm but my voice came out exactly how he always made me feel.

He smiled in response. My fear satiated him.

"You're going to get in so much trouble with Mama and Baba!"

"Am I though, Maya?"

He was right, of course. My parents wouldn't do anything. My poor, immigrant parents were too busy trying to navigate through the western world to notice that their precious son was in desperate need of some medical attention. Not that they would have done anything even if they had realized. They were raised in a place and at a time when mental illness wasn't a thing. If you weren't physically broken, then you didn't need fixing. My parents saw his anger as something normal. He's a boy, Maya, and boys get mad.

He just had a bad day, Maya.

Stop being so sensitive, Maya.

He's your brother, Maya.

And when his anger continued to intensify, they saw it as a test from God, and the only solution was to pray, pray, pray . . .

That wasn't the only reason. My parents were also raised to abide by one simple principle. The same principle that the rest of the world seemed to follow as well.

Family. Over. Everything.

So it didn't matter if Mikhail was toxic. It didn't matter if he was a bad son and an even worse brother. He was family, Ana, and that was the end of it.

I should've just walked away like I usually did, but I was so mad at him for ruining my birthday and I let that anger choose for me. I went inside and I tattled on him.

One decision, Ana. One split-second verdict was all it took to change the course of my life forever.

Which immediately prompted Act II.

I ran upstairs just as the yelling started, grabbing the home phone on my way up as my snack of choice. My brother was already cussing at the top of his lungs by the time I closed my door and sat in my closet. I wanted to cover my ears, but I couldn't. I needed to listen. As long as I heard their voices I would know they were safe.

I heard stomping as Mikhail went up to his room, my parents right behind him.

They were screaming now, and Mikhail was calling me a liar. Insisting that I was doing it for attention.

And then he punched the wall . . . for emphasis? Ostentatious effect? The scene wasn't playing out as melodramatic as he wanted? Whatever the reason, it worked. The vibrations from the impact were so strong, they rattled every bone in my body.

My parents backed off after that, retreating to their room without any punishment or discipline for his chaotic and uncalled-for behavior. I stepped out into the hall and saw Mikhail's door wide open in my peripheral view. Before I could stop myself I slowly moved to his room and, after a quick sweep to make sure he wasn't around, I walked inside.

Sure enough, there was a fist-sized hole in our adjoining wall. It looked like his hand had gone completely through, and there were pieces of drywall littered all over his bedspread. I wondered what he was picturing when he did that.

Or who.

I didn't want to be there anymore, so I turned around to leave and nearly jumped out of my skin when I saw Mikhail standing directly behind me.

"Jesus Mikhail," I said, my hand flying to my chest. "You scared me."

He didn't respond. He just continued to stare at me, scattering goosebumps all over. I couldn't understand my body's reaction, or why I suddenly felt like I was exhaling more air than I was inhaling, but my instincts were telling me to escape. The floor was suddenly made of glue, but I forced my feet to move around him. I stepped onto the landing above the stairs and felt the same hand that was previously through the wall wrap around my arm.

"Let go of me," I whispered. I tried to move my arm out of his iron grasp but he wouldn't budge.

He leaned in, closing the small space between us. "Do you think I don't know what you're doing?" he asked, clutching my arm tighter. My teeth sunk into my bottom lip before I could cry out. "You keep making up lies about me to get me into trouble."

"Lies? I just saw you destroying my bike——"

And then he slapped me across the face, swiftly launching us into Act III.

I was confused. Shocked. Unsure if it even happened. If he actually hit *me. But then my cheek started to flare, and my eyes brimmed with tears and my heart, Ana. My heart hurt.*

"I was just trying to teach you a lesson, Maya. Make you better.*"*

I didn't respond.

He hit me, Ana. My brother fucking hit me.

I twisted and turned to get away from him but his grip was airtight, and then suddenly he smiled at me, and I thought oh, okay, this is a joke. *We didn't have that silly and playful brother/sister relationship like other families did, but I forced a smile back anyway and it worked. He let go of my arm . . . before shoving me down the stairs.*

I always imagined falling would be like how they showed it in the movies. My body would soar down in slow motion, defying all the rules of gravity while a coming-of-age song commenced somewhere in the distance. Then, just before the main character fell to the ground, they would wake up in their big comfy bed and sigh in relief because it was just a dream.

But my life wasn't a movie and this wasn't a dream. My back hit one of the thirteen tiled steps first, and then I tumbled the rest of the way down. My limbs were paralyzed from the impact for a few seconds as I lay there feeling nothing, and I briefly wondered if it really was a dream. But then the pain hit me from every angle and I knew it was real.

After a thorough inspection from my mother it was concluded that, besides the bruises covering every inch of my body, I was fine.

I looked fine.

I was completely and utterly fine . . . except I wasn't.

I tried talking to my mom, but she shushed me and then helped me up the stairs and into my bed. It wasn't until later that night when I could finally get myself to take a shower, that I noticed it. Five long bruises were hugging my forearm vertically with one large circle in the center.

A handprint.

I let my anger take over again and decided to give my parents a second chance to redeem themselves. He marked *me, Ana. They couldn't ignore that. I reached the foot of the stairs and could hear my parents in the kitchen talking in hushed voices. Mikhail wasn't with them, which fueled my determination even more.*

"Eviction notice?" Mama said, her voice full of panic. "But it's only been two weeks since the rent was due!"

Her words halted me mid-step.

"It's okay, Fatma, I'm going to call Elizabeth tomorrow," Baba reassured her. "We've never been this late before. I'll just explain our situation and she'll understand."

It was obvious from the strain in his voice that it wasn't going to be easy. I could hear my mom's quiet sniffles as she tried to contain herself, but one painful sob managed to slip through.

Sympathy replaced my anger, and for the second time that day, I made a decision that changed the course of my life forever. I never tattled on him. I was furious with myself for even considering it. My parents already had enough to deal with, and all I would end up doing was add more hardship to their tired souls. And for what? Because I was mad at Mikhail? Because we didn't get along? Siblings fight, Ana. No one's family was perfect. I wasn't special, or different, or one of a kind.

I went back upstairs and spent the next few weeks wearing long sleeves during the sweltering summer. I took the incident with Mikhail and shoved it deep into my mind, never speaking it into existence until I started to wonder if it even happened at all.

I wish I could tell you that was the first and last time, but it wasn't. Mikhail's third act never ended. With each nightmare, I became more and more reluctant to tell my parents and now here I am, lying in a hospital bed with a broken body, a broken mind, and a heart that doesn't belong to me. Maybe things would be different if I'd pushed past my guilt and told my parents what really happened that day. Maybe not. Maybe this is just how my story is meant to go. All I know is that my birthday will never just be my birthday, Ana. It will always be the day my brother decided to punish me for being born.

I'm not ready to talk about that car accident, but I want someone to know. I want you to know, Ana, because you're the reason I'm still here.

Do you regret saving me yet?

NOW

Get up.

No.

You have to.

I'm supposed to be dead.

But you're not. You failed as a daughter, you failed as a sister, and yesterday you failed at death. Now you have to suffer the consequences.

I can't.

We don't have a choice.

My lap buzzed loudly again and with a regretful sigh, I shoved my closet door open, letting the harsh sunrise streaming through my open curtains blind my eyes. I stood up and paused, waiting for the dizziness to pass. Waiting for the numbness in my limbs to get replaced with pins and needles. Waiting for the reality that I was still *here* to hit me in full force. I tried to recall if I slept at all, but I couldn't. The last six hours of my life simply didn't exist in my mind.

I lived in the golden age of social media, where *men* and *women*, *boys* and *girls*, and *children* and *adults* all loved to glamorize and profit from this troubled state of mind. They documented their tears and the hours they laid in bed doing nothing in an aesthetically filmed fifteen-second video, with a pop song in the background, and ten different hashtags intentionally chosen to prey against their target audience. It was a fetish. A *trend* to be mentally disturbed and people were so quick to hop on the train and get their brief moment of relatable content.

They had it all wrong, though. It wasn't *cute* when I had to brush my teeth for double the amount of time just to make up for my lack of oral hygiene the night before. It wasn't *quirky* when I could barely bring myself to scrub away the grime left over from all the food and bacteria in my mouth before it rotted my gums. It wasn't *special* when I could scarcely get myself to take a fucking shower even when it'd been a week since the last one, and my hair was a knotted bird's nest hidden under naturally hectic curls and a shit ton of coconut scented dry shampoo. And then after I finally managed to drag my body into the tub, I couldn't get myself back *out* until eventually, the water would shrink me into the pruned version of a corpse. That was the only part of it I liked. When the cascading water withered me into a raisin and suddenly I felt small and weightless and it was easier to carry myself upwards . . . but that feeling was always fleeting. The same could be said about every other basic human necessity. Everything that was supposed to be *simple* suddenly turned into a draining and time consuming task.

But of course, no one wanted to broadcast any of that. They only wanted to accept the parts they believed to be charming. The ugly parts needed to stay hidden, not acknowledged. The dirty parts needed to be wiped clean until they were unrecognizable and meaningless.

I turned the tap off and closed the mirror compartment, but hesitated before turning away. I usually avoided looking at my reflection but as much as I hated to admit it, I was curious. Curious what the man at Ana's grave saw when he looked at me. Curious if he could tell what I was thinking.

I pushed away a stray ringlet—my bangs were growing out and needed a trim. Detached eyes stared back, the bags carved beneath them enunciated with lack of sleep. It didn't matter that I wasn't successful yesterday because I still looked like something that belonged six feet under the ground. I could see my years of loneliness slowly starting to transform my features. My pupils mirrored how painfully vacant I was inside, like there was an essential part of my existence missing. My *spark* being the essential thing. It had been violently destroyed and ripped out of me before getting burned to the crisp right in front of my eyes, and I hadn't been able to revive it since.

Sometimes I feared this was all I was and all I would ever be, but other times—*most* times—I honestly couldn't bring myself to care. I kept staring at her as the minutes ticked on, unable to identify the girl reflecting back at me. Every time she blinked it crucified another piece of my awareness. I continued to look anyway, suddenly desperate to find some flicker of resemblance but there was nothing. What was I like before? Was I happy? Was I full of life? I *had* to be. I had to have been better than this. There had to be a before this. A before *girl*. If there was a before girl, then that meant there could be an after girl. This damaged, semi-suicidal coward stranger was just the in-between. She wasn't *me*—

I squeezed my eyes shut against the image and fled the bathroom. There was a reason I never looked in the mirror, but at least my curiosity was satisfied now. I didn't know if he could tell what I was thinking, but I did know that he went to the cemetery to mourn the dead only to be forced upon the gaze of a zombie.

As pitiful as it was that I had to work this early, it was undoubtedly my favorite time during the day. It was early enough that everyone else was still sleeping, which in a way meant that I had the house to myself. Peace and quiet weren't usually a luxury of mine, so I liked to take full of advantage of it whenever I could. I took my time making my coffee and packing my lunch, before changing into my scrubs.

My schedule was the same every day—I worked as a medical receptionist in the ER department at the Mountain View General Hospital from six to three. Then I had a two-hour break where I would escape my existence with a book, before rushing to Tysons department store where I worked retail from five-thirty to ten. Then I went home and my miserable routine continued, over, and over, and *over* again.

To say that I didn't like my jobs was an understatement. I *despised* them. I always had my heart set on working in healthcare, but I didn't feel any passion for sitting behind the reception desk. My retail job wasn't any better, seeing as it triggered every fiber of my antisocial tendencies to the core. I hated talking to people. I hated folding clothes and organizing every section, only to turn back around a minute later to find the shelves completely destroyed *again*. I hated that every day at least three people would tell me I looked tired—when did that become an acceptable conversation starter? I hated how tedious the work was. I hated how slow time went during my shift, but somehow on the drive home every night I always wished I could go back and start my shift over. Every twenty-four-hour period I lived was a never-ending cycle of not wanting to be in this house, but not wanting to be at work either. Why wasn't there a third option I could choose from?

I rearranged my cold features into a smile, just like I practiced, and swiped my key card against the door. I waved at the janitor who was mopping the hallway. I asked Gwen about her daughter's dance recital and cooed as Helen showed me pictures of her grandson taking his first steps.

Nobody ever fucking noticed.

~

I usually headed to the Starbucks near Tysons before my shift, but I heard about a new café from some coworkers and decided to go check it out. I glanced around *Espresso & Chill* while I stood in line but thankfully didn't see anyone I knew.

It didn't look like your traditional café. There were plants and tapestries made of leaves hanging down the walls. The tables were an ashen wood material, accompanied by amber green plush seats, and the aroma of freshly ground coffee beans filled the air around me. At the far end of the café, the wall was covered with white plastic. It seemed like some renovations were being done on the other side, but I couldn't hear any construction. Instead, there was a steady beat of classical tunes in the background, along with the whir of the coffee machines and the light chatter from customers.

"Hi, what can I get for you today?"

Thump, thump—

Ana recognized the sound of his voice before I did. I turned to look at the front to place my order but my words got lodged in my throat, cutting off my air supply.

It was *him*.

He instantly recognized me too and his smile slowly faded. I couldn't decipher the expression on his face. Was he angry? Would he demand I tell him who I was, and why I was at Ana's grave? Was he going to kick me out and humiliate me in front of all these people?

I could see why Ana chose him—heterochromatic eyes, hairline gap between his two front teeth, ears that pointed out a little more than they should, but it was okay because they somehow still aligned perfectly with his sharp jaw and long neck, and a head of dark and fluffy curls that looked like they'd never met the bristles of a brush in their life, but I knew they would still feel silky and soft between my fingers.

Thump, thump—

But I couldn't notice those things. I couldn't notice men. Especially not *this* man.

"Was that you?" he asked quietly, slightly unsure. Like he couldn't believe I would have the audacity to show up here after yesterday's disaster. "At Ana's grave?"

He looked harmless and didn't sound aggressive—quite the opposite, actually. But he was still a man, and unlike the day before, we were in a public place. So without responding, I turned away and quickly headed for the door.

"Hey, wait!" he called out to me, just like yesterday. I didn't want to cause a scene so I didn't run. It wasn't like he was going to abandon his line of customers and come after me.

"Hey, wait up," I heard him say again, but this time it was at a much closer proximity, and then suddenly, he was right there, standing in front of me. My eyes saw him before my feet did, and they continued their brisk pace straight into his body. I stumbled back and he instantly reached out to steady me, but before he could touch me, I involuntarily flinched away from him. Violently.

"I'm so sorry," he said quickly. "Are you okay?"

I could feel his gaze looking me up and down to see if there was anything physically wrong with me, but besides my flushed face, the humiliation searing through my veins wasn't visible to the naked eye.

I thought . . . for a moment there I actually *thought* he was going to hit me. In public. Where everyone could see.

Insane.

Not insane, though. The most brutal monsters were the ones you didn't see coming.

I was still embarrassed. Not just because my reaction was so fucking obvious and there was no way he could've missed it, but because I had no power over my body . . . *he* did. A vital piece of myself had been forever altered, forever tainted, forever controlled by the puppet strings attached to *his* fingers. The worst part, though? I allowed it to happen. I didn't *ask* for it, but I also didn't try hard enough to *stop* it either.

Maybe that was why I always avoided my reflection. Maybe it wasn't because I didn't recognize that girl, but because I *did* recognize her as the person to blame for who I'd become. Not Mikhail. Not Ana. Only me.

I finally glanced over to see if he had hopefully disappeared so I would never have to face him again. He hadn't. That uniquely attractive and slightly nerve-racking man was still standing beside me with a concerned look on his face. I slipped my headphones out and took a second to evaluate the rest of him that was previously disguised by the counter, my brain immediately doing some quick calculations with his approximate volume, mass and density. He was taller than my 5'10 inches tall—which I hated—and his body was built like a spaghetti noodle—somewhere between fettuccine and linguine. My favorite was angel hair, but I was confident I could take him.

Not that he posed a threat.

Yet.

"Can I help you?" I asked, quirking an eyebrow.

"Um, no, but can *I* help you? You seem shaken up."

"I think it's pretty normal to get nervous when someone you don't know is chasing you down the sidewalk," I said with forced indifference. If I didn't act like my reaction was weird, then it wouldn't be weird.

He gave me an apologetic look. "Sorry, I realize now how that must've seemed. You just keep running away from me."

"Most people would take that as a hint."

"True," he said absently, his ornate eyes suddenly moving rapidly across my face with vigorous acuteness. "I'm getting hit with an extreme wave of déjà vu right now. Have we met before?"

Thump, thump—

I swallowed hard and shook my head.

He continued to stare at me without breaking eye contact before finally shrugging it off. "Yeah, you don't seem like someone I could easily forget. I'm Noah. Noah Davidson."

Is it possible he might . . .

"Maya Ibrahim," I replied cautiously.

Nope. Not a single flicker of recognition. The hospital did its job well.

"Maya . . ." he repeated, a shadow of a smile gracing his face. "Would you like to have a cup of coffee with me, Maya Ibrahim? So maybe by the end of the day, I can become someone that you know?"

I hated the way he said my name with that voice filled with curiosity and fascination like I was the most interesting part of his day instead of his worst *nightmare*. There were two ways this could go—I could politely decline his offer, get back into my car, and never look back. I was blessed to live in a huge city filled with thousands of tasteful coffee shops and libraries where I could pass the time. *Espresso & Chill* was probably great, but it was worth the sacrifice.

Or . . . I could do something crazy. *Different.* I could go against every instinct I had and say yes. I could accept this seemingly kind man's offer and go have a cup of coffee with him. He *owed* me after ruining my already ruined plans yesterday. He owed me a new routine. And he didn't seem to know how he knew me, so maybe he wasn't there the day they begged for her heart. Maybe he wasn't that close to Ana after all?

Thump, thump—

No, they *were* close. I could feel it. He might not know he knew me, but he did know me. I was probably imagining it, but her heartbeats sounded more . . . ecstatic. It recognized his proximity. Did he really want to know me, or did his spontaneous coffee invitation have to do with the girl's heart trapped in my body?

I could never tell him who I was because he would undoubtedly hate me—why would he want to be friends with the girl who survived in place of *his* Ana? And if I didn't tell him and he inevitably found out, he would hate me even more because I was a liar—why would he want to be friends with a liar?

So option one then. It was the right thing to do. But why did the right thing make me so mad? Maybe because despite always doing the right thing, nothing positive ever came from it. I was never rewarded for my stellar behavior. The universe still threw shit my way, completely fueled by my obedience and not giving a fuck about how good of a person I was.

"Fine," I agreed. "But only because I love coffee."

Fuck you too, universe.

THEN

Dear Ana,

Four weeks. That's how long it took him to strike again.

My birthday changed everything for me, Ana. I was a new person. My universe completely tilted on its axis, revolving around one thing: Mikhail. He was all I thought about. I memorized the way he walked— quick when he was fine, slow and enunciated when he was angry. I memorized his smile—when it was genuine, when it was cruel. I memorized his body language. I memorized the way he breathed and talked. I memorized the way he smelled so I could sniff him out from behind every corner before making myself seen. I noticed every small shift in his energy. Every vibration that radiated off him. Every tiny detail and stroke in his tone.

Our relationship was different now, Ana. Before, I was always waiting for him to be angry, but now I was always waiting for him to be angry at me. I went to sleep every night going over all the ways I could be better. I went over every mistake I made that could possibly trigger him, and I remedied it.

On top of being the perfect daughter, I was also the perfect sister.

But perfection wasn't enough.

I was reading at the dining room table when my parents announced they were going grocery shopping. They asked me if I wanted to come, but I refused because I needed to finish my readings before school started.

That wasn't the real reason. I didn't want to go and have to watch them check the price tag on every jug of juice in the aisle. I didn't want to notice my dad muttering the calculations under his breath every time they added another item to the cart. I didn't want to feel my mother's aura radiating waves of unease while we waited in line. But mostly, I didn't want to feel the fierce sting of embarrassment spread when my dad asked the cashier to take something out after he heard the price total. And then, once the embarrassment wore off, I didn't want to feel the immediate stab of guilt for being embarrassed in the first place. They didn't choose this. They were trying their best.

I didn't hear Mikhail come downstairs. I kept my head down as he walked through the living room and into the kitchen, my body automatically aware of his sudden presence. I listened carefully as he shuffled around in the cabinets, and after confirming that he was still ignoring my existence, I went back to my reading. A few minutes later I heard a loud bang echo throughout the small space.

I didn't move a muscle—reacting only made things worse. I locked all my limbs into place and kept my eyes glued on the page, not comprehending a single word. All my brain power was focused on not drawing any attention to myself.

He started banging around in the kitchen again, opening and closing the cabinets roughly. I couldn't tell what he was looking for, but I knew it was time for me to make my escape.

Everything happened quickly after that.

He pulled open the silverware drawer to grab a spoon. After counting to three I carefully pushed my chair back slightly, cringing when the wooden legs dragged loudly against the carpet. Then, out of nowhere, something hard and cold hit me in the eye.

I touched my eyebrow lightly, flinching away at the stinging sensation that followed. There was a spoon lying on the floor beside me, and Mikhail had dumped all the contents of the drawer onto the kitchen counter.

"Why are all the spoons dirty?" He wasn't yelling, but his voice still *impaled through me.*

I stood up without responding and Mikhail immediately stormed toward me. After weighing my options for half a second, I swiftly ducked down under the table.

"Why are you running away, huh? Why are you scared?" he asked lividly, grabbing one of the chairs. I crawled to the opposite end, panting heavily, but the length of the table wasn't very long. I was just about to shove one of the chairs out of the way so I could scurry out through the other end when I felt a very familiar hand wrap around my ankle.

He tugged on my leg roughly, pulling me to him. I reached out to grab onto one of the chairs, but my fingers grasped nothing but air. My chest hit the ground as he dragged me out, causing my glasses to slip off my nose and tumble onto the floor. I squinted desperately and tried to focus on my surroundings, but my vision was completely obstructed.

I kicked and thrashed against his hand, frantically trying to escape, but he only tightened his grip on me. He released me once I was out from under the table, and I quickly turned to flee but his fingers were back. They wove through my hair, yanking me up and onto my feet.

"Let go of me," I said, trying to step away but that only made him jerk my hair harder. He shoved me into the kitchen and pushed my face down toward the pile of cutlery on the counter.

"Tell me, Maya, do these look clean to you?" he breathed into my ear. The heat from his body in my proximity was making my skin crawl. I willed my corneas to magically fix themselves, but all I could see was a blob of color, and my eyes welled up, eclipsing my vision further.

"Answer me!" he screamed, making me jump.

"I can't see!" I told him, causing him to thrust my face right into the pile, a million sharp edges digging into my skin at the same time.

"Can you see now?" he demanded, but my lips wouldn't stop sobbing long enough to form a coherent answer. I couldn't understand what was happening. How did we get to this point? What was wrong with him?

"Take them all to the sink and wash them properly," he ordered. "You need to be better than this, Maya. I need to watch you scrub them until they're clean."

I swiftly grabbed a handful of spoons, knives, and forks in my fists and tried to turn but he was still clenching my hair tightly, preventing me from moving. Without warning, he let go and pushed me to the sink. I attempted to take a step blindly but inevitably tripped on the mat and stumbled to the floor. I managed to empty my hands to break my fall, but before I could right myself I felt Mikhail's foot on my back, ramming me violently into the cabinets.

I cried out from the force of the impact. There was a throbbing ache erupting from every inch of my body, each sting fighting for my attention but I ignored them. I felt around the floor, collecting everything I dropped before standing up and tossing them into the sink.

I could feel him standing behind me as I vigorously scrubbed away, scrutinizing my every move and suddenly everything was too much. My cloaked vision was getting fuzzier and my heartbeat was thrashing painfully against my rib cage. The sponge slipped through my fingers and I hastily splashed through the sink to retrieve it, terrified of the repercussions that were soon to follow because of my clumsiness—

"Maya?"

I froze at my mom's voice, before quickly turning and collapsing in her arms.

"Maya, honey, what are you doing?"

I couldn't control my sobs long enough to answer her. She held me tightly, letting me cry until eventually, my trembling subsided.

"I dropped my glasses," I whispered, wiping my eyes. "I can't see."

I vaguely saw my mom rush to the dining room to retrieve them. I looked around, but Mikhail was nowhere to be found. The chairs were all pushed back into the right place around the table. The pile of cutlery that I could have sworn was on the counter had disappeared.

"Maya, what's going on?" Mama asked, looking at me with concern and confusion. I opened my mouth to speak but stopped when I noticed the single limp grocery bag she was carrying.

The pile of unopened bills in my dad's hand.

The stress lines etched deeply into my mom's forehead.

"Nothing," I whispered. "I wanted to clean up before you came home, but I . . . lost my glasses and got scared because I couldn't see."

She continued to analyze my face carefully but didn't say anything. She didn't comment on my frizzy and tangled hair. She didn't question the scratch on my eyebrow that was bleeding. She didn't ask why I was shaking and crying and kept jumping in fright at every noise. I know she noticed, but she just never asked.

And in turn, I never told.

I went up to my room while she put away the groceries so I could clean myself up. I stared at my reflection in the mirror, horrified by the person I saw before quickly flipping the mirror compartment open so I couldn't see her anymore.

Siblings fight, I reminded myself as I covered the gash in my eyebrow with a Band-Aid.

Siblings fight, I reminded myself as I washed his fingerprints off my skin.

Siblings fight, I reminded myself as I ran my trembling fingers through my hair and watched the clumps fall into the sink, one by one, along with my tears.

I stayed in my room until everyone was asleep. There was an itch in the back of my brain, and I needed to soothe it. I went into the kitchen and inspected all the silverware.

They were all clean, Ana, but I checked again just in case.

And then again once more.

Again because I lost my place.

Again, Maya.

Did you check that one, on the right?

You need to be better, *Maya.*

Is that just a smudge or is it food?

You need to be perfect, *Maya.*

But perfection wasn't enough . . . so I checked again, and again, and again, and AGAIN—

I never stopped.

He never stopped either, Ana. I was his new addiction. His favorite toy to play with whenever he wanted to because he knew that toys couldn't talk.

Which brings us back to today. Three years later. On my way back home after months in the hospital.

I'll let you know when he strikes again.

NOW

"Thanks," I said, as Noah placed a cup of coffee in front of me and took a seat.

He smiled, waiting. "Well, are you going to try it?"

"I never told you how to make it."

"I'm pretty good at guessing how people take their coffee," he assured me. "Barista secret."

I glanced down at the steaming mug with a smiley face frothed on top. "I don't drink hot coffee."

"I thought you said you love coffee."

"Yeah, I love *iced* coffee."

"It's freezing outside," he pointed out as if I wasn't just outside *with* him.

"Why should the weather dictate what I choose to put into my body?"

He opened his mouth to respond, but no words came out. I couldn't tell if I sounded rude, or if he could understand my sarcastic wit. It had been so long since I engaged in a conversation outside of work and my parents, that I'd completely lost the few social skills I managed to pick up within the last twenty-five years.

He was still looking at me like . . . he was trying to figure me out or something. I wasn't a puzzle that could be solved though, so to spare him I carefully lifted the mug to my lips and took a small sip. The scorching hot bitterness slid down my throat and I almost gagged. Where was the sweetener? Where was the almond milk? Where were the four pumps of vanilla syrup?

Regardless, I managed to maintain my expression. "Delicious."

"Told you so," he grinned, exposing that gap and an unsymmetrical dimple. I could still feel that one sip of venom trickling uncomfortably through my system and failing to elicit even an ounce of warmth in my ice-cold body. I couldn't bring myself to disappoint that smile, so I continued to choke down my mug of unsweetened toxins.

"In the future, I'd recommend a less conspicuous way of inviting someone for coffee."

"Haven't you heard the phrase '*go big or go home*'?"

"Yes, and it reeks of desperation."

"Noted," he said, letting out a throaty chuckle. After a few seconds, I felt myself doing the same.

"Still," I continued hesitantly, "there must've been another reason you were trying so hard to catch up to me. Aside from the offer to satiate my caffeine fix."

"Yes, well, I couldn't let my mystery girl disappear on me for a second time without at least knowing her name."

"Mystery girl?"

"You were at Ana's grave yesterday."

Not a question—a statement.

I looked away and searched my brain for an acceptable reason that I could have been there but came up blank. What kind of deeply unhinged human would just hang out in front of someone's tombstone if they *weren't* visiting them? I had no choice. I was going to have to tell him the truth.

Would he get mad and throw his hot coffee in my face? Or would the café full of people lessen the blow of his anger, and give me time to flee?

"I am *so* sorry, Maya," Noah said instead.

Huh?

"I could see how much I scared you yesterday, confronting you the way I did. And, clearly I didn't learn my lesson because I went ahead and did it again today."

"It's fine."

He shook his head. "No, it's not. I'm not usually an asshole, it's just that yesterday was . . . the anniversary of her death. You could say I let my emotions get the best of me for a moment. But that's not an excuse, and I just wanted the chance to apologize."

The deep sincerity in his voice sent a stab of guilt my way. *I* was the only person here who needed to be apologizing.

"Grief has that effect. It's fine, really."

He smiled lightly. "So I'm assuming you knew her from school?"

I gave him a puzzled look, and he glanced pointedly at my keys that were hanging from a University of Calgary alumni lanyard.

Thump, thump—

I swallowed the bundle of nerves back down my throat and nodded slowly. "Yeah, we met briefly. I barely knew her, though. I was actually at the cemetery visiting someone else when I . . . recognized her name."

I observed his face carefully for any sign of suspicion, but if he had any he didn't show it. I waited for him to ask who I was visiting, and to pester me for more details but he didn't.

"Hey, are you cold?" he asked suddenly, gesturing to my gloved hands. "Do you want me to turn up the heat?"

"Boss? Can I get your help for a second?" the barista

behind the counter called out, saving me from trying to come up with an acceptable answer.

He nodded. "Sorry, excuse me for a moment."

I watched him head back and help the boy with his customer. It looked like he couldn't get the woman's drink right, and she was making a fuss. Noah remained professional though, apologizing for the inconvenience, and showing him how it was done with the utmost patience. He stayed and helped with the rest of the line, before strolling back to our table.

"Are you the manager?" I asked.

"Owner, actually," he smiled shyly. I noticed then that he wasn't wearing an apron and a name tag like the other barista was. Just a simple white shirt with a red and blue flannel over top.

"How long have you been open for?"

"A few months now."

"By the looks of it, you're doing very well for a start-up."

"Thanks. The idea to open my own business was kind of sudden, but I'm glad I did it."

"What were you doing before this?"

"I was a software engineer," he said, laughing. "That's what I majored in, so it made sense to make a career out of it, but there was just something *missing*. My days had become almost robotic. I woke up at the same time every day, put on clothes I didn't feel comfortable in and went to an office filled with people I didn't connect with. I just wasn't excited about life anymore, you know?"

Of course I knew. He was describing every day of my existence.

"Anyway," he continued. "I could feel this routine starting

to affect me negatively. It's extremely draining, doing things you aren't truly passionate about, so I quit. I had some savings to hold me over for a good while and I spent most of my time trying to figure out what I really wanted. I didn't want outside forces to play into effect during my thought process—like income or my family's opinion—so I spent a few weeks at our cabin in Banff."

I nodded to show I was listening. I didn't want my voice to betray what I was feeling.

"You've probably been there yourself—" I hadn't "—so you know what I'm talking about when I say the air is just different. Refreshing. It helped to clear my head and just focus on myself." He took a sip of his coffee. "I found this hidden gem while I was there and I fell in love. It was a cozy little coffee shop that just radiated warmth, and I remember wishing we had something like it here in the city. That's when I decided to just open one up myself, but make it my own."

My head continued to bob up and down robotically.

"My parents hated the idea at first, saying that I was wasting my potential and that I didn't know the first thing about opening up a business. But I had taken a few related courses in school, so I wasn't completely blind. Don't get me wrong, they had every right to be hesitant about it. There was a part of me that was scared too, but for the first time in years, I felt excited about something. I woke up every day with a sense of purpose and joy, which was enough motivation for me." He paused, looking around his shop and at all the happy customers. "It was hard, but I'm proud of myself. It's been a long time since I've felt this way."

His success was nice, but it was almost *comical*, seeing how easy things were for other people when they were completely impossible for you. He didn't like his job, so he quit—why continue doing something when it was no longer fulfilling? What would he gain from that? He had money saved up because he didn't have to take care of anyone but himself. Sure, his parents disapproved in the beginning, but it was *his* life. They weren't relying on him for anything and, in the end, they trusted him enough to make the right choices.

It was easy. *Simple.* One plus one equaled two.

He didn't even realize how fucking privileged he was. Typical men.

I forced a smile his way. "I'm glad everything worked out for you."

"Thanks, I appreciate it," he replied genuinely. "What about you? Are you still in school, or are you working?"

I squared my shoulders and prepared all my well-rehearsed answers on the tip of my tongue.

"Both. I'm getting my master's degree in physiotherapy right now, but I work part-time in the evenings—"

Liar.

But of course, my nuisance of a roommate decided to join in as the silent third wheel.

"Wow, good for you. You probably came here to get some work done and I completely monopolized your time," he said sheepishly.

"You didn't."

"So you want to be a physiotherapist?"

"Well, my plan A is medical school, but I decided to get my masters just in case I don't get accepted—"

Liar, liar—

"Wow, medical school? Did you write your MCAT?"

"Not yet," I replied, fiddling with my hands anxiously.

What was with the third degree? "But I'm studying for it—"

Liar, liar, pants on fire—

"That's impressive," he said in admiration.

He's only admiring the idea of you. If only he knew who you really were—

"I'm just going to use the restroom, excuse me for a minute." I stood up carefully but quickened my steps once I was out of his eyesight.

I locked the bathroom door and turned the faucet on high so no one could hear me, but also so I couldn't hear myself. What was I *doing*? Why the fuck was I *here*? Was I so desperate for change that I was making small talk with someone who was connected to the worst thing that ever happened to me?

"Stupid," I muttered. "Stupid, stupid fucking *liar*—"

Knock, knock.

"Maya?" Noah's calm voice floated through from the other side. I turned the tap off and opened the door. "Are you okay?"

I paused, suddenly confused. "Sorry, what?"

"I asked if you were okay."

Oh. *That.* What a silly question. Of course I wasn't okay. I was never okay but it had been a while since anyone asked.

I smiled. "I'm fine."

He nodded. "And fine is code for . . . ?"

My smile disappeared. He was going off-script.

"Excuse me?"

"*Fine.* It's such a filler word. It doesn't mean anything, you know?" he sighed and leaned against the doorframe. "There are so many other adjectives that could be used to better describe how you're feeling—excellent, top-notch, exceptionally splendid. Saying you're fine is basically like

41

saying you're nothing."

I stared at him blankly for a moment before looking around to see if anyone was watching this bizarre interaction, and could confirm that I was indeed imagining the words coming out of this man's mouth.

"Who are we looking at?" Noah whispered, his face suddenly level with mine, following my stare.

Nope. I wasn't imagining.

I fixed my gaze on him again. "Is this a small business owner thing—to follow new customers to the bathroom for a quality assurance check? Are you *that* desperate for a good Yelp review?"

"Is that what you are? A customer?"

Thump, thump—

"What else would I be?"

"A friend . . . ?" he suggested, but it came out as a question.

"You don't even know me."

"That's typically how friendship works," he said slowly. "You start by not knowing someone, and then you *get* to know them. I have this theory that it only takes one minute to know if you want to be someone's friend."

"And how's that theory working out for you?"

"Well, I only just came up with it, but—" he gestured between us "—I'd say it's already proved to be flawless."

I raised my eyebrows in disbelief, suddenly determined to prove him wrong. "You seem like a decent person, Noah, so I'm going to use my *one minute* to give you a disclaimer about what it's like being friends with me. I'm not fine, excellent, top-notch, or exceptionally fucking splendid. I could lift a semi-truck over my head with all the effort it takes for me to get through what should be an effortless day. My brain is a menace and gets triggered by the most minuscule occurrences. Don't bother asking me what's wrong because I won't tell you."

I paused, giving him an out, but he stayed put.

"My social battery is extremely limited. We could be in the middle of a conversation and I will literally just stop talking. I cancel plans last minute. I always say the wrong things. I'm awkward and quiet and honestly, Noah, I'm just a really *sad* girl." I exhaled deeply, instantly regretting my unexpected honesty, humoring this ridiculous conversation, accepting his offer to have coffee and, most importantly, not racing through that red light yesterday. "So, no disrespect, but I think your theory has actually been proven to be extremely *flawed*. Lucky for you, there are one point two million people in this city. One point two million opportunities to test your theory on someone who isn't a complete mess and get a better outcome."

He glanced at his watch. "You still have five seconds."

I rolled my eyes. "I'm also scared of birds."

"Why are you scared of birds?"

"Because they're basically rats with wings."

He gave me a look. "No, you're thinking of bats."

"Bats, birds—same thing."

"I mean . . . they start with the same letter."

"I'm sorry, do you have a pet bird or something?" I asked, crossing my arms. "Why are you so offended?"

"I'm not offended," he said, raising his hands in defense. "I just think it's an unusual fear to have."

"We met in a cemetery, but *this* you find unusual?"

"I'm an unconventional guy, what can I say," he laughed. "You know, for a sad girl, you're kind of funny."

"Humor is a textbook self-defense mechanism."

His eyes softened and he tilted his head slightly to the side. "Why are you sad?"

"That's none of your business."

He ignored the edge in my voice. "What are you right now, on a scale from one to ten? One being extremely sad and ten being deliriously happy"

"I find it really interesting that you assume my emotions can easily be ranked between the numbers one and ten."

"Just tell me," he insisted, biting back a grin.

"Why? Because you made me a free cup of coffee and I *owe* you now?"

"No. From this moment on you can expect all your coffees at *Espresso & Chill* to be on the house," he said with a playful smirk. "Honestly, you seem like you could use a listening ear and I just happen to have two."

"Right, because I'm just some helpless girl dying to profess all her tragic first-world problems to the first pretty boy to ask?" I scoffed. "I'll pass on the opportunity to feed your ego, but thanks."

He stared at me for a second, expressionless, before the corner of his mouth slowly lifted into a smile. "You think I'm pretty?"

"Wow." I was stunned. "Is your selective hearing a medical condition, or is it just a side effect of being chronically complacent?"

"You're also kind of mean for a sad girl," he pointed out. "Is that another textbook self-defense mechanism?"

"No, that's all me," I assured him. "Sincerely and wholeheartedly *mean*."

My words only brightened his eyes. "Just to be clear, we can't be friends because you're a mess?"

44

Thump, thump—

"Among other things."

"Everybody's a fucking mess."

"Oh really? Because the cookie-cutter life story you spent twenty minutes going on about begs to differ."

He laughed again, louder this time, head thrown back, lips stretched wide and breathless. "It seems that way on the surface, but it's not all rainbows and sunshine. Promise."

I wasn't convinced.

"*Pinky* promise," he said when I didn't respond. "Where I come from, that's the highest and most honorable kind of vow."

"Is that a line?"

"That depends . . . is it working?"

"Not in the slightest." That playful smirk was back. "This has officially been the weirdest conversation I have ever had with a stranger."

"I think I've earned my way up to acquaintance status by now, Maya."

"Okay, settle down," I said, rolling my eyes again, and headed back to our table to collect my things.

"You're leaving?"

"Yeah, I have to go to work."

He was quiet for a minute. "So . . . *Maya Ibrahim*, was this a one-time thing, or am I ever going to see you again?"

"Do you *want* to?"

"Shockingly yes," he replied. "But also sincerely *and* wholeheartedly. Hold on a sec."

He went behind the counter and started fiddling around before coming back with a to-go cup. "Pick me up before your shift."

I grabbed it from him reluctantly, and there were ten digits scribbled across the side.

"Do you give all your female customers your number?"

"Only the ones I like. So far, you're the first."

"And when you say that exact phrase to all your female customers, how do they usually respond?"

"I wouldn't know, but I'm assuming not like *that*."

"Right," I agreed awkwardly. "Okay, well, thank you for the coffee. Goodbye."

"Goodbye," he echoed, giving me once last warm smile as I turned away.

I let my car idle for a bit to heat the engine and took the lid off my coffee. Sure enough, there was another design, but it wasn't a smiley face this time. It didn't matter that I never answered his question because he knew the answer anyway.

1<

It could only get better from here.

~

I pulled into my empty driveway with a sigh of relief. The hint of a smile on my face hadn't moved all day, even when Sheila made me mop up an unknown substance in the women's fitting room. It looked like vomit, but it definitely smelled like urine.

I was always immune to men. Mikhail had tainted the male species for me so much that I had eventually convinced myself they were all the same. I *needed* to believe that because I refused to live in fear at the hands of a man ever again. I knew what men were capable of. I knew from experience how charming they could be, and how quickly women succumbed to their spell after a few seconds of memorized sweet talk. They were masters at collecting precisely what you were looking for and pretending to be exactly that, only to throw you away like a sack of garbage after they successfully took everything from you. Men were animals. They fed off your weaknesses. Instead of taking a woman in fear as a sign to *stop*, they saw it as an urge to continue.

My fear wasn't the only reason I shied away from men. Behind the abnormalities in my life, there was still a pile of all your typical insecure bullshit. I wasn't *pretty* enough, *funny* enough, or a *pleasure* to be around. I wasn't *captivating* or *interesting*. Boys and girls had walked by me all my life without so much as a second glance. My social awkwardness radiated off me in fumes of unfriendliness, and my cold aura scared people away like I had the plague.

I didn't blame them. I wouldn't want to know me either.

"Salam Mama," I greeted her, slipping off my shoes. I dropped my bag at the foot of the stairs and headed for the kitchen.

"How was work?"

"It was okay," I said absently between mouthfuls of food. I was still thinking about Noah.

"Can you sit for a second? I need to talk to you about something."

I looked up at her and finally noticed the tense atmosphere.

"What's wrong?" I asked immediately, taking a seat beside her. "Is it Baba? Is he sick again?"

"No, no everyone is fine, it's just." She hesitated. "It's Mikhail."

Of course it was. How was everything in my life somehow revolved around the one person I hated?

"Don't start," Mama snapped before I could even respond. "He's trying to be a better person."

"Oh, is he now?" I laughed humorlessly. "The first step to becoming a better person is apologizing to the people you've wronged. I've never heard anything *close* to an apology come out of his mouth."

"He *has* apologized to Baba and me," she insisted.

That's great, but what about me?

I shook my head and resisted the urge to press my hands against my ears like a child. I didn't want to think about this anymore. I didn't want to have this conversation *again*.

"What did you need to tell me, Mama? I want to go to sleep."

She looked away and started fidgeting with her fingers nervously. "Well, your brother came by to talk to us about something yesterday, and . . ." She paused, taking a deep breath. "He's going to be moving back in with us for a little while."

Her words were rocks being chucked at the walls that made up my existence and the world around me shattered, its sharp pieces slicing my skin open on their way down. But I couldn't feel that pain, because all the memories of my past had come flooding back into my head, *crippling* me.

"Maya, honey?" She put her hand on my shoulder but I moved away. For a moment, I couldn't tell the difference between her hands and *his* hands.

"Why are you doing this to me?" I whispered between trembling lips.

"I'm not doing anything to you. Your brother needs a place to stay—"

"This city is filled with a million other places where he could *stay*."

She sighed. "I don't know what you expect me to do. He's

my *son*, I can't turn him away when he needs me. Are you so full of hatred that you would let him live on the streets? What would people think of us? What would my *friends* think? I know you've had your issues, but you need to move on. You're being selfish right now . . ."

Was I supposed to feel sorry for him? He was always the fucking *victim*. The *sufferer*. The *focus* of all their love and attention.

She was still talking but I had stopped listening. I barely survived it last time. I was barely surviving *now*, but at least I didn't have to see him every day. At least I didn't have to feel his presence lurking around every corner. At least I didn't have to tiptoe around my own house, praying I wouldn't run into him. At least I could try to sleep at night without the fear of something happening to me while I was unconscious. Why didn't I get rid of myself when I had the *chance*? Why did I wait so *long*, why, why, *why*—?

"Are you forgetting why you kicked him out in the first place?" I asked shakily.

"No, of course not, but he's different now."

I snorted. "I don't believe that for a *second*."

She gently put her hand on my back and started rubbing soothing circles. "I'm sorry, Maya, I really am. I just . . . I don't know what to do anymore."

I knew she didn't—it wasn't her fault. She didn't truly know the extent of Mikhail's behavior. Maybe if I had told her about it from the very beginning, things would be different. Maybe if I had told her about it from the very beginning, she wouldn't have been able to build an indestructible bond with her son, making it impossible for her to ever let him go.

Don't be a fool. Nobody ever believes you.

"I'm only going to give him one chance, okay? If he crosses the line again, he's gone."

Her effort was admirable, but she wouldn't be able to notice the line until it was covering my dead body. And how could she? She was a *mother*. She had the hardest job in the world. No mother was going to expect this. No mother was going to prepare for this. No mother was going to be able to come to terms with *this*.

I forced a small smile on my face. "It's okay, Mama. Is he going to at least help out with the bills and stuff?" Maybe some of the financial weight would ease off my back a little bit.

"Well, no, not for a while. Once he finds a new job, I'll tell him he needs to start helping out."

My smile disappeared.

"You need to let go of all this resentment you have toward your brother, Maya."

Where do I put it? I wanted to ask. *How do I get rid of it?*

"Please don't make this harder for me," she pleaded.

Like I said, he was always the victim . . . and I was always the villain.

"You're right," I told her. "I'm sorry."

I grabbed my bag off the floor and headed upstairs, my eyes immediately zeroing in on all the evidence of Mikhail stained permanently in my room. I quickly pressed my hands against the door, making sure it was securely shut. Even though I knew he wasn't there, I still dragged my plastic storage compartments away from their designated spot and jammed them under the handle anyway . . . just in case.

I changed into some sweats, but my exhaustion had vanished. I *knew* he wasn't there, but I needed to stay awake anyway . . . just in case.

50

I paced back and forth, listening for my mother's soft footsteps going up the stairs. She didn't make me wait long. As soon as I heard her click their door shut I immediately dropped down on my stomach. I took a deep breath and pushed my chest off the floor with fatigued arms. It *hurt*, but I forced myself to keep going, fear fueling my nonexistent strength.

Up.

You need to be stronger, Maya.

Down.

You need to fight back this time, Maya.

Up.

God, you're so fucking weak, Maya.

Down.

You're such an easy target, Maya—

Up

No wonder he wants to hurt you, Maya—

I collapsed—my lungs heaving and my muscles shaking. I only let myself rest for a second before I started the next set again, and again, and *AGAIN*—

I didn't stop until the sun rose.

Just in case.

THEN

Dear Ana,

I met his girlfriend today.

It's only been a few weeks into my junior year of high school, but I'm already crammed with work. I refused to let my accident set me back in school, so I spent the entire summer getting caught up instead of resting. I gave up on the idea that life was going to change, and the only way out was . . . out. I was going to get accepted into a university far, far away and my parents wouldn't be able to say no. Or maybe they would, but I didn't care. I couldn't *care. I had to cut the cord and escape*

I was in the middle of writing my biology notes when my mom knocked on my door.

"Maya, your friend is here. Why didn't you tell me you invited someone over?" she asked, crossing her arms.

I stared at her blankly. "I never invited anyone over."

"Well, there's someone downstairs saying that you did."

I didn't push it. I headed for the stairs but stopped when I saw Mikhail round the corner. He continued in my direction, forcing me back into my room. I was pressed up against the farthest wall and he was right there with me, in my bubble, sharing my air.

"Go along with it or I'll kill you," he whispered into my ear, lips just barely grazing skin.

And then he left.

The old me would have been shaking, Ana. I would have slid down the wall in a slow and exaggerated way, choking on sobs and tears like the pathetic and naïve child I used to be.

That was the old me, though. The new me didn't even blink an eye. The new me had an agreement with Mikhail. He could do whatever he wanted, and I would keep my mouth shut or else I would be reunited with four white walls and a thick file labelled Ibrahim, Maya.

I headed for the stairs a second time without interruption, and just like my mom said, someone was sitting on the couch in the living room. It was a girl, who looked to be about my age. She was short and pretty, and I had no fucking clue who she was.

"Hey!" She greeted me excitedly like we were long-time best friends.

I racked my brain for a memory with her or even just what her name could be, but I was coming up blank. I did not know this girl.

"You look confused. We said that we were meeting up today, right? You were going to help me study for our biology test?" She held up the same textbook that was sitting on my bed.

"Um . . . yeah," I replied hesitantly. "Let's go downstairs."

She slipped her shoes off and followed me to the basement. "You can set up your stuff on the table, I'm just going to grab my things. Can I get you anything to drink?"

"Just water, please. Thank you, Maya."

She was saying my name with such familiarity it was starting to freak me out. I forced a smile her way and ran back upstairs, where my mom was in the kitchen pouring some water and juice into glasses.

"Hiba seems lovely. Why haven't you mentioned her before?"

I wanted to tell her that I had never met Hiba before today. I wanted to tell her that I never invited Hiba over. I wanted to tell her that something weird was going on, and I was positive Mikhail had something to do with it.

But I didn't, Ana. Nobody ever believed me.

I grabbed my books and went back downstairs to help this stranger *study only to find Mikhail sprawled on the couch, deep in conversation with Hiba.*

"You didn't have to grab your stuff, silly. We both know I'm not here for biology help," she said, giggling. "Anyway, Mikhail, did your mom say anything about me so far?"

I was too stunned to speak. My eyes flickered between them as they continued talking like there was nothing strange going on, and Mikhail's threat from earlier suddenly made sense. I was just a pawn in his perfectly calculated plan to hang out with a girl in our house, unsupervised. They never acknowledged my existence for the rest of her visit. I just stood in the corner, quietly suffocating under a cloud of heavy awkwardness and confusion.

I could've just left. It wasn't like he was going to drag me back by my hair in front of her if I tried to leave, but I couldn't, Ana. My feet were glued to the floor and my eyes were glued on Mikhail. Following his every movement and studying him intensely. The way he was smiling at her tenderly. The way he was speaking to her so gently and sweetly. The way his tone was so low and calm.

Something was beginning to simmer underneath my layer of numbness. I tried shoving it away, but that ugly green-eyed beast was starting to spread quickly. God, I sound so fucking creepy, but I just felt . . . I don't know. It's stupid. I'm stupid. My entire fucking life is stupid but it doesn't matter because that hopeless longing was consuming me and it was disgusting. How could I want that? How could I still want anything to do with him after everything he did to me? After everything he put me through? But if he was truly so rotten to the core, why was she still here? Why was she smiling at him and playing with a piece of her hair? Could she really not see what I saw?

She wasn't the only one—my parents, the doctors at the hospital, his friends. They were all trapped under his spell. It was just me, alone on the other side, crying about the monster hiding in my closet but every time someone checked it was suddenly empty. If you were the only one who could see the devil in a room full of people, did that make you smarter, or did that just make you delusional?

I couldn't help but start to notice all our differences . . . do you think he would like me more if I was prettier, Ana? Like Hiba?

If I was short and small?

If I was more talkative?

If I played with him more as a baby, instead of crying every time he held me?

If I was a better sister?

If, if, if—

"Well . . . I have to go," Hiba said, pulling me out of my existential crisis.

"I'll show you out," I mumbled. I was almost at the top of the stairs when I heard them.

"Your sister probably thinks she's crazy," Hiba giggled quietly.

"She is. She's been making my life a living hell since the day she learned how to talk," Mikhail replied.

"Awe, it's okay honey," Hiba crooned. "I'll see you later, okay?"

I covered my mouth with my hand before I could make a sound and waited for her by the door. I stared at her while she put her shoes on, hoping that she would say something to redeem herself, but she didn't. I quickly ran up to my room and paced back and forth in the small space, trying to process what had just happened.

It was obvious they were together romantically. So he . . . what? Invited her over? Told her to pretend that I had invited her over so our parents wouldn't know they were dating? And she—without questioning my brother's sanity—just went along with his act? She couldn't see his true colors because she was just as manipulative as he was.

I wanted to slap myself, Ana. I wanted to bang my head against the fucking wall for letting his charm confuse me. For being jealous of her.

I thought I was so sure of myself. Even after everything that happened with my accident, I didn't let him faze me. But it was already happening and I just never noticed. He planted a seed of doubt into my brain long ago and it was growing rapidly. I needed to escape before it took over everything that I knew to be true.

I flung open my closet and started throwing clothes out. Besides my very old and used laptop, I had managed to save up every penny from tutoring over the last few years. I grabbed my bawled-up scarf and turned it upside down on my bed.

Nothing came out.

"No, no, no," I whispered as panic started to crawl up my skin. I went back into my closet and searched every inch, but it was no use. All my money was gone.

Stolen.

Mikhail stole all the money I was saving up for school.

My numb was gone, Ana. The new Maya was gone and the old one was back, and I could feel everything, everywhere, all at once. I flipped my mattress over and ripped my curtains off the window sill. I tore my clothes off their hangers and I screamed into the fabric. I screamed and I screamed and I screamed, and when it wasn't enough I took my fist and shoved it straight into my reflection.

Cracked. Broken. Angry.

Just like me.

Just like him.

I was truly my brother's sister.

There was a long shard of glass next to my foot. I imagined picking it up. I imagined it would feel cold and hard in my palm. I imagined taking it and slicing my wrists. I felt the pain. I felt the warm blood trickling down my hands and onto the floor. I felt your pulse slowing and then stopping completely.

But then something dawned on me, and I immediately came back to life. The shard of glass was still next to my foot, my wrists were intact and all my blood was in my veins.

What if today wasn't just an act of manipulation? What if Hiba only went along with his plan because she wanted me to know that she existed? What if this visit was a cry for help? Was it possible that Mikhail was doing the same thing to Hiba that he was doing to me?

I stepped into the empty hallway. His door was open, and I could hear the shower running in the bathroom. Without thinking it through I quietly entered his room and grabbed his phone, sighing in relief when he didn't have a passcode. I went to his contacts with shaky fingers and found Hiba's name.

The water stopped.

I tossed his phone back on his bed and ran back to my room, whispering her number under my breath so I wouldn't forget. I grabbed my notebook and scribbled it down before shoving it into my backpack.

I know siblings fight, Ana. Sometimes they hit you, threaten you and try to kill you. Sometimes they steal your money, and sometimes they treat their girlfriends better than they have ever treated you. But she's not his sibling, which means anything he did or didn't do to her was wrong and completely unacceptable.

I can't protect myself, Ana, but maybe I can protect her.

I know what I have to do.

NOW

I checked my phone for the hundredth time. It was eleven-fifty.

She's not coming.

I lifted my phone to my ear anyway and waited.

"Hello?"

At least she answered.

"Hey Bayan, where are you?" I said cheerfully. *Too* cheerful. Synthetic.

"Home."

One-word responses. Just like her texts.

"Oh . . . I thought we were hanging out today. Did I get the day wrong?"

I *didn't* get the day wrong. I had our hangout marked in my calendar because I was so excited to see her. I was so excited that she texted me back—three weeks later, but *still.*

"Oh my God, I totally forgot," she apologized. It sounded genuine. "My mom has been super extra every time I ask to leave the house—you know how she is—and I've been really busy lately with . . ."

I listened while she vented about her overly strict parents, and her busy, *busy* schedule. Regardless, I still drank in every scrap of her life she threw my way—a dog begging at the foot of the dinner table. I didn't mind. I missed her voice.

". . . but anyway, rain check?"

"Yeah, that's fine. What day did you have in mind?"

"I'll text you," she promised.

She won't.

"I'll talk to you soon, okay?"

You won't talk soon.

"Bye."

And just like that, she was gone.

Things weren't always this weird between us. There was a time when our friendship ran deep. There was a time when there wasn't a single second of silence between us because we couldn't stop talking, and laughing . . . until I ruined it by being sad. I mean, I was always sad, but it was background noise. I could tune it out when I was around her because she was a ray of blissful and charismatic sunshine without even trying, and it was contagious. But eventually, my world darkened to a point of no return and everything I was holding back came tumbling out, tainting our friendship forever.

It wasn't like I ever told her anything. I never once vented or cried or dumped all my trauma onto her unwilling shoulders to make myself feel better. I was simply but completely a little *sad*. My smile was a little smaller. My laugh didn't come from the gut. My height lost a few inches from the new slump in my shoulders. My eyes were a little less bright. And she just . . . never questioned it. She accepted the sudden shift in my personality without acknowledgement, causing our relationship to dwindle into a series of unanswered messages and meaningless hangouts every few months. We would meet up, she would talk, I would listen, and then she would leave.

My phone was still pressed against my ear.

But what about you, *Maya, how are you doing?*

59

"Not good," I whispered into the screen.

Why, what happened?

"Mikhail's moving back in," I told no one. "He's moving back in and I'm so terrified and *mad*. I'm so fucking mad at them for doing this. For being so oblivious and *gullible*. It's not fair. It's not fucking *fair*. He put me through hell and they're just—" my voice broke "—welcoming him back with open arms."

Silence.

"I met a boy yesterday," I continued. "He seems nice, and he's kind of cute. Really cute. Exactly my type."

Let me guess—tall, lanky, dark curly hair?

"Yes," I laughed. "But then I made it weird. I had this whole bitchy, *Shakespeare*-level dramatic monologue. It was mortifying."

Typical Maya. How did he react?

"He reacted . . ." I paused. "He *didn't* react. He just carried on the conversation."

See? Stop overthinking it.

"He gave me his number. Should I text him?"

Yes!

"There's something else."

What?

"He knew her. *Ana*. He knows I knew her too, and when he asked me how I lied."

So. Everyone lies.

"But this is a big lie. What if he finds out?"

That you were about to die in a car accident and needed a heart to survive?

"*Her* heart," I corrected.

So what. You're just another transplant patient, Maya. It doesn't need to be deeper than that.

"I guess . . . I don't know. Every time he spoke, it was like she was reminding me of her existence in my ear with her thumps."

Your thumps, *Maya. There is no her. Ana's dead.*

"I know. It's still my fault, though, kind of. Sort of? And I know he'll agree with me if he finds out."

Then don't tell him.

"I won't," I promised.

Silence.

I swallowed and glanced around the cafeteria, peeling my phone away from my face. I didn't look alone and crazy. I just looked like a girl talking on the phone with her best friend. I grabbed my wallet and pulled out the ripped piece of polystyrene with Noah's number on it. I didn't know why I kept it—I already had it memorized. But I liked having a piece of that hour. Proof that it really happened.

I smiled as I replayed our odd conversation. The only reason I accepted his offer for coffee was because I knew it would be a one-time thing. I didn't think I would want to see him again . . . but I did. I *hated* that. I hated how quickly my loneliness clung to people. I hated how quickly I became obsessed.

But this was different. *Noah* was different. He already knew I was sad, so I couldn't ruin it this time.

He could find out, and that will ruin it.

I added him as a contact anyway . . . and then before I could overthink it I sent him a message.

Hey, it's me

Three dots immediately appeared.

Who's me?

61

> Maya, obviously

How could that possibly be obvious?

My mouth twitched.

> Because you've been desperately waiting for a text from an unknown number since the moment I left

Damn, you caught me

Come to the café

I smiled.

> I'm busy

After you're done being busy

My smile widened.

> I'll see

The best two words I heard all day

> Okay, settle down dude

I'll try my best, chick

My alarm rang. Five minutes left for lunch.

> I have to go

Okay

I'll maybe see you later

> I'll maybe see you later, too

Maya?

> Noah

I'm so glad you texted me

Thump, thump—

One more time, Ana, I promised, *and then I'll never see him again.*

~

I opened the front door of *Espresso & Chill*, my gaze immediately searching every inch of the perimeter for him. A set of mismatched eyes locked with mine from behind the front counter, and his face lit up with that beautiful, toothy grin.

62

"For you," he said, handing me a steamy mug before taking a seat across from me.

"Are you sure you're okay to take a break?" I forced down a sip. "It looks like it's getting busy."

"I'm here if they need me."

"How many baristas do you have?"

"I only needed to hire *one* . . . until this morning when I decided to hire a second one."

"Why the impulsivity?"

"I had a feeling I was going to be preoccupied this evening," he said, giving me a pointed look.

"Don't flatter yourself, Noah. I had to fish your number out of the trash."

One corner of his mouth tugged upwards. "Fishing my number out of the trash is a much bigger compliment than if you had simply added me as a contact right away."

I looked away, letting my short curls mask my expression. "Permission to withdraw my last statement?"

"Permission denied," he laughed. "I caught you red-handed. Or, in your case, red-*faced*."

"Okay, settle down."

"I'm settled. *You* on the other hand . . ."

I shook my head in annoyance but then started laughing despite myself, the spontaneous sound coming from the deepest part of my belly. It felt different. It almost felt nice.

"Can I ask why you felt inclined to get rid of my number in the first place?"

"I'm not usually eager to face people after throwing an emotional bitch fit in their presence."

"I'm used to that—it comes with the job description," he assured me. "I make girls drinks, and in return, they cry and tell me all about their problems."

"I did not *cry*, okay," I scoffed. "And you're describing a bartender, Noah, not a barista."

He shrugged. "Bartender, barista—same thing."

"They start with the same *letter*," I echoed smugly.

He chuckled lightly. "Tell me about your day."

"I had work at six am and I finished about thirty minutes ago," I told him, forcing down another sip.

"I thought you only worked at night?"

"Well, I do." What was I trying to hide? "I have two jobs. I work at the hospital from six to three every day except Sunday, and I work at Tysons from five-thirty to ten most nights."

"Wow," he replied, his eyes widening in surprise. "How do you juggle both jobs with classes?"

My face immediately flushed with shame. "I differed my enrollment for two years last September. I'm sorry I didn't tell you that yesterday."

"That's okay, but why did you defer? You seemed excited about it."

"I can't work two jobs *and* go to school, so I figured I would just focus on saving up for now."

It was crazy how the more I told that lie, the more I started to believe it myself.

"Have you tried looking into financial aid?"

"I have financial aid, but six years is a lot to pay back." I focused my gaze on the mug in my hands, wishing he would just drop the subject but it was too late. His question already triggered one of the prohibited boxes in my mind and it was wide open now. Financial Aid? More like financial *debt*. I didn't even know what the amount was after all the

64

accumulated interest because I couldn't bring myself to open any of the envelopes or emails they sent me. There was *years'* worth of unopened letters shoved into the back corner of my closet. I had changed my number countless times to avoid their constant calls but they still ended up figuring out the new one, sending me into a frenzy of panic every time my phone buzzed with an unknown caller screen.

But what could I do? How could I explain that the reason I couldn't pay them back wasn't that I was irresponsible or that I didn't care, but because my money was not my own? They didn't care about my sob story. Every cent I earned went to paying the bills, groceries, and gas. By the time I was done, I could barely treat myself with a simple cup of coffee because the thought of spending *my* money on *my*self felt like . . . theft. Or some other outrageous crime against humanity. I didn't even bother trying to make a payment plan because what was the point? My dad's health was a chronic issue, making it impossible for him to get a job with a livable wage. Mikhail was fucking *useless*, so the burden fell on me. I was going to have to press the permanent pause button on my dreams and take care of my family for the rest of my life while dodging creditors hiding in every corner.

I blinked against the lights that were suddenly too *bright* and my hands twitched to cover my ears from the low background music that suddenly wasn't *low* anymore and my lips were trembling to tell the people chatting casually around me to stop fucking *yelling* so I could just think of a solution to my never-ending problems—

"Maya? What are you thinking about?"

"Just thinking."

"Is your brain being a menace again?"

"Not again, Noah. *Always*."

He hesitated. "I find that fresh air usually helps, but I know how you feel about birds. The outdoors is kind of *their* territory."

"It's December—they're already long gone and won't migrate back until early spring. The smart ones would've escaped as soon as the temperature started to drop, and any stragglers left in the city will get hit by natural selection soon enough—except for crows, of course." My mouth kept moving, spouting useless information to distract me from thinking. "Did you know that a group of crows is called a murder? I mean, there has to be a reason for the name. Can you blame me for being terrified? They're basically just mini dinosaurs."

"For someone who's scared of birds, you sure do know a lot about them."

"Isn't that always the case? To obsessively memorize and consume all pieces of information pertaining to the thing you fear the most?"

"To put it *eloquently*," he agreed with a chuckle, standing up. "Come on. I'll protect you from all the mini dinosaurs."

The wind hit as soon as I opened the door. I quickly took in mouthfuls of air, looking up at the grey clouds. Noah stood beside me, far enough to give me some space but close enough for me to feel his presence and know he was still there.

"Please tell me you're finally regretting the choice to ignore my helpful warning."

"Not quite," he smiled and started walking down the sidewalk. "Why are you so desperate to prove your point?"

"I'm not," I sighed, shaking my head. "This might shock you, but I'm not usually like this," I laughed. "Well, I am, but not at first. I normally like to get to know someone before revealing how emotionally unstable I am."

"Everyone is emotionally unstable, Maya. Some people are just better at hiding it."

"*I'm* good at hiding it," I insisted. "Seriously, it's like my only talent. Or *was*."

"Hiding isn't a talent. It's just a delay on something that's destined to happen."

I rolled my eyes. "You just have all the answers, don't you?"

"Nope. Only the lessons I learned the hard way."

"Oh my *God*, do you hear yourself?" I asked in disbelief. "You sound like a walking self-help book."

He laughed.

"Is that what this is? Do you have a book you're trying to sell? Are you a barista, bartender, bird-lover *and* author? No, not an author—" I paused for dramatic effect "—a *book* writer."

"Gotta keep it consistent," he agreed, still laughing. "I do sound like a corny douche, don't I?"

"*You*? No. Never," I replied sarcastically.

"I swear I'm not some entitled white man," he promised. "I only speak from experience."

"You keep hinting at this secret messy life of yours, Noah. Enlighten me."

He chuckled. "Well, once upon a time there was a little boy named Noah . . ."

"Here we go," I groaned.

". . . who woke up on his tenth birthday and found his mom dead in the kitchen."

My teasing grin disappeared.

Fuck.

I squeezed my eyes shut. "I'm an asshole, Noah. I am so sorry."

"You're not," he disagreed softly. "And it's okay, it happened a long time ago."

I *was* an asshole. I was so consumed with my own life that I forgot shitty things happened to other people too. Worse things.

"How did she . . . ?"

"Overdose." He spoke soberly. Business like.

Overdosing was clean. Simple.

"I thought she was asleep," he continued. "I didn't realize what happened until she started to smell."

No one would even know at first.

"You were so young, of course you wouldn't think she was . . ."

"Not really," he replied, looking straight ahead. "Physically I was a kid, but mentally . . ." he sighed, shaking his head. "My mom struggled with severe addiction for most of my childhood, and it was hard for her to take care of me. Eventually, I had to start taking care of myself and *her.* Cooking, cleaning, taking money from her purse every night to make sure the bills would get paid on time."

"And your dad?"

He laughed humorlessly. "Yeah, that piece of shit took off when I was six and left us to fend for ourselves."

"But who . . . you mentioned your parents to me yesterday, didn't you?"

"My adoptive parents. I was put in the foster care system after my mom overdosed, and a few years later I was adopted. That's how I met Ana."

Thump, thump—

Brother, *not* boyfriend. It hit me then, how ridiculous it was to immediately assume his relationship with Ana had to have been a romantic one. Sometimes I forgot that brothers loving their sisters was completely normal.

"We were placed in the same foster family, and we were inseparable ever since. My adoptive parents originally came in wanting a girl—Ana—but she insisted that she wouldn't leave without me," he chuckled lightly.

Did I really call her a bitch the other day? She was a fucking *saint*.

"That was incredibly nice of her."

"Ana's the definition of nice. Or . . . *was*."

Thump, thump—

Abandoned father, addict mother, foster care and two intimate deaths all in the span of twenty-eight years, and *I* was the sad one. Pathetic.

"I know we just met, but for what it's worth, I'm glad she did that. You deserve a family that loves and takes care of you."

"My mom loved me, Maya. I know it sounds terrible, how we were living, but she tried her best. People are so quick to judge, but they just don't understand that addiction is a *disease*. She wasn't selfish, or neglectful. She was just fighting demons' that no one else could see."

I nodded in understanding. I knew the feeling.

"She tried her best," he repeated. "Even though she didn't always show it, I know she loved me."

"Are you trying to convince me or yourself?"

He didn't respond. Just kept looking straight ahead with his eyebrows scrunched together.

"It's okay to be mad, Noah," I told him after a few minutes of silence. "Just because there was a reason for her actions, doesn't make it okay."

He exhaled deeply before speaking. "I begged her to pick me over using for my entire childhood. But one day I just . . . stopped? And then when she died, it was like . . . my inner child died with her. Now I just have these days where I hate myself for not trying harder to help her." He paused. "It's been so long though and it just feels silly to keep thinking about it, you know? It's not helping anyone by continuing to fester over it. What's done is done. I'm over it."

"Who says?" I asked, irritation creeping into my voice. "Who made it a rule that *family* can get a free pass to treat you however the fuck they want to and you just have to accept it and move on."

His gaze immediately cut to mine, startled by my sudden outburst. I didn't say anything more, but the deed was done. I wasn't talking about his mom, and he knew it.

"It wasn't like that, Maya," he said slowly.

"I know, I just—" I took a breath. "You don't need to be over anything. Even if you convinced yourself you were over it but it hits you all over again. There is no *timeline*. It's not supposed to be easy and clean and *short*—it's supposed to be messy. That doesn't make you weak, or a bad son. It only makes you human."

He smiled and nudged me with his shoulder gently. "Who's the corny douche now?"

I rolled my eyes at his teasing tone, but I still felt guilty for judging him so quickly. I hated how optimistic and buoyant he was and automatically perceived him as some privileged white male. He *was* privileged, in a sense, but the way he spoke yesterday . . . he wasn't bragging, he was just thankful. He knew how it felt to be on both sides of the coin.

We started heading back to his café, just as the evening rush began. I had no choice but to step closer to him, and our hands bumped against each other.

"Sorry," he murmured after each accidental touch.

I glanced down at our hands with curiosity—one gloved, one bare—and carefully shifted my pinky finger, hooking it with his. I felt his eyes on me, but I continued looking forward. After a moment his finger tightened around mine, securing it with his and our hands started to swing lightly between us. My lips inched up in a tentative smile, and in the corner of my eye, I could see his doing the same.

Thump, thump—

My finger slipped out from his and my grin evaporated. I felt his eyes on me again, but I ignored him. A minute passed before he looked away, and put his hand in his pocket.

I only held his finger for a second, but it was enough. A second was all it took to wonder if I could be touched by a man without being in *pain*. If I could be ignited into flames without being *burned* to ashes in the process.

"I'm sorry you had to go through that," I told him sincerely once we reached my car. "But your optimism and lust for life . . . it's refreshing."

He shrugged and smiled brightly. God, he was always *smiling*.

"How do you do that?" I asked.

"Do what?"

"Stay so . . . positive? And *happy*? It's weird."

He tipped his head back and laughed.

"I'm being serious," I insisted. "Is your café just a front to sell *special* deserts? Are you on cloud nine right now, Noah?"

"Is it really so unbelievable that I could simply choose not to let a few shitty things dictate the rest of my life?"

Yes.

"So this is how the other half lives?" I muttered. "Interesting."

His eyes softened. "Whatever you're going through right now will pass, Maya. Things will go back to normal. The way they used to be."

I looked at him sadly, and for the first time since I met him, I told him the truth.

"That's what I'm afraid of."

He waited to see if I would continue, or give more details, but I didn't. I let my cryptic response float uneasily in the air between us until my alarm went off in my pocket.

"I have to go to work," I said reluctantly.

"Will I see you tomorrow?"

"I don't usually hang out with my acquaintances multiple times in one week."

"Well, that ship has already sailed. We're currently at *three*."

"Three?"

"Running away at the cemetery, antagonizing me at my café, a trauma dumping stroll downtown." He tallied them off on his fingers. "We're basically a married couple."

I snickered at his word choice. "I don't know if the cemetery counts as a hangout."

"I'll take what I can get."

"Yes, Noah," I consented. "You will see me tomorrow."

"Promise?"

"Promise."

"*Pinky* promise?"

I groaned. "Is that going to be a thing?"

"Do you want it to be a thing?"

"No," I replied immediately. "The only thing you can *pinky* promise me is that you'll never say the words *pinky* promise again."

"Bye Maya," he grinned and turned to leave.

"Wait!" He looked back. "I hate your coffee."

"What?"

"The coffee you keep making me? I hate it. It's disgusting. The thought of drinking it ever again makes me want to vomit."

His eyes widened in shock.

"You told me a secret," I explained. "I wanted to tell you one too."

"So, I gave you deep and heartfelt, and you're giving me an *insult*?"

"Yes."

He raised his eyebrows and then realization hit him. "It's *disgusting*? But you drank it."

I shrugged. "Yeah, to be nice."

"You're not very good at being nice." A laugh burst through my lips. He watched me for a minute before cracking a smile. "What about the cute little designs I frothed?"

"*Super* cute," I agreed. "But I don't want to admire my coffee, I kind of just want to drink it."

"Okay, how *do* you take it?"

"Iced double shot of espresso made with almond milk—" he cringed "—four pumps of sugar-free vanilla syrup and a shit ton of stevia."

"It should be considered a crime for you to order that at

any café," he said painfully.

"No one likes a coffee snob, Noah."

He laughed again and shook his head. "You're something else, Maya. I'll see you tomorrow with that caffeine abomination waiting."

I waved and got into my car, my phone beeping before I'd even put my seatbelt on.

I might still be your acquaintance, but you are most definitely my friend -Noah

Thump, thump, THUMP—

"I know, Ana," I whispered. "I *know.*"

THEN

Dear Ana,

My plan was simple. I was going to call her, tell her that Mikhail was terrible and she should break up with him, and then this guilty obligation I was feeling like Mikhail being terrible was somehow my fault would go away and I could go back to feeling nothing.

Did my plan go as intended? No. Did my plan completely blow up in my face? Yes.

Step one was to get a phone. I had two options, Ana. I could ask my friends who I stopped sitting with at lunch without notice because they weren't very good friends, or I could ask the girl whose name I didn't know that sat at my table in the library. We had an unspoken agreement, this mystery girl and I. We shared a table in the library at lunch—her at one end, me at the other—and we just didn't speak. There were no introductions or fake small talk. She did her chemistry homework while I read my cheesy romance novels, and it was nice, sitting in silence, not having to force conversation.

I chose option one because I didn't want to disrupt the equilibrium we had created between us.

Do I regret my choice? Yes, yes I do.

"Hey Dania," I said, standing by our usual lunch table. Not 'ours'. I hadn't sat with them in months. "Do you mind if I use your phone for a minute? I need to call my mom."

"No . . . I guess it's fine," she replied hesitantly, giving Lena a look.

"Thanks," I said, giving her an awkward smile. I quickly left the cafeteria, eager to get away from their judgmental stares and shared looks.

I walked around school until I found an empty hallway and opened my fist revealing the balled-up piece of paper. I carefully smoothed out the wrinkles so I could read the numbers, and dialed with shaky fingers.

"Hello?"

My breathing stopped.

"Hello?" she repeated, louder.

Still no lung movement. There was no way that could be humanly possible, right?

"Hello?" she said, irritated now. "If you prank call me again, I am going to report this number—"

"It's me!" I blurted.

"Maya?"

"Yeah."

"Oh, hey . . . what's up?"

And then everything I'd rehearsed disappeared from my mind.

"I'm sorry, I don't know why I called you," I backtracked quickly, hoping she would just hang up and I would never have to face her again.

"Are you sure? You can tell me anything. I would love to be friends."

Despite her manipulative performance yesterday, Hiba sounded kind of . . . sweet? Didn't I owe it to her then, to do the right thing? To save her from having to experience the things I did, if she hadn't already experienced them?

"Look Hiba, I don't know the right way to say this so I'm just going to say it. You need to end things with Mikhail."

I held my breath, waiting for a response. A sound indicating that she heard me. Anything.

"Excuse me?" she said, an edge to her voice.

"I know I have no right to tell you what to do, and this may be none of my business. But, you have to understand, he is not a good person."

"*Mikhail is the best thing that ever happened to me,*" she said after a moment.

"*No, Hiba, listen to me. He has you fooled, okay? He's just pretending to be a good boyfriend and a good person, but I'm his* sister. *I live with him and I see a side of him that you don't see. He has done terrible things. He—*"

I stopped, but it wasn't intentional. It was like my mouth suddenly didn't know how to work anymore, or my vocal cords ran out of battery.

"*He what?*"

I opened my mouth to respond but nothing came out. Why couldn't I just say it? Why did I feel so . . . guilty? Like I was lying? That seed of doubt was starting to sprout branches in my mind, intertwining with all my memories. What was real and what was my imagination running amok?

"*He . . .*" *I tried again, my voice so faint I couldn't tell if she could even hear me.*

"*Did Mikhail hurt you?*"

I always told myself that if only someone would just ask, then I would tell them. My parents never asked. The doctors at the hospital never asked. But now this girl that I didn't know was asking if Mikhail had ever hurt me.

The word yes was on my tongue, ready to be said, but when I opened my mouth the only thing that came out was an unintelligible sound—like I was choking—and then suddenly I was *choking. Choking on air. Choking on that stupid word made of sand in the back of my throat.*

"*It's okay. I understand, Maya.*"

She understood, which meant she knew. She knew I was trying to say yes and she believed me. Maybe this could be the start of something. Maybe we could take this further, to my parents, and the doctors I saw and maybe even higher up. Two people were always better than one. Something was brewing inside me, Ana. A tiny sliver of hope was starting to bloom . . .

"You put on a convincing act."

. . . and just as quickly that sliver shriveled up into nothing.

"He warned me that you would try something like this."

"What?"

"Mikhail warned me about you when we first met," she said, laughing humorlessly. "He told me all about that car accident. You know, I thought he was exaggerating. It didn't occur to me that anyone could be cruel enough to make up lies about their own brother."

Lies, *Ana.*

"How dare you?" she seethed through the phone and into my ear. "How dare you treat him like this when all he's ever done is love you? This has gone far beyond trivial sibling banter. This is toxic, Maya. You are toxic.*"*

"No, he's lying to you," I said quickly. "He's the toxic one. He has severe anger issues and it just comes out of nowhere, you'll never see it coming! You have to get away from him, Hiba, please, before he—"

"Shut up!" She demanded loudly, interrupting me. "Do you even hear yourself? How manipulative you sound? You're trying to drive me away from him because you don't want him to be happy. Your victimized tactics may have worked on your parents, but they won't work on me."

"My parents? I have never—"

"Just stop, Maya. I really hope one day you'll accept the help you need."

"Wait, Hiba, just listen—"

"Goodbye."

"Hiba."

Silence.

"Hiba please," I whispered into the dead phone, but the beep of the dial tone started, so I slowly dropped my hand limply to my side.

It was over.

I should've known Mikhail would cover his bases from the get-go, just like he did at the hospital. I guess he knew me better than I thought he did.

I leaned back against the lockers as the disgusting cloud of humiliation dawned on me. What was I thinking? What part of me thought this would end well? Why would she believe anything I ever said?

"Stop," I pleaded quietly, covering my ears tightly with my hands, willing the thoughts to come to an end. The harder I tried to push her words out of my head, the stronger they pushed back and forced themselves into the sliver of space between my irises and closed eyelids.

The first warning bell buzzed, signaling the end of lunch. The sound of students rushing into the hallway, and opening their lockers broke me out of my reverie. I saw Dania and the others on my way back to the cafeteria and quickly headed their way.

"Hey, here's your phone, sorry I took so long—"

"Where have you been?" she snapped, snatching the phone out of my hand. "You said you would only be a minute."

Her words stung my fresh wounds. I opened my mouth to apologize again, but she turned on her heel and walked away, her posy one step behind her. Before she was out of earshot her next words still reached me, clear as day.

"What kind of teenager doesn't have a phone anyway?" she asked rhetorically, her voice deprecating.

"I know right," Lena laughed.

The second bell buzzed, saving me from having to hear any more of their conversation, and the rest of the school day passed in a blur. As soon as my mom came home I went straight to my closet and curled up in a tight ball. I was still in disbelief at how things had panned out, but there was only one thing on my mind.

Was she going to tell Mikhail that I called her?

Tears pricked the corner of my eyes as her harsh words whispered in my ears again. She was so convinced I wasn't telling the truth. What could he have said to make her believe that? What lies did he feed her about me? Most importantly though, were they even lies? The more I tried to remember, the more confused I became. All the details were getting jumbled together with her words, and nothing made sense anymore. There was no way I could even validate the things in my head. How could I prove myself when it was just me? I was so sure of myself before but now . . . the weeds of doubt were sprouting quickly, their stems thick and sharp, knocking a few pegs off my ladder of confidence.

I heard the front door open with a sudden bang, and my body immediately switched on high alert.

"MAYA!"

His feet were running up the stairs loudly, quickening my breath with every step. The closet suddenly flung open, and before I knew what was happening I was off the floor and slammed into the wall with Mikhail's hand wrapped around my neck like a noose.

"What the fuck do you think you're doing, huh? Why the fuck would you call my girlfriend?" he whispered. His face was close, only a millimeter away, his saliva sprinkling me with sparks of lava.

"How dare you threaten her?" he said louder this time, enunciating his question with another shove, and my head once again banged against the wall. I could feel my brain shudder with the impact.

"I didn't threaten her." I could barely get the words out from my compressed airways. "I was just trying to warn her."

"Warn her?" he laughed. "I'm the best thing that ever happened to her."

His words echoed Hiba's exactly. He must have trained her well.

"Are you jealous of her?" His voice was lower now, a murmur in my ear. "She is twice—no—a million times the woman you will ever be. Do you understand me, Maya?"

His fingers pressed deeper into my skin, imprinting his mark.

"Do you think you can tell her lies about me? Do you think she'll believe you? She loves me, okay? She adores me. She lives and breathes

just to cherish and obey me. You will never understand how that feels. You will never be loved, Maya. Do you hear me?"

I tried to inch away and wiggle out of his grasp, but that only made his grip tighter.

"I thought things would be different. I thought that car crash would have taught you a lesson, or made you better," he sighed in disappointment. "But you're still the same. You're still so desperate for attention that you've gone and tried to interfere with my relationship."

I pounded and pushed against his body frantically, starting to feel lightheaded.

"Do you think I like doing this? You make me do this," he explained desperately. "This is your fault, Maya."

"Mikhail what are you doing? Let her go!" Mama shrieked from behind him but he didn't move. His manic eyes were zeroed in on me, and his crushing grip squeezed tighter around my neck until black spots started popping up in my vision.

"Mikhail stop, she can't breathe!" My mom grabbed his arm and pulled. A shocked look appeared on his face like he genuinely didn't realize she was there, which momentarily loosened his grip. I quickly slipped out from between him and the wall and ran for the stairs, coughing and clutching my chest. I grabbed the phone on instinct, before going into the bathroom and locking the door.

I gasped at the girl looking back at me in the mirror. Finger-like bruises were starting to blossom across the surface of her neck. Her eyes were red and splotchy from lack of oxygen and exploded blood vessels were leaking into her pupils.

I leaned against the sink trying to catch my breath, but it felt like my throat had permanently molded into a smaller airway. My breaths were coming in and out constricted and scratchy, barely giving me any clarity. I hunched over as my body started convulsing with dry heaves and desperate sobs.

I could hear yelling from above. I needed to go and protect my mom, but how could I protect her when I couldn't even protect myself? I held the phone in front of me with trembling hands, ready to make a call. But I had no one to call. No one could help us.

I continued to stare at the numbers as the yelling grew louder. As long as I heard yelling, that meant she wasn't hurt.

I ran my thumb over the buttons gently, waiting.

A loud bang thundered from above, making me jump out of my skin, and before I knew what I was doing my finger was moving on the dial pad.

"Maya?" Mama called, her footsteps coming down the stairs.

I breathed a sigh of relief. She was okay. My mom was okay. Everything was okay . . . until a woman's voice floated through the phone.

"9-1-1 what's your emergency?"

NOW

"Movie?"

"*Eagle Eye*."

"Never heard of it."

"That's concerning."

Noah chuckled. "I'll add it to my list. Season?"

"Winter."

"*Winter?*" he repeated in disgust.

"Yes. I love the cold. I hate the sun. I love when it gets dark early. I wish daylight savings was never-ending."

"Well," he said doubtfully. "I guess that explains why you're always wearing gloves."

I looked away and took a sip of my coffee instead of responding to his not-so-subtle way of trying to get me to uncover something about myself. It was Friday night and we were at *Espresso & Chill* after hours. I wasn't scheduled at Tysons and usually I would pick up a shift, but once we started talking the time flew by and it was too late. Noah and I had come up with a system over the last few months. I clearly laid out all the topics of conversation forbidden from being discussed, and after that, everything was . . . easy. I hadn't had easy in a long time.

Noah had no issues filling my silence with his life. His story was heartbreaking and inspiring, with a happily ever after to tie it all together. The plot to a touching movie, or a sentimental memoir. He talked about his café. He talked about his loving brothers. He talked about the close relationship he had with his parents.

He talked about Ana.

I thought I'd felt the worst of it. That never-ending, all-consuming, always *there* guilt. But listening to him speak so highly of her . . . it hurt. God, it fucking hurt. Ana was everything I wasn't and everything I would never be. If only her best qualities had gotten donated as well. I still couldn't bring myself to stop asking, though, to stop *torturing* myself because somewhere, deep down in the corrupted barrel I called a soul, I knew I deserved it. The questions kept steamrolling through, questions I didn't even know I had until suddenly this boy who had access to all the answers fell right into my lap.

I hesitated before bringing her up, certain he would hear the irrational eagerness behind my innocent curiosity, but he didn't seem to notice. It was obvious he was holding back when he spoke of her, but I didn't mind. I took the crumbs he fed me fervently. *Desperately.* A mouse trapped in a home with a vegan family but eating the dairy-free cheese anyway just to survive.

So while Noah gave me depth, I gave him minor and nonessential facts about myself. I was sure he would get sick of my answers, but every night ended the same way.

"Will I see you tomorrow?"

And I would nod.

"Pinky promise."

"What about baked goods? You only ever get a coffee when you're here," he said suspiciously.

"I'm more savory than sweet and I put hot sauce on

everything, but if I was in the mood for it, I would choose anything with chocolate. I hate cheese, except on a well-done pizza or in a double-toasted bagel. I hate nuts and anything peanut butter flavored, but I do *love* pb&j sandwiches, and my favorite chocolate bar is definitely *Reese*. I know that sounds contradicting—"

"Everything you said sounds contradicting—"

"*But* the fuzzy math makes sense in my head. I prefer processed snacks over real food. I love candy. Hate rabbit food. Fruit-based pastries are a *no*, except for banana—oh!" I clapped my hands together loudly. "Okay, I have my answer. I would never eat a banana, like, by itself—that's gross. But my mom makes this chocolate chip banana bread that is to *die* for."

"Chocolate chip banana bread?" he repeated, shaking his head. "Did you have to choose the *one* thing that's not on my menu?"

"I'm just trying to improve your business."

"I appreciate the input. Chocolate chip banana bread has also been added to my list."

"Good."

"*Good.*"

I was leaning casually on the table with my chin in my right hand and my left hand resting beside me. He was sitting back against his chair, arms crossed, eyes never leaving mine, giving me that look I'd become so accustomed to. It was focused and fascinated, one green orb, one blue orb, and suddenly I was flying in the sky and laying in the grass at the same time.

Thump, thump—

"What? Is the interrogation over? Did I finally bore you?"

"Not even close," he assured me. "I'm giving you an

opportunity to offer something up voluntarily."

"I just gave you an entire speech about what I like to eat."

"And it was *truly* invigorating."

I grinned and pointed to the white drape covering the right side of the café. "Are you still renovating?"

He ignored my question. "What's your favourite color?"

"Green. Does someone else own that part of the building?"

He huffed playfully. "I'm the sole owner of the building, but I still have no idea what to do with the rest of it. I think I might just expand the shop once it starts to get more foot traffic."

"This place is packed every day," I reminded him. "I'm starting to suspect that you're shoving some innocent person out of this chair seconds before I walk in because it's conveniently always *empty*."

He looked down, his cheeks tinted pink. "It's the least I could do, seeing as my café is always packed because of the continuous *anonymous* glowing Yelp reviews."

"Oh, those aren't me. I mean, your café is nice and all, but I definitely wouldn't rate it five stars."

"Sure it's not, hotcoffeeh8ter101."

"It's not," I insisted, biting back a smile. "But I would *love* to meet them."

"I'll set you guys up," he promised jokingly.

I kept looking at the tarp and an idea occurred to me suddenly. "You should turn it into a bookstore."

"A bookstore?"

"Yeah, reading is super *in* right now."

"I didn't realize you kept up with the trends."

"I don't," I agreed. "I'm part of the generation of readers that spent lunch in the library because I had no friends."

"Wow . . . no wonder you're sad."

"Those are happy memories, Noah. Reading is much more fun than socializing."

"Okay, reading has also been added to my list," he said. "So, what are we talking—*Austin? Dickinson? Atwood?*"

I stared at him blankly. "None of the above."

"Oh. I assumed you'd be into classic literature or intellectually stimulating novels."

"Intellectually stimulating?" I repeated with a chuckle. "My favorite book series is *Twilight*. Which was very stimulating, just not intellectually."

"Oh God," he groaned. "You were one of those girls?"

"No," I replied. "I still *am* one of those girls. Present tense, Noah."

"I'm sorry, I just can't picture you fangirling like the girls did at my school."

I laughed at that. "It's not cool to be a hater. Besides, I was more of a *silent*-obsessed fan. I didn't express it in fits of squeals and giggles, but I was exactly like them. And yes, *Edward Cullen* was and will forever be my one true love," I told him with conviction.

"Really? A sparkly fictional character is my competition?" he teased.

Thump, thump—

"Fictional men are definitely the standard, but it was the unconditional and irrevocable love concept that gripped my attention."

He contemplated my words for a moment. "Have you ever been in love? With a *real* person?"

I coughed as the coffee went down the wrong pipe.

"Are you joking?"

"No, I'm seriously asking."

"Um, well, in order to fall in love, you would have to get to know someone. Date someone. *Talk* to someone. None of which I have ever done. You're actually the first guy I've ever been . . . friends with."

When did the word 'friends' become such an ugly word?

I glanced at him when he didn't respond, and Noah was smiling brightly.

"What?" I demanded.

"You called me your *friend*."

I rolled my eyes. "Don't let it get to your head."

"Too late." He winked. "You've really never been in a relationship before?"

"Are you *surprised*?" I looked at him skeptically. "It's so obvious how awkward I am. That's not exactly a turn-on for people."

"That's not how I see you. I mean, you're certainly difficult at times. *Most* times."

My lips twitched. "I have no idea what you're talking about."

"Mhm," he agreed sarcastically. "You're also a little mean."

"*Only* a little?" I scoffed.

"Extremely pessimistic."

"Okay, I'll give you that."

"You're so . . . secretive. But somehow you're also remarkably blunt at the same time." He shook his head. "You're an enigma, Maya."

"See?" I said, laughing. "Getting to know me is too much work."

"*But*," he continued. "You're also funny. Smart. You listen in a way that I *know* you're listening, even though I can't physically see the action. When I talk to you . . . I don't feel like my words are just bouncing off. You absorb everything I say," he said softly. "I like the way you think. You never respond or react to stuff like I expect you to. It keeps things interesting."

"You're making me sound like a science experiment."

"You're pretty," he pressed on. "Effortlessly, painlessly, fluently *pretty*."

Thump, thump—

"If only that's what men want."

"What do you mean?"

I rolled my eyes. "Don't play dumb, Noah. I may have been single for a lifetime, but I'm not naïve. Men don't care if a woman is smart—actually, most would prefer the opposite. You know, to protect their fragile ego. And, I don't have proof, but I'm almost positive the first rule in the male pledge of allegiance is that a female can't be funny. Literally *and* figuratively."

He raised his eyebrows in shock. "You've read it?"

I ignored his mockery and kept going. "*Listening*, Noah? If I let a single brain cell comprehend what was coming out of a man's mouth, it would only take half a second to hear something sexist, misogynistic, or just plain cruel." I shook my head in distaste. "Men don't want *unpredictable*. They want easily controlled, and someone willing to accept the bare minimum."

He regarded me skeptically. "For someone who isn't a fan of real men, your words carry the fumes of a scorched past relationship." His eyes lit up suddenly, and he gave me a suggestive look. "*Girls*?"

I sighed longingly. "Yeah, I wish."

He paused, thinking. "Your dad?"

"We're not *close*, but he still fulfilled all the fatherly requirements."

"A male stranger on the street? A creepy professor?" He was grasping at strings. "I've got nothing."

Of course he didn't. Those were always the immediate assumptions—boyfriend, father, or a fucking *stranger*. Those were the only possible ways a man could ever hurt a woman. There were no other scenarios. Everything else didn't count. *My* story didn't count.

It wasn't Noah's fault for thinking that way. We lived in a world that chose to only recognize the *right* kind of abuse, and that chose to only believe the *right* kind of victim. If it wasn't previously psychoanalyzed in a published document, or artistically displayed in the media by an Oscar-winning celebrity then it wasn't real. If you didn't relentlessly perform your victimhood with calculated tears and a striking, *unmistakable* image of frailty during all hours of the day then it must not be true. It was deemed unacceptable and therefore couldn't be heard. And if your story couldn't be heard, then it also couldn't be helped. And as the days went on . . . as the minutes of being ignored and invisible continued to tick loudly in a never-ending cycle of despair you inevitably started to believe it too.

But so be it. You got blamed when you fought back. You got blamed when you didn't speak up sooner. You got blamed for being too *sensitive*. Too *dramatic*. Too *emotional*. You got blamed when the situation you described wasn't common or ideal. You got blamed when you didn't have proof because obviously, the first thing I felt like doing after getting beaten and strangled was to take a fucking *selfie*. I refused to humiliate myself any further. I refused to fold myself into society's version of the perfect damsel in distress, and if that meant my story would remain unspoken until it died with me then so *fucking* be it.

"The silent monologue raging on in your head looks good," Noah said when I continued to reel quietly. "If only I could hear it too."

"It's extremely rusty," I assured him, forcing my unyielding anger back into its forbidden box. "You're not missing out."

"Well, on behalf of my very fucked up species, I apologize."

I gave him a small smile. "You're not *all* bad."

"A select few aren't," he agreed reluctantly. "You'll find your match, Maya. Any guy would be lucky to date you."

Thump, thump—

"Who said I was looking?"

"You just told me that you only read about cheesy romance and everything *love*."

"I do."

He gave me a look. "So you enjoy reading about it, but you don't want to experience it?"

"Not necessarily." I hesitated. "I guess I just don't believe in it."

"There's nothing to believe in. Love isn't a theory or a hypothesis—it exists."

"I believe in love as an *emotion*," I clarified. "I believe that love can be strong. I believe that love can be beautiful. But I also believe that love is conditional and subject to change. It can happen in a split second, or after a prolonged sequence of time . . . but it always happens. Real and unconditional love is as make belief as vampires, and werewolf's and any other mystical creature or fairytale ever written on paper."

"Do you really believe that?" he asked doubtfully.

"There's always *something*, Noah. There's always going to be something that you can't forgive, or look past." I swallowed noisily, all remnants of humor gone. "Sometimes you don't even know what it is that made them change their mind—that made them decide to *hate* you—but it always happens."

He was quiet for a second, before suddenly leaning into the table, his chair squeaking against the tile. "They're wrong."

"Who's they?"

"*They*," he repeated firmly. "Them, he, she, *it*. The person who told you that you couldn't be loved without restrictions or limitations. They're *wrong*."

His face was so close to mine, I could count every eyelash, and freckle, and smile line, and hair follicle beginning to sprout over his lip.

Thump, thump—

I leaned back in my chair, pushing it away from the table.

He would never forgive this.

"Maya?"

"Sorry," I replied, standing. "I have to go . . . my mom's going to be wondering where I am."

He nodded. "Drive safe."

I walked to the door but stopped with my hand on the knob.

"Thank you," I said, looking back at him.

"For what?"

"Calling me pretty."

He grinned. "No need to thank me for being honest."

"Okay, settle down." I rolled my eyes. "Bye, dude."

"See ya, chick."

I pulled onto my street with a smile on my face, just like I'd been doing every day since December. Somewhere within the hours of laughter and shared words, I always found myself forgetting . . .

. . . but then that same smile disappeared as soon as I saw my brother's car in the driveway, just like it did every day since December.

I walked to the front door slowly, counting each stride. After three tries it finally took exactly 52 steps. I *knew* 52 steps. 52 steps was *real*. 52 steps confirmed I wasn't imagining. I could hear them all talking in the living room, and they sounded so . . . normal. But everything would change as soon as I stepped through the door. My presence would shatter the illusion they'd created for themselves—a tornado ripping through on a cloudless day. Or maybe it wasn't an illusion. Maybe they *weren't* pretending. Maybe they genuinely felt like an ordinary, loving family and it was *me* who made it feel incredibly dishonest and illegal.

"Salam Mama, Baba," I greeted, tilting my head in their direction but keeping my gaze on the floor. I could feel Mikhail's eyes burning a hole through my skin like bleach.

"Maya, honey, we've been waiting for you. We wanted to have dinner all together tonight. Like a family."

"I already ate," I lied quickly, my stomach growling in response. "I'm really tired, I just want to—"

"Maya," she interrupted. "*Please*."

I shifted my stare to her pleading eyes. I spent my whole life pretending, couldn't I do it for one more night? For *her*?

"Okay," I agreed. "I'm just going to change."

After getting dressed in some sweats, I went to the bathroom and leaned against the door, staring at my hand. I swapped out my leather gloves for my cut-off cotton pair today. They were meant to be used for arthritis or carpal tunnel, which was what my mom thought I had because that's what I told her. Not because I had anything to hide or because I was doing anything wrong, I just didn't know how to explain whatever *this* was. I liked to think of it as grooming. It was equivalent to shaving your legs or popping a pimple. I was only cleansing my body of its noticeable flaws.

I carefully slipped them off and examined the skin on the dorsal side of my right hand—for some reason, my deranged hyper fixation excluded my left hand, but wearing one glove was more conspicuous than wearing two. It wasn't as bad as I thought. Most of the scabs had healed into a faded pink spot, but there were a few that were still bumpy and protruding from my skin, which meant the glove remained necessary. All I had to do was leave them alone for a few more weeks and they would disappear completely, freeing me from this disgusting bad habit. As long as I couldn't see or feel them, I wouldn't have the compulsive urge to *pick*.

There was one though, near the bottom, that hadn't healed quite as nicely as the others. The corner was black, which I assumed was dried blood I hadn't wiped away from the last time I was picking at it. I was positive the black and crusted part would be pink underneath, it just had to be removed so it could heal smoothly. So it could heal *perfectly*. I gently rubbed the scab, careful not to go too fast. Speed usually resulted in accidentally pricking my skin too hard and causing it to bleed.

"Maya, come down!"

I ignored her and slipped my nail underneath the scab

slowly. I washed my hands, satisfied with the result, until I noticed the stream running red in the sink.

It was bleeding. I must have nicked my skin without noticing.

I ran my hand under the water to stop the flow, ignoring the tender sensation—

"Maya!"

I turned the water off and put my gloves back on, letting out a shaky breath. It was gross and weird, and after every picking session, or episode, or whatever the *fuck*, I would tell myself that it was the last time. But then after a few minutes, or days, or—if I was lucky—weeks, my brain would go into overdrive and my fingers would absently go searching and prodding for a fresh scab or bump or scratch on my skin to pick, pick, *pick*.

"Sorry, Mama. I was in the bathroom," I told her, taking my usual seat at the table. They had already started eating which meant our *family* dinner would end quicker. I still hadn't set my eyes on Mikhail or acknowledged his presence in any way, but I knew he was sitting across from me because I could feel his gaze. They followed my hands as I reached for my spoon, and kept watching as I scooped up some rice and brought it to my mouth. I swallowed forcefully—my hunger had vanished and was replaced with nausea.

"How was work today?" Mama asked.

"Good," I responded, my voice monotone. He was still trying to get me to look at him. He wanted me to address his existence. He wanted to see the fear embedded in my eyes and confirm that I was still scared of him. That the panic he instilled in me all those years ago had never left. That, even though he'd been gone for almost five years, I was still haunted by the mere mention of his *name*. He could stare all he wanted. I was never going to give his sick and twisted mind the satisfaction it craved.

"Did you call the university yet to make sure your enrollment deferral is still active?" Baba asked.

Did he mean *fake* enrollment?

"Yeah, they said it's fine. I have two years, Baba," I replied, pushing food around my plate to make it look like I'd eaten more than one bite.

"I don't know why you differed anyway," he said disapprovingly. "You're just going to be behind. Everyone has got it figured out except for you."

My resolve slipped for a moment and I scraped my spoon harshly against my plate. My father was a prideful man, but *this*? Letting his wounded dignity speak to me like I was burdening him with my existence. Like I wasn't reminded every day that I was behind in life.

"Honey, you know she's helping us out," Mama told him quietly, but he kept eating without giving her a response.

I bit my tongue and swallowed the burning sensation starting to grow deep in my chest at his unjust disappointment. I put my whole life on hold for them. I sacrificed my happiness and well-being for *them*. I would have left ages ago. I would have run away from this nightmare they called a family but I didn't. I *stayed*. I stayed and they still weren't satisfied. Nothing I ever did was good enough.

My mom stood up an eternity later and gathered my dad and Mikhail's plates. I got up quickly and took my plate to the kitchen as well.

"I'll do them, Mama, go sit down," I insisted, taking the plates from her. I covered the sponge with soap and started scrubbing the dishes clean. I was almost done rinsing when I felt him walk up behind me and my movements instantly halted. He reached over to grab a glass from the drying rack, his arm brushing my shoulder gently and I jumped back, dropping the plate. It hit the ground between us and shattered loudly, glass flying everywhere—

The vase shattered against the wall less than a millimeter away from my head. Shards of glass sliced through my cheek.

"Why are you running away, huh?" Mikhail goaded—

"Are you okay?" he asked, grabbing my arm.

He grabbed my arm tightly and shoved me into the wall—

"Let go of me," I demanded, yanking my arm out of his grasp.

"Maya, I just—"

"Get *away* from me!" I was screaming now, backing into the counter, but he was blocking my only exit so I couldn't escape. I slowly slid down the cabinets and onto the floor.

"Please, leave me alone," I pleaded, covering my ears so I couldn't hear his yelling. "Leave me alone, leave me alone, leave me alone . . ."

I put my head down on my knees, praying for it to be quick. After several minutes I shifted my hands away from my ears, checking to see if he was done yelling but there was only silence.

Was he gone? Did he change his mind? Did I black out again and not notice him leaving? I lifted my head slightly and opened my eyes.

My mom, dad, and Mikhail were all standing in the kitchen, staring at me with shocked expressions. My mom had tears in her eyes, and my dad held her hand, regarding me apprehensively. Why were they just standing there? Didn't they see what he did to me just now? Weren't they going to—?

And then it dawned on me.

My memories had mixed in with reality.

Nothing was real.

I stood up quickly, and everyone took a step back like . . . they were afraid of me.

"I'm fine," I told them. "I just thought . . ."

Thought what? That Mikhail was attacking you?

"Maya, what's going on with you?" Mama whispered with the same frightened look on her face.

"Nothing, I'm fine. I just got startled—"

"Startled?" Baba repeated. "You had a psychotic breakdown!"

A psychotic breakdown? A laugh slipped through my lips before I could stop myself. There was no way they were being serious.

"Maya, if you need . . . *help* again, that's okay. There's no shame in struggling . . . mentally. Let us get you some help, honey."

My humor quickly disappeared as I realized they *were* serious. So it was normal when he did it, but as soon as I took a step out of line I needed psychiatric help? *Again?*

"Yes, Maya," Mikhail said suddenly. "Please, let us help you."

All my efforts to avoid looking at him flew out the window, and my eyes flickered to his at the sound of his voice. My mom said he'd changed, but he still looked exactly like I remembered. Even his smug look was the same.

Disgust pooled in my mouth. I was going to be *sick*.

I ran out of the kitchen and up to my room, slamming the

door behind me. I could still see their expressions judging me through the closed door, Mikhail's standing out over the rest, and before I could stop myself my fist rose and struck the door once, twice, a third time. Each bang harder than the next as I desperately tried to break the images out of my mind. I pulled my arm back to swing again, when I caught a glimpse of myself in my full-length mirror and paused.

Wild, knotted hair. Tear-stained cheeks. Lips pulled back into an animalistic sneer as I destroyed my door. Spots of blood leaking through the glove covering my right hand. Blood from my *own* neurotic doing.

I dropped my fist to my side. They were right to look at me that way. They were right to be terrified by my presence. Everyone should be terrified of me. *I* was terrified of me. Who was I? When had I become this person? I didn't slam doors and get consumed with so much fury I could only see red. That was Mikhail's role in this family . . . wasn't it?

I'd been constantly aware of my genetics for my entire life. I took numerous biology and psychology courses because I needed to know and understand what made up our brains and our minds, and how they both connected to make up who we were as individuals. Did we have a say in how we turned out as humans or did our genes and brain chemicals call all the shots? How much of who we were and what we were capable of was predetermined? Inescapable? Unpreventable? I didn't need to know because I was interested in the subject. I needed to know if there was even the *slightest* possibility I could end up just as fucked up as Mikhail.

I tried so hard not to be like him. I tried so hard to smother every ounce of anger that ever raged through me. I told myself over and over again that my brain was different. That *I* was different. But trying to fight science was useless. Trying to fight my genetics was useless. We were both created and marinated within the same womb, so it was highly likely the mutation that dominated his mind would dominate *mine* as well, no matter how hard I tried to deny it.

As I continued to stare at myself, I suddenly couldn't tell if it was me or Mikhail standing there, and pure revulsion filled my core up to the brim. I was slowly turning into everything I hated about him. Whoever said the apple didn't fall far from the lunatic tree was right . . . I was truly my brother's sister.

Quicker than seemingly possible, I grabbed my bottle of cleanser from the shelf behind me and hurled it at my mirror. I watched, satisfied, as it hit my reflection's face perfectly and shattered my image into a pile of glass on the carpet. The only thing facing me now was a half-empty wooden frame with sharp fragments clinging on for life. Even without the mirror, it was still accurately *mirroring* the person standing in front of it.

I flicked my light switch off without bothering to clean up the mess and curled into a ball of misery under my covers. I held my phone in my hand, the need to let everything out before I rotted from the inside out was strong, but who could I talk to? Who would understand?

And then almost like it was planned, almost like he sensed it, Noah texted me.

My lips twisted into a watery smile at his name lighting up my phone. Poor boy. He thought he knew me. He thought he had me all figured out, but he was wrong. He only saw what he wanted to see. I couldn't even bring myself to be upset about it because who would want to know the real me? I brought destruction with me everywhere I went.

It was supposed to be easy, Noah and I, that's why I kept seeing him. But after one simple interaction Mikhail reminded me why I couldn't have easy. After one simple interaction, Mikhail torpedoed the charade I had managed to uphold since December. The play I'd been putting on where I starred as a girl who had coffee dates with a boy, and Noah fell for it because Noah was a *believer* and I was a *liar*. He didn't deserve this. No one did. Which was why I had to do the right thing and . . . let him go.

I could physically feel her heart and my mind cracking at the thought. Two parts of two different people writhing in synchronized pain. This was it. *This* was my life. There was no one I could text about my day. No one to see after work. Nothing in the next week, or the next month, or the next year to look forward to. I was entirely alone. But not the kind of alone people loved to romanticize. No, there was nothing *poetic* about this. I was living inside a body that was forcing me to survive when my soul didn't want to, and I didn't even have it in me to do anything about it. I couldn't live and I couldn't die. I couldn't fight and I couldn't give up. I was just stuck here, sinking in the quicksand, standing *still* and patient and silent so it didn't suck me under because that was how you survived the deathly quicksand, but it was still pulling me under anyway and I was starting to suspect there was no bottom.

I was starting to suspect this was forever.

My phone beeped again and I reluctantly opened his message.

You sidetracked me with your anti-men/anti-love speech, and I forgot to ask...will I see you tomorrow? -Noah

I swiped left and deleted our chat.

"No," I said. "You'll never see me again. Pinky promise"

I chuckled. *Promises* . . . they were like threads. One hard yank from both directions and it would break in half. In this case, I was holding both ends.

THEN

Dear Ana,

"9-1-1 what's your emergency?"

The phone slipped through my fingers and onto the floor.

"9-1-1 what's your emergency?" she repeated louder.

My world stood still. All the pain vanished as my focus zeroed in on the fact that I had just called the police. I had dreamt about doing this so many times, but never in a million years thought that I actually would.

"Hello? Can you hear me?"

The only sound in the room was your pulse vibrating off the walls around me, and my breath coming out in short bursts. I didn't know if that was because Mikhail permanently destroyed my windpipes with his fingers, or because I didn't want her to hear me on the other end.

"Maya?" Mama banged on the door. "Come out please."

I wanted to tell her to be quiet so the officer wouldn't hear her, but I couldn't open my mouth to speak.

"Are you in danger?" the lady asked.

I didn't know, was I in danger? I assumed my mom was okay since she could talk and walk, and I couldn't hear any movement from upstairs.

"Listen to me, we're tracking your location right now. Help is on the way, okay?"

"No, wait!" I blurted into the phone.

"Maya?" Mama said through the door.

"Hello?" the lady said through the phone.

There were too many people talking to me at once, and I was getting confused. I forced myself to take a deep and steady breath and brought the phone up to my lips.

"I'm so sorry, I dialed by mistake," I told her calmly. My mom was quiet behind the door.

"Are you in danger?"

"No, no," I said quickly. "I'm not in danger. I heard some noise and called without thinking. Everything is fine. I'm sorry."

She was quiet. I held my breath, making a silent prayer to God that she would just let it be, and that this nightmare could finally come to an end.

"Did you know it's a felony to call the police without cause?" she asked seriously.

"I'm sorry," I whispered, unsure if she could even hear me.

"It's okay, honey," she said sympathetically. "We've tracked your location, and an officer is going to stop by soon to check on you just to make sure."

"No, I told you everything is fine. They don't need to come here."

"Someone has to be dispatched on every call, it's protocol."

A fresh wave of dread washed over me as I tried to make sense of what she was saying.

"Hello? Can you hear me?"

I quickly ended the call and dropped the phone in my lap.

"Open the door right now," Mama demanded.

I got up slowly, my brain in a heavy fog, still unsure of what just happened.

She gasped in surprise as I opened the door and revealed myself. My eyes quickly analyzed her from head to toe to make sure she wasn't harmed.

"Oh, Maya," she said, putting her hands on my cheeks. I flinched away from her touch, my body no longer able to tell the difference between a loving and a punishing form of human contact.

"Please honey, I'm not going to hurt you. I just want to make sure you're okay," she assured me.

She reached for me again and this time I let her. I watched closely as she examined the damage in front of her, tears streaming silently down her face. I knew I had to tell her the police were on their way, but I didn't know how to. She was going to be so angry and worried. But watching her fret over me, and feeling her fingers stroking my face and my neck softly . . . lovingly . . . would she be mad? She just got a front-row seat to what Mikhail was capable of, and when I finally came forward about all the other things he'd done, she wouldn't be able to deny it any longer. Mikhail needed to leave. He needed to be taken far, far away from us, and get some serious help. She had to know that by now.

"Everything is going to be okay. Just go take a warm bath, and I'm going to make you some dinner."

"Mama, I . . ."

"Yes?"

"I called the police."

All the color completely drained from her face and she snatched her hands away from me.

"You did what?"

She was pissed. Of course she was.

"I . . . I called the police——"

"Oh my God, Maya, why? Why would you do that?" she asked frantically.

"I was scared! I didn't know what else to do. I heard yelling and then a loud bang, and I thought he was going to hurt you——"

"He's my son, how could you think he would ever hurt me?"

"Look at me!" I screamed hoarsely. "He did this to me right in front of you! What makes you think he won't do the same to you? I did you a favor, he needs help. He needs help that you can't provide for him."

"Your brother loves you——"

"This is love?" I interrupted, pointing to the marks on my neck.

"It was just a misunderstanding. He was upset because you called his girlfriend and were unkind to her, so he just—just reacted in the moment! He's not a monster. He's human and he's your brother. Siblings fight, it doesn't mean you call the cops to come and take him away!"

"You can't be serious," I whispered. I was in shock. I couldn't believe she was defending him after everything. I couldn't believe she was still making excuses for his horrific behavior.

"Maya, please." She put her hands on either side of my face, bringing me down to her eye level. "Please, you have to tell them it was a mistake. They can't take him away from me, he's my only son. What he did today was not okay, but calling the police isn't the solution. Are you really so cruel a sister? Is your heart truly this black?"

She did that a lot, Ana. Insinuated that I was a mean, cold, terrible, terrible sister. It's funny, though. I've never once heard her say that Mikhail was a terrible brother.

"He's not like this all the time. He's never acted this way before. You really can't forgive one mistake?"

This is your chance, I told myself. Open your mouth, speak, scream about every other mistake he's made and watch the truth poison her with pain.

But I couldn't, Ana. My pathetic lips stayed pressed together and my eyes continued to stare straight into her tortured soul. I hated what this was doing to her. What I was doing to her. Mikhail's actions weren't her fault, but she was going to be the one who suffered the consequences in the end. I couldn't do that to her. I didn't understand the strong urge she possessed to protect Mikhail, especially after the way he treated me, but how could I? I wasn't a mother. I couldn't possibly comprehend the deep and unbreakable bond that was coiled tightly between a mother and her son. I just wished the same could be said between her and I.

I was constantly being torn between empathy and betrayal. The natural maternal instinct in me that came with having a womb understood, but the daughter in me that she failed over and over again did not.

"Maya," she said urgently. "Please!"

I nodded quickly as bright headlights flashed through the curtains in the living room.

She kissed my cheek and ran upstairs. I didn't move from where I was standing, still surprised and disturbed by the events that had transpired. My mom hurried back and shoved something over my head. A turtleneck sweater. To cover up the bruises, of course.

There was a loud knock on the door. I could feel the panic starting to bubble up, but I shoved it back down. I couldn't afford to break down right now. She needed me to be strong, for the both of us. I had to protect her from any torment threatening to come her way, which meant I had to fix the problem I created. I had to convince the police it was all a misunderstanding. A mistake. That I was fine.

Completely and utterly fine.

I took a deep breath and turned to the door, but before I could take a step, Mikhail rushed down the stairs and beat me to it.

"Hello officers, how can I help you?"

I closed my eyes tightly to keep myself from making a disgusted expression. I would never get used to how easily he could pretend to be a friendly and charming man.

"We received a call from someone in your household today," one of the officers replied. They both stepped inside, taking a look around before their stare landed on me.

Despite my mother's attempt to make me look presentable, it was obvious they could tell something was wrong. I don't know what she expected, but I wasn't a magician. I couldn't just erase all traces of trauma from my appearance at a moment's notice.

I forced myself to smile back at them. My facial muscles felt like they were moving through cemented concrete.

"That was me who called," I said, my voice rough and scratchy. I cleared my throat a few times, swallowing down the shooting pain. "I tried explaining to the dispatcher who answered that it was a mistake."

"We still have to come out," he replied, regarding me intensely. "There's a lot of situations where people are forced to say that on the phone, even if it's not true."

I nodded. "Yes, I understand, and I appreciate you coming out here, but everything's fine."

They didn't look convinced in the slightest.

"So what happened?" he asked. "You seem pretty shaken up."

"I'm fine, really," I started, scrambling to come up with an excuse that made sense, but Mikhail spoke before I could.

"That would be my little sister's fault, officer. We got into a simple argument and, in an attempt to get back at me, she called the police without thinking," he lied smoothly, walking over to me. "Isn't that right, Maya?"

It took everything in me to keep my smile from wavering. So that's how he was going to get out of this? By placing the blame on me? It wouldn't be the first time.

"Is that true?" the officer demanded.

"Yup," I replied bubbly. Too bubbly. I sounded phony even in my own ears. I couldn't help myself. I had to over-compensate to hide the fact that I was reeling inside. I was a ticking time bomb, ready to eradicate everything in my wake.

"Are you sure you're okay?" the other officer asked. He had been quiet up until then, watching me the entire time while the other one did all the talking, analyzing my every movement. There was something about the way he was staring at me that made me extremely uncomfortable. Like he could see straight through my charade.

"She's fine," Mikhail answered for me and, taking it way too far, put his arm around my shoulder. My body immediately tensed up at his proximity. Fear raced through my blood and my bones were threatening to *explode in distress. "Siblings fight, it's not a big deal."*

"I was asking her,*" he said, scowling at Mikhail.*

"Listen, bro——"

"I am not your bro,*" he interrupted sharply.*

Mikhail didn't respond and just smiled politely, but I could feel his rage coming off his body in fumes. His arm, the same arm that was trying to kill me not even an hour earlier, tightened around me.

"Everything is fine. I'm sorry to have inconvenienced you guys," I told him sincerely. Well, the last part was sincere.

"It wasn't an inconvenience," the quiet one said softly. He walked up to me and slipped a small card into my pocket before looking away and glaring at my brother. "Next time we won't let you off so easy."

Mikhail continued to stay quiet and followed them to the door. He stayed with his back to me until their car pulled out of our driveway and drove off, before turning around.

"Are you out of your fucking mind?" he fumed, stalking toward me.

"Mikhail, it was an accident," Mama said, stepping in front of me. Her intention to protect me was useless, though, because Mikhail wasted no time roughly shoving her out of the way.

"Don't touch her!" I shrieked, reaching out and pushing him. He stumbled back in surprise. "Get away from——"

I didn't see his hand until it made contact with my left cheek sharply. The loud smack of his blow cracked through the air like a lightning bolt. I didn't have time to react before he plunged his hand into my pocket and roughly grabbed the card that the police officer had given me. I watched silently as he shredded the card and threw the pieces into my face.

"You disgust me," he whispered, and then left, slamming the door behind him.

"Maya, honey, are you okay?" Mama asked quietly. I opened my eyes and stared at her defeated frame. She looked exhausted, and her shoulders were hunched down with the weight of the world.

"I'm fine."

"I'm sorry, I know this is hard," she said, pulling me into her arms. "I'll speak to him tonight. Things will get better, I promise."

I didn't respond. I just rested my chin on her frail shoulder, letting her think she was comforting me, but in reality, I was already shutting down. Her words had lost all meaning. Her touch, once capable of alleviating all my pain, had lost its impact. She was holding the empty, inhuman, untethered shell of the girl I used to be, whoever the fuck she was. I couldn't even remember. Fragments of myself had been chipped off and scattered along the way through this never-ending web of suffering without my notice and now they were lost forever.

Life becomes so much more peaceful once you detach yourself from the truth, Ana. My family had made me feel so lonely and unwanted, but I didn't have it in me to be bothered about it anymore. I could scream, and cry, and beg the universe to please, please, please save me because I couldn't handle it anymore, but what was the point? I knew that I would wake up the next day and everything would just be ten times worse.

To be completely honest, Ana . . . I really felt like ending it all tonight, but I know I'll never do it because there's always this stupid part of me that gives the next day a chance. I tell myself that maybe, finally, something good will happen. Nothing good ever does happen, but for some reason, I still hang on to that part anyway.

Hey, what time are you coming by today? I have a surprise for you ;) –Noah
Hey, it's getting kind of late, are you okay? –Noah
Maya, I'm getting really worried, call me –Noah
Please call me so I know you're okay –Noah

There were about forty more messages and double the amount of missed calls, all sent to voicemail and then deleted without listening. It wasn't because I didn't know what to say to him—the complete opposite, actually. I had *too* much to say. *Too* many reasons. I could tell him about Mikhail. I could tell him that my parents thought I was a mental case and I was starting to believe them. I could tell him that I was extremely disconnected from reality and my days were all blurred together, making it really hard to maintain a conversation. I could tell him that only months ago I was seriously considering death. I could tell him that the sister he lost . . . the sister he loved more than anything's heart was living in my chest, pumping two thousand gallons of blood a day, and the guilt was eating away at me with every painful beat.

Or I could lie. I could say that I didn't know what was wrong. That *nothing* was wrong. That the chemicals in my brain just decided to be scrambled and unbalanced, refusing to provide me with the necessary levels of serotonin and dopamine to get through the day. That the imaginary tiny pills I placed under my tongue every morning just to survive were suddenly out of stock. That I lost my phone, or accidentally dropped it in a ditch, or was out of town, or was super, duper busy—*anything*. I could come up with any lie that I knew he would believe, and then we could continue with our uncomplicated and fake routine.

Which was easier? When Noah asked me what was wrong and I lied and said *I don't know*, or when Noah asked me what was wrong and I told him the ugly truth? Neither of them were easy, so instead I chose option three. The option I always chose when things got hard. Instead of dealing with it, I simply stuffed him away in a box of problems I avoided in the hopes that they would somehow just fix themselves. I cut Noah out of my life so that he could never *ask* and I could never *answer*.

I missed him, though. I tried not to. I tried to forget about Noah Davidson and that dimpled, lopsided smile that brightened his face every time he looked at me. I tried to forget about that dorky little gap between his two front teeth, and his constant charismatic attitude, and how he would call me *chick* and I would call him *dude*, and that feeling I felt where I wanted to tell him about everything, and anything, and nothing at all. But then, like a punch to the gut, I'd realize that one day I actually *would* forget and suddenly all I wanted was to remember those simple, yet lovely things forever. As much as I hated to admit it, the last few measly months—eighty-six and a half days to be precise—were the closest thing to happiness I had felt in a very long time. He'd become my best friend quickly, bit by bit, and so effortlessly that I didn't even realize it until after he was gone.

"Maya, what are you doing?" Sheila demanded,

interrupting my reverie.

"I'm putting away the recovery from the fitting room," I replied, pointing at the clothing rack I was pushing onto the sales floor.

"Did you do a round of maintenance?"

"Yes."

"Are you sure?"

For fucks sake.

"Yes," I repeated, not able to hide my annoyance any longer.

"Okay, you can finish doing this rack, but when you're done just focus on cleaning the store. Make sure when you're cleaning the bathrooms you're actually wiping the toilet seats."

As soon as she walked away I closed my eyes and focused on my breathing so I wouldn't *scream*.

I had somehow managed to avoid working retail for twenty-three years, up until a year and a half ago when I applied to work at Tysons. I assumed at the time I would just be organizing clothes and merchandise, which didn't sound *too* bad, only to realize once I got hired that wasn't exactly the case. Working retail was honestly code for *labor*. Dirty work. I was constantly dealing with ignorant customers, drug addicts who only came in to hide in our bathroom to snort some coke, and gangs of thieves who came in to openly rob the store because they knew we weren't allowed to confront them about it.

But despite all that, it was my assistant manager who was the reason I wanted to quit after every shift. I wasn't sure what I could have possibly done to piss her off—I seemed to just have that effect on people—but she was dead set on making each of my shifts miserable. And, coincidently, I was always scheduled on maintenance when we were working together.

"Maya?"

I jumped in surprise at his voice behind me.

"Noah? What are you doing here?"

"You wear glasses?" he asked instead of answering my question.

I adjusted them slightly on my nose. "Yeah . . . surprise! I'm blind."

He smirked at my weak attempt at being funny. "They suit you."

"I usually wear contacts, *obviously*, but I was too tired to put them in today. Sometimes I don't wear either though, because I just don't feel like *seeing*. It sounds weird but it's actually kind of nice."

He didn't pretend to laugh this time and examined my face with concern. "You look exhausted, Maya."

I *was* exhausted. Although Mikhail pretty much avoided me, I still couldn't bring myself to surrender into unconsciousness. I needed to stay alert at all times . . . just in case.

"Hey, talk to me," he said quietly, stepping closer. "What's wrong?"

"Maya, what are you doing?"

This bitch is seriously spying on me.

"I was just directing this customer to where we keep our bedding supply," I said, looking back at Sheila.

"I can answer any questions you have. She's cleaning," she told Noah, smiling.

Yeah, because you need a fucking Ph.D. to answer questions about thread count.

"Maya is more than capable to assist me," Noah said, an edge to his voice.

Sheila glanced between us, sensing something there. "Well, don't take too long. You still have to finish your rounds."

"Actually," I said, putting my cleaning spray back on the cart. "I'm going to take my break. It was scheduled thirty minutes ago."

She narrowed her eyes at me but nodded and walked away.

"Someone's got a stick up their ass," he said, glaring at her retreating figure.

"Come on," I told him and started toward the door. A harsh breeze immediately hit me the second I stepped outside. I quickly walked to the far corner, away from prying eyes, and stopped. "What are you doing here?"

"Are you seriously asking me that?"

I looked away, rocking back and forth slightly to keep warm. I saw him move from the corner of my eye and watched as he held up his jacket. After a few seconds of hesitation, I carefully slipped my arms through and let him button me up. He adjusted the collar to cover my exposed neck and pulled his hood up over my head to protect my face from the wind. His fingers grazed my cheeks slightly, erupting every nerve in my body into flames. Despite the brisk cold licking my skin, I suddenly felt warm. *Too* warm.

Thump, thump—

"Maya," he whispered. "What happened last week? I was so worried about you. After going to three different Tysons across town, I finally tracked you down here."

Lie or truth, lie or truth, lie or truth—

"You didn't have to do that, Noah. I'm fine."

"Enough with that fucking word, Maya. If you were really *fine*, then why didn't you say that after the hundreds of messages I left you?"

My once opaque lies were suddenly becoming translucent.

"Look," he started. "I know I probably came off pretty strong the last time we talked. I didn't mean to make you uncomfortable; I just couldn't help myself. I can't seem to think logically when I'm with you, which sounds ridiculous since we haven't known each other for very long," he smiled sheepishly. "But I'm sorry. I know you need to take things slow and I respect that."

Option four—he blamed himself for my actions. An option I never considered. An option I didn't *accept*.

"You didn't do anything wrong. It's me."

He looked confused for a second before realization sparked on his face. "Is this the part where you give me the whole speech about how you're a messy sad person, and there's a million other people I could be friends with? Because I still have it memorized."

"I'm sorry for the inconvenience," I assured him sarcastically.

"You're not an inconvenience, I'm just . . . I'm worried about you. What's going on?"

"Nothing's going on."

"That's obviously not true," he disagreed gently. "You can trust me, Maya, with whatever it is."

"*Trust* you? We've known each other for five seconds and I'm just supposed to trust you now?"

"I trust you."

And he *did*. I already knew he did. I could hear it in his voice when he spoke to me about his past with raw vulnerability. I could see it in his eyes when he looked at me, pupils open and ready, wholeheartedly inviting me into uncharted territory. It was a wholesome kind of honor to be trusted by someone like Noah. To be seen as a person *worth* his trust. But it was also a mistake.

I took a deep breath to soothe the sudden ache in my chest. "I'm sorry. I know I'm being mean, and secretive, and *difficult* . . . just do yourself a favor and leave."

"You're confusing my flattery for an insult. I *like* those things about you. I like everything about you."

Thump, thump—

"Leave."

He didn't move.

"I'm serious, Noah, go."

I waited silently for him to leave. To accept it and walk away, but he just continued to stand there.

"Are you bored?" I asked incredulously. "I mean, that's why you quit your fancy engineering job, right? Because you were *bored*. And now your cute and artsy café isn't fulfilling enough, so you've decided that your next entertaining challenge is going to be me?" His eyes hardened, but his feet stayed firmly planted, never wavering, fueling my newly accepted rage. "Leave."

He didn't. He stayed put, scrutinizing me intensely.

"Who hurt you?" he asked suddenly.

"Excuse me?"

"Who *hurt* you?" he repeated, taking a step closer. "Tell me who did this to you. Tell me what happened to make you so closed off, and *cynical*."

"Nobody hurt me," I lied. "God, Noah, I *warned* you. I warned you about me, but you still went ahead and made me be your fucking friend anyway."

"*Made* you? I don't remember holding a gun to your head for the last three months, Maya. Besides, if anyone's at fault here, it's you."

"Me?"

"Yes, *you*," he stressed icily. "If you didn't want me to like you, you shouldn't have made it so fucking easy."

"*This* is easy? Having to track me down for days just to see if I'm okay, only to get bitched at as a thank you?" I laughed humorlessly at his ridicule. "Nobody wants this, Noah. I just need a *minute*, okay? All my friends know that this is what I do and they're fine with it. Why can't you be fine with it too?"

"Don't lump me in with your friends, and not just because they're doing a shitty job fulfilling that title," he snapped. "*I* can be a better friend than them . . . but I don't want to be your friend."

Thump, thump—

"Stop," I interrupted him.

"I want to be so much *more* than just your friend, Maya. I want to hold all your deepest secrets in my heart. I want to spend all my seconds of the day with you. I want—"

THUMP, THUMP—

"I said *stop*," I repeated louder, to *both* of them. This conversation wasn't going as planned. I didn't want to hear this. I didn't want to feel the thrilling warmth spreading through me at his words, and wrapping around me like silk. I needed to hold my ground—

"I want to be with you through everything. The good *and* the bad."

"That's just it, Noah, there is no good."

"I know that's not true because I've *seen* your good. Even

the bad things are good."

"You don't know what you're saying."

"Maya, I can't be here for you if you don't talk to me."

"This isn't a modern day Cinderella story," I said, rolling my eyes. "I don't need some man to swoop in and magically solve all my problems for me."

"I'm not some *man*. I'm a person who cares about you." He ran his hands over his face in frustration. "Why do you *do* that? Why do you insinuate that needing someone makes you weak and pathetic? Everybody needs help sometimes."

"You *can't* help me!" I shouted, and the people walking in and out of Tysons looked in our direction. I didn't care. All the emotions that had been festering inside me were starting to bubble over and I was so *done* pretending. "*This* is who I am! You're so desperate to convince yourself otherwise, that you're not even paying attention to what's right in front of you."

I squared my shoulders. "You really want to know what's wrong? *Everything* is wrong. I have had things thrown at me from every direction for my entire life, and nothing ever works out in my favor and it's exhausting. It is so incredibly *exhausting* to be me. To hear my thoughts, and to speak my words, and to feel my emotions, and to exist in this body, this vessel—" I glanced down at my long unfamiliar limbs clad in clothes I could barely remember picking out "—this *thing* that doesn't feel like mine. That feels like a stranger." My voice slipped into a whisper. "And sometimes, Noah . . . sometimes I really, truly, desperately, with everything I am and everything I have, don't want to be me anymore. I don't want to exist anymore." I let out an unsteady breath. "I'd give anything to know what it's like to wake up and feel rested. To wake up and not think *again*? *I have to do this all again*? To wake up and not have to walk on eggshells around my own mind. To wake up and feel like I'm not just surviving, but *living*."

"Maya," he started softly, but I kept talking.

"I'm not pushing you away because I want to, Noah. I guess I just don't want to see the day when you finally look at me—and I mean *really* look at me—and realize how exhausted I make you too. I know you think you've got me all figured out, but I'm not the girl you get to know as *more* than a friend. I am the damaged and emotionally unstable girl that will drain you with all her endless problems until you can't take it anymore and leave." I looked away, the truth behind my words hitting hard. "You can't try to fix me without getting broken in the process."

"You don't need fixing," he disagreed immediately. "This isn't forever, Maya. It'll get better."

I scoffed. "It will get *better*, Noah? Really?"

"Yes, it will get better," he repeated, a fierce fire burning behind his stare. "Maybe only for a second, or an hour, or a day, but things *will* get better."

"Sometimes things don't get better—at least not for everyone. Sometimes things only get worse."

"Do you think I don't know how that feels?" he demanded. "Do you think I don't know what it's like to have your whole world fall apart around you and there's nothing you can do to stop it? I've been through shit—you *know* that—and most of the time I didn't think I was going to make it out, but here I am. *Still* standing, and trying to tell you that you can make it through too."

"We are not the same, Noah. You blossomed from the rubble and wreckage of your past and evolved into a thriving, and happy, and amazing human, but I *didn't*. I didn't find meaning in my pain. I didn't learn a beautiful and heartfelt lesson. The only thing it taught me is how to push people away."

"You'll get through it——"

"No, *you* got through it," I interrupted harshly. "I will never *stop* going through it."

"So . . . what? That means we can't even . . ." He ran his fingers through his tousled hair. "You don't need to wait until you're all shiny and polished to have someone in your life, Maya. You don't need to wait until your life's not *hard* anymore to try and be happy."

"It's not that simple, Noah. You don't understand."

"Then explain it to me. Help me understand. *Fuck*—just tell me what's going on."

I could feel myself slipping into his words. Every part of me wanted to cave in and believe him.

"What's really the problem here?"

I glanced up at him, and once again got caught in his stare and couldn't look away. I could feel him tugging the truth right out of me.

"I'm scared."

"Of what?"

"You." He recoiled like I slapped him. "I'm scared of how attached I'll get. Of how attached I *already* am. Of how much I already crave your presence. I'm terrified that I'm going to put what little I have into whatever *this* is between us, and then end up getting left with nothing. I don't want to know you, Noah, and you're making it really fucking hard."

Slowly, he brought his hands up to each side of my face, hovering inches away for a moment, never quite connecting with my skin . . . like he was afraid to touch me . . . before dropping them back to his sides.

"Maya," he whispered firmly. "I would *never* hurt you."

I didn't reply. What did he see in my eyes? Why didn't he touch me? Why was he terrified of me too?

"I get it, okay? Where you are right now—I've *been* there. I've *felt* that. But you're never going to reach a point in life where bad things don't happen to you. You're never going to reach a point where life's not *hard* anymore. You're just going to waste all your time trying."

There was nothing but pure sincerity in his eyes, burning intensely into mine. I begged myself to believe him. To open up my heart and let him in. Not *my* heart, though. It always came back to *her*. Out of all my terrible secrets, *she* was the ultimate reason. It wasn't my tight grasp clutching me back from going to Noah, it was *Ana's*. She was acting as my moral compass and my constant reminder of why I could never be his friend or *more* than his friend. How could I truly give him my whole self while lying about this huge part of my life?

"You still want me to leave?" he asked finally.

I swallowed back the *no* in my throat. "Yes."

"And you're okay with that? Never seeing me? Never having coffee with me?"

I looked away, the word *yes* on my tongue but I couldn't spit the lie out. It didn't matter, because he nodded in understanding and took a step back.

"I'm going to go, but only because you want me to. This is *your* choice, but . . . it doesn't have to be." His words were coming out breathless and desperate. "Life is short, Maya. Life is short and it *sucks* ninety-nine percent of the time, but that other one percent can be so bright and wonderful that it'll make the rest of it durable." His nervous fingers were back in his hair. "You have this idea of me—that I'm this guy who went through a lot and is now a happy, positive, sunshine being, but . . . has it ever occurred to you that maybe I'm only like that when I'm with you? Have you ever considered the possibility that *you* make me happy?"

Thump, thump—

He sighed and smiled lightly. "Thank you for giving me the moments that you did. I'm not going to pressure you, but if you ever find yourself willing to try to make another choice . . . choose me. *Try* with me. I'll be your stranger, or your acquaintance, or your friend . . . I'll be your anything, Maya. I'll wait, no matter how much you don't want me to. And if *this* isn't something you end up wanting . . ." He looked at me sadly. "I hope you can heal from the things that are silently tearing you apart. I hope you can find happiness."

He started to turn, but stopped and glanced back at me. "I may not know exactly what you're going through right now, but I do *know* you, Maya. I *see* you—the real you—and I can assure you that what I feel is the complete opposite of exhausted."

And then he walked away.

I willed and pleaded with all my might for my body to *go*. For my legs to run and chase after him. For my lips to yell his name and tell him to come back because he made me happy too. But I did nothing. I just stood there, my pathetic feat glued to the concrete, and watched as my breath of fresh air vanished.

I hope you're happy, Ana.

~

I floated through the remainder of my shift, barely aware of anything going on around me. The only perk to being scheduled on maintenance for the day was that no one told me to do anything else. I spent the rest of the night doing round after round, spraying and wiping and *spraying* and *wiping*. The only thing flashing in front of my eyes was Noah's expression before he walked away.

I was the last one in the parking lot after clocking out. I sat in the driver's seat waiting for the car to heat up, huddled inside Noah's jacket. If I wrapped my arms tight enough around myself and closed my eyes, I could almost trick myself into believing I was in *his* arms. His scent was still freshly rooted into every thread and fold of his jacket, encircling me entirely, getting me completely hooked. I wanted the particles of his fragrance to get submerged into my skin, so I could have a piece of him with me forever. So I could feel connected to him for eternity.

Something was crumpling in one of his pockets. I didn't want to be nosy, but I couldn't help myself. I pulled out a piece of paper he must have forgotten in there, and smoothed out the crinkles, examining it carefully.

Maya's list

- 1<

- Sad

- Pretty

- My mystery girl

- Iced coffee

- Eagle eye

- Chronically cold hands?

- Scared of birds

- A little mean

- Mostly kind

- *No phone calls*
- *Listens*
- *Pessimistic*
- *Winter*
- *Real*
- *Chocolate chip banana bread*
- *TWILIGHT*
- *Bookstore?*
- *Make a library card*
- *Insomnia?*
- *School and family off-limits?*
- *Pinky promise*

And the list continued on both sides, filled with things . . . about *me*? Every time he said that he was adding it to the list, he was *actually* adding it to a list. Most of the stuff on here wasn't anything I'd ever told him. I never noticed how closely he studied me, probably because I wasn't used to such deep scrutiny. People didn't pay attention to me, which was fine because I didn't like attention. I spent my whole life making myself small and unnoticed to avoid problems. The closer people watched you, the harder it was to keep up the image I was so desperate for everyone to believe was true.

But I didn't mind this. It was sweet. *He* was sweet. Noah was so, so sweet and I didn't know how to accept it. I didn't know how to let it infect me. What if it turned sour as soon as it touched my tongue? What if it turned to poison as soon as I swallowed? What if I was allergic? What if I got addicted and could never live without it? What if, what if, *what if*—?

And then there was Ana, of course. The one responsible for me meeting him in the first place. The one responsible for every shade of scarlet that flushed on my cheeks and every flutter that erupted in my chest whenever I was in his presence. Was I translating her beats wrong? Was she urging me forward or holding me back?

It wasn't just Ana, though. It was also exactly what he said. I wanted to be better first. I wanted to be healed. I wanted to be shiny, and polished, and *new* before I could even think about stepping into the next phase of my life. The problem was that I never truly believed it was possible to get better, which was why only months ago I was so desperate to make the next phase of my life start in a coffin. But that wasn't a phase of life . . . it was an ending.

I hadn't been paying attention to where I was driving, but I wasn't surprised to find myself at *Espresso & Chill*. It was closed, but I could see some light inside so I knew he was in there. I stood outside, still unsure of what I should do until my feet moved on their own accord, up to the door. My fist raised without any effort from me and knocked.

Once.

Twice.

A third time.

I counted to ten before I heard the lock turn. The door opened slowly and Noah stepped through the shadows. His eyes widened slightly in surprise when he saw me, before softening so intensely his pupils melted into two green and blue glittery pools staring deeply into mine.

"I *want* more moments with you, I just—" I paused, pathetic longing leaking through my words and making my voice crack.

He didn't respond. Instead, he reached his hand out slightly, letting me make the next move. Letting me choose to take it, if I wanted to. And I did want to, but still . . . I hesitated.

I lived my whole life treading water. Always on the verge of drowning, with only enough legroom to keep my mouth barely above the surface. I could breathe, but only if I didn't let my guard crumble. Only if I spent every second fighting with gravity trying to drag me down. Only if I used every ounce of strength wrestling with the weight of the world on my shoulders, and with all the people in my life who were trying to pull me under.

"What do you choose, Maya?" he asked.

I looked at his hand. A life jacket falling from the sky and into the water next to me at arm's reach. I wasn't saved, but maybe—just *maybe*—I didn't have to choke on water anymore.

My hand moved, not on its own this time. I *told* it to.

My decision was made.

I grazed his palm with my fingertips and slowly trailed a path up his arm. I only paused for a second before letting them explore his neck and his face. I touched his cheek, his nose, brushed the hair out of his eyes. They fluttered shut and he leaned his head further into my grip like it was pleasurable for him. A low hum vibrated up his throat, parting his lips.

Thump, thump—

I pulled my hand away . . . and then lightly placed it in his.

I was choosing to float.

"I'm sorry I was mean."

"You weren't—"

"I *was* mean," I interrupted. "And I'm sorry."

He was silent for a minute before speaking. "A genuinely mean person doesn't genuinely apologize for being mean. That's how I know you are kind."

My lips twitched into a smile. "Well, I'm still a *little* mean."

"I wouldn't want it any other way." His grin mimicked my own. "Can I . . . hug you? Strictly platonic, I swear."

He was staring at me a little too intensely and gripping my hand a little too tightly to be *platonic*. I probably was too . . . but I couldn't. Not yet. Maybe not ever.

"There has to be an off switch."

"To what?"

"Your *endless* thinking," he groaned.

"I thought you liked how I think."

"Just because I like it, doesn't mean it doesn't drive me insane."

"That won't stop," I warned him. Giving him one last out before I crossed over. One last opportunity to run away from something that had no chance of ending well because nothing ever ended well with me. "If I can guarantee you anything, it's that I will never stop driving you insane."

But just like every other time, he didn't take it.

"Insanity with you is the only sane thing I've ever wanted," he replied. "Hug me. Please."

I let go of his hand and wrapped my arms tightly around his neck. Goosebumps erupted everywhere our bodies were connected—hands behind back, chest on chest, stomach against stomach. His warmth radiated through all the layers between us, melting the first coating of my flesh, and suddenly it *hurt*. It hurt how content I was in his embrace. He quickly folded his arms around me, pulling me tighter against him, nuzzling his head into the crook of my neck. His heart was beating in my ear and it was the most glorious tune I had ever heard.

Thump, thump—

I'm not letting him go, Ana.

I didn't realize how long it had been since I hugged someone. I didn't realize how much I *needed* a hug. I'd been deprived of physical affection for so long, and it was incredibly surreal to finally experience it without any repercussions threatening to follow. Somehow he sensed this because he pulled me even closer.

"Promise me something?"

"What is it?" I asked warily.

"When everything starts to feel like too much . . . or when you wake up one day and wish that you didn't . . . don't go silent. Don't push me away. Just *tell* me. I promise I won't ask questions and that I'll always respect your privacy, but please don't disappear on me. I can't think properly or go about my day if I don't know you're okay."

"I'm sorry," I breathed. "I don't consciously decide to do it; I can't help it. I wasn't trying to ignore you or make you worry, I just . . . sometimes things happen, and the only way for me to get through it is to detach myself. I just barely go through the motions day after day, hoping tomorrow will be better but knowing that it probably won't be," I sighed. "But I didn't realize . . . I guess I'm just not used to people noticing."

"*I* noticed. I will always notice. I can't just *not* see you anymore. Promise me."

"I . . . okay. I'll try my best. Pinky promise."

He pulled away slightly, tipping his head down so it was resting against mine, forehead to forehead. His bright, optic globes gazing at me fiercely. "Your best is more than enough for me, Maya."

THEN

Dear Ana,

I've never had a boyfriend.

I don't know why I'm telling you this as if it's not painfully obvious. If I can't even get a female to love me platonically, how the fuck can I get a boy to love me romantically? There is no answer because it can never be done, which is okay because I hate men anyway. And don't start with all the 'not all men' bullshit. Yes, I know not all men, but just one man can ruin it for you, Ana. Not all bees will sting, but you still keep your distance anyway right? Besides, any man would run in the opposite direction once he saw the suitcase of damage permanently attached to my hip. And if he didn't run? Well, now I'm even more concerned.

There's another reason apart from not believing that anyone could ever love me, though. A new reason. A worse reason.

I was home alone. My parents and Mikhail were out, and it was nice. I could leave my room without checking corners and holding my breath. I could use the bathroom without being terrified of someone banging so hard that the door might snap in half. I could make myself a sandwich in the kitchen without my head being thrust into a pile of cutlery. It's the little things that mean the most.

I heard someone at the door, and after seeing the driveway empty of my parent's and Mikhail's car, I didn't hesitate before opening it.

I should've hesitated, Ana.

Three men were standing on my porch. They were all impeccably dressed—*freshly ironed khakis, crisp cut button-ups, shiny loafers*—and *reeked of old money.*

"*Can I help you?*" *I asked with a smile on my face.*

I shouldn't have smiled, Ana.

"*Does Mikhail live here?*" *one of them asked, smiling back.*

"*Yes, but he's not home right now.*"

I should've lied, Ana.

They all looked at each other and then looked back at me. "*Tell us the truth, sweetheart,*" *the one in the middle said.*

That's when I noticed how big and bulky they were.

The baseball bat in the left one's hand.

The way the right one was looking at me everywhere but my face.

I took a step back, but I should have stayed still, Ana, because they noticed and took a step closer.

The middle one leaned down to get to my eye level. "*Tell him we want our money, sweetheart. Tell him that if he doesn't get his ass outside with our money* right now, *we're going to come inside and take it.*"

I was noticeably uncomfortable but they seemed to enjoy that. The right one licked his lips.

"*He's not here. I'll tell him what you said when he comes home*—"

I tried to slam the door shut but the middle one immediately stopped it with his large hand, and forced it back open and right into my face. I stumbled backward and before I could make a move, they all barged into my house. I didn't bother trying to stop them. They were twice my size and could squash me like an ant under their shoe if I tried to get in their way. Besides, I wasn't *lying. Mikhail wasn't home, and if they needed to see that for themselves to leave me alone then fine.*

I waited by the door for them to check every room in the house, but I should have just gotten the fuck out of there, Ana.

We lived in a mid-sized duplex so it didn't take them very long to do a thorough search before coming back.

"Did you find what you were looking for?" I snapped.

"No," the middle one replied. "Which makes things more complicated."

"Whatever complication you're referring to can get dealt with out of my house," I said, tapping the door as a signal that they needed to leave.

They didn't leave, Ana.

"You're feisty, but we still need to get paid, sweetheart."

"Take it up with my brother," I insisted, and they all shared another look.

It wasn't a nice look, Ana.

"We can settle our payment differently," the right one said suggestively, looking me up and down.

I scoffed. "Yeah, I'm not interested."

"Who said I was asking permission?"

Before my brain could fully process what he said, the one holding the bat roughly thrust it into my abdomen and shoved me backwards. The middle one shut the door, while the right one stalked over to me. I ran for the stairs but one of them grabbed my hair and pulled me back. I shrieked as multiple strings of my hair got ripped out of their follicles, but whoever it was clamped his other hand over my mouth and silenced the noise.

He turned me around, and I came face to face with the one on the right. The one who kept looking at me. He was ugly, despite his perfect clothes. It was always the ugly ones who felt the need to prove their fragile masculinity in such a demeaning and loathsome way.

He didn't hesitate before pushing me against the staircase. Pain sprung up through my spinal cord, but I was too focused on the three men standing over me to pay attention to my injuries. He let go of my hair and I immediately tried to push past them, but the middle one smacked me across the face which momentarily halted my movements. He took advantage of that and grabbed both my hands, locking them in his grip above my head. He leaned his face close to mine and pressed his body against me, letting *his free hand wander. I squirmed and protested, but he just smirked at my discomfort and kneaded my breasts painfully.*

"Hey, me first," the right one protested.

Me first, he said.

Me fucking first.

The middle one reluctantly pulled away from me, and I raised my free leg and kicked him in the knees. His legs buckled, but he didn't release his iron grasp on my hands. My movement just made him smile. The fight thrilled him.

He popped the button of my jeans open.

I screamed, but he just shoved his fist into my mouth so hard I tasted blood.

His other hand was suddenly in my pants, gripping me tightly.

I fought and thrashed against him.

He thrust two fingers inside me, tearing through my barrier of innocence with a silent pop.

I cried out in pain.

"Since your hand's already down there, take her jeans and underwear off, will you? And you," the third one looked at the one holding the bat, "hold her legs down. Whack her in the fucking head with that thing if you need to. I'm not going to last long and I don't want any pushback from this bitch. Once I'm done with her, you guys can get your turn." He looked back at me and smiled smugly. "If you're a good girl, then maybe I'll let you please me more than once."

Bile bubbled in my stomach.

I shouted and I fought and I begged myself to wake up because obviously, I was having a nightmare.

But as I watched the third one fumbling with his belt, I knew.

I knew, Ana. I fucking knew *what was going to happen and there was nothing I could do to stop it. I just hoped my mind would shut down, and I would wake up and not know if it really happened.*

But just before my life changed for the worst, I heard a car door slam.

They heard it too because they all froze. A second passed, and then we heard the car beep. It sounded close, Ana, and I prayed that it was my parents or even Mikhail—

The men moved. The third one pulled up his pants from where they were wrapped around his ankles. The middle one let go of my hands and stepped away from me. The one with the bat pointed to the back door and they all rushed toward it. Seconds later I heard Mikhail yelling after them, and then he came rushing inside, stopping abruptly when he saw me.

He looked at my flushed cheeks.

He looked at my shirt that had risen mid-way, exposing my stomach. He looked at my unzipped jeans.

His eyes flickered back up to my face, and he slowly walked over to me and leaned down.

"Whore," he spat, saliva hitting me square in the face.

And then he stepped over me and walked up the stairs to his room.

I was in shock. A million thoughts were flying around in my mind but I heard a second car pull up to the house, and I knew it was my parents. I forced myself to push through the throbbing in-between my legs and stood up, heading straight for the bathroom. I turned on the shower and stripped out of my clothes before going in. The water was scalding, but I couldn't bring myself to adjust it. I couldn't even bring myself to stand, so I just sat down. I curled up in the tub, letting the water fry my skin one cell at a time, and pretended not to notice the stream turning red beneath me.

I felt gross, Ana. I felt violated and rotten, but I didn't have the right to feel that way because . . . nothing happened. They never saw anything. Any fondling and touching was above my clothes . . . for the most part, so it doesn't even count as . . . right? I felt gross, Ana, which only made me feel guilty because I should have felt relieved. *Relieved that the thing I thought was going to happen didn't end up happening after all.*

That wasn't even the worst part. The worst part was that I couldn't even let myself process the fact that three men were on top of me, because all I could think about was what happened after. When Mikhail chased them away, and for a split second I thought he was coming to help me. The humiliation was searing, Ana. And then he called me a whore because he thought I . . . what? Offered myself up to them one by one in exchange for the money he owed them? The only reason they were there in the first place was because of him. I was put in that horrific situation because of him. Every terrible thing that has ever happened to me was linked to him, him, HIM.

I want to find the despicable human who decided that 'all siblings fight' was an acceptable explanation, and tell them to shut the fuck up. They say blood is thicker than water until your blood is quickly surging out of you from wounds that your blood created. They say blood is thicker than water until you're pinned down and about to get assaulted by three strangers—coincidentally three men—because of something that your blood did. Fuck all siblings fight. How long could that stand as a valid excuse? How many things could that statement justify? When does it cross the line? I couldn't even see the line anymore, Ana. It wasn't blurred, it simply didn't exist. This shit wasn't normal. He wasn't normal. Why was everyone acting like I was being dramatic? Why was everyone making me feel so fucking insane? Why was I the only one who could see him for who he was? Why was I the only one getting hurt? Why didn't anyone believe me?

Why?
WHY?
WHY!

NOW

"Hi?"

"مرحبا."

"Marhaba."

I gave him a thumbs ups and threw a gummy bear at him—he caught it in his mouth. I ate two.

"Coffee?"

"قهوة."

"Kohwa."

"No, you're pronouncing it with a *K*," I corrected him. "It's more of a *Q* sound."

"Quahwah?"

I shook my head and laughed. Not a small snicker, or a cute and flirty giggle. I was full-on laughing, my face a complete blubbering mess. I ducked my head into my elbow to stifle the noise but it continued to echo through his café. Minutes passed before I could breathe again. I wiped my face and glanced at Noah, who was silently watching me with a small smile on his face.

"I'm sorry."

"No, you're not. You *love* this."

"You're right," I snickered again. "I have never heard someone butcher the Arabic language so terribly. You deserve a prize."

"Seeing you laugh is the best prize."

"Right," I agreed sarcastically.

"I'm serious," he insisted. "It's a nice look you've got going on right now—snot and tears smeared across your cheeks."

"Oh yeah? You like that?"

"Yes," he grinned, standing up. "I have a surprise for you."

"That's too bad because I hate surprises."

"Okay, I'll add that to the list. But since I didn't know, can you just humor me this one time?"

"I ghosted you for several days yet you're giving *me* a surprise?" I shook my head. "I guess enigmas only attract other enigmas."

"You're attracted to me?"

I snorted. "Yeah, you wish."

"You have no idea."

Thump, thump—

I laughed again, harder this time, ignoring Ana and the unmistakable hint of longing in his voice. "Now you're just trying to be funny."

"Close your eyes," he demanded lightheartedly.

"طيب," I replied, and Noah raised his eyebrows. "*Okay*."

I covered my eyes as he walked back behind the counter, and started rustling around with pans and dishes.

"Open up."

I moved my hands away eagerly. "Banana bread?"

"*Chocolate chip* banana bread," he corrected. "From scratch. I seem to remember this being someone's favorite baked good."

"You remember correctly."

"It's not your mom's recipe, but I've been playing around with it for a few weeks and I *think* I nailed it. But you are the ultimate taste tester."

"I'm honored to be chosen for such an astound role," I teased, cutting a piece off with my fork. I could feel his eyes watching me as I raised it to my lips and slipped the cool metal into my mouth. If I was being honest, I couldn't concentrate enough to tell if the first bite was good or not. His gaze was like a laser burning a hole right through my skin. The rich flavor hit my taste buds then, and I momentarily forgot about his presence.

"Mmm, this is so good," I moaned, taking another huge bite. "Seriously, Noah, you have magical hands."

He smiled while I continued to scarf down his delicious creation.

"I'm sorry, did you want some?" I asked when there was only one bite left, but he stayed quiet. "What?"

"You've got a little . . ." he said, pointing to the corner of his mouth.

"Oh jeez, my bad." I rubbed my face aggressively. "I'm such a messy eater. Is it gone?"

He didn't answer. Instead, he reached out to me steadily, his eyes never leaving mine. I felt his soft finger touch the corner of my mouth, wiping something off. I looked at his finger and saw a little piece of chocolate chip. Before I could react, he brought that same finger to *his* lips and I watched, unblinking, as the tip of his tongue peeked out and licked his finger clean.

Thump, thump—

"I agree. It is delicious," he murmured.

I swallowed the blazing rush bubbling up in my chest, and it burned all the way back down into the inferno that had been raging a fire in the pit of my stomach from the moment I set eyes on Noah Davidson. It was all his fault. I wasn't susceptible to these emotions until he opened his mouth and said he *liked* me, which immediately made me aware of how much I fucking liked him too. I spent twenty-five years being immune to whatever *this* was, but now *this* was all I wanted.

"It's a crime what you're doing to me, Maya."

"What am I doing?"

"Thinking but never sharing." He narrowed his eyes. "It's selfish."

"I'm curious, Noah. You keep commenting on how much I think, but you know what's really concerning? How much you *don't* think. I mean, how can a gifted and accomplished man like yourself be so . . . thoughtless?"

"It's always either or with you, isn't it? Overthinking and under thinking are not the only two options. There is such a thing as simply *thinking*, period. You should try it sometime."

"I can't help it."

"Your face says otherwise. You don't even try to hide it. Your eyes literally *vibrate* like they're trying to keep up with a million different thoughts. Your left brow slightly scrunches. You bite your lower lip. It's like you *want* me to know you're thinking something good and that I'm missing out. It's taunting. If I didn't enjoy looking at you so much, I would almost describe it as cruel." He leaned into the table, smirking. "Do you want to know what I think?"

I kept my voice nonchalant but my insides were aching. "Not really, but you're probably going to tell me anyway."

"I think you were thinking about *me*."

"I wasn't."

His smirk didn't falter.

"Stop giving me that look," I demanded.

"What look?"

"You *know* what look."

The smirk just got bigger. His hands were on the table, and I watched as he slid one of them forward until the tips of his fingers were just barely touching mine.

Thump, thump—

I didn't move my hand.

"Are you ever going to tell me why you're always wearing gloves?"

No.

"It's a fashion statement," I lied. "I like looking different from all the basic bitches in this town."

He chuckled. "You don't dress like someone who cares about fashion."

I gasped in mock horror. "How dare you insult my wardrobe?"

His fingers inched closer, laying partially over my hand.

Thump, thump—

"I wasn't complaining," he assured me. "You make jeans and sneakers look good. *Runway* good."

I glanced down at our matching shoes. "Your sneakers are cleaner than mine, though. And newer."

He kicked my foot playfully.

Thump, thump—

I kicked him back.

"Are your feet longer than mine?"

"Duh, I'm taller."

He nudged me again. "No, you're *not*. I'm at least a head taller than you."

"Tall for men and tall for women are completely different."

"What does that have to do with anything?" he asked,

Dear Ana

nudging me again. "I'm still taller. In women *and* men. When I hugged you the other day, I could practically tuck you under my chin."

"Okay, settle down. You're like two, *maybe* three inches taller, max."

"If only there was a quick and easy way to see who's right . . ." he said, sighing dramatically.

"I let you hug me *once*, Noah, you need to get over it."

He smiled. His foot was pressed against my foot, rubbing my ankle gently, and his hand was entirely covering mine.

Thump, thump—

"My God, even your *fingers* are longer."

Thump, THUMP—

I slipped my hand out from under his and took my foot back.

"I'm going to go get another piece," I explained quickly before he could get offended.

He stood up and grabbed my plate. "I'll get it for you."

His voice was light and his smile was bright, but his *eyes.* His eyes were hurt.

~

The living room light was off as I pulled up to my house—that meant no one was up.

The weeks following my breakdown in the kitchen were awkward, to say the least. I avoided Mikhail like an infectious disease, even if it meant not having dinner multiple nights in a row. Even if it meant asking my mother to do my laundry because he'd decided to set up camp in the basement, instead of in his old room. It made me feel slightly less terrified knowing he wasn't on the other side of the wall, but not enough for my mind to let me actually go to sleep for more

141

than a few hours a night. It was getting harder to function with all the all-nighters I was pulling. I found myself dosing off at both my jobs, at the café with Noah, while I was driving . . .

It was a mess. *I* was a mess. The dark contour permanently stamped under my eyes wasn't helping to keep my nightly activities a secret, and I knew Noah was starting to notice. As promised though, he never asked.

I unlocked the door quietly, not wanting to trigger anyone's attention with my arrival. To my surprise, I found my mom sitting on the couch in the dark.

"Salam Mama," I greeted her, taking off my shoes.

"Wait, come sit with me for a bit," she said when I was about to head upstairs.

I sat down at the edge of the couch and looked at her, waiting.

"Where have you been?" she asked. "Do you think I haven't noticed you staying out later for the past few weeks?"

"Well, you haven't been hounding me with texts like you usually do, so . . ." I shrugged.

"I don't want to fight, Maya."

"Neither do I," I snapped.

Get a grip.

I took a deep breath to calm my nerves. "I'm sorry. I've just been going to . . . Starbucks after my shifts to get some work done. You know, to stay on top of things for when I go back to school."

"Starbucks stays open past eleven PM?"

"Fine, not Starbucks. This café downtown." I started to get annoyed again. "What's with the interrogations? I'm not a child."

"I don't care how old you are, it's not okay for a girl to be out this late." I immediately rolled my eyes at her cultural double standards and she sighed. "Like I said, I don't want to fight. Baba and I are just worried about you, especially after what happened."

I fidgeted with my fingers as the discomfort started to settle in.

"I know Mikhail being here makes you uncomfortable, and I understand, Maya, I do. I just . . . is it so much to ask for us to be a family? Can't we just leave the past in the past and move on? Please?"

I wanted to laugh. As if it was so *easy* to move on. How could I move on when nothing was ever discussed or acknowledged? How could I forgive someone who had never *asked* for my forgiveness? Why was that so hard for them to understand? I wasn't a kid anymore; I was a full-grown *adult*. My brain had already molded into itself, with all my memories deeply rooted in its core. I couldn't forget, and I *wouldn't* forgive.

"If you guys want to act like nothing happened that's up to you," I said without looking at her. "I don't want to argue anymore and I don't want to fight with anyone, but that's only going to work if he doesn't talk to me or come near me." I pushed back the emotions festering in my chest. "I feel physically *sick* every time he speaks to me like . . . like he did *nothing*! Like the last twenty-five years of my life didn't happen. My brain can't handle any more chaos, Mama. My skin crawls whenever I'm near him, I can't . . ."

She reached over and started rubbing my arm soothingly. "I know, Maya, I know. I'll talk to him okay? But . . . he's changed. I wouldn't have let him come home if he didn't."

I didn't doubt for a second that she believed that, but my

mother's vision would forever be tainted by her unequivocal love for Mikhail. It was common in immigrant households for mothers to absolutely cherish their sons like they walked on water. Nothing he ever did would change how she felt, and Ana's heart beating in my chest was proof of that.

I told Noah I didn't believe in unconditional love, but that was a lie. I believed it existed, I just didn't believe it could ever be felt for me, and *this* was one of the reasons why.

"I'm tired," I whispered, the exhaustion suddenly hitting me like a tsunami.

"Okay, go to sleep."

No, Mama, I wanted to say, *I'm* tired, *I'm tired, I'M SO FUCKING TIRED—*

"Night," I said instead and started for the stairs, but not before I saw a shadow move through the sliver underneath the basement door.

~

I laid out all the bills and my most recent bank statement on the passenger seat and took out my calculator. It was *that* time of the month.

−2300$, −120$, −60$, −150$, −135$, −50$, −200$

I looked at my almost empty gas tank.

−80$

Zara's birthday dinner was next weekend and I still hadn't purchased her present.

−100$

Mama was going grocery shopping this week, right?

−150$ roughly?

No, Mikhail lived with us now and spent twenty-four hours *eating*.

−200$

Which left me with . . .

1.12$

At least I wasn't in overdraft.

I could feel a sharp pain in my chest and my hand immediately flung to my throat, clutching at nothing. The water was starting to rise around me, submerging my body completely into a pool of harrowing heartache.

"Fuck," I whispered to myself, hitting my fist on the steering wheel. "Fuck, fuck, *fuck*!"

I continued to cuss at my poor car until the intense tightening in my chest eventually stole the breath I needed to keep speaking. *Good*, I thought bitterly, *difficulty breathing will lead to suffocation which will ultimately lead to my death.*

But then who would help my parents pay their bills?

I knew I had no right to complain. I had a roof over my head, food in the fridge, a vehicle to get me from place to place, and two jobs that paid me every week. Some people had it worse. Some people had to live in their cars or on the streets. Some people couldn't afford food or clothes or shelter, in this devastatingly freezing weather we were having.

I *knew* that.

That didn't mean it wasn't hard living paystub to paystub. That didn't mean the financial stress didn't constantly weigh me down like a backpack filled with bricks. That didn't mean I wasn't continuously worrying and agonizing about my family's future, and how they were going to survive if something ever happened. That didn't mean I wasn't endlessly telling myself I needed to get a third job, that I should be investing, that I wasn't *trying* hard enough—I mean, who needed eight hours of sleep anyway? As much as I did and as hard as I worked, there was always going to be that voice in the back of my head chanting more, more, *do more, YOU CAN DO MORE!*

The worst part was there was no end in sight. No light at the end of the tunnel. My neuroscience degree was fucking useless on its own. The only job I could really get with it was a clinical research position, but after thousands of rejected applications, it was clear they didn't care about my above average transcript, all my extracurricular activities, or the hundreds of hours I spent volunteering. The only thing they required was experience. Sorry, I was too busy studying and going to school to get *experience*. I needed to get a job first to get *experience*, but every place needed *experience* to hire me, so it was essentially a lose/lose situation.

So the solution would be to get a higher education, right? Well, how the fuck was I supposed to go to school full-time *and* work full-time? I was trapped in a tiny box with two impossible ways out and no room left to breathe. How long was I supposed to stay imprisoned? When was my confinement going to end? I was born poor and I was going to die poor, and there was nothing I could do about it.

My phone beeped in my lap, but I didn't need to check to see that it was Noah. It was Sunday, so *Espresso & Chill* was closed, but he'd asked me to come by later today because he wanted to show me something. I told him I would, feeling giddy and excited at the time, but no part of me wanted to see him right now. I promised I wouldn't disappear again, so with a heavy chest, I turned on my car.

I forced the bundle of emotions eating away at me to a lower and subtler level, plastered a smile on my face, and started to drive. I reluctantly parked in front of a black pickup truck that was always there, but quickly looked away as a sense of déjà vu hit, not wanting its presence to stir up any unwanted memories. It didn't help that more than half of this city drove a black fucking truck.

"Noah?" I called when I didn't immediately see him inside.

"Coming!" I heard from what seemed like above me, accompanied by movement and footsteps. I took a seat on one of the plush chairs and waited.

"Hey, sorry, I was just washing up," he said, appearing a few minutes later through the door behind the counter.

"Washing up where?"

"My bathroom upstairs. I live here."

"You live *here*?"

"Yup."

"Since when? You tell me *everything*."

"Since always," he said, smiling. "And, I don't know, you never asked."

"There's an apartment above the café?" I said in awe. "That's so cool."

"I guess," he chuckled lightly. "So, what did you do so far on your one day off?"

His question immediately triggered the heaping pile of anxiety I was desperately trying to keep at bay.

"I just ran errands all day. What have you been up to?"

He narrowed his eyes slightly. My quick subject change didn't go unnoticed, but surprisingly he didn't comment on it. I knew he was just respecting my space, but I wished he would ask anyway. And when I didn't tell him, he would continue to ask me again and again, and when I still refused he would proceed to beg and plead and *grovel* on the floor until I told him.

You are literally a walking red flag.

"That's actually why I wanted you to come by," he said. "Well that, *and* I wanted to see you."

I rolled my eyes, but I could feel my face heating up.

"Thanks to *you*, I finally decided what to do with the other half of this space."

"What do you mean?"

"Come with me." He stood up and started toward the white tarp separating his café, and swiftly pulled away a corner so we could walk through. I looked around the room, trying to understand what he was talking about. It was empty, and the floors were covered in plastic to protect them from the paint. There were paint cans littered around the room, along with paintbrushes, tape, and a sketchbook.

"I still don't get it."

"I'm turning it into a bookstore," he said excitedly. "A second-hand, thrift book store. You mentioned how expensive books were so I'm hoping to keep the prices low or let people pay for a book by donating a book they already own. I was thinking of keeping the same theme as the café, so I'm going to do deep mahogany shelves all along this back wall here." He pointed to the far wall where he had started painting it a light sage green color. "I'll add a few chairs by the windows where people can sit and read if they want, and maybe keep some board games and puzzles and stuff. I don't know, I'm still working on the details."

He looked back at me, pure delight twinkling in his eyes. "And the best part is that since it was *your* idea, and since your job at Tysons sucks ass and I hate that you have to work with such a bitchy assistant manager every day . . . I think you should work here. I *want* you to work here with me. You can choose your own hours and you can quit whenever you want, or whenever you decide to go back to school. It's completely up to you, Maya."

"I . . ." I started, but I was too astonished by everything he had just said.

"You don't have to decide right away," he said immediately. "Also you don't have to do it if you don't want to, but . . . I think you do. I think you'll enjoy it. I know *I'll* enjoy seeing you for more than an hour or two a few days a week."

I was at a loss for words. Not because I didn't agree with him—he was right. The most consistent question you were asked while blossoming from child to teenager to adult was *what do you want to be when you grow up?* As if what you wanted mattered. As if the universe didn't decide what you were going to be for you. As if you had a *choice*. There was a time when my naïve mind fell for it, though. There was a time when I had aspirations and dreams and a zest for life. There was a time when I wanted to *be* everything and *do* everything, but somewhere along the way that stopped. Somewhere along the way, this idea of having a job that you wanted became this inconceivable concept. *Job* and *want* used together instantly turned the sentence into an oxymoron. They were opposite sides of a magnet that couldn't be forced together. When I thought of the word *job* all I thought of was *survival*.

But maybe I was wrong. Maybe I only felt that way because soul-sucking jobs were all I ever knew. Maybe I only felt that way because all the jobs I ever set my eyes on weren't actually what I wanted, but what *other* people wanted. All the jobs I ever considered, all the careers I ever aspired to have, as different as they were, they were also all the same. They were big and loud, with a money sign stamped permanently into the title. But that wasn't me. That wasn't what I wanted for me. I wanted quiet and soft and *Noah*.

And now he was offering me the chance to spend more than a few hours a day with him, which was even better than working in a bookstore, and he looked so fucking happy to be doing it.

"This isn't the time to kill me with silence," he said, disturbing my thoughts. "Say something, Maya. Say *yes*."

"I, um," I started again, but I was too overcome by my emotions. The feelings of sentiment were mixing in with the accumulation of grim despair that I had barely packed away earlier. I couldn't feel one without feeling the other and everything was brimming to the top and threatening to topple over into existence.

"Hey, what's wrong?" he asked, coming closer. "It's okay if you can't. I know you're busy with work, and thinking about school and—"

"I'm not in school," I interrupted.

"I know; I'm talking about *after* your deferral."

"There is no deferral," I said, looking him straight in the eye so he knew I was serious. "I lied to you."

He continued to stare back at me with a puzzled expression. "I don't understand."

I took a deep breath and finally did the one thing that I'd never been able to do. I told him—I told *someone*—the truth.

"I told you I was doing my masters and decided to differ so I could work and save up for school, but the truth is . . . I dropped out after my first day."

I watched his face for any signs of hatred or anger while he processed my words. It was strange, though. I was prepared to feel ashamed—which I *did*—but I also felt a little relieved. It felt as though the bag of bricks I was carrying on my back at all times had suddenly lost a few pounds of weight. My airways, which always felt constricted and tight, started to feel a little looser. Was this how normal people breathed all the time?

"I still don't get it," he said after a few minutes. "Why would you tell me that if it wasn't true?"

"Um, habit?" I said, unsure. "To be honest, I don't know why I told you that. I guess I was just too embarrassed to admit that I wasn't working toward anything and that being a medical receptionist and a sales associate were currently my only occupations."

"Why would I *care*?"

"Because everybody does." My words came out harsh and glaring. "Everybody cares about that stuff, Noah. The first thing out of people's mouths after you graduate is 'Congrats, so what are you doing next?' Not commenting on what stage of life someone else is in, even if it doesn't fit into the social norm, seems easy right? Well, apparently not." I looked away from his face, focusing on a piece of lint stuck on my shirt.

"Everybody had a plan. All my friends knew what they were doing—whether that was going to teacher's college, grad school, writing the MCAT, or getting accepted into law school—and then there was *me*. Me, who *barely* graduated university. I got offered two outstanding scholarships when I started because my grades were so high, but by the end of my four years they had redacted both of them." I crossed my arms over my chest in an attempt to hold myself together. "All I talked about for *years* was going to medical school. I dreamed about becoming a doctor and saving lives every day for the rest of my life. Everybody knew this and no one could doubt me on it either because I had the grades and the drive to accomplish it. I was high off the academic validation I got, and that spark of pride in my parent's eyes. All I wanted was to make them proud, and to give them a better life than the one they could give me."

I squeezed my eyes shut. "But then . . . something happened. My brain just stopped working. I don't remember the exact moment when *I need an A* turned into *as long as I pass*, which ultimately turned into *nothing fucking matters anymore*. I didn't have it in me or the time to study, let alone go to class. That's when my grades started to slip, and then my first academic probation email came in and I—" I broke off, my voice suddenly wobbly and high pitched and I was pushing back tears.

"Hey, hey, it's okay," he said immediately, reaching out to me, but I backed away. I didn't deserve his comfort.

"The fear of failure was enough to jolt me awake and I managed to pull my grades back up within the next two years. I graduated with honors just like everyone expected me to, but I was . . . gone. I thought I was home free. I thought I was finally going to be able to *breathe* a little bit, and maybe take a break or something to think about what I wanted but that didn't happen." My voice slipped into a whisper as my mind drifted to the past. "Everybody just kept *asking* me all these questions—Maya what are you doing now, Maya did you schedule your MCAT, Maya are you applying for jobs, Maya, Maya, Maya, *MAYA!*"

I covered my ears to block out their voices as the hysteria started to build in my chest.

"I was forced to watch everyone else achieve their goals while I was just trying to *survive*. I'm so happy for them, please don't miss understand me but . . . what about me? When is it my turn?"

"It's okay, Maya," he repeated, his calm and empathetic voice soothing me from afar.

I took another deep breath and pressed my sleeve against my eyes before the tears could fall.

"I spent the next year working and trying to study for the MCAT, but my parents wouldn't get off my back, so I told them I was going to do my plan B first and applied for my masters. That way, if I didn't get into medical school, I would still have something to fall back on. I had no interest in studying physiotherapy, but it gave me some time to stall. I wrote all the required admission tests and got accepted, but, um . . ." I trailed off.

"But what?" Noah asked quietly.

"After my first day, I had to drop out and I . . . lied about it. I told everyone I was deferring my enrollment for two years so I could save up for school because I didn't want to be in more debt," I whispered, the shame clouding my vision. "I didn't mean to lie to you or anyone else. I swear that's not who I am, and it kills me to keep it up, but I'm so *humiliated*. And I figured it's not a lie that's hurting anyone . . . I know that doesn't make it right, but that's just how I chose to handle it."

I held my breath, waiting for the question that I knew was coming.

"Why did you drop out?"

Was I really about to tell him my truth? Something I went out of my way to make sure people would never suspect? I couldn't. I *wouldn't*. But . . . glancing around at the beautiful bookstore he was trying to create, all for me. All because he noticed how much I hated my jobs. Didn't he deserve more than what I was giving him?

"I dropped out because after seeing the syllabus, I realized I wouldn't be able to go to school full time *and* work full time."

"But why do you need to work so many hours while you're in school? They have payment plans available after you graduate—"

"Because I'm financially responsible for my family."

I still couldn't look at him.

"What do you mean?"

A laugh slipped out before I could stop it. "It's pretty simple, Noah. I go to work so that we can have fun things like food, and a roof, and a car—you know, basic human necessities."

"Okay, but *why*, what happened to your parents?"

"Nothing happened to them. My dad has a job, but he's just an online math tutor so it's not exactly a steady or an *adequate* stream of earnings."

I finally glanced at him briefly but there weren't any traces of judgment. Just concern and confusion.

"But the jobs you're working are probably only paying you minimum wage, so how are you even . . . ?" He paused, the wheels in his mind spinning, and then his face slowly changed into that look people gave you when they felt *sorry* for you, but all it did was make you feel disgusting and mortified. "Oh . . . Maya, why didn't you tell me? I could've helped—"

"It's fine."

"It's not fine, though. A minimum wage job in this economy basically makes you p—"

"I'm not . . . *that*. My job at the hospital pays a lot more than minimum wage. I'm just low income," I interrupted, my face heating up and internally cringing at that word. "My dad is the smartest person I know, okay? He moved here with a student visa and went to school to become a physics teacher, but by the time he finished school, the economy turned to shit. He applied for jobs every day but the need for teachers was extremely low and the only position he ended up finding was overseas. It wasn't ideal, and the salary they were offering wasn't great, but it was better than nothing. My mom and I would do our best to live beneath our means to make the money last, but it wasn't easy with all their bills, and credit card debt and inflation . . ." I paused, trying not to get angry thinking about all the money my mom had to spend cleaning up Mikhail's messes.

"He lived internationally for ten months during the year and he stayed there for four years. He would've stayed longer, but . . . his health started to take a turn for the worst and he had to move back home." I looked down at my fingers, knotting and unknotting them together in agitation. "That's why I lost my scholarships. It wasn't only because I was mentally burnt out, but because I couldn't just let them struggle alone. I got a full-time job and worked as many hours as I could to help pay all the bills. I made enough that we didn't get evicted and always had food on the table, but my grades suffered the consequences. I thought I could juggle it all but I failed. Everybody around me is chasing their dreams and living life, and I . . . am a failure."

I couldn't stand still anymore so I walked to one of the windows and watched as people scurried up and down the sidewalk, trying to get out of the cold. It was crazy how big my own life seemed when in reality I was just a tiny ant trying to survive among a billion other ants doing the same.

I felt him walk up behind me and touch my shoulder.

155

"Maya, I am so sorry," he whispered. "I'm so sorry you had to go through that, and are still going through this right now. I had no idea how tough things were for you."

You still have no idea.

"I don't mind helping them, it's just . . . for how long? I feel so *stuck*. Like I'm backed into this tight corner without any direction to go. My parents had such high hopes and standards for me that I just couldn't live up to. I want more for myself and for my family, but I just don't know how to do it. *I* am their wallet. *I* am supposed to be their retirement fund, but I just don't know how to—" I closed my eyes and let out a shaky breath. "I've had a job since I was thirteen. I worked my ass off in school, and all I got from it is a stem degree collecting dust in my room and a mountain of student debt that keeps growing like *mold*. I did everything right but still, nothing is enough. Nothing I ever do is *enough*."

I glanced at his reflection through the window. He was staring at me with pity filled eyes.

"Stop," I whispered, closing my eyes to block out his expression.

"Stop what?"

"Stop looking at me like that. I didn't tell you this so you can feel sorry for me. I told you because I'm tired of lying. You deserve better than that, Noah."

"I don't pity you, Maya, I *care* about you. I can't imagine the burden of stress and tension you must carry with you everywhere you go. You shouldn't have to deal with this. You're young, this kind of financial strain isn't healthy and it isn't fair. Please, just let me help—"

"Don't," I interrupted, turning around to face him. "Thank you, but the answer is no. Please don't ask me again."

He shook his head in frustration. "So, let me get this straight. You get to take care of everything and *everyone* . . . and then what? Who takes care of you?"

"I do," I said firmly, my chin tilting up in defense.

"Bullshit."

"Excuse me?"

"Every day you come in here with circles under your eyes, and you smile, and you laugh, but I can always tell you have a million other things going on beneath the surface. You never hesitate to jump behind the counter when the line gets hectic, and you help me clean up every night that you're off from work. I catch you staring off into space all the time. You take shit from patients in the morning, and then you take shit from customers and from that bitch Sheila at night, but you don't do anything about it. You just suck it up and you deal with it, and you neglect yourself while continuing to put everybody else first."

"So what do you want me to do? I don't have a *choice*. I can't just be selfish and abandon my family."

"It's not selfish to take care of your own needs first. You only feel like that because you're not used to doing so. It's not your responsibility to take care of your parents' financial issues."

"Yes, it is."

"No, it's not—"

"*Yes*, it is. It's not my dad's fault. It's not his fault he's *sick*. He tried his best. He moved here to give his family a better life, but he didn't realize how difficult it would be to navigate through a country that isn't developed to help people within the minority. An immigrant that didn't move here with prior connections or a pile of gold. My parents worked so hard, and they have *nothing* to show for it." I couldn't imagine how he must have felt every day knowing that he couldn't fulfill his dreams.

"It's not his fault," I repeated quietly. "And it *is* my responsibility. You did everything you could to try and help your mom, and you were only a *child*. I know it was a long time ago, and I'm happy that you eventually got to have a family that loves and takes care of you, but I know there's still some part of you that understands where I'm coming from."

"Maya," he started, but I spoke before he could.

"Sometimes you can't put yourself first. Sometimes you have to sacrifice the things you *want* for the things other people *need*. Sometimes there is no way out," I sighed. "All I know for sure is that I would feel a million times worse if I had stayed in school, knowing full well that my parents needed me."

He rubbed his hands on his face in exasperation. I hated how stressed I was making him with my problems, so I quickly planted a smile on my face.

"It's fine, Noah. Things don't usually work out for me, but I'm used to it," I assured him. "I shouldn't have said anything. Just forget about it, okay?"

He lowered his hands. "No, it's not *fine*. Don't ever apologize for letting me know you," he said fiercely. "And you're wrong. We will always work out, no matter what happens . . . so get used to that."

"I'm sorry I lied to you," I said quietly.

"There's nothing to apologize for."

"I disagree."

He fixed his gaze on me seriously. "You're not a bad person, Maya. If anything, this just proves you are the *best* person."

I chuckled humorlessly, "I *disagree*."

"Look at me," he insisted, waiting until I reluctantly met his unrelenting stare. "You are *not* a failure. That's a pretty hefty declaration for a girl in her twenties. It's a privilege to be able to only focus on school while you're in school, but not a lot of people understand that. I understand, though, and I know you did everything you could." His lips twitched into a small smile. "Your best days are still ahead of you, Maya. You have time to accomplish everything and anything you've ever set your mind to. I just wish you weren't so hard on yourself. I just wish you didn't feel like you have to deal with everything alone."

"Alone is the only way I know how to live."

He cocked his head to the side and looked at me sadly. I stepped toward him slowly, leaning my forehead against his chest, arms crossed tightly into my abdomen, breathing deeply.

"This isn't . . ." He hesitated. "There's *more*."

He wasn't asking, but I answered anyway.

"Yes."

"Worse?"

Yes.

He sighed at my silence and finally moved. One hand was rubbing my forearm while the other was stroking my hair, pressing me deeper into him. I could hear his heart thrumming, blocking out *hers*. "When you're ready, Maya."

I wasn't ever going to be ready. He had no idea how much I wanted to continue. How much I wanted to finally break down and let go of all the gut-wrenching burdens that had rested on my shoulders for what felt like an eternity, but I couldn't. The comfort of having Noah's understating was *fleeting.* It only lasted a minute before Ana's thumps reigned my guilt back in at full force, dragging me into the deepest trenches of hell.

If only this was the most deceitful lie.

THEN

Dear Ana,

I couldn't sleep.

It was way too hot in my room. I opened the window, but the air flowing through the screen was humid, so I ended up going downstairs after everyone went to sleep. I lounged on the couch for a few hours, flipping through channels on mute, until eventually, I drifted off.

I don't know how long I was out. All I remember is suddenly jolting awake, facing the inside of the couch with my back to the room. I was going to turn around so I could spend the rest of the night in my bed, but something in my gut stopped me from moving.

And then I felt him.

He was breathing deeply and loudly right behind me. I didn't need to have eyes behind the back of my head to know it was Mikhail. No one sparked a raging fire of fear in me like he did.

He didn't speak. He just stood there, watching me. I kept my eyes and lips closed tight, breathing in and out through my nose. I knew he could tell I was awake, but I was hoping he would just leave me alone. After a few minutes that felt like hours, I heard him move and to my horror, he came closer. His hot breath was on the back of my neck, and something fluttered lightly across the side of my body, but I pretended it was a spider and not Mikhail's fingers—

And then he left.

I waited, frozen in shock and distress. After a few moments, my body slowly started to unlock my joints, one by one. I turned around slowly and, after confirming he was nowhere around, tiptoed back upstairs. I paced around my room, waiting for my body to relax but it wouldn't. What if he came back into my room? What if he decided to hurt me, knowing I was defenseless in my unconscious slumber? Most importantly though, how many times had he done that? The thought of him coming into my room at night, staring at me with those menacing, and hatred-filled eyes that made my skin crawl in disgust . . . I had to grab my pillow and shove it against my mouth to keep from screaming.

After a few hours, my exhaustion started to creep back, so I slipped into bed and under the covers. I wrapped my blanket around my' body tightly, wishing it was a cloak of invisibility instead of a thin piece of cotton held together by a low thread count and incapable of shielding me from anything. I tried to close my eyes and clear my mind but I kept seeing his face. The wall separating our room was gone and I was lying right beside him, in the same bed, under the same covers. His breath was on my neck, and his voice was whispering profanities into my ear, and his spider leg fingers were dancing over my clothes, but then a second passed and I could feel them tickling my skin—

And then I felt it. My skin was suddenly cold, right between my legs. It started from the top and then quickly spread lower, accompanied by sticky dampness. The light fabric of my pajama bottoms started to feel heavier as it soaked up the weight of all the moisture secreting from my body.

Humiliation tainted my face red, Ana. My mind has already failed me; I guess it was only a matter of time before my body did too.

It's okay, I told myself. It's nothing, just don't look under the covers.

The muggy wind blew the sudden rancid air into my face and my eyes started to water.

Don't look under the covers, Maya, I repeated.

The wetness reached my ankles.

Don't look under the covers, Maya.

God, it smelled so fucking bad, Ana.

Don't look under the covers, Maya.

I didn't need to look to see the urine soaking into a puddle of disgust beneath me—

And then he was gone. Mikhail was gone, and his breath was gone, and his fingers were gone, and the wall that separated us was back in place. It was just me, alone in my room, marinating in my own filth.

That was the last time I willingly fell asleep at night. It wasn't the last time I wet the bed.

NOW

Some idiot took my usual spot, so I had to park a block away from the café.

I was dreading the walk—not because of the frigid weather, but because it was so long. I never ended up walking, though. I was skipping. Yes, *me*, Maya fucking Ibrahim was skipping down the sidewalk to meet her favorite boy. Her new best friend. Her first *non*-fictional crush. I was blushing just thinking about him.

My happiness was interrupted when I saw the café closed. It was four PM on a Wednesday—when we usually saw each other. When it was always open. But from what I could see it was dark inside, and the window blinds were drawn. I checked my phone and I had no new notifications. I tried not to be offended, but I couldn't stop that *stupid*, silly, inconsequential hurt that instantly stung through me.

I took my keys out of my pocket and picked the one he'd given me a few weeks ago. The key to his cafe. I wasn't trying to pry, but I just needed to make sure everything was okay.

I unlocked the door and walked inside, looking around. I'd never seen it look so quiet and dead. After confirming Noah wasn't there I turned to leave, but the heavy wind from the open entryway ruffled the tarp concealing the bookstore. That's when I saw him standing by the window. If he knew I was there, he never made any inclination. I hesitated for a moment before walking in his direction.

"Noah?" I said softly, stepping through the tarp. He didn't look at me, and he didn't respond . . . he just stood there. I went over to him and gently touched his hand. He jumped at the contact, startled, and looked at me in shock.

"Sorry, I didn't mean to scare you . . ." My voice trailed. His face was off. "What's wrong?"

He turned back to the window. "My dad died."

My hand flew to my chest. "No," I breathed. "What happened? Why aren't you with your family—?"

"Not my adoptive dad," he interrupted. "My birth dad."

"I'm so sorry. How did you find out?"

"He'd been trying to reach me for a few months now, but I never returned any of his calls." He closed his eyes and sighed. "His lawyer showed up this morning before I was supposed to open. He told me that my dad was diagnosed with stage four prostate cancer and that it quickly spread throughout his whole body . . . he died two days ago. Before his lawyer left, he handed me an envelope."

My eyes landed on the thick envelope strewn on the floor, unopened.

"Are you going to open it?"

"I don't need to open it, Maya, I already know what it is. It's his fucking *will*," he chuckled humorlessly. "He gave my mom *nothing* when she was trying to take care of me after his sorry ass left us, but then *years* later he decides to leave me money? I'm not opening it. He can't just—" He shook his head angrily. "He can't just be a terrible dad, and then suddenly decide to reach out because he's *dying*, leaving me with all of this . . . guilt. Guilt for not answering his calls. Guilt for not letting him redeem himself before his time on this earth was done." He pressed his clenched fists against his eyes. "Maya, I need you to leave, please."

"I get it, okay? I always want to be alone when I'm upset, or mad, or in pain. But here's the thing, Noah . . . deep down under my urge to be alone there's always this tiny, yet *burning* need to be with someone. This gnawing wish that someone would push back and *stay*. You can tell me to leave, but I'm not going anywhere."

He was silent for a moment, staring solemnly out the window. "I don't want you to see me like this."

"See you like what?" I asked, confused. "See you *sad*?"

"No," he scoffed. "See me *angry*. I'm not sad that my piece of shit father died, I'm fucking pissed."

"Then *be* angry. I don't understand why I need to leave—"

"Do you think I don't notice every time you flinch?"

The rest of my words got lodged in my throat.

"Do you think I don't notice every time you jump at a sudden noise? Or when you cringe away from someone—a *man*—stepping too close to you?" I looked away from his intense gaze. "You did it with me before, at Ana's grave. And again the next day when I blocked your path outside the café. I could see it on your face—how absolutely terrified you were. How your body got all tense like you were bracing yourself for something . . . I'm sorry. I never should have done that."

"Noah, it's fine. *I'm* fine. You don't need to walk on eggshells around me," I insisted.

"I'm not, I just . . . I don't ever want to be the reason behind your fear," he said. "I'll be okay, I promise. Please don't make yourself uncomfortable for me."

He turned away and continued to stare out the window

silently. I never realized he noticed when I reacted like that. Most of the time *I* didn't even notice when I reacted like that, but of course, Noah did. He was always watching me, memorizing everything I did and everything I said . . . but if he wanted me to leave, I would. I didn't want him to have to hold back because I was a broken little girl who couldn't get over her past.

But before I took a step back toward the café, my eyes paused on all the paint cans he got for the bookstore. We were supposed to start painting today . . . I *wanted* to start painting today. I changed direction and grabbed one of the buckets. It was heavy, but not as heavy as the mountain of emotions sitting on my chest. Noah wasn't the only one who was angry. I was angry with him. He didn't deserve to go through what he was feeling. He was healed. He was *happy*. Fuck his dad for opening up old wounds and making him feel guilty. Fuck his dad for trying to ruin everything Noah worked so hard to build.

I lifted the paint can above my head, rage fueling my muscles, and chucked it at the wall. I watched it hit the drywall loudly and explode open at the impact, sprinkling paint all over me. I didn't care. I was *trembling* with the slow burn of fury racing through my veins. I went to grab another can and felt Noah come up beside me.

"What are you doing?"

I met his gaze. "I'm angry too."

He lifted his hand and gently stroked my paint-splattered cheek. "I'm not this person."

I held out the paint can. "I know you're not this person, but right now you need to be."

He hesitated for a moment before taking it from me

cautiously. "I don't want to ruin your bookstore."

My bookstore. Even though I never said yes, he was still giving it to me. Even though I never said yes, it was still mine anyway, waiting patiently until I could bring myself to accept it.

"Nothing can stay ugly forever."

He didn't waste any time throwing it effortlessly against the wall and spraying us with more paint. I stayed put beside him, making sure not to recoil from the loud sounds his throws were making. Every smack reverberated against the wall and bounced onto me, eliciting sharp memories. How was it possible that a paint can hitting the wall could sound just like a human *body* hitting the wall?

If I was being honest, I didn't want to see him angry. I didn't want to know him as someone that could *be* angry because I associated anger with my brother. In my eyes, anger meant you were a bad person. It was a dirty emotion that I refused to let myself feel because if I did then it would confirm all my worst fears . . . that I was just like him. That I would *like* it. It was there, though. Even when I didn't let myself feel it or enjoy it, I could always hear it humming in the background. Sometimes it was quiet. Sometimes it was clawing and begging and roaring to come out. Sometimes I let it.

That's the thing about *sometimes*, though. *Sometimes* couldn't last forever—not really. It eventually had to stop being *sometimes*. It eventually had to fall back into *never* or transform into *always*. Was my *sometimes* anger slowly transforming into an *always* anger?

But when my gaze flickered toward him I didn't see any anger that I recognized. He was mad, but it was a soft mad. His rage didn't feel directed at *me*. His rage didn't want to hurt *me*. His rage was simply pain, and there wasn't a single ounce of my being that was scared of him.

Maybe anger didn't make you bad. Maybe it was how you chose to deal with that anger. Maybe we were all bad. Unavoidably, inexcusably, absolutely *bad*.

He stopped moving. All the cans were completely demolished, and the white walls were covered in green paint.

"Noah?"

"Yes, Maya?"

"I'm sorry it took him twenty-eight years to want to get to know you," I told him. "I'm sorry it had to take dying for him to realize the mistake he made when he abandoned you, but don't let him ruin the amazing person you've become *despite* him."

He nodded slowly. "Okay."

"I'm going to hug you now, okay?"

"*Okay.*"

I wrapped my arms around him, and he immediately crushed me into his chest. We stood there, our clothes wet and sticky, and I let him hold me. After a while, I finally felt him release the gust of air trapped in his lungs. I waited for her to thump in protest, but Ana was quiet. She was letting me comfort him without any interruptions.

"I'm all right, Maya. It was just a moment. Thank you."

I didn't respond. I just breathed him in completely and begged some of his relief to replace the fire screaming inside me. God, I was so *fucking* angry. I was angry at his father for not loving him. I was angry at Mikhail for making me this way. Above all though, I was angry at *myself* for making Noah feel like I couldn't be a source of comfort for him. For making him feel like I was the only one who was allowed to be in pain. For making him feel like he couldn't express himself for fear of hurting me in the process. What kind of person did that? What kind of *friend* did that?

He pulled away from me slightly and rested his forehead against mine. "Your body feels tense."

"Oh, those are just my hunky muscles."

"Funny."

"I prefer *hilarious*, but funny will do."

"Maya," he said seriously. "I gave you my pain, it's only fair that you give me yours too."

"You promised you would never ask."

"I know, but I didn't say I would never break my promises," he replied, leaning closer. "Tell me."

"Why do you want to know so badly?"

"So I can be there for you like you're always there for me." I felt his velvet finger at the corner of my mouth, tugging it upwards. I couldn't help smiling half-heartedly under his touch. "So I can cheer you up like you're always cheering me up."

And for a second I considered it. I really considered giving him what he wanted, but even the idea of it was too preposterous for my mundane mind to comprehend. I felt like I was constantly trying to speak about things that were unspeakable. The words were there, scratched into my throat, but they just . . . couldn't be said.

"I can't."

He sighed. "How long?"

"How long what?"

"How long until you'll be able to tell me? Is it going to be forever? Are you going to keep hiding everything *forever*? Because I can't do this forever, Maya. I can't keep watching you hurt alone forever."

I stared at him, a million thoughts and secrets and letters swirling around behind my eyes, bursting to come out in a sea of shrieks and sobs. I settled for a light chuckle instead. "There's so much I wish I could say, but I don't know how to, because no one has ever *asked*. No one ever wanted to know about my pain and now . . . the words are poison on my tongue, Noah. The memories are acid in my brain and I——" I swallowed back the lump in my throat. "Nothing good ever came from talking, so I just stayed quiet. Now I only know how to be silent."

"I'm sorry your ears stayed open for everyone's words, despite no one ever taking a second to hear yours," he said softly. "But maybe talking wasn't the problem. Maybe it was the *people* you were choosing to listen."

"It doesn't matter anymore. The damage is done. It's too late."

"Don't let the bad things fool you, Maya. It's never too late." He wiped away the lone tear that had managed to escape without my notice. "You're going to be okay too, I promise. And this is a promise that I will never break."

He was wrong. A soul could only hold on for so long before it eventually let go and ceased to exist . . . but I nodded anyway. He didn't need to know he was holding onto a corpse.

~

"Do you want to lick the spoon?"

"Does a bear shit in the woods?"

Noah paused and glanced at me with confused eyes. "I assume so, why?"

"That was a rhetorical question," I said, laughing. "You asked me an obvious question so I asked *you* an obvious question back."

He looked back at the bowl. "You're a weird chick."

"And you're a weird dude," I replied, taking the spoon covered in batter from his extended hand. "When are you adding my banana bread to the menu? I don't think it's fair that only *I* get to enjoy all this finger-licking delectableness."

"Did the paint fumes get to you?" he asked, grinning. "Are you on cloud nine right now, Maya?"

"It's possible," I mused. "It's concerning how much I enjoyed throwing that paint can at the wall. I feel . . . lighter or something."

Almost like how Mikhail feels after he throws you *at the wall.*

"You should come on my runs with me," he suggested. "You'll get the same feeling without all the mess."

"The only way I'll be going on runs with you is if *you* are doing the running while *I* ride on your back," I said, sticking my tongue out and scooping up the last chocolate chip. "Besides, I like the mess we made in the bookstore. It gives it character."

My eyes flickered in his direction when he didn't respond. He was staring at me intensely, his darkened eyes zeroed in on my *mouth*.

"Stop," he demanded.

"Stop what?"

"Stop *torturing* me," he whispered, walking toward me. He lifted his hand and gently pried the clean spoon from my fingers.

"I'm high on paint fumes, remember? I legally can't be held accountable for my actions while I'm under the influence."

"That is definitely incorrect," he chuckled, shaking his

head. "You are an incredibly well-spoken woman, Maya, but I swear sometimes you say the weirdest shit and I fucking *love* it. I can listen to you talk nonsense for all hours of the day and never get sick of it. You told me once that getting to know you was *work*, and you were right. It's the dream job I never knew I needed to have and I'll willingly do it free of charge, for the rest of my life."

Thump, thump—

"Did you just call my intellectual speech *nonsense?*"

He laughed again and stepped away. I watched silently as he erased the item written under the specials section on the menu, and wrote a new one in bright pink chalk.

Mayas Finger-licking Delectableness Banana Bread

"No one's ever going to order that," I told him.

He shrugged and wiped his chalky hands on his pants. "More for you."

The oven timer went off and he carefully removed his delicious masterpiece and placed it on the cooling pad. "Am I grabbing plates, or packaging this up for you?"

Noah's voice was casual, but I could hear something else simmering beneath the surface of his smooth tone.

"I'm sorry."

"Don't be," he insisted. "At least let me go turn on your car so it can heat up for a few minutes. It's been sitting there for a while now, it's probably a rolling ice box."

"I can do it," I said quickly, standing up.

"It's freezing," he stressed, grabbing my keys. "And you're always so *cold*. I'll be quick."

"Wait!" I said, and he turned back. "You have to—I mean; you *might* have to like, try it a few times."

"Try what a few times?"

My face was red with humiliation. "You know . . . the *ignition*," I explained awkwardly. "It's an old car . . . so sometimes it doesn't start on the first time, especially in the cold." Or the second time. Or the *third* . . .

Understanding replaced his confusion and his eyes softened. "It's okay, Maya."

I didn't respond, so he grabbed his jacket and headed outside. I held my breath and prayed that it would run smoothly this *one* time, *please, please, please*⸺

My bones cringed painfully as the loud groan and splutter of the engine flowed into my ears, but I breathed a sigh of relief when it turned on after the first try. Noah came back in after a few minutes, his dark curls windswept and his nose a rosy pink. He immediately came up to me and rubbed his cold hands against my cheeks.

Thump, thump⸺

"What was the point of heating up my car, if you were just going to come back in and make *me* cold too?" I protested but made no move to push him away. My face was cold, but the rest of my body was sizzling with *warmth*.

Thump, thump⸺

"Thanks for calling in at work," he said after a moment. "Is it terrible that I'm willing to commit some murders just so you feel obligated to stay here and comfort me?"

I laughed. "Yes, it is terrible."

"And thank you for making me dinner. Your impeccable culinary skills truly *illuminated* my kitchen."

"Hey—I put out that fire before it did any real damage. Don't act like the grilled peanut butter and jelly sandwich I made for you wasn't the best thing you've ever eaten."

"The very best," he agreed and released my face to start

packing up my banana bread. "Thank you for staying even though I asked you to leave."

"Are you going to be okay?"

"I'm already okay," he replied. "I grieved my father a long time ago. *Physically*, he died two days ago but he died in my heart when I was six."

I nodded as he took his jacket off and put it on me instead. "That's good because being sad is *my* thing," I reminded him sarcastically. "I called dibs on it the first time we met."

He laughed. "Technically it was the second time."

"Right, well, you can . . . call me, you know. If you need to talk or whatever. I'll probably be awake."

His eyebrows shot up in surprise. "You *hate* talking on the phone."

"Yeah, I do," I agreed with a chuckle. "But I think I would hate it a little less if it was you on the other end."

He smiled, his eyes beaming through the dimly lit café. "In that case, I hope you have unlimited minutes on your phone plan."

"Okay, settle down." I rolled my eyes, but my skin was flushed. "Don't make me block you."

"Try not to finish this on the ride home," he teased.

"No promises." I took the container from him. "See you later dude."

"Bye, chick."

I stepped outside and rushed to my car. I was going to get there later than usual, but surprisingly my mom hadn't hounded me with any messages. I didn't have to wonder why for long though, because when I got to the house the answer was clear. The living room light was on through the curtains, and three shadows stood out. She wasn't texting me because she probably didn't even realize I wasn't home. She probably assumed I was locked up in my room, instead of going up there to actually check. She didn't care where I was because she was too preoccupied with *them*. Her husband and her son. Her family.

"Do you think I haven't noticed you staying out later for the past few weeks?"

"Bullshit," I spat, opening the container and tearing off a piece of banana bread.

Fuck them and their happy little bubble.

I shoved another bite into my mouth before I was even finished chewing the first one.

Fuck them for acting like *I* was the black sheep in the family. Like *I* was the reason behind all the chaos and drama, and not *him*.

I crammed another chunk into my mouth, but I couldn't even taste the finger-licking delectableness anymore. All I could taste was the salty tears coating my lips.

Fuck them for only giving me attention when they needed something from me. They loved me when I was paying their bills and keeping quiet about their *precious* son, but after that? After their debt was cleared and I was so deeply traumatized that I couldn't utter a single word about him even if I tried? I was nothing. Nothing but a burden. Nothing but the miserable outcast threatening to contaminate their clean and polished air.

The container was empty now. The only thing left was some crumbs on my shirt and chocolate smudged on my fingers.

Fuck them for making me feel useless when I couldn't be used. *Fuck* them for making me drain everything I had on them, only to be left completely dry and shriveled up. *Fuck* them for consuming me with the overpowering urge to take care of them, and now I had no idea how to take care of myself. *Fuck* them for making me question if my need to comfort Noah was genuine, or if I was just doing it because I didn't want him to realize I was a valueless excuse for a friend and he could find better. He *deserved* better.

I muffled all my pain for them. I swallowed all my anger for them. I concealed all my wounds for them. I was the perfect daughter for them. I chose my parents every time, but they always chose him.

I shook the container again, not believing that it was empty. If it was truly empty, then why was *I* still empty? Why didn't I feel full?

My phone buzzed in the cup holder. I pressed it against my wet cheek.

"Hey," I greeted cheerfully. "Are you okay?"

"I *was* okay," Noah replied. "I'm better now, though. Amazing."

A laugh tumbled through my chocolate and tear-stained lips, and I quickly muted myself just as my laughs turned into sobs.

"Maya? Are you still there?"

I forced a deep breath through my clogged chest. "Yeah, sorry, my reception is bad." Another deep breath. "So . . . if you're *better* than okay, why did you call?"

He was silent for a moment before speaking softly, a gentle caress against my ear. "You told me that I could."

Someone finally chose me.

THEN

Dear Ana,

I never wanted to have kids.

Most girls aspire to be a mother. Most girls aspire to get married and have children and create a family of their own. Most girls do . . . but I'm not one of them. It's not without reason—I mean, giving birth sounds like the most painful and terrifying experience a person could ever go through. It seems unnatural to try and shove a watermelon through a keyhole, so why do that with humans? There has to be an easier way, but I guess we just never discovered it yet. Or maybe we have, and we were just choosing to do it the hard way. Isn't it crazy how the fate of the human population is entirely dependent on women in pain?

The pain isn't the only thing holding me back. I just can't imagine finding someone that I would even want to start a family with. I don't know a lot of things, Ana, but I do know that I am not a person people can fall in love with.

Maybe I'm just missing the maternal bone every other woman seemed to be born with. I could list a million reasons, Ana—the economy is shit, the world is filled with racism and war and discrimination and guns, so why the fuck would anyone in their right mind want to throw an innocent fetus into all that chaos? But none of that matters. I don't want to have kids because what if that kid turns out to be like Mikhail? You can have amazing parents but still have a shitty child. I'm not saying my parents were amazing, but they weren't necessarily terrible enough that it could justify why Mikhail turned out the way he did. I already had to deal with him in one lifetime, I couldn't imagine having to deal with him in another.

And if my child did turn out like Mikhail . . . would I stop loving them too?

My answer to that question is why I should never be a mother, but it doesn't matter because I never wanted to have kids anyway.

Mikhail didn't know that, though.

He didn't know that when he came down to the basement while I was studying. I didn't even notice he was there until I got up to use the bathroom, and nearly had a heart attack when I saw him. I ignored him and walked to the stairs but he immediately moved and blocked my way. He didn't look mad, Ana. He looked . . . weird. Sad, or something, I don't fucking know.

"I had sex with Hiba," he said suddenly.

I was shocked at first. Why the fuck would he tell me that? Then I was disgusted because that wasn't an image I ever wanted to flash through my brain. I took another step to go around him, but he spoke again.

"She wanted to wait for marriage, but I convinced her to do it with me anyway."

I froze.

"She wanted to use protection, but I convinced her not to. I told her that it would ruin her experience, and she agreed."

I covered my ears. I didn't want to hear him anymore.

"That's not why I wanted her unprotected, though."

"Stop talking," I whispered, my body quickly filling with dread.

"She wanted to wait until her doctor could prescribe her birth control pills, but I told her no. I wanted to do it now . . . and she agreed."

I closed my eyes against the scene playing in my head, but it kept playing anyway.

"Like I said she agreed, but she told me to pull out so she couldn't get pregnant."

I already knew that he didn't.

"But I didn't."

My eyes flashed open and I looked at him, rage replacing my dread. "You disgust me. You are a horrific excuse for a human. I hope she reports you. I hope she presses charges against you, you piece of shit——"

And then he punched me in the face.

I didn't see it coming, but I felt the blow of his fist against my jaw and the metallic blood coating my tongue. I tried to swallow but there was something solid rolling around in my mouth. I spit the contents into my palm, and among the red, there was a speck of white. My glasses had flown off from the force of his impact, but I didn't need them to recognize my fucking tooth.

"Please don't interrupt me, Maya," he said calmly. "It's rude. That's what you get for being rude."

My trembling hand dropped my tooth onto the floor and into the puddle of blood dripping at my feet.

"Like I said, I didn't pull out because I wanted her to get pregnant. If she got pregnant then she could never leave me."

My whole body was shaking at that point. I was covered in blood and spit, and my face was burning with pain. His words though . . . his words clawed through my chest intensely.

"She was nervous at first, but then she didn't mind. She realized that she also wanted to have a kid with me too."

I fucked up, Ana. I should have fought harder to get her away from him.

"Months went by, Maya. Months went by and she still wasn't pregnant."

Thank God, I thought.

"It didn't make sense. I asked her if she had any problems, but she said no. I didn't believe her though, so I made her go to an appointment and get checked. They told her that she was fine, and at first I was happy.

A woman who can't bear children is not a woman." He paused, and I felt his eyes burning a hole into my face but I kept mine closed. I didn't want to look at him. *"I'm the problem, Maya. I can't have kids."*

And then I thanked God again. I thanked the stars and the moon and the masters of the fucking universe for taking this away from him. He should never be a father.

"How did you do it?"

I didn't respond.

"I asked you a question!" He shouted, his calm demeanor gone and replaced by the brutal anger I was so accustomed to. *"How did you do it?!"*

"Do what?" I snapped, backing away. He didn't answer. He simply lifted his foot and shoved it into my abdomen, ramming me onto the floor.

"What did you do to me, huh?" he asked, standing over me. *"Why can't I have kids?"*

He was crazy, Ana. He was out of his fucking mind. How could I have done anything to him? How could I have possibly accomplished what he was implying?

"If I can't have them, then neither can you," he said suddenly, kicking me again. *"You should be thanking me. I'm doing you a favor. I'm giving you a gift. I'm making this decision for you so that you'll never have to make it for yourself."*

He kicked me in the ribs. *"Thank me,"* he demanded.

I tried to get up but he just shoved me back to the floor.

"I said thank me!" he shouted, ramming his foot into my lower stomach.

"Thank you!" I cried out in pain. I didn't understand what he was saying, but I would've said anything to make him leave me alone.

He didn't leave me alone, Ana.

I stopped trying to fight back. I learned after a few years that fighting back only encouraged him. My attempts at defending myself thrilled him.

181

But if I just stayed still . . . eventually he got bored and, if I was lucky, ended things earlier than planned.

He kicked me in the same place a second time, and then a third time, and that's when I realized what he was aiming for.

My uterus.

And then everything made sense.

He kicked me again, but this time he kept his foot there. He pressed down with all his body weight, his toenails cutting into my skin like daggers. His foot kept crushing deeper into my body, trying to compress my organs into a pancake until I could almost feel his foot touch the bones that made up my spine.

Here's the thing, Ana. I didn't care what he was doing to me in that moment because all I could think about was Hiba, and what he did to her. *All I could think about was how it was my fault. I inherit all his sins. I become the monster because I created the monster. I was the first person he ever hurt. He only knew he had power because I gave him the power and let him continue to keep it without any consequences.*

I shouldn't have given up on her so fast. So what if she lied to him and almost got me killed? She was a girl in love. Her mind was infested with all the terrible lies Mikhail fed her about me. Why would *she believe me? Maybe she would've believed me if I had tried again? Maybe she would've believed me if I had shown her all my scars and bruises?*

As much as I hate to admit it, maybe she had it worse. I don't think I ever loved Mikhail, so it was easier for me to hate him. She did *though. She got hurt by someone she loved which is the worst kind of pain. She got hurt by someone she loved, and the worst part is she probably doesn't even realize it.*

I don't know when he stopped, or when my mom came home, or how I got off the basement floor. I lost all my perception of time. But eventually, I woke up from my haze and found myself in my bed and under the covers. I was clean of blood, and my mouth was one tooth short. I blinked a few times to bring back some moisture into my dry eyes because they felt like they'd been open for hours, and then the memories came crashing back. I lifted my shirt and examined my tender and bruised abdomen, wondering if . . . I didn't want to wonder, Ana. I didn't want to think anymore. I desperately tried to summon that dissociating feeling again, but nothing came. Every ache and crack penetrated through me over and over again.

I don't know if he succeeded, Ana . . . but it doesn't matter because I never wanted to have kids anyway.

My period is late, Ana . . . but it doesn't matter because I never wanted to have kids anyway.

I don't deserve to be a mother, Ana . . . but it doesn't matter because I never wanted to have kids anyway.

NOW

Noah asked me out on a date.

It happened a few weeks after his father died. Noah and I went to his funeral so he could make peace with it, and then things went back to normal. All he needed was a moment. He let himself feel *bad* for a moment, and then he just . . . moved on. I didn't believe him at first, certain his childhood pain would come creeping back into his life. I waited for the self-sabotage, the shutting down, the unrelenting *anger* . . . but he was fine. And not my kind of fine—the other kind. The real kind. The healthy kind. The content, satisfied, exceptionally fucking *splendid*—

And I was happy for him.

We were painting the bookstore. Well, *I* was painting the bookstore and Noah kept flicking paint at me. He grabbed a washcloth and was in the middle of cleaning his playful mess off my face when he suddenly paused.

"Go on a date with me," he whispered. It wasn't a question—it was a *plea*. He was staring at me fervently and his hand was on my cheek and Ana was pounding her heart against my chest so hard it *hurt*.

"Okay," I whispered back without thinking. And then he smiled so big and so bright—how I imagined the sun would smile at the midnight sky in the alternate universe they got to exist simultaneously—and suddenly I couldn't remember why

I was supposed to say *no*.

And now here I was, a week later, staring at my closet for the last forty-three minutes, waiting for an outfit to magically create itself without any effort from me. I'd texted Noah earlier asking him what I should wear, and he said I should wear what I always wear. I never imagined wearing jeans and sneakers on my first date, but I wasn't mad about it either.

I smiled. Just thinking the word *date* made me giddy. I was nervous at first——my brain couldn't resist second-guessing his intentions at every corner. But for the most part, I was excited. I liked him. God, I liked him so fucking much and I knew I shouldn't, but I *did* and I couldn't terminate my feelings even if I wanted to.

I was convinced things between us would change after my confession, and they *did*, but not in the way I assumed. My honesty somehow broke down one of my many barriers and brought us closer together. I was still uncomfortable with the vulnerability I'd expressed and asked him to, respectfully, refrain from bringing it up ever again. He obliged begrudgingly, but his words still rang vividly in my ears.

"Please, just let me help——"

I flinched away in embarrassment and blocked the conversation out. It wasn't like I never expected him to say that——he was the kindest person I'd ever met——but that didn't make it any less awkward. I hated when people spent money on me and I didn't want or *need* his help. We were both born into a broken world. The only difference was that he managed to get handed a way out, and I . . . didn't.

"Who takes care of you, Maya?"

I stared at my reflection in the mirror——well, what was left of it after my episode. My once long and thick hair had been falling out in chunks until I just chopped it off mid mental breakdown. I didn't mind—short was better. Short was harder for him to *pull*. The brown curls hovered above my collar for the last several years because I couldn't be bothered to learn how to style them. My ivory skin was in desperate need of some sun and sleep, and my bone structure was sharp with inconsistent nutrition.

I forced my eyes to continue downwards, reluctantly dropping the damp towel I was wrapped in. My body—tall, lithe and lean—was a torture chamber. A permanent reminder of what I needed to know was *real*. It wasn't easy to stare at myself when I basically looked like a crime scene, with all the car accident scars, Mikhail scars, and a few lingering bruises that simply refused to fade. I tried to imagine what I would've looked like without them. I tried to picture myself with pristine and unspoiled limbs, straight out of the box. I wanted to believe that I would've been beautiful. I wanted to believe that in another universe where I was a simple girl living a simple life, I could've been beautiful . . . if it weren't for him.

But at least I had proof. I couldn't rely on my mind, but I could rely on my body as irrefutable, undeniable *proof*. I could rely on 52 steps. I could rely on my letters to Ana.

I carefully examined my hand, hoping I could go gloveless today. It had been a few days since I had a picking session, but the scabs were still a little noticeable. I rubbed the rough callouses with my fingers over and over again, and carefully started to tap them with my nail.

Pick, pick, pick—

It was a persistent itch in the back of my brain that could only get soothed if I picked the scab off. I imagined how I would do it. I had a process to it. I was an *expert*. I wasn't doing something wrong, I was just cleaning it. It looked messy right now, but if I fixed it, it would heal neater next time. It would heal *perfectly*.

Carefully—*slowly*—I peeled away the dead skin and exposed the moist second layer. I smiled in satisfaction, but then frowned as it started to pink up and fill with blood.

"Fuck," I muttered under my breath, pressing a tissue against it until the flow stopped.

I looked away and quickly covered the awful sight with clothes. I pulled on the jacket he loaned me that I never gave back, and closed my closet door.

Noah saw right through me. No one took care of me, not even myself.

~

I jumped out of my car and skipped over to Noah, who was waiting for me in front of his café with his hands behind his back.

"Hey dude," I said, stopping to a halt in front of him. I watched his eyes trail over the white cotton slip dress I put on instead of jeans, and then linger slightly on the small portion of skin exposed from my calves down to my ankles. "I couldn't bring myself to lose the sneakers—they're part of my identity."

"You, um—" he stammered. "You look really pretty, Maya."

"So do you," I told him, tapping his nose, and his blush echoed my own.

"Are you ready to go on your first date *ever*?"

"You don't need to keep reminding me that I've never been on a date," I groaned.

"I love it," he replied softly. "That just means I get to be your first."

And my last.

"These are for you," he said, revealing what he had behind his back.

I looked down and he was holding four perfectly carved wooden flowers, all painted white. They were so life-like and so perfect, if I didn't reach my hand out and gently feel the grain of wood beneath my fingers I would've sworn they were real. But as I took a closer look, I noticed little scribbles on each of the petals, and I immediately recognized the words.

Quotes scrawled in his handwriting.

Book quotes.

A bouquet of all my favorite book quotes.

"Did you make these?" I breathed in awe. He really *did* have magical hands, but clearly not just in the kitchen.

"I wanted to get you flowers, as they're a first date rite of passage, but I didn't want to get you real ones because I knew they would eventually die." I looked up at him and he was staring at me intensely. "I don't want what we have to ever die, Maya."

His voice was barely above a whisper, gently caressing me with his words.

"They're beautiful," I told him sincerely, grabbing the bouquet from his hands cautiously. There was a small, folded paper tucked between the twine that held it together.

"Um, you can read that later," he said nervously. I smiled and threw my arms around him, careful not to squish his heartfelt gift.

"Thank you," I said, hoping the depth of my emotions was clear enough without me having to enunciate them.

He tugged me closer, nuzzling his head into the crook of my neck. I pulled away after a minute and put them in my car.

"So, what's next?" I asked eagerly.

"We need to go catch the city bus. Can I . . . ?" He nudged my hand with his finger, and I nodded.

He took my hand, intertwining our fingers and swinging them lightly between us as we walked. I wore my cut-off cotton gloves, so my long fingers were exposed at the knuckles. I bit my lip at the new sensation of skin on skin. The rough and smooth texture of the pads of his fingers was extremely pleasurable. I lightly untangled my fingers from his and put his hand into both of mine. He watched me with confusion but smiled when he saw me start tracing his palm with my exposed fingers.

We stopped at the bus stop and waited a little ways away from the other people standing. I was still clinging to his hand, doodling circles and other shapes on the surface of his palm. I lightly grazed the length of each of his fingers and studied each line and crack in his perfect skin. He lifted his other hand toward me after a few minutes and I felt his index finger under my chin, tilting it up. I grinned sheepishly at him, not sure how to explain why I was so entranced by his hand and how it felt under my naked fingers.

He gently smoothed back my windblown hair, tucking it behind my ear and stroking the length of my jaw. My eyes fluttered shut and I shuddered slightly as his finger tickled my neck. I was fully aware that the way we were interacting wasn't exactly on a friendship level. Or maybe it was; I never had a male friend before, so I wasn't exactly sure. While I was comfortable being near him, I had never experienced contact like this. It felt intimate, but also kind of strange. I was always a little tempted to pull away, worried it would be too much all of a sudden and I would panic, but that never happened.

That's how I knew it was *right*.

Thump, thump—

It was hard to enjoy it when I still felt guilty, especially now, watching the way he gazed at me with intense adoration, not caring if people were staring. I couldn't keep hiding the truth from him. I had to tell him. And I would, *tonight*, after I was positive about how he felt. If he cared about me as much as I cared about him, I knew we could get through it. There was nothing he could tell me that I wouldn't understand.

Did you hear that, Ana? I'm going to tell him. Just let me have this day.

The bus announced its arrival behind us with a loud squeak of the breaks. I grabbed my wallet to take out some change, but Noah placed his hand on mine, stopping me.

"I got you a pass, don't worry about it," he assured me, placing it into my hand.

"Noah," I started but stopped when I saw the words on the pass. "Wait, why did you get a monthly pass?"

"I always get monthly passes," he replied. He let me in first, waiting for me to hand the driver my ticket before giving him his. He pointed to empty double seats beside the window.

"Do you take the bus frequently?"

"Yeah," he said, looking away. "I don't drive."

"Wait," I snickered. "You still don't have a *license*? Do you need me to give you lessons?"

My laughter immediately subsided when I realized it was one-sided. His head was down and his eyes were closed tightly like he was trying not to remember something. He almost looked like he was in . . . pain.

"I was just kidding," I told him quickly.

He didn't respond, but he did grip my hand tightly in his.

"Are you okay?"

He took a deep breath and looked at me, his eyes bright and haunted by the tortures of his past.

"It's not you, Maya. I have a license, I just . . . don't drive," he said finally.

"Why not?"

He studied my face carefully for a minute. "I'll tell you later, okay?"

"Are you sure? We can reschedule. I don't mind."

"*I* mind."

I nodded slowly as he pulled out his headphones and slipped the right one into my ear. I leaned my head on his shoulder, watching the city passing by through the window. I felt him shuffle slightly, moving me closer, clasping my hand firmly in both of his.

"I came across this place while I was looking for locations to get inventory for the bookstore," he explained as we exited the bus, pointing to the place we were going to. It was a bookstore—a huge one at that. He opened the door for me and I stepped inside, taking in the magnificent space. It was filled with floor-to-ceiling shelves and large windows that illuminated the room with natural light. I waved at the old man behind the counter absently, my eyes completely fixated on the rows and rows of books, comics, and magazines. I hadn't been around them in so long and I immediately felt at ease, their pages welcoming me back with open words.

Noah stayed behind, watching me silently with a small smile on his face.

"I wish you could enjoy this as much as I am."

"Watching *you* enjoy it is very joyful for me. Pick out all the books you want."

I looked back at him questionably.

"It's part of the date," he insisted.

"Noah," I sighed. "Don't make this weird."

"I'm definitely the normal one out of the two of us."

"Okay, true," I chuckled. "I just mean . . . I know I told you about some personal things, but I can take care of myself."

"I never thought you couldn't. You are the strongest and most capable person I've ever met," he said, eyes sparkling in awe. "This is what guys *do* on dates—at least, the good ones."

I smiled. "I appreciate you wanting to give me the full date experience, but I don't need all the extra stuff. Being here with you is more than enough."

He took a step closer to me. "Just because you're easily pleased, doesn't mean you deserve anything *less* than everything."

I reached up and lightly touched his cheek. He was so sweet, and I wanted to accept his kindness but it was almost painful to do so. How could you convince someone they were worthy of everything when they spent their entire life believing they were worthy of nothing?

"How about this? What if I pick out all the books that I want *you* to read?"

I could tell he was about to argue so I spoke again quickly. "I'm compromising with you, Noah. You suggested something and I'm not saying *no*, I'm just giving you another option that I'm more comfortable with."

"I already have a stack of books you told me to read," he reminded me.

"Oh, Noah. That stack is only the beginning."

He regarded for a moment but eventually nodded. "*Difficult*," he said pointedly.

I grinned and took his hand in mine. "Come on, let me turn you into a bookworm. And don't worry, I'll definitely be borrowing these from you soon," I promised, winking at him.

We spent the next few hours thoroughly going through each shelf. I chose about thirty books, all from different genres, and read him the synopsis of each one. I didn't want to force him to read a book that he wasn't at least a little bit interested in, but he still went with every single one I suggested.

"I'm so excited for you to read these," I said. He laughed, grabbing the custom tote bag and led us out of the store. We went to the farmer's market next, and Noah picked up all the ingredients for the surprise dinner he was going to cook for us later that night. After strolling casually through the streets, hand in hand, we grabbed some sandwiches from a deli nearby and went to the park. It had warmed up considerably since the morning so he insisted on sitting outside.

I leaned back and rested my head on his legs, staring up at him as he played with my hair.

"I love your hair," he said softly. "It's so curly."

"You love it because you never have to tackle *brushing* it."

"I would brush it for you every day if you'd let me."

"It's a deal," I replied, hesitating for a moment. "Noah?"

"Yeah?"

"Why don't you drive?"

His fingers stopped in my hair.

"You don't have to tell me if you don't want to. I understand," I assured him, immediately regretting bringing it up in the first place.

He stayed silent, but his fingers resumed their movements. I was just beginning to accept that he wasn't going to answer before he spoke.

"I got into a car accident."

I inhaled sharply. "What happened?"

"I don't . . . want to get into details, but . . ."

He closed his eyes and tensed. I stroked his face, trying to smooth the stress lines. He leaned into my hand, his muscles loosening slightly.

"Ana died in that accident. I killed her."

Thump, thump——

"What do you mean?"

He took a shaky breath, and I braced myself. I spent the last ten years wondering how she died. How we ended up in the *same* hospital on the *same* day. "We weren't supposed to be there; my flight wasn't leaving for a few days but . . . we got into a fight. She told me to leave early, and I did, but she had to come with me to drive my truck home. There was a disruption in the road on our way and I . . . Ana didn't make it."

Thump, thump——

She was in a car accident *too*——?

Thump, thump——

A part of her *did* make it, and it was beating only inches away from him.

I quickly pushed myself up and sat on my knees in front of him. "That doesn't make it your fault, Noah. It was out of your control."

He shook his head at my words. "It was my fault we were *fighting*. If we hadn't fought, then I wouldn't have left early and there wouldn't have been any commotion on the road, causing us to crash."

I continued to touch his face, brushing his hair out of his eyes, waiting for him to continue. He smiled at me for a second, before looking away. "You're probably wondering why we were fighting."

I didn't say anything. *Of course,* I was wondering. I had been wondering what happened between them from the moment I saw him that day at her grave. I immediately assumed at the time that she was his girlfriend, but when he told me they were adopted together . . . I still couldn't shake the feeling there was more to their story.

"Ana was . . . my person. She was my first point of comfort after my mom died and I got thrown into the system. I needed her just as much as she needed me. I loved her. I *love* her."

Irrational jealousy coursed through me at his words.

"Nothing changed when we moved in with our new family, except, well, *everything* changed. We still loved each other but it was different. It *had* to be different, I mean, we were technically siblings. I didn't think she . . ." He shook his head. "I didn't think we had to discuss it."

"Discuss what?"

He sighed. "My feelings were confusing at the time. I was in pain and I was grieving the loss of my mother and Ana was all I had. We thought we were going to be stuck in that hell hole forever. We never expected to get adopted."

Thump, thump—

"What happened, Noah?" I asked quietly.

"I got my acceptance letter from British Columbia," he whispered. "I took a gap year after graduating high school because I didn't know what I wanted to major in, and Ana had already started at the University of Calgary. I was so excited and immediately bought a plane ticket so I could go see the campus, but Ana was upset. We'd talked about staying here for school. I *told* her I was going to go to school with her and I just needed a year off, but on a whim, I sent them my application too and never told her about it. I knew she was going to be mad, but I just . . . I needed to leave. I needed to be on my own for a bit and figure out what I wanted to do. God, I sound like such an ass," he muttered.

"No, you don't," I assured him automatically.

"She was my best friend, but it was still hard—at school, I mean. I always felt like the odd one out, until my junior year when I met a few guys on my robotics team. It wasn't a big deal at first because usually we just hung out during our meetings. One day, Freddie invited us to his house after school to see the remote control plane he was working on and I went. Ana was . . . *livid* when I came home. Accusing me of abandoning her just like her parents did," he looked at me with tormented eyes. "I wasn't abandoning her, Maya; I would *never* do that. After hours of consoling her, she finally forgave me, but I didn't want her to ever feel like that again, so I stopped accepting their invitations. Eventually, they stopped asking."

I rubbed his arm gently.

"She was acting weird ever since I told her about BC. I asked her to come with me to see the campus, but she denied the offer. I was worried she would think I was trying to leave her again or something, but I couldn't tell because she wouldn't talk to me . . . until the day I was supposed to leave."

"The day of her death," I whispered.

The day of my rebirth.

He nodded, taking a deep breath.

"She knocked on my door while I was packing saying she needed to talk." He looked away again. "She stood in front of me and she started *crying*, and begging me not to go. I told her

196

I was just going to see the campus and that I would be back in a few days, but she was so upset. She said she knew that if I went it would make my decision for me and I would end up leaving her. And then . . ."

Thump, thump, THUMP——

". . . she kissed me."

My eyes widened.

"She kissed me and then pulled away and told me that she loved me. That she was *in* love with me and that it didn't matter because we weren't really related."

What. The. Fuck.

I waited for a moment, listening . . . but she was suddenly quiet. *Too* quiet. I touched my wrist subtly, but I could still feel her pulse.

"I was . . . shocked. I mean, I was conflicted too at first, but after a few years, I realized my feelings were strictly on a familial level. I assumed the same from her, and that our close bond was just a sibling thing. I never expected *that* at all. When I didn't respond to her confession right away she got embarrassed and ran to her room. I followed her obviously, and tried to explain . . ."

He rubbed his eyes in distress. "After I was done talking, she told me to leave. I thought she meant to my room, but she wanted me to leave for the airport. She said she needed some space and that she wanted me to get an earlier flight out to BC. I agreed; I didn't want her to feel uncomfortable around me. Nobody was home, so she came with me to drive my truck back and . . . well, you know the rest."

I nodded sadly.

"I'll always wonder if it was my fault," he whispered regretfully. "I'll always wonder if I led her on without realizing, or if I was unintentionally giving her any kind of inclination that I felt the same way. Maybe if I had pushed her away a little in the beginning she wouldn't have felt . . ."

I wrapped my arms around him tightly.

"It wasn't your fault, Noah," I said firmly. "You loved her like a brother and like a friend, and instead of taking advantage of her like most men would have, you *respected* her. I don't doubt for a second that if Ana were still alive, she eventually would've thanked you for pushing her away. I'm sorry you never got to hear the words from her. I'm sorry you lost your best friend."

I'm sorry her heart is beating inside me instead.

He rested his head on my shoulder and returned my embrace, squeezing me closer.

"It's okay if you . . ." I started slowly. "It's okay if you felt, or . . . *feel* the same way. I mean, all that matters is that you didn't act on it. We can't help who we love."

"I wondered that too," he breathed into my shoulder. "I spent the last ten years wondering if what I felt for her was *more* than familial love. I spent the last ten years experimenting with other women, desperately searching for someone to convince me that I was right and she didn't just die because I was in *denial*."

He lifted his head and looked into my eyes, his face not even a millimeter away from mine.

"It took me ten years, Maya . . . but I know now that I wasn't in love before."

I had a feeling I knew what he was implying, but I didn't want to guess. I wanted to *know*. I needed to know for sure. No more fooling around. No more playful flirting. His gaze flickered down to my mouth and then back up to my eyes, asking, *pleading*. My face felt so hot, and Ana's frenzied heart was suddenly pooling blood into my open skin. His closeness was making me nervous; I wanted to stay in it forever and run away from it at the same time——

His phone beeped loudly, interrupting us, and he leaned away. "We have to go, the last bus is about to leave."

He stood, pulling me up with him. I looked around, only now noticing that the sun had gone down and the moon had taken its place. He grabbed his bags and grinned wickedly before dipping down and throwing me over his shoulder.

"Noah!" I shrieked into his back, but he just laughed and quickly ran back to the bust stop. He set me down gently, my cheeks flushed, and I gave him a questioning smile.

"You said the only way you would ever go on a run with me was if *I* was doing the running with *you* on my back."

Before I could reply, the bus came. We got off at our stop and walked quietly back to his café, our hands intertwined in his pocket, just as the flurries started to fall. I smiled and looked up at the sky, but Noah groaned beside me.

I chuckled. "You don't like the snow?"

"You're the only person who does, Maya."

I turned toward him and brushed the snowflakes out of his hair. "Do you want to make snow angels? You know, so you can associate snow with a good memory."

"There's not enough snow on the ground yet, weirdo," he teased. "Besides, every memory with you is a good one."

I blushed. "I think you're just scared mine will turn out better than yours."

"Oh yeah?"

"Yeah," I breathed.

"Okay, tomorrow when there's more snow on the ground,

I am officially challenging you to a snow angel *and* a snowman-making contest."

"I'd prefer to make a snow*woman*, actually."

He laughed loudly. "Of course, my mistake. A snowball fight will be the grand finale."

"Get ready to lose, Davidson," I warned, grabbing his other hand and lifting them above our heads before twirling under his arm. "But for now, let's dance."

He grinned in surprise. "You don't dance."

"I didn't do a lot of things before I met you."

His gaze softened and intensified at the same time under the moonlight, boring into mine. He extended our hands to the side and placed the other on my hip and started to sway. I leaned into him and we moved back and forth on the empty sidewalk. No music. No people. Just us.

"Maya," he whispered, his lips hovering over the sensitive skin of my ear. I was too overwhelmed to form a coherent thought, let alone answer him. "I think I'm falling in love with you."

Thump, thump—

"God, it feels so fucking good to finally say that out loud," he laughed breathlessly. "I keep waiting for this feeling to go away, or for it to die down . . . but then I wake up the next day and all I can think about is *you*. Your smile . . . your voice . . . your laugh . . . the way your air mixes with mine and effortlessly ignites all these things I never knew existed." He grazed his nose against mine, inhaling deeply. "I know we haven't known each other for very long, but it doesn't feel that way. This *thing* between us is so strong, I feel like I've known you forever."

"That's because you *do* know me," I said, pulling away.

"What do you mean?"

I looked at his confused and beautiful face as he waited for me to respond, his eyes glazed like he was intoxicated by my very existence. My existence that was a *lie*. This was what I was waiting for, right? I was waiting for him to tell me how he felt so I could finally tell him the truth. I *needed* to tell him the truth before we went any further. He deserved to know.

"Noah, there's something I have to tell you."

"You can tell me anything," he assured me.

I took a deep breath. "I'm—"

"Noah, is that you?"

He whipped his head around. "Mom? Dad? What are you guys doing here?"

"You didn't come to family dinner today, so we wanted to check up on you," his mom said as they approached us.

"Sorry, I was on a date," Noah responded sheepishly.

"We can see that."

"Hi, I'm Maya," I said awkwardly. "It's nice to meet you."

"Likewise," his dad said, smiling. I smiled back and glanced at his mom, but she wasn't smiling at me like his father was. Instead, she was scrutinizing my face.

My smile disappeared.

No way.

No *fucking* way.

There's no way she recognizes me, I pleaded silently to whoever the fuck was listening. Please, please, *please*—

"Do I know you?" she asked curiously, coming closer.

"No, I don't think so," I told her quickly.

She took another step closer, standing directly under the street lamp, and gasped.

She knew.

Panic gripped me tightly as recognition dawned on her face. I had to act quickly. I had to tell him before they did. I had to, I *had* to—

"It *is* you," she whispered and then glanced at Noah. "Noah, I told you not to go looking for her. Does she know who you are?"

"What are you talking about, Mom?" he asked, looking between us with a perplexed expression.

"You don't know?" She looked back at me. "Honey, this is the girl who received Ana's heart."

THEN

Dear Ana,

I want to know what you were thinking when you decided to give me your heart.

You weren't a registered organ donor—I heard them say that—which means they would've had to ask first. So I want to know the exact thoughts that framed your mind and the exact emotions that overwhelmed your body when you realized you were going to die. I want to know how you even ended up at the hospital that day. How is it fair that you saved my life, but I don't even know how you died?

Did they tell you who I was while you were laying on your deathbed, clinging to life? Did they tell you about my accident, in a sick attempt at guilt-tripping you into saying yes? Did they tell you that I was just a poor little girl, broken from head to toe, and was going to die if you didn't help her? That I was too young, and still had so much life to live and so many more moments to experience? If you were in a state so ghastly and irreversible that all your doctors decided you weren't going to make it, how is it possible that you were even able to give your consent? The answer is that you didn't. *You didn't give them consent, Ana, someone else did. You didn't choose this, Ana, someone else chose for you. Someone else thought they knew you so well and so intimately that they were qualified enough to make such a drastic decision for you.*

I hate *them.*

I hate that person.

I want to find the soulless monster who thought they could play God, and mix and match organs like we're just two pieces of a puzzle instead of real humans. I want to show them the life they brought me back to. I want them to experience just a fraction of the dreadful misery I had to experience every day.

I want to tell them that I'm currently hiding in my closet because my dad and my brother are at each other throats. I want to tell them how four hours ago my dad found a black trash bag filled with needles in the basement, and that Mikhail was the one who hid it there. I want to ask them why someone would just casually have a bag filled with needles. Is he doing drugs? Is he selling drugs?

I want them to know that the first thing I did when I heard this was run up to my room and strip out of all my clothes. I want to demonstrate how I desperately analyzed every inch, and crevice, and vain on my body for any needle pokes. How I scrutinized my entire physique for hours, searching and prodding for any evidence of a recent puncture wound, or a prick from a syringe sticking into my skin because I was so convinced he had used them on me. How suddenly, I could feel a strange and unknown substance flowing through my system. How I was starting to sense something repugnant and vile pouring into my bloodstream. There was something that wasn't supposed to be inside me, and it was fueling my organs until they would be reliant and couldn't function without it. I couldn't find any marks, but I was positive, Ana, so I checked again. And again. And then again after that.

Mikhail must be skilled, I told myself, that's why I couldn't find any evidence. Something was living inside me though, I was sure of it. I could feel it in my core. Whatever he injected me with was making my skin crawl, like a thousand invisible spiders creeping all around and gnawing away at my insides. It was making me so itchy until eventually, I couldn't help myself anymore, and I started to scratch. I desperately dug my nails deep into the thin outer layer of my skin and dragged them all along my body but the spiders just kept burrowing faster. I scratched my arms, my legs, my chest and my back but the repulsive creepy-crawly feeling of something burning my flesh only got worse. It was so strong and present that it blocked out any physical pain I was inflicting on my body.

I want them to know how I continued to claw and scrape at my skin until an hour later my body was ripe and raw from head to toe. It must be out though, right? The burning had sizzled down. The spiders escaped. That thing he tried to poison me with was finally gone.

I want to tell them that after I cleaned myself off and hid the evidence of my panic attack with layers of clothing, I came and sat in my closet and after a few minutes of being enveloped in complete darkness, I began to realize that it was my fault. A couple of days ago, I was so exhausted. I knew I shouldn't sleep because sometimes Mikhail watched me while I slept so I always forced myself to stay awake. But the other night I was so drained and worn out, and it was four AM and my covers were so warm, and my bed was so comfy, and my eyes kept slipping closed, and before I could help myself I was falling, falling, falling. I opened my eyes after only a second, Ana, but the sun was up, so I knew it had to be longer than a second. Long enough for Mikhail to use that bag full of needles on me.

It was all my fault.

Except that it wasn't.

It was their fault.

That's what I want to tell them, Ana. That's why I want to know who they are. They did this to me. They're the reason I'm still here. The universe was finally going to set me free but they stopped it from happening. I saw the light, Ana. I felt its brightness on my skin. I was so close.

I was finally going to rest in peace.

But instead, I'm here, in this cramped closet with damp eyes and heavy breaths, forcing myself to listen to their screams just to make sure my dad is okay.

I.I.E

I may be alive, but my soul died that day. They thought they were doing me a kindness, but in reality, they just dragged me back to hell.

And I will never, EVER, *forgive them.*

NOW

Everybody froze.

The world froze and stopped spinning on its axis. The wind froze and stopped mid-blow. Even the clouds froze and stopped crying snowflakes.

Noah was the first to move. He looked down at me, completely dumbfounded.

"No, Mom, this is Maya . . ." he whispered, his voice suddenly uncertain.

". . . Ibrahim," she finished.

He continued to stare at me, analyzing my face carefully

"*That's because you do know me*," he repeated my words from only minutes ago.

And that was it. The last puzzle piece finally clicked into place in Noah's mind.

"Oh my *God*," he said, taking a step away from me.

"Noah, please, just let me explain," I said quickly.

"*Explain*? You knew this whole time and you never said anything? How could you do that to him?" his mother demanded angrily.

This can't be happening.

"Honey, let's just . . . let them talk," Mr. Bennet intervened before things escalated.

She glared at me for another minute and stalked away with her husband, disappearing around the corner.

"Tell me it isn't true," Noah spoke from behind me. I turned to face him, my heart breaking at his betrayed expression. "Tell me you haven't *known* this entire time. Tell me you haven't been *lying* to me this entire time."

"It's not what you think. Just let me explain."

He looked at me expectantly, waiting, but my mind suddenly went blank. Why hadn't I prepared for this? Why hadn't I prepared what I would say when he inevitably found out? God, I was so *stupid*.

"Why aren't you talking?"

"I . . ."

But nothing came out. All the air had been sucked out of my lungs.

"Show me," he said suddenly.

"Show you what?"

"*Show* me," he repeated, looking pointedly at my chest.

A wave of unease washed over me as I realized what he was asking, but he couldn't be serious. How was that going to help anyone? But the longer I stared into his hectic eyes, the more I realized how completely serious he was.

"Noah," I pleaded quietly. "Please don't—"

"I said show me!" he demanded loudly and I flinched away from his sudden hostility. He regretted his tone instantly, the words *I'm sorry* burning behind his stare, but it was too late. I finally came face to face with the anger I'd convinced myself he didn't possess.

I took an unsteady breath and unbuttoned his jacket, ignoring the cold wind whipping harshly at my newly exposed skin. I pulled down the collar of my shirt with shaky fingers and exposed the deep, long scar that ran down my chest.

He sucked in an intense breath, closing his eyes at the sight.

"I can't believe you," he said quietly. "I can't believe this whole time I've been trying to prove myself to you . . . I was trying to make *you* trust *me*, but you were the one lying."

"I'm so sorry," I told him, my voice trembling.

"I don't want your apologies, Maya. I want you to tell me that this is a *joke*. That my mom mistook you for someone else. That you haven't been playing me—"

"I wasn't *playing* you—"

"You fucking knew who I was. You knew who I was when we met and instead of telling me the truth when I asked who you were, you *lied*."

"I didn't know who you were, Noah," I explained. "I didn't even know who Ana was, only her name."

"What makes you think I can believe a single thing that comes out of your mouth? You're a liar."

I was a liar.

"All those moments you spent asking me about her . . . asking about our time in the foster homes . . . I thought you wanted to know *me*, but you didn't. You wanted to know *Ana*, and you were using me to do it."

I was insufferable.

He looked at me again, eyes filled with hurt. "Do you have any idea how devastating it is to realize that the best part of my life was *fake*?"

I brought destruction with me everywhere I went.

"I mean, was *anything* real?"

"It was real," I insisted.

He shook his head. "Give me my key."

"What?"

"The key to my café, Maya. Please." His voice was taught with repressed emotion. Even now, when he had every right to lash out, he was holding himself back.

I did what he asked, not wanting to rile him up further. My fingers were shaking hard, but I eventually removed it from my keychain and handed it to him. He snatched it from my hand and started to walk away.

"Wait, where are you going?" I asked, following him.

"I'm leaving." His harsh voice flew back at me through the wind. "Isn't that what you always do when things get tough? Now you know how much you've *influenced* my life."

"Just let me explain," I begged, reaching out for his hand but he pulled away immediately.

"I gave you time to explain, I'm not waiting anymore. I'm done, Maya, *we're* done."

His words pierced through me sharply.

"What?"

"We're done," he repeated, facing me again. "I can't—"

He stopped. A flicker of hope went off inside me but he wasn't looking at me. He was staring at the black pickup truck that was always parked up front.

He finally met my gaze and I inhaled sharply at his expression. He looked absolutely *horrified*, and his eyes were wide with disbelief.

"No," he whispered franticly. "No, no, no, *no*—"

"Noah, what's wrong?" I asked, my eyes raking over him to see if he was suddenly hurt. I stepped toward him but he backed away. He gave me one last tortured look, before quickly turning away and heading to the door of his café.

"Noah, wait!" I called after him. I was only a step behind him when he slammed the door in my face.

What just happened?

Did he just . . . break up with me?

No. No, there was no way.

I hesitated for a minute before knocking on the door. "Noah?"

Silence.

I knocked again, harder this time. "Noah!"

Silence.

A rush of dread crashed over me as the minutes ticked on. I continued to knock, each bang louder than the next, pleading with him to open the door but he never did. His last words rang loudly in my ears, blocking any other thought from entering my mind. I was trembling. Something was *breaking* inside me. My eyes were blurry and I struggled to keep myself in check until something between a scream and a sob finally escaped from my lips as I crumbled to the floor at the foot of his door. Betrayal and pain, stronger than I had ever experienced were colliding into me from every angle, burying me under a mountain of rubble and destruction until I couldn't see. I couldn't *breathe*. His infinite silence was an iron rod shredding me to pieces until I was just a pile of sizzling flesh on the concrete. I couldn't handle this. I needed to turn this torture off. I needed it to stop, *please, God, make it stop—*

"You know what, Noah? *Fuck* you!"

It worked. The pain was gone . . . but something else had to take its place.

"You could've left me alone!" I shouted at the door, smacking my fist into the glass roughly. "I *told* you to leave me alone! I gave you an out but you *stayed*! You stayed, and you pinky *fucking* promised you would be patient and that you'd be there for me. You pulled me into your arms with your sweet and kind words, and made me *trust* you! You forced me into your life and made me rely on you, just so you could throw me out onto the streets and stab me in the back!" I smacked my forehead against the door, desperately welcoming the throbbing pain so it could diminish the agony crushing my chest. "You ruined *everything* I spent years trying to build, what the fuck am I supposed to do now?!"

I continued to hit the door with my hands, letting that new but old anger infect me completely, taking pleasure in its toxicity.

"God, you think you can *hurt* me, Noah? You don't know what it takes to live my life!" I screamed, my resolve slowly breaking down. "You don't know the kind of *excruciating* pain I have felt! You don't know how long I've suffered *alone*, over and over, day after day! The agonizing torture never ends for me, so *this*," I pointed at him through the shuddering doorframe, "is nothing! It's fucking *nothing!*"

My fists were still hitting the door robotically, bruised and bloody from the force of the impact. I rested my forehead on the door as the numbness finally started to seep in, protecting me from my emotions.

"You think you can hate me, Noah?" I whispered. The only way he could still hear me was if he was leaning directly on the other side of the door. "Well, you better get to the back of the *fucking* line," I chuckled humorlessly. "Actually, don't even bother getting in line. You could never feel even an *ounce* of the amount of hatred that I already feel for myself."

I turned away and stormed back to my car, remnants of my anger still pulsing through my body where the numbness hadn't yet reached. I turned my key in the ignition and stepped on the break, but before I moved the gearshift something caught my eye.

The flowers from earlier tucked under the passenger seat.

I made sure the car was still in park and reached for them, gently brushing the white petals. How could a day that started so amazing, end in such a terrible way? I carefully took out the folded note and smoothed it open.

Maya,

You told me once that to fear something meant to obsess over it. To memorize it. To learn everything and anything there is to know about it, but I disagree. I think that's what it means to love something because that's how I feel about you. If anything, Maya, the only thing I fear about you is that you'll never love me back. But even that isn't enough to diminish my feelings. Whether or not I can have your heart, I'll continue to love you more than I did yesterday, and I know I'll love you more tomorrow than I did today.

—your Noah.

And there it was. I wanted to know how he felt before I told him the truth and he had already written it down for me, waiting in my car, this entire time. Was love really so fragile that it could disintegrate within minutes, or was it just the love that people felt for me? How could *I love you* turn into *I hate you* so quickly?

A harsh sob shook through my entire body and suddenly I was crying. Over a fucking *boy*. He wasn't just a boy, though. He was warm and soft and safe, and I was kind of, sort of, sincerely and wholeheartedly in love with him and he seemed to think that he was in love with me too—sad, mean, difficult *me*—and now . . . now he was broken because of me. I was so determined to never let another man hurt me, that I went and did the hurting instead. I took the excellent, top-notch, exceptionally fucking splendid boy and ruined him.

A chuckle slipped through with the tears and I couldn't tell if I was laughing or crying anymore. How was it possible to fuck up the best thing that had ever happened to me to the point of no return? I mean, this was it. It was *over*. There were no words, no apologies, no *explanations* that could ever repair the damage I'd caused. It wasn't so much that I wanted to *fix* this—he had every right to hate me. I just wanted him to know that it wasn't all a lie. I needed him to know that it wasn't a game to me. But how could I get him to listen to me long enough to understand?

My thoughts drifted to the back corner of my closet, where it sat hidden . . .

I quickly put my car into reverse and backed out of the parking space, before racing back home. I could survive if he didn't want to be with me anymore, but I couldn't live with myself if he had to spend another second hurting because he thought my feelings were fake.

I slammed on the brakes in front of my house with a screech, not bothering to turn off the engine before running to the door.

52 steps—

Shut up.

I hastily unlocked the door with a bang and ran up the stairs with my shoes still on.

"Maya?" I heard my mom call from downstairs. I ignored her, not even seeing them sitting in the living room when I came in. I flew to my closet and started chucking clothes left and right until I saw my childhood jacket. I shoved my hand into the sleeve, desperately searching until my fingers finally landed on the smooth leather of my journal. I pulled it out and ran my hand over the bound cover. I hadn't touched this thing in years. What was the point of writing in it anymore? I had eventually decided that I was going to . . .

I shoved the thought from my brain before it could fester with my emotions and distract me. I didn't have time to go down memory lane, but hopefully, Noah *would*. I ran out of my room and down the stairs but was immediately stopped by my mother who was standing in front of the door.

"Maya!" she gasped. "What happened?"

In my haste to give my journal to Noah, I had completely forgotten what I must've looked like.

"Nothing," I said, stepping around her. "I'll be back. There's something I have to do."

"It's late, you're not going anywhere," she insisted, taking my arm.

I slipped my arm away gently and took another step toward the door. I would explain later; I didn't have time right now—

I felt another hand wrap around my arm tightly and I stiffened. Terror flooded through me, gluing my feet to the ground, not letting me escape.

"Mama said *no,* Maya," Mikhail scolded from behind me. My body started to tremble at his sudden proximity. I closed my eyes and took a staggering breath, begging myself not to start hyperventilating.

"Let go of me," I demanded.

He didn't fall for my act of strength.

"I said let *go*," I repeated louder and to my surprise, I felt his hand release me. I stalked outside, forcing myself to keep it up. As soon as I heard him slam the door shut behind me my fake strength disappeared and I stopped, almost falling to the ground. I leaned against my car unsteadily.

He let go so easily—

"Shut up," I whispered. Out loud this time. I looked back

at my house, at Mikhail, 52 steps away. I looked at my car, still running, waiting for me. At the flowers, at the note, at *Noah*, waiting for me.

I faced my house again. Noah could wait.

"*One.*"

~

After seven tries and finally 52 steps later, I found myself in front of *Espresso & Chill*. I realized as I went up to the door that I had no clue what I was going to say.

"Noah?" I called, knocking on the door despite my swollen knuckles. "It's Maya."

I waited a few seconds, not shocked when the door remained closed.

"I don't know if you're there or not, or if you can hear me or not but I'm just going to talk anyway," I said into the door. I placed my hand against the frame and imagined Noah on the other side, his hand pressed against mine. "I am . . . *so* sorry for the things I said earlier. I was hurt and overwhelmed, and instead of accepting responsibility for my actions I decided to blame you." I felt my eyes well up for the hundredth time today. "You didn't deserve anything I said, and I'm sorry."

I took a deep breath to steady myself. "That's not all I'm sorry for. I'm sorry I lied to you about how I knew Ana. I should have told you the truth when you asked me at her grave, but I was scared. I was scared that you would get . . . angry. But you have every right to be angry, Noah. I took the one thing that could have given her life and shoved it into myself instead.

"I didn't expect to ever see you again after that, and I had *no* idea who you were and that you worked here, I *swear*. My co-worker told me about this new café downtown and I decided to try it out. I always went to the same Starbucks every day after work and I wanted to be spontaneous and try something different," I chuckled. "I know it sounds silly, but *that's* how boring and depressing my life was."

I leaned my head on the door, closing my eyes. "I recognized you immediately and I tried to leave, but you caught up to me and," the tears started to spill over, one by one, "I felt something between us almost immediately. Your presence kindled this powerful flare of emotions inside me and it felt . . . it was unlike anything I'd ever felt before, so when you asked me to have coffee with you, I said yes. I should've declined, but I said yes instead because I wanted to know you, just *once*. But then once turned into twice, and I couldn't stop myself anymore.

"I hated myself for lying to you, Noah, I still do, but I don't regret it. How could I regret meeting you, when meeting you felt like the one-billion-pound elephant finally lifted one of its feet off my chest? The other three were still pressing down but it was okay because I wasn't suffocating anymore. I was so *sad*, Noah. I was so miserable and I was dealing with so much, and you . . . you made me feel better. You made me feel better without even knowing about any of the things going on in my life." I paused, the truth behind my words was almost too much to bear. "I was constantly floating around, rarely connecting with people and just silently observing others live their lives to the fullest from the sidelines. You were the first person who ever fought for me. Who *noticed* my absence. Who *felt* it when I was suffering. You saw through my façade and despite the broken mess you found hiding, you still wanted to know me. The *real* me.

"For so long, my identity was deeply rooted into being single. I got so used to being no one's first choice and going through life alone, that I didn't know how to live any other way. My solitude was my safety net . . . until you." I knelt down, not having the strength to hold myself up anymore. "Every day that went by it got harder and harder for me to tell you the truth because I didn't want this to end. I told myself this morning that as soon as you told me how you felt, I would tell you about Ana because if you truly cared about me then . . . we could get through anything. But there was no reason to wait because you had already shown me how you felt over and over again."

I wiped my eyes and sniffed vigorously. "I get it if you . . . never want to see me again. You deserve so much better than what I can give you, and I hope you find what you're looking for. There is something though." I placed the journal down carefully. "I always felt connected to Ana, from the moment I heard her name at the hospital. I felt responsible for her death even though I never *wanted* to have her heart. I wrote her letters for years and I want you to have them. I want you to read them so maybe you can believe me. So you can *understand* me and . . . why I am the way that I am." I traced the door, what I wished was Noah's face, one last time. "Thank you for being my comfort person. You're such a bright light in this world, I hope you know that. I hope you know I appreciate you more than I will ever be able to express. No matter how this ends . . . thank you for being here."

My hand dropped limply to my side. "For what it's worth, I tried not to like you. I tried even harder not to love you, but it was just too easy, too effortless, too *right*. If you can only accept one thing as the truth, accept this: it was real for me,

Noah, I just wish it was still real for you. It was *real*, you and I
. . . I just wish you and I weren't past tense. Goodbye."

I stayed for a moment, clinging onto that last shred of
hope. Grasping at the strings of the life jacket he'd once
provided me with but was now trying to snatch back.

Silence.

Not just from Noah, but from *Ana* as well. I stopped
hearing her beats blaring in my ear the second he found out.

I nodded in understanding and walked back to my car.

Nobody ever believed me.

THEN

Dear Ana,

It happened on December 4ʰ, 2010.

I was getting ready to go tutor one of my students when my mom came into my room and told me that my brother was going to be driving me instead of her.

"Mama, please," I begged, desperation leaking through my voice and coiling around every single word that slipped through my lips. "Can't you just drive me?"

I was standing by the front door, my eyes frantically flickering around to make sure that Mikhail wasn't in earshot.

"Maya, stop being dramatic," she demanded. "I told you I'm helping out with the parent's night at school, and I can't just cancel on them because you and your brother won't stop bickering. I need them to know they can count on me so they'll call me in more often."

Her words sent an intense blaze of fear straight through me.

"Honey, siblings fight. It doesn't need to be a big deal. One day, when you're older, you guys will start to get along. No one will ever be there for you like your brother will, Maya."

She was right. No one would ever be there for me like my brother would.

I walked slowly to his car, not knowing whether to sit in the passenger seat or in the back. He did seem quieter that day, but oddly enough that only made me feel more anxious. It wasn't a serene calm he was exuding,

Ana . . . it was an eerie calm. An unnatural *calm. I couldn't stop wondering what he was thinking about in that manic head of his, and how long it would take until he snapped out of his trance. Most importantly though, was I going to be a causality in one of his outbursts again?*

I reached his car and decided to just act normal and sit in the passenger seat. My body didn't seem to get the memo because my hand was trembling as I grabbed the door handle. He never looked at me while I was getting in, he just kept staring straight ahead, his face expressionless.

That still wasn't enough to ease my nerves. Every inch of my existence was hyper-aware of the danger sitting only a few inches away from me, and it was on high alert. My brain was sending me warning signals left and right, telling me to get out, go, RUN! I slowly inched closer to the door to create more space between us, glancing at him from the corner of my eye to make sure he wasn't paying attention and wouldn't notice what I was doing. He didn't. Or if he did, *he didn't make it seem like it. He continued to stare at the road in front of him as he drove at exactly the speed limit. One hand was loosely wrapped around the wheel and the other hand was resting on the clutch between us. The same hand that had dug deep into my arm until it touched bone. The same fingers that had squeezed my throat so tightly I saw black, and so firmly that his handprint was engraved into my skin for weeks.*

I closed my eyes as I fought a losing battle with the hysteria threatening to take over my body. I tried to focus on my breathing instead of on the war raging in my brain . . . exhale for three seconds and inhale for three seconds . . .

"We're here," he said.

My eyes snapped open and I jumped at the sound of his voice.

"Um, thanks," I muttered awkwardly and quickly got out of the car. I was expecting him to rush off to go to . . . wherever it was that he went in his spare time, but I could still hear his engine rumbling behind me. Almost like he was waiting for me to go inside. Almost like he wanted to

make sure that they were home, and that I would be okay before he left.

I was so confused, Ana. My brain simply couldn't comprehend the almost ordinary interaction I had with Mikhail. My mom's words were echoing in my ear and I couldn't help but wonder if she was right and I was just being dramatic. But how could she possibly know that when she was never there? I was the one who felt his wrath. I was the one who heard his verbal stabs. He was just trying to manipulate me. He knew that he had his sharp talons sunk deep into my mind, and he was just trying to drag me around like his own personal puppet.

But it didn't matter, Ana, because that seed of doubt in my brain had already started to grow stems of hope. God, I was such a fucking idiot. I actually started to wonder if he was trying to have a fresh start with me. It had only been three years since my disastrous twelfth birthday, and my deep hatred for Mikhail hadn't quite settled into my bones yet. I wasn't clueless, Ana. Even as a kid, I was aware that Mikhail and I's relationship was unmistakably different from the way I'd seen other siblings interact with each other and . . . I was jealous. I wanted what they had. I wanted a brother, Ana, and if this was his way of trying to turn a new leaf with me then my heart was willing to accept it. My heart was willing to forgive him.

"Hey Maya, come on in," Taryn's mom greeted as she opened the door. I smiled at her in response and took a step inside. Before I could stop myself, I glanced back at Mikhail and saw him looking in my direction. I was about to turn away and walk through the door but before I did, I saw him smile.

He fucking smiled at me, Ana, and those stems of hope blossomed into flowers. I was so excited and preoccupied with Mikhail and I's newly found relationship that I didn't pay attention to the time.

I didn't realize I was late.

"Perfect Taryn!" I congratulated after marking his practice quiz. "Do you have any more questions?"

"No, I think I got it now. Thanks, Maya."

"Of course buddy." I ruffled his hair. "I'll see you next week."

I packed up my things and headed downstairs, meeting his mom at the front door.

"I'm sorry you had to stay longer than usual," she apologized as I slipped on my shoes. "I put a little extra in there this time."

"Oh you didn't have to do that," I said, taking the envelope from her. "Thank you, I appreciate it."

"No thank you. You're really helping Taryn out, Maya. I'll see you next week."

"See you." I waved and headed outside, smiling on my way to Mikhail's car that was idling next to the curb. I peeked inside the envelope and opened the door, overjoyed with what I saw—

"Why the fuck are you late?!" Mikhail screamed from the driver's seat, causing my heart to nearly jump out of my chest. I quickly grabbed the handle to close the door so Taryn's mom wouldn't hear him, but the car lurched forward before it could even click into place.

"I go out of my way to drive you somewhere, and you don't even have the decency or respect to be on time?!" he yelled, his loud voice reverberating against every corner of the small car's interior. I flinched away from him and pressed my body tightly against the door.

"Answer me!" he shouted, and before I could see it coming his fist reached out and slammed into the side of my face. The car swerved to the side of the road as Mikhail momentarily lost control, and the cars around us started beeping at the disruption we were causing. He quickly put both hands back on the wheel and drove straight again. Straight and fast. Too fast to be legal.

My fingers lightly touched my injured cheek and a sob cracked through my lips. He continued to speed and weave in between the cars ahead of us in our lane, my pain seeming to fuel his anger even further.

"Stop crying. Don't make it seem like I'm the bad guy, Maya, you

223

brought this on yourself! Whatever happens now is your fault!"

A cold sense of terror started to creep up on me at his vile words. I knew something was going to happen. My gut was screaming at me earlier, warning me with waves of unease that I should not step inside his car. But I ignored it, and for what? Because my mom told me too? She was completely oblivious to the incidents happening right under her nose! How could I be so quick and naïve to fall for his perfectly engineered manipulation? I was a fucking fool, Ana. I felt that flower of hope die and another harrowing sob burst through my lips at the heartbreak.

"I said stop crying," he snapped, pressing his foot harder against the gas pedal. The cars and trees whizzed by us quickly through the window, blurring together until I could no longer tell them apart.

"Slow down," I said quietly, my tears spilling into my open mouth. I saw him smile in my peripheral vision and the car surged forward even more rapidly.

"Please!" I begged louder. "You were right, okay? I was wrong. I shouldn't have come out late, just please slow down. Please, Mikhail, please . . ." My voice cracked and veered off into nothingness as I continued to mouth the words silently.

My poor attempt to console him was useless. I clutched my seat tightly as he continued to zoom forward. I looked around wildly, trying to find some way out, and my eyes paused on the door handle beside me where the latch was still unlocked.

I weighed the odds for a moment. Jumping out of cars only looked smooth in movies, and I highly doubted I could walk away unscathed. On the other hand, Mikhail was going to wrap us around a tree like a car pretzel at any minute if I didn't do something.

"I'm not stopping," he muttered to himself. "I'm just trying to make you better. This is what you deserve."

I touched the door with shaky fingers, but paused . . .

"Why do you hate me?" I asked, and his mumbling stopped. I glanced

at him when he didn't respond, but he was still staring straight ahead.

"Can't you hear me? Can't you see me? Look at me!" I was screaming now but he didn't even flinch. "Tell me what I did to make you hate me!"

Maybe if I had just waited for a second longer he would have given me an answer. Maybe I didn't give him a chance to answer because I didn't really want to know what it was. Either way, it didn't matter because I heard the car's engine spur even faster and I knew I needed to get the hell out of his car.

So I pulled the handle and jumped.

I was right—jumping out of a moving car was only smooth in movies. The car was speeding so fast that I landed at least a meter away from the place where I jumped. My arm hit the ground first, scraping harshly against the pavement and twisting at an odd angle. I looked down and saw a flash of white poking through the penetrable skin in the center of my elbow. Bile bubbled up in my stomach at the gruesome sight.

I heard a loud screech of a car slamming its brakes and I whipped my head toward the noise. Mikhail had stopped in the middle of the road without giving the cars around him any signal, causing them to start beeping and swerving obnoxiously.

The stench of blood sent another wave of nausea over me, but I had to keep moving before he could catch me. I had to get away. I took a step into the road, not paying attention when I heard a loud horn. I turned around, and to my horror, there was a black pickup truck heading straight for me.

I lost my glasses when I jumped so my vision was fuzzy, but I was positive about what I was seeing, Ana. I knew I had to move, but I was frozen in place, so I just stood there and watched as the driver pressed on the brakes and veered to the side, right over a patch of ice. The truck continued hurtling toward me like I was a magnet and the laws of physics were too strong to keep it away from me—

And then everything went black.

NOW

People always assumed the worst day of my life was the day of my accident, but they were wrong. The day of my accident was the *best* day of my life. The worst day of my life was the one after my accident. The day I woke up. The day I came back to life.

Until last week, that is. Last week, the day I came back to life got bumped down a peg and was replaced with a new day. The day Noah left me. And no, it wasn't the worst day of my life *because* he left me. As much as I would love to say that was the worst kind of pain I'd ever experienced, it wasn't. I had encountered much worse trauma and had suffered through the deepest, most unbearable trenches of purgatory before I knew that a man named Noah Davidson even existed.

That didn't mean his sudden absence in my life didn't rip open a raging hole inside me and burn my soul with the fire of a thousand suns. The edges were so raw and scorching, no amount of water or tears could soothe them. It was a part of me now, and as sick as it was, I didn't want it to go away. The pain was a reminder that he was real and not one of the cursed maladaptive fantasies I conjured up to distract myself from the realities of life. It hurt, but it was comforting at the same time. I welcomed the throbbing stings of torment because I knew the numbness would eventually follow. That's when I realized what the real problem was, and it was the most powerful and intense ripple of distress I'd ever had to endure.

I was *addicted* to being sad.

It sounded crazy and ridiculous, but the more I thought about it the more it made sense. My life was always filled with stress. From the day my brain was coherent enough to understand what was going on around me, I was hurtled into a wave of chaos. Sadness was all I knew. Fear was the natural state my body was in at all times because it didn't know how to relax. My brain was in a constant phase of fight or flight to protect my mind from going through any more irreversible damage. I couldn't be happy, not because good things didn't happen to me, but because I didn't know *how* to. It was a foreign emotion that my mind couldn't recognize and instead of letting myself be vulnerable and just experience them, I chose to take comfort in my misery because it was familiar. I was never going to get better because deep down inside there was a part of me that didn't want to. I didn't want to open myself up to new feelings because the only way to do that was to expose all the old wounds I had incorrectly bandaged in my haste to feel nothing, instead of allowing them to *heal*.

I lived within emptiness and emptiness lived within me, and I was ashamed of myself because I let that happen. I ripped everything down and sat idly by, waiting for the universe to write me a new path without putting in any effort. Waiting to move out. Waiting for my problems to fix themselves. Waiting to feel better without trying to feel better. Waiting, waiting, waiting, *waiting*.

The world didn't want me to suffer, *I* did.

So what now? I thought desperately. *How do I stop?*

I listened patiently for the answer to appear. For the solution to magically reveal itself, but it never did. So I just sat in my car, watching as the snow slowly turned into rain, and wondered if maybe, God was crying with me too.

~

16 days.
384 hours.
23,040 minutes.
1,382,400 seconds.

That's how long it took for Noah to text me. Sixteen long and slow treacherous mornings and nights, but eventually, he did. And during those sixteen days I just . . . kept going. Because life didn't stop when you wanted it to. Life didn't stop when you needed a *minute*, so I went to work every day, I choked down dinner with my family every night and I did push-ups in my room until the sun rose. My old routine picked up exactly where it left off as if it had never paused in the first place.

I'd be lying if I said I didn't cheat. I drove by his café a few times, hoping to sneak a glance but it was always closed. I wrecked his heart and his business. The only climactic thing that happened during those sixteen days was when Mikhail came home one night with a broken nose. He claimed that someone jumped him for no reason, and my parents ate it up, just like the obedient little pets they were. Whoever it was had a reason, I was sure of it, and I wished I could thank them.

The chances of Noah reaching out after everything were slim, which was crushing. I told myself not to hope. I told myself that even if he *did* reach out to me, it might not be to reconcile . . . whatever we had. Maybe he needed closure. Maybe he wanted the chance to yell, and scream, and properly end things with one final *bang*. I didn't care. I would take it. I would grovel on my knees for hours if that would make him forgive me.

Whatever the reason was, I still flew to *Espresso & Chill* faster than he could finish typing. I saw him through the window, stacking up the last few chairs in the empty cafe. My body immediately yearned to be near him, to feel his hand in mine, on my face, in my hair. I couldn't though, not until we talked. I took a deep breath to contain myself and pushed the door open.

He turned at my arrival and I stifled a gasp at his appearance. His dark and fluffy curls were longer, and he'd let his facial hair grow out. He looked . . . disheveled, and rough, and *beautiful*. I quickly skimmed him over, memorizing his body and all his features just in case this was the last time I would ever see him. I needed him to be engraved into my memory for eternity. My eyes stopped on the bandage wrapped around his right hand.

"Coffee burn," he said, following my gaze. "It'll heal in a few days."

I sighed in relief as my stare found its way back to his face. My fingers itched to push the hair out of his eyes, but I stayed put. *He* had to make the first move. He stared right back at me and his lips slowly turned up into that small, lopsided smile I loved.

"Maya," he whispered. "I missed you."

"I missed you too, Noah, so much," I said quickly, my voice cracking under the weight of my emotions. I couldn't stay still any longer, I needed to go to him. He was too far. I took a step, but his next words stopped me.

"We need to talk."

Fuck.

I'd never been broken up with, so I wasn't an expert, but

I'd read enough books and watched enough movies to know that the phrase *we need to talk* was never a good sign. His solemn voice wasn't making it any better.

"I think you should sit down." He gestured to the only chair that wasn't stacked up already.

I nodded and took a seat, pushing back the nerves threatening to overpower me. He didn't pull out another chair and instead stayed at the counter.

He can't even be near me.

"Maya . . ." he started slowly, looking away.

We're done.

I don't want to see you anymore.

I wish it was you in the ground instead of Ana.

". . . I never told you the whole story. About what happened to Ana."

"Um, okay. She didn't die in a car accident?" I asked in confusion.

"No she did, but I left out some details. Not intentionally," he assured me. "I would have probably told you eventually, I just wasn't ready to talk about it. And I was also worried about what you would think of me if you knew the whole truth."

"There's nothing you can say that could change the way I think about you," I told him sincerely. I didn't want to talk about Ana—I wanted to talk about us. If there was still going to be an *us*.

He scrutinized my face, his expression guarded and uncertain.

"Noah, I don't *care*," I insisted, standing up from my chair. "Whatever you did, whatever details you left out, it doesn't matter to me—"

"I hit someone," he blurted.

The rest of my words dissolved in my throat. "What?"

He closed his eyes tightly, wincing, but forced the words out anyway. "I hit someone with my car . . . a *girl*. That's how Ana died. She wasn't wearing her seatbelt and flew through the windshield from the force of the impact. She was declared brain dead before she even made it to the hospital."

I stared at him in shock as I tried to process what he was saying. For the past ten years, I had wondered what happened to make her *die* but still have a beating heart, ready and healthy to live inside me instead.

"And the girl? What happened to her?"

"She survived." His voice was a mix of relief and anguish.

"Okay, that's great," I told him, smiling.

He was still staring at me intensely, his eyes pleading. Pleading for what, though? What did he need? How could I protect him from the torment he was feeling?

"We were driving to the airport," he started again.

"You already told me this." What was happening? Why was he repeating himself? I felt like there was an elephant in the room that I just couldn't see. What was I *missing*?

"We were driving to the airport, when . . . this black sedan came out of nowhere and swerved in front of us."

Oh.

"They were speeding like crazy," he continued quietly. "They stayed in front of us for a bit before cutting in front of the next few cars, almost getting hit by the traffic in the opposing lane."

All the color drained from my face.

"Ana yelled at me and told me to drive better. It was the first thing she said to me since we were in my room. We started to talk, and then we started to argue, and suddenly the sedan

231

stopped, causing a blockade, and all the cars were swerving into the other lane to get around. One second the road was empty, and the next this *girl* walked into the street—"

I took a step into the road, not paying attention when I heard a loud horn. I turned around, and to my horror, there was a black pickup truck heading straight for me—

"I beeped for her to move, but she just *stood* there—"

I knew I had to move, but I was frozen—

"I slammed on the breaks and started to swerve so I wouldn't hit her, but everything was happening so quickly and the roads were icy—"

The truck continued hurtling toward me like I was a magnet and the laws of physics were too strong to keep it away from me—

"I was too late," he said, his voice cracking.

And then everything went black.

I looked out the window but the only car there was mine.

"The black truck that was always parked outside . . . it's yours?"

"Yes," he admitted after a moment of silence.

Of course it was. How didn't I see this coming? Why didn't I expect this? Of course *I* would fall in love with the person who almost killed me.

Clearly, I had a type.

"How did you . . . I mean, how did you not *recognize* me this entire time?"

He ran his fingers through his hair frantically. "I only saw you for one blurry, split-second moment. When I woke up, I was in a hospital bed and they were saying Ana didn't make it—" He inhaled desperately. "I tried to find you, but no one would tell me anything or let me fucking see you."

I didn't realize I was crying until my vision was suddenly

obscured. What was I supposed to do with this information? How was I supposed to proceed?

"*Maya*," Noah whispered, rushing toward me. He fell to his knees and wrapped his arms around my abdomen tightly, pressing his forehead into my stomach.

"I'm *so* sorry," he moaned into my shirt. "I am so fucking sorry. I can't believe I—I fucking *hit* you with my car. This nightmare has haunted me for the last ten years, but when I found out that it was *you* I couldn't even—" His voice broke and I felt wetness seeping through the thin fabric of my top and onto my skin.

He was crying.

And his pain . . . his pain felt worse than all my pain.

"I couldn't live with myself when I found out," he choked. "Finding out you were the girl I ran over almost killed me. I wish it was me. If there was some way I could change the past and put myself through all the pain I caused you, I would do it in a heartbeat."

I combed my fingers through his curls, my own tears falling alongside his. He clutched me tighter, holding on for dear life.

"Please forgive me," he begged desperately. "I will spend every last breath trying to make this up to you. I will *grovel* on my knees for the rest of my fucking life. I don't deserve your forgiveness, Maya, but I *need* it. I need *you*. You make everything better. Please, please, *please* forgive me, it was an accident. I *swear* I tried to stop. I swear, Maya, please, please, *please* say you'll forgive me . . ."

"It's okay, Noah, it's okay." I continued stroking his hair until I finally felt his shaking diminish into a tremble.

"Stand up," I said, running my fingers down the sides of his face and nudging his chin lightly. "I want to see you."

He gave me one more squeeze before standing up slowly. He kept his head low, refusing to make eye contact.

"Look at me," I told him, pushing his head up and holding it tightly between my hands. "It's not your fault,"

He finally met my stare with red and crushed eyes.

"I can't forgive you because there is nothing to forgive. It's *my* fault. I'm the one who jumped out of my car and walked onto a busy road—*of course* you wouldn't have seen that coming. I should have stayed put. None of this would've happened if I didn't *jump*."

"Maya," Noah said fiercely. "His driving was *lethal*. If you didn't jump you wouldn't have ended up on the road, but in the morgue instead."

I tensed. "Did you . . . did you read . . ." I swallowed anxiously. "Did you read my letters?"

He cradled my face gently. "Not all of them. I couldn't, um . . ." He winced, his eyes turning glassy again. "I read *enough*, and I can't believe you . . . I can't believe all this time *you*—" He leaned his forehead against mine, breathing raggedly. "I understand, okay? I understand why you never told me. I am so sorry for how I reacted. I am so sorry for *everything*, but you're safe now, baby, I promise. I'm never going to let that son of a bitch hurt you ever again."

He read my letters.

He knew about Mikhail. He knew about *everything*.

Someone finally knew.

Something was happening to me. My limbs suddenly felt flimsy—had they turned into rubber? My brain couldn't comprehend—my mind didn't know *how* to—

"You know?" I whispered, and he nodded strenuously. "And you . . . believe me?" His eyes shattered at my question, but I could still see his answer through all the broken pieces.

Yes.

But I couldn't bring myself to properly process that information because it wasn't enough.

"Still, it doesn't excuse anything," I said, shaking my head. I couldn't handle his understanding, but I could handle his anger. I needed it. "I lied to you. If I didn't jump, Ana wouldn't have died. Don't you get that, Noah? Everything is *my* fault. I killed her. I always felt responsible for her death and this just proves it. To make matters worse, they donated her heart without Ana's permission to the person who *murdered*—"

"It was me," he said quickly, interrupting me.

"What?"

"Ana wasn't a registered organ donor," he explained. "I was listed under her emergency contact and as her POA, so when they came in and told us that . . . *you* were dying." He paused, grimacing. "I told them to give you her heart, Maya. I told them to save you."

I told them to save you.

"Why did you do that?" I asked shakily.

They thought they were doing me a kindness, but in reality, they just dragged me back to hell.

My hands dropped from his face and before I could make any distinct decisions, they rose to his chest and shoved him. He stumbled away from me, not expecting my sudden movement.

And I will never, EVER, forgive them.

"Maya, what—?"

I reached out and shoved him again, *harder*. "Why did you do that?"

235

He looked at me, completely baffled. "What are you—?"

"Why did you tell them to give me her heart?!" I shrieked hysterically, all the years of pain crashing down on me all at once. "I was *dying*, Noah, why did you let them save me?!"

He stopped moving at my words. "Maya . . ."

"I was finally dying. I was finally going to be *free* from him, why did you let them save me?!" I banged my fists against his chest roughly, but he didn't make a move to stop me or to protect himself. He just stood there, motionless, and let me take out all my despair onto *him*.

"Why did you let them save me?" I repeated irrationally over and over again, the tears coating my lips and pouring onto my tongue. "Why didn't you let me die?" My movements slowed as I exhausted all my energy. Sensing this, Noah grabbed my hands and pressed me into the counter gently, holding my arms above my head. My stamina had been completely drained, so I didn't bother trying to struggle against his grasp. I hung my head and succumbed to the weight of my tears, grieving the future I never got to have.

"Let it out baby, it's okay," he murmured into my hair.

"I wanted to die," I sobbed, my resolve shattering as all the memories echoed loudly in my ears, torturing me all over again. "Why didn't you let me die?"

"Shh, don't let him *win*," he breathed into my ear. "I couldn't help my mom, okay? No matter what I did or said, she always chose her addiction over me until she . . . until it *stole* her away from me for good. I wasn't enough for my dad to stay and love me like a father *should* love his son and Ana—" His voice snapped into bits. "Ana wanted more than what I could give her, and before she even had the chance to find her true soul mate and forgive me, she *died* right in front of my eyes, and there was nothing I could do to stop it. But saving you . . ." He grazed my cheek with his nose, inhaling deeply. "Knowing that a decision *I* made gave you life . . . it saved me, Maya. *You* saved me."

He carefully lowered my arms and stroked my face tenderly, wiping away the remnants of my tears.

"I don't get it," I whispered dejectedly. "Why don't you hate me?"

"I could *never* hate you," he stressed.

I pushed away his hands and crossed my arms. "Oh really? Because it didn't seem that way when you stayed in here while I was screaming, and crying, and *begging* you to open the door for me," I snapped, the hole inside me throbbing.

"I'm so sorry about that, Maya, but I had to call my parents to confirm that it was you who I . . . hit. And yeah, I was mad that you lied—"

"Exactly, you were mad."

"Yes, I was *mad.* Anger and hatred are not synonymous with each other, Maya," he retorted. "Of course I was mad and embarrassed that you . . . that I was so *clueless* this whole time, but I don't hate you for fuck's sake, I'm in *love* with you!"

My breath seized in my throat at his words, and I shook my head. "No, you're not, Noah. Not after everything I did. Not after everything you *know.*"

His eyes narrowed. "I love you, Maya."

You will never be loved, Maya.

"I love you," he repeated louder.

You're going to live the rest of your life alone.

He grabbed my face in his hands, forcing its movements to a halt. "I love you."

You will never be loved, Maya.

"Maya," he pleaded. "I love you."

"I don't believe you."

"*Don't*," he snapped. "Don't do that. Don't pretend you can't see how I feel about you. Don't pretend you can't *feel* how I feel about you just because you're scared." He stared at me intensely for a moment, his eyes dazzling and brimming to the top with emotion. "I know everything seems fucked up right now, but I can't help and feel . . . *ecstatic*. I'll forever be indebted to the universe for allowing us to exist in the same lifetime. I hate the twisted ways fate used when trying to bring us together, but ultimately . . . it worked. You're here, and I'm here and I love . . ." He inhaled deeply, suddenly breathless. "I *love* you, and being with you over the last several months has made me feel whole and complete in a way that makes me certain I've been in love with you forever." He paused, smoothing my hair back gently. "So you can say that you don't love me back, Maya, but you can't say that I don't love you. You can't say that my love for you isn't limitless, unconditional and *real*."

I closed my eyes and let the tears fall, surprised I had any left. "I can't."

He cupped my face in his hands, running his thumbs under my eyes to capture the moisture. "Is that really what you need? Even after everything, you *still* need to push me away? Why?"

"I wish I found you when I was healed," I explained desperately. "I wish I was healed before I found you so that you could only know the best version of myself. The perfect version. I can be *better* than this, Noah, I promise."

"I love *you*, Maya. Even the parts of yourself you think are too broken. Even the parts you don't love about yourself. You are the best fucking thing that has happened to me, *exactly* the way you are. I'm sorry he made you believe that you need to be better. I'm sorry he made you believe that you couldn't be loved." He leaned in closer, the tip of his nose brushing mine. "But it's been ten years and you're still in pain from the past. Maybe the reason is that you're not supposed to heal alone. We're both made up of broken pieces, but when put together they seem to fit perfectly. Let me love you, Maya. Let me help you heal. Let's heal together."

He tilted his head lower, his lips just barely grazing my cheek, and I gasped, my heartbeat accelerating at the contact. He pulled back slightly, his eyes seemingly black in the dim light of his café, and I was suddenly hypnotized. My mouth was dry and my breathing was shallow——

"Can I kiss you?" he whispered into my ear. "I know you want me to, Maya. I can taste the desire emanating from you and luring me in like a Venus fly trap. Except I know your bite won't be filled with poison . . . only lust and passion."

He placed a small kiss on my earlobe and my eyelids fluttered shut at the sensation, everything around me disappearing as I drowned in the feeling of his lips on my skin.

"I know you don't know how . . . let me walk you through it." He placed small kisses up to my temple. "Your pulse is *erratic*; I can feel it beating against my mouth. Is that because of me? Do I make your heart race, Maya?"

I nodded quickly, the needful ache returning full blast. My eyes were closed but I knew he was leaning in closer because my skin was tingling with his proximity. His warm breath was on my face and his scent was swirling around me, mingling together with mine. Very gently and very slowly his lips brushed against mine, pressing down with the slightest bit of pressure before pulling back, testing the waters.

My breath caught and I touched my lips in astonishment, not believing these feelings could exist in real life but it wasn't the same. The only person capable of provoking that intense thrill of euphoria inside me was *Noah*. I looked up at him, his eyes dark with desire, and without another thought, I knotted my fingers into his hair and pulled him back down toward me fiercely.

I fumbled around blindly for a second, not knowing what to do but *needing* to satisfy the overpowering hunger raging in my veins. I felt him chuckle against my lips before moving them with mine, sending shockwaves of passion and fire through me. I returned the pressure, mimicking his movements until our lips were in tune and moving simultaneously. Noah tilted his head slightly to the side, opening his mouth and kissing me harder, faster, *frantic*. I followed his lead, inhaling him in as my body registered the connection of our mouths in overwhelming elation. His hands stroked down the length of my body and curled around my thighs, lifting me onto the counter. My legs immediately wrapped around his torso and I dug my heels into his back, pushing him into me even closer.

He released my swollen lips and dragged his mouth across the length of my jaw and down my neck. I leaned my head back, my breathing unsteady as he peppered kisses in the indent of my collarbone, sucking gently on my flushed skin. I felt his hand slowly pull down the front of my shirt before brushing his lips against my scar. He looked up at me, pure love and devotion radiating through his eyes. "You never told me, Maya . . . do you love me too?"

"Do I *love* you?" I chuckled erratically at his stupid question. "You are my miracle, Noah Davidson. My heart used to form a new crack every day I woke up and realized that I was still alive—" I leaned in closer, not breaking away from his endearing stare. "Although it's borrowed, fractured, and imperfect . . . my heart is still completely and undeniably yours."

"And I, my love, am completely and undeniably yours," he vowed against my lips.

I opened my mouth to kiss him again, but a gut-wrenching sound cracked through my lips instead.

"What's wrong?" he whispered breathlessly.

I couldn't speak. The relief or the pain—*something* was too overpowering for my mind to grasp.

"Maya, you're scaring me."

I met his gaze and forced myself to take a breath. I forced myself to finally take a proper breath of air. "I just—" my chest was heaving "—you *know*, Noah, and you . . . believe me."

He wasted no time pulling me down from the counter and crushing me into his body. His arms wrapped around me tightly in an iron cage of safety. "I believe you, Maya."

My bones were breaking.

My body—

My *soul*—

Someone finally believed me.

He lowered us to the ground because I couldn't hold myself up anymore. I was on my knees and my head was in his lap and my core was shaking uncontrollably. Noah didn't speak. He tilted his head down so it was leaning on mine. He stroked my face and my hair and my arms and continued to hold me as I desperately tried to comprehend the painfully relieving possibility that I was no longer alone in my torturous world.

THEN

Dear Ana,

It took me a minute to understand what happened.

I remembered being in pain, and I remembered all the doctors scrambling in a panic around me. I couldn't understand why until I realized that the frantic beeping sound was the heart monitor. My *heart monitor. I knew enough to know that wasn't a good sound, and then I finally grasped what was happening.*

I was dying.

And I was relieved.

God, Ana, you have no idea how fucking relieved I was when I put the pieces together. If my face didn't feel like I was getting electrocuted with a thousand powerful bolts, I would have smiled from how alleviated I was by that news. I felt the load I'd been clinging to for so long completely disappear. My back felt light. The pain was slowly but surely melting away.

I always thought people were exaggerating when they said 'go to the light' but it was true. You would know, I guess . . . I saw the extremely luminous and beaming light flashing directly into my eyes, and it was getting closer and brighter, and if I could only move my hand and reach out I was positive I could feel it burn my fingertips.

Then the heart monitor stopped, and the world went quiet and I was . . . nothing.

I felt nothing. The light was gone. Everything was gone. Time was gone, my senses were gone, Maya *was gone.*

Until suddenly I was back.

The pain was back. My senses were back. That stupid beeping heart monitor was back.

I knew something was off the second I touched my chest but I couldn't put my finger on it. My thoughts were flowing through cement and it hurt too much to try to think a single coherent thought, but there was one thing I remembered. One thing I was extremely sure about.

"My heart stopped beating," I whispered.

"What did you say, honey?" Mama asked from beside me.

"My heart . . ." I started again, taking a deep breath to clear my raspy voice, and cringed back from the pain. "I heard it stop. I felt it stop, Mama. I . . . died."

"Honey," Mama started, taking my hand carefully.

"I died," I repeated louder. "Why am I still here? *I died Mama, I died!"*

I was screaming now. The monitor was thumping erratically alongside me, as the heart in my chest thrashed against its bandages with hysteria.

"Maya, you're okay now," Mama said, trying to soothe me. She grabbed my hand but I yanked it out of her grasp.

"No!" I screeched, yanking at the needles attached to my body. "I died! Why am I still here? Why am I alive?"

A dozen nurses flooded into my room at that point and rushed toward me. I fought and clawed against their hands aggressively, but they restrained me and injected me with enough sedatives to instantly knock me out.

I don't know how long it took, but eventually, I woke up. I opened my eyes and stared at the rusty overhead light hanging from the ceiling. I tried to take a deep breath but my throat was rough and scratchy. Inhaling and exhaling made it feel like my trachea was rubbing against a cheese grater. I waited a few minutes for my brain to regain its motion before willing it to signal my arm muscles to move, but they still wouldn't budge.

I heard the lock turn, and a nurse walked in. "This should help," she said, slipping my glasses onto my face. My vision immediately cleared, and that's when I noticed the thick leather cuffs binding my good hand and leg to the bed rails, restricting them from moving.

They tied me to the bed, Ana. They actually . . . shackled me to the bed like I was a mental patient. I looked around frantically, trying to find my mom so she could explain what was happening when I saw the bars on the window.

The multiple locks on the door.

The stark white walls.

The empty room.

I wasn't just chained to my bed, Ana; I was chained in my room. From the looks of it, I was literally in some kind of psychiatric ward.

I looked back at the nurse to demand that she take them off, but I paused. She looked so familiar, but I couldn't recall when I had seen her before. I focused my gaze on her appearance, and my eyes froze on her arms which were all bandaged up.

Memories flooded back to me then. Flashes of screaming . . . my screaming . . . blood . . . nurses trying to help me and I . . .

"Did I do that to you?" I whispered, my voice cracking.

She sat beside me slowly and nodded. I closed my eyes against the tears that were bubbling in my throat.

"I'm so sorry. I didn't mean to, I just didn't—I don't know what's happening—I thought I died and then I woke up," I stuttered, my words stumbling over each other.

"It's okay," she soothed softly. "I know you're confused and scared, but a psychiatrist will come and explain everything to you soon."

"A psychiatrist?" I asked, coughing.

"Your throat must be sore. I'm going to bring you some water, okay?"

She came back in after a few minutes and brought me some water. I looked at my one good hand expectantly, thinking she was going to untie me, but she didn't. She leaned in close and pressed the Styrofoam cup against my lips, waiting.

"Can you take these off?"

"I can't do that."

She didn't trust me enough to let me drink my own water, Ana.

I separated my trembling lips and let her tilt the cold liquid down my throat.

"The psychiatrist will be here soon," she promised, before exiting the room. The locks clicked back together loudly in the empty space.

Hours went by. Nurses came in every little bit to check on my vitals, and on all the tubes pumping God knows what inside my system. From what I could tell, my left leg was in a full cast, suspended in the air. My right arm was also in a cast, and I distinctly remembered the flash of white and the snapping sound cracking in the air like a gunshot.

The psychiatrist finally arrived, locking the door behind her and taking a seat.

"Hello Maya, I'm Dr. Silverstein," she said, introducing herself.

"Hi," I muttered.

"The nurses told me you're still a little confused about what's going on, is that correct?"

I nodded.

She took some notes in her notebook before looking back up at me. "Yes, that's normal considering all that you went through."

"My car accident," I stated.

"Yes. And your psychotic episode."

I froze, my eyes widening at her statement.

"I didn't have a psychotic episode," I snapped. "I was just confused. I'm sorry about the nurses I hurt, but I'm not crazy."

She scribbled in her notebook. "Why don't you tell me what happened from the very beginning? Your brother was picking you up from the *students' house you tutor, correct?"*

"Yeah, he picked me up and . . ."

Suddenly I was back in the car and he was beside me again. I could feel him in the room with me, breathing in my ear, making my skin crawl. I looked to my side, but there was no one there.

"Do you see something?" she asked, pen on paper.

"What are you writing?" I demanded. "I'm not seeing anything."

"I'm just observing you. I have to before I can make an official diagnosis."

"Diagnosis?" I repeated. "Diagnosis for what?"

She looked at me carefully before putting her notebook down and clasping her hands together on her lap. "Maya, honey, your brother told us what happened."

Her words were a bombshell exploding in my brain, and I knew then that everything coming out of her mouth would be bad. Something very, very bad was happening, Ana.

"What did he tell you?" I asked quietly.

"He said that while he was driving home, you suddenly started to freak out. When he tried to help you calm down, you started hitting him, similar to the way you did to the nurses, causing him to swerve the car and almost crash. You told him to drive faster, and when he didn't oblige, you tried to push him out of the driver's seat and out the door. He struggled against you, accidentally punching you in the face, and before he could lock the doors you jumped out."

I closed my eyes as the tears finally brimmed over the edge, and the story she described played out in my head. A similar version to what I remembered, only in a different font.

"You survived the fall unscathed," she continued. "But before he could stop the car and restrain you, you ran in front of a truck."

Of course Mikhail would use my time unconscious to his advantage. Of course he would try to place the blame on me.

"He's lying," I insisted. "This is what he does. He takes the truth and twists it to fit his own story."

"Maya, it's okay. Now we just need to focus on getting you better," she said softly.

"No, just listen to me," I pleaded frantically. "He was the one who was speeding, and I was begging him to stop. I didn't feel safe in the car anymore, that's why I jumped. I didn't think I had any other choice."

I stared at her, breathing hard, but she didn't respond.

"Why aren't you writing this down?"

"Maya . . ." she started. "Your brother told us you would say that."

It was like a bucket of cold water was getting drenched over my head. "Well, he's a liar! Just ask my parents—they'll tell you. They'll tell you about his anger problems."

I couldn't understand why she was just sitting there. Could she not hear the desperation in my voice? Could she not see the fear in my eyes?

"I did speak with your parents," she said. "They told me you had some kind of . . . resentment toward your brother, but that they never actually saw him do anything to you."

"He's lying," I whispered through a mouthful of tears. "Please, why don't you believe me?"

"I believe that you believe that," she replied calmly, closing her notebook.

The irrational terror was starting to build up in my chest. I couldn't believe my parents actually believed him over me.

"Just let me talk to my parents," I begged, my hand starting to twitch nervously against the binds. They would believe me, all I had to do was explain.

"I can't do that."

"Why not?" I snapped, hating how calm she was. Hating the condescending edge to her tone, like she was talking to a child who was on a time-out for throwing a tantrum. "Take these off me."

"You're under observation right now," she repeated. "Once we can determine that you're not a danger to yourself or to others—"

"Why aren't you listening to me? He's lying!" I shrieked hysterically, thrashing my one good hand against the bandages restraining it. "He's manipulating the story, please, you have to believe me. Just get me out of these!"

She continued to sit there patiently, watching me struggle without making a move, which only pissed me off more.

"What is wrong with you?" I asked angrily. "Why are you just sitting there? What happened to always believing the victim?"

"That's just it, Maya. I don't think you are one."

I slowly halted my movements as the fatigue hit. My energy was limited and I only had two working limbs, but the pain of not being believed . . . the pain of my parents not coming to rescue me from this terrible mess . . . it was paralyzing. It drained all my sustenance in one big gulp and left me with nothing.

"I'm a sister too," she said suddenly. "I have five brothers—all older than me. I'm a sister too, Maya, so I know. I get it. They always messed with me and it drove me crazy," she laughed lightly. "They played pranks on me, pulled my hair, practiced wrestling moves. They were . . . boys. Boys are boys. Boys will be boys. Their definition of fun is just different than ours." She paused and fixed her gaze on me seriously. "But just because they didn't want to have a tea party with me and ripped the heads off of all my dolls doesn't mean they were bad brothers. It didn't make me hate them."

I've never said that out loud before, Ana. That I hated Mikhail. I've never even thought it, but when I heard her say that I realized it was true. I hated him. I hate him. I hate my brother. I am a sister who hates her brother.

"Maybe you didn't know because you only have one sibling, so let me relieve your confusion. This is normal. Siblings fighting is normal.

Siblings not getting along is normal. Your life is normal, Maya, but your behaviour? That's *what's not normal."*

She was right, Ana. I wasn't normal. I was a fool. A fool for jumping out of his car. He was doing me a favor and I ruined it. He was giving me an out and instead of taking it, I backed down. I should've let him kill me.

"I've seen this before," she continued, not noticing how I was slowly shutting down. Some fucking psychiatrist she was. "I've seen teenagers your age—younger siblings especially—act out when they don't feel seen . . ."

I was invisible.

". . . when they don't feel heard . . ."

I had been screaming *for years and no one had blinked an eye at the high-pitched noise.*

". . . they start to feel like the only way to get attention is by creating false scenarios, or by harming themselves . . ."

I didn't want attention. I just wanted him to leave me alone.

". . . until eventually they're convinced that the 'fake scenarios' are real."

I wished they were fake.

"What I'm trying to say, Maya, is that you've created this victim mindset for comfort, and to gain pity and sympathy from others."

I continued to stare at the ceiling with dry eyes. If I truly wanted pity and attention, then why hadn't I opened my mouth years ago?"

"I see this all the time, but you're still different than the others. You're smart. *Straight A student. Top of your class. Never missed a day. Never got in trouble. You're a good kid and sometimes the good kid doesn't get as much attention as the others, but that doesn't mean you're neglected. That doesn't mean you're not loved."*

Straight A student? Never missed a day? Was she implying that if I got bad grades and had a long history of truancy then she would've taken me seriously? She was fucked, Ana. The system was completely fucked up. If I was lying in that hospital bed claiming that a stranger, or my boyfriend, or my parents tried to kill me, she wouldn't be sitting there calmly, scribbling all her stupid assumptions in that stupid *notebook. Why does it stop being real just because we're siblings? Suddenly you're just the little sister who's acting out because her big brother got all the attention. Because she couldn't take her big brother's innocent teasing. Because her big brother sucked up all their parent's love. Because her big brother didn't want to play dolls, or stop and get some ice cream on the way home.*

I wasn't a victim of anything, and that was that.

He probably felt so fucking proud of himself, Ana. Proud that he finally pushed me over the edge and I was now medically diagnosed as a crazy person, which was exactly what he wanted. No one would ever believe someone that was clinically insane.

"But don't you see how out of control your behavior has gotten? You almost died*. You almost died for good, but you got a second chance. That doesn't happen very often. You were lucky they were able to find a match so quickly."*

It took a minute, but eventually her words moved sluggishly to the left hemisphere of my brain, where my straight A frontal lobes began to comprehend what she was saying.

"Emergency heart transplants are risky and not many people survive. But you did*, Maya."*

My eyelids collapsed into darkness as all the air escaped my lungs in a painful gust.

"This outburst, although extreme, can be remedied. This doesn't have to be your story, Maya. Let me help you," she said softly. "Don't waste your second chance."

Didn't she understand? I wasn't given a second chance; I stole it from someone else.

"We're going to wait for your injuries to fully heal, and then we'll start to work on the internal injuries that no one else can see." She stood up and gently patted my shoulder. "You seem like a lovely girl, Maya, and you have a bright future ahead of you. I know you can do this."

I didn't respond. Somewhere in the distance, I could hear a door being shut and locks being clicked, but I didn't care. I wasn't in that room anymore. My spirit had seeped out of my body and through the hospital floors, all the way down into the molten lava bubbling under the earth's core. I knew something was off the second I woke up, but I never imagined . . .

I was finally settling into a desensitized daze, but her words obliterated through the tough exterior shell my brain had created against the devastating pain. It was right on the surface, waiting for the first sign of weakness so it could attack me again and invade my composure. Heart transplant? Whose heart? Was it a girl? A boy? Were they young? Old? Was their body still warm? Did they feel it when their heart was suddenly removed from its home? I'm not stupid, Ana. I know that they—you— were dead when it happened, but you still had a beating heart pumping warm blood through your veins. Some part of you must have felt it, right? You had to have felt it when your primary source of life was removed. Did you feel it when your soul's battery ran out? Did you feel it when your light was flicked off forever?

I turned and, to the best of my ability, shoved my face into my pillow in a weak attempt at muffling my tortured scream, but it still erupted loudly in the small room. I fought against my restraints as the bodily tremors plagued me roughly. What was this game God was playing with me? Was I truly just the Lord's guinea pig? Let's see how much one girl could suffer before she simply combusts into thin air under the weight of all her crippling despair?

Or maybe I really did die and this was just my specifically curated hell. To continue reliving the same nightmare over, and over, and over again until I finally learned my lesson? But what was the lesson? What sin did I commit, and why couldn't I remember it? What form of repentance would be strong enough to set me free? I would do it all. I would do anything.

Whoever said what doesn't kill you makes you stronger is a fucking liar, Ana. What doesn't kill you does not make you stronger. It just makes you wish that it did kill you.

I waited, writhing in mental and physical agony for the numbness to settle back in. For the pain to freeze my nerves until they were senseless. It eventually did, and I was able to think logically instead of emotionally. Fighting was useless so I just played along. I healed quietly. I did my time under psychiatric observation and made sure I was the perfect patient until they finally signed my release papers. It was during my last week at the hospital that I heard them.

"He came in again today," one of the nurses said, adjusting my tubes.

"Really?" the other one asked in shock.

"Yeah, it's so heartbreaking. I can't imagine losing someone you love so abruptly. She was so young too."

"Why does he keep coming back?" she mused thoughtfully. "Do you think he wants to see . . ."

She trailed off, and I felt their stares boring holes into my face. I made sure to stay very still.

"He keeps asking to see Ana, but they already had her funeral, so he must be looking for her. He doesn't know who she is though, or where to even look."

They both crooned in synchronized compassion and pity for this mystery boy, but I wasn't paying attention anymore. There was only one thought running through my mind, blocking out any and all background noise from interrupting it.

Ana. The heart I stole belonged to a girl named Ana.

NOW

"*Stay*," he mumbled into my neck, tightening his grip around my waist.

"I can't," I repeated regretfully.

"Tell them you're staying over at your friend's house," he pleaded. "I haven't seen you in so long. I just want to keep you in my arms forever."

"I was never *allowed* to sleep over at my friends' houses."

"I don't get it," he groaned. "Why are they still so strict on you?"

"Because I'm not white? Age isn't a thing for them, Noah. As long as I'm a girl living under their roof, they don't want me sleeping anywhere else."

He pulled back slightly, looking at my face carefully. "It's not like you're sleeping under their roof anyway." He traced the circles under my eyes gently. "They can notice when you're not home, but be completely oblivious to what your brother's presence is doing to you?"

"Don't start this again, *please*."

"I don't know how else you expected me to react, Maya," he said, looking at me in disbelief. "Did you seriously think I would be comfortable with you living in the same house as that piece of shit?" He ran his fingers through his hair in frustration. "Thinking about you being around him after *he*—" He took a breath. "He's lucky I only broke his nose. I should've broke—"

"You what?" I interrupted.

He didn't answer. I grabbed his hand, and my eyes widened at the purple bruises peeking through under the bandage.

"That was *you*?"

He stared at me, anger radiating intensely through his ornate eyes. "Yes."

I sighed, hating his sudden animosity. I knew how he felt. I *knew* that he was just trying to protect me, but it didn't make it okay.

"I don't accept violence."

"Maya—" he started.

"I don't *accept* violence," I repeated. "God, you think *he's* lucky? *You're* lucky. Lucky you caught him by surprise. Lucky he didn't kill you."

He scoffed. "I could easily take him—"

"I don't care," I cut him off sharply. "This isn't a toxic masculinity contest, Noah."

"It wasn't planned," he said, looking away. "After reading your letters I was . . . *livid*. I'm not a violent person. I have never felt rage like that, even during the lowest times in my life, but he *hurt* you, Maya. He hurt you, for *years*, in the worst ways possible—" He shook his head. "I went for a run to blow off some steam, and then suddenly . . . there he was."

"I don't know how I recognized him, but I did. I went up to him and asked if he was your brother . . ." He squeezed his eyes shut in anger. "The disgusting smirk on his face when he said *yes* . . . something exploded inside me, and before I could stop myself I was . . ." He trailed off, lifting his bandaged hand. "My swollen and bruised knuckles should prove this isn't something I do often because *obviously*, I don't know how to throw a punch correctly," he chuckled, embarrassed.

"Good," I said, taking his hand carefully and running my fingers over the damage. "That means you can't ever throw a punch at *me*."

He winced. "That's not funny."

"You're right, it's not," I agreed. "But I'd rather think of it as a joke than as something real."

"You know I would never hurt you, right?" he whispered desperately.

I nodded. "I know."

"But . . . ?" he probed.

"But," I continued. "You can't *do* stuff like this."

He stared at me fiercely until I met his gaze. "You can't ask me not to protect you. I'm sorry, but I won't agree to that."

"That's not what I'm saying," I replied. "He deserves it, okay? He deserves to know what it's like to . . ." I closed my eyes against the images. "To feel small, and defenseless and scared. But it's not my job to do that. It's not *our* job. I've spent my whole life being resentful at him, and at my family, and at the world and I just want to move on," I sighed deeply. "But that means I can't be around *that*. No anger, no shouting, no violence, nothing. I just want peace, Noah. I'm tired and I just need some peace."

"I know, baby, I'm sorry."

"Don't be sorry." I brushed my lips against his injured hand. "When he came home that night claiming someone jumped him for no reason, I didn't believe him. I *knew* there was a reason behind it, and I wished that I could thank them." I looked up at him. "Thank *you*."

"Don't you know, Maya?" he asked gently. "Don't you

know that there isn't a single thing I wouldn't do for you?"

I stroked his lips lightly, my heart overwhelmed with feelings I didn't recognize and words I couldn't seem to speak.

"Kiss me," he said in a breathless plea.

"Okay." I threaded my fingers in his hair and kissed him, his new scruff tickling my skin and eliciting a rush of electricity throughout my entire body.

"Is the *hair* your new look?"

He rubbed his cheek against mine playfully. "I'll get rid of it. I know how you feel about men who look like *men*."

"I actually kind of like it," I admitted. "You look . . . hot."

His eyebrows shot up and he grinned. "Okay, how about I keep it, and whenever you start to miss my old face, you can shave it off for me."

"Deal."

"I love you, *habibti*," he murmured, peppering kisses all over my face.

"I never taught you that word."

"The app on my phone did," he whispered into my skin. "A much better teacher than you, I might add."

"You should watch what you say, Noah," I warned him. "I can get pretty competitive."

"I love the way you talk," he chuckled against my mouth, tracing my bottom lip with his tongue. "I'm *obsessed* with your lips. My mouth has been begging to touch them since that first day. I want to make up for all the moments I didn't spend kissing you. I want to kiss you *forever*, Maya. I want to learn what your body likes and how it will respond to me. I want to memorize the way your skin feels under my hands. *Fuck*, the things I want to do to pleasure you, Maya . . ."

"Noah," I breathed erratically. "You need to stop talking

before I combust and die a virgin."

He laughed. "Call me as soon as you get there?"

I nodded. He grabbed my hand and led me to my car, but then pulled me into another tight hug before I could get in, holding me like he was afraid I might disappear. All I'd ever wanted was for someone to *know*. To believe me. To make me feel less alone. Now that I had that, there was also an unmistakable feeling of guilt because he was now just as tortured about my past as I was.

"You'll tell me right?" Noah whispered.

"Tell you what?"

"If he ever tries to . . . hurt you again. You will leave right away. You will leave and come to *me*, Maya."

"It's not like that anymore." I paused, thinking of my breakdown in the kitchen. "I barely even see him."

My words didn't reassure him because he still didn't release his hold on me. I pulled back and placed my hands on both sides of his face. "I'm still *here*, Noah. My brother has hurt me more times than I can count. He has tried to *kill* me more times than I can count, but I'm still here. Please don't worry about me. There is nothing to worry about."

He covered my hands with his. "I won't stop worrying until I have you back in my arms."

"I'll be fine," I assured him again. "I'll call you soon okay?"

He sighed and reluctantly released me. He looked at me silently for a moment, fear and love fighting each other behind his colored eyes. His fingers grazed my cheek one last time, before finally stepping away from the car.

I watched him stand outside his door through my rearview mirror until I was far enough away that he was just a dot on the horizon. My foot instinctively pressed harder on the gas pedal so I could get home faster. Not because my house was home, but because *Noah* was. I was already anxious to hear his voice again. His existence brought a powerful surge of calmness into my chaotic life, and whenever I left its vicinity the disruption hit me so much harder.

He called while I was brushing my teeth. I quickly rinsed and spit, before closing the door and tucking my storage containers under the handle.

"Eager much?" I teased, flipping my light switch off and getting into bed.

The sound of his laughter flowed through the phone and immediately warmed my heart. "Are you in your room?"

"Yup. Teeth brushed and pajamas on."

"Tell me, Maya . . . what does your sleep attire consist of on this lovely night?"

A burst of laughter slipped through my lips and immediately got muffled by my pillow. "Are you joking?"

"No, I'm genuinely curious. I need all the details so I can complete your image in my mind while we talk."

"Okay, but it's nothing pretty," I warned him. "There are two types of girls—the ones who wear a matching set to bed and the ones who don't. I am, unfortunately, part of the latter."

"Matching sets are boring," he said softly.

This conversation was slowly moving away from being *silly* and into something else entirely. I tucked my knees under my chin, pushing back whatever emotion was slowly starting to bubble up in the pit of my abdomen.

"I'm wearing an oversized, bleach-stained t-shirt and gray cotton sweats."

"How is it that you can make the most ordinary and basic

clothing items sound so . . . sexy?" he whispered, his smooth voice clouding my mind into a haze.

"I hope you know that you're the only one who thinks that."

"Highly unlikely," he replied. "But as long as I'm the only person you *want* to be thinking that, no one else matters."

I was quiet for a minute, the air around me heavy. "What is this feeling?"

"You tell me."

"You've been in relationships before, Noah."

"Not like this. Never like this."

I smiled and continued to listen to his breathing, matching my pace with his until our breaths were synchronized.

"Thank you for calling," I whispered, snuggling deeper into my covers. I slipped my earbuds in so I could be more comfortable. "Whenever anything *happened*, I would always grab the phone on my way to hide in the bathroom or my closet. Just in case, you know?"

He didn't reply, but I could hear him breathing louder as he pressed the phone closer to his face, listening.

"It wasn't just to call the police though, if anything happened. I mean, it's not like they would even do anything," I said truthfully. "I always had this urge . . . this desperate need to call someone—*anyone*—but there was no one for me to call." My voice cracked in the dark room. "Now I do. Thank you for being my someone."

"I'll be your everything," he vowed fiercely. "I'll stay on the phone with you all night until you fall asleep, okay?"

"You don't have to do that."

"I want to," he insisted. "I *need* to."

Another ripple of guilt flooded through me. I hated that

my pain was now *his* pain too. I also hated how, deep down, I was comforted by that. If he needed to be sure that *I* was okay for *him* to be okay, then I could do that.

"Okay. What do you want to talk about?"

"Actually, I have a confession to make."

"What is it?"

He chuckled at my anxious voice. "I started reading another book."

"Really?" I said excitedly. "Which one?"

"Oh, you know, just a silly little book about vampires . . ."

My eyes widened. "Stop—what chapter are you on?"

"Three."

"Damn, dude, you're *slow*."

He laughed. "Hey, don't be mean. I'm trying to internalize every word so I can love it as much as you do."

"Impossible. No one can love it as much as I do."

A deep yawn suddenly erupted from my chest, interrupting his next words. "Sorry," I apologized quickly. "What did you say?"

He ignored my question. "Maya, when's the last time you slept?"

"Yesterday."

"For *more* than a few hours," he clarified.

"I don't remember," I whispered honestly. "I try to force myself to stay awake most nights, but sometimes I slip without noticing. Terrible things always happened when I slipped, Noah."

He was suffering quietly. "Why did I let you go?"

"You didn't *let* me go. I didn't have a choice."

He didn't reply, breathing rapidly, and then the line suddenly went dead. I was just about to call him back before

260

my phone started ringing with a video chat request.

"Hi again," I greeted his face.

"Sorry, I needed to see you. Try to sleep, Maya. I'll stay on the phone with you."

"Noah—" I started to protest.

"*Please.*"

I opened my mouth to argue but another yawn slipped out in place of my words. The mention of sleep was already lulling me into dreamland. Sleep deprivation was like existing with tunnel vision. My brain only absorbed what was directly in front of me. Eventually, the two openings got clogged up and enveloped my entire tunnel into complete darkness, until I was mentally and physically drained of light. I was *tired*. Tired of being tired. Tired of constantly straddling the line between reality and unconsciousness.

"Okay," I finally consented.

"Thank you," he said, relieved. "Just close your eyes, Maya. I love you."

"Love you," I murmured, already falling under. I pulled my covers higher and adjusted my limbs until I was comfortable. His soothing voice started to flow through the phone again, but he wasn't talking.

He was *reading* to me.

I recognized the lines instantly, having read that sacred book series so many times it was permanently inscribed in my mind. I imagined that Noah was beside me, whispering the sentences into my ear, his warm breath fanning over my face. I was pressing myself closer into his chest, admiring how the moonlight emphasized his peaceful and beautiful expression until I slowly subsided into a deep and dreamless slumber.

~

"I can't believe you're making me do this," I groaned.

"I'm not *making* you do anything," Noah replied. "Just say the word and we'll get off at the next bus stop."

"Your mom was so . . . *angry*. And she has every right to be. I broke her family. I can't even imagine being in her shoes and having to meet me."

He wrapped his arm around me tightly and pulled me closer. "You didn't break our family, Maya. The situation the other day was . . . confusing. Everyone's emotions were heightened," he reminded me calmly. "But I explained everything—"

"*Explained?*"

"Not *that*, I would never . . . betray your trust." He kissed the top of my head lightly before resting his forehead against mine.

I stared at his face closely, hating how tired he looked and how *rested* I looked. He was trying to steal all my burdens and carry the weight on his own. Did it have to be either or? He suffered or I suffered? Was there no middle ground?

The bus stopped and he grabbed my hand, leading me to the door. As soon as we stepped outside my jaw dropped to the ground.

"*This* is your neighborhood?" I asked incredulously, taking in all the immaculate and flamboyant houses lined neatly down the street.

"No, it's my parent's neighborhood. *I* live in a tiny, one-bedroom apartment."

"Says the former software engineer, and current owner of a very popular café—soon-to-be café bookstore." I rolled my eyes. "It's okay to be rich, Noah."

"I'm not," he insisted. "My parents are."

"Something only rich people say."

He laughed, swinging our hands between us.

"You don't have to be modest," I assured him. "I actually grew up around a lot of wealthy people."

"Really?"

"Yeah, most of the women in my community, and my mom's friends, are married to doctors," I told him. "Their kids were all nice, but it was still vividly glaring how different our worlds were."

"I'm not . . . *this* isn't me." He looked at the houses on either side of us. "Even when I moved here, I never really accepted this lifestyle. I always knew that I would leave one day."

"I don't think I could ever live like this."

He glanced at me in surprise, raising his eyebrows, and I rolled my eyes again. "I swear people always assume that if you grew up poor, all you ever dream about is becoming rich." I shook my head at the thought. "I always dreamed about providing this life for my *parents*, but for myself . . . not having to stress about money would be absolutely alleviating, don't get me wrong, but all I've ever really wanted was to just be comfortable, you know? To have a . . . gentle day, every once in a while. To not have to force myself to go to work when I'm sick. To not feel guilty after buying myself a cup of coffee, or a new pair of shoes, or going out to dinner with my friends because that's money I should be *saving*, even though all the money in my savings account ends up going toward bills anyway."

He kissed the back of my hand. "You shouldn't feel guilty for spending money. You work so much and so hard—you deserve to treat yourself."

"All I'm saying is that some people don't need to have a lot to be content."

He nodded in understanding. "Money doesn't buy happiness."

"True . . . but it does buy *freedom*," I said wistfully. "If you're financially stable and suddenly find yourself unhappy, you have options. You can *pay* for a therapist. You can *pay* for a vacation. You can *pay* to go out and have fun or meet new people or literally do anything that will bring you happiness again. Not everyone has that option."

"Is that how you feel right now? Trapped?"

I felt the box I was in suddenly getting smaller around me. "You have no idea."

He let go of my hand and wrapped his arm around my shoulders. "I *do* have an idea," he whispered. "It's not the same though, and I know that. Things are going to change, Maya. I promise."

"I miss when I was so naïve to all of it," I told him. "When I didn't notice how small our house was, or that all my clothes were from the thrift store. I remember the first time I went over to a friend's house, it was like the veil got ripped off and suddenly I was aware of *everything*. How our fridge was white instead of silver, and how we didn't have a dishwasher or a garage. We had to hang up our clothes to dry, instead of having a dryer. Bills were always the topic of discussion at the dinner table, and I was on a first-name basis with the manager at the gas company because they always had me call to set up the payment arrangements—every immigrant daughter's duty. It was all so obvious to me all of a sudden, and my house physically started to feel so cramped and claustrophobic," I sighed. "But I think the worst part was later, as I got older and started to notice when no one ever asked to come over to *my* house. My friends always assumed the movie nights would be at *their* house, and if we were baking cookies it would be in *their* kitchen. I mean, I know why *I'm* embarrassed to invite you over, but why are *you* embarrassed to come over? It wasn't ever discussed; it was just . . . decided."

"Nice friends," he commented sarcastically.

"It's not their fault. All my overthinking and insecurities' is an outcome of my own doing, not theirs."

I could tell he was going to disagree. "Anyway, it doesn't matter," I said quickly. "Thrifting is popular now, so technically I'm ahead of the game. Besides, I never really minded any of that stuff. I just hated seeing my parents stress about it. Still, though, I would take money problems any day over . . ."

My brother.

He stopped suddenly and I looked up. We were standing in front of a big brown house, with a basketball net over the garage and three sleek cars in the driveway.

"This is it."

"It's really beautiful."

"I'll be sure to let my parents know you think so," he teased.

He was trying to make me laugh, but the air around us was suddenly . . . awkward. Did he think I was going to be *jealous* of his lifestyle?

"Maya," he said, cupping my face in his hands. "If you want to leave or feel uncomfortable just tell me, okay? My brothers . . ."

Oh, *that's* what he was nervous about.

"You don't have to go near them, but they're nicer than

they look, I promise. I wouldn't have brought you here if I wasn't positive about that."

"I'll be fine," I assured him. "I'm more worried they're not going to like me, than . . . *that*."

"They'll love you," he said softly. "How can they not?"

He leaned down slowly, barely brushing his lips against mine, letting me make the next move. Always letting *me* lead. Always going at *my* pace. I clasped my hands behind his neck and kissed him fervently. And then I kept kissing him. And he kept kissing me back—

"Noah, Mom said to stop kissing your girlfriend and come inside!"

I broke away from him abruptly, my face immediately heating up, but Noah just laughed.

"Come on," he said, grabbing my hand and leading me up the front steps where one of his brothers was standing.

"Sorry to interrupt," he smirked. "I'm Oliver."

He was tall, the same height as Noah, and lankier. He had a friendly smile on his face and was extending his hand toward me. Noah squeezed my hand slightly.

You don't have to shake his hand, he said silently.

But I did have to. I was trying to move on. I needed to move *on*.

I reached out slowly and grasped his hand in mine. My heart was beating anxiously in my chest at the contact but I couldn't detect any negative vibes from him.

"Hi Oliver," I smiled. "It's nice to meet you. I'm Maya."

"Likewise, come on in," he replied, releasing me. He opened the door wider, letting us in, before locking it behind us. The interior of his home was just as big and beautiful as the outside—marble floors, spiral staircase, high ceilings, a

266

fancy sitting area that looked like it had never been used—but that wasn't what caught my immediate attention. It was . . . light. Warm. Sometimes when I walked into my house it almost felt like I was stepping off Earth and onto a separate planet. An unknown asteroid that had yet to be discovered because it was so far from the sun. It felt cold and dark, and it was hard to breathe because the planet wasn't fit for human life but for some reason, we were refusing to evacuate.

Noah guided me through the house and toward the living room, where three people were deep in conversation. I glanced at the first person, a man I didn't recognize—Noah's other brother. My eyes only paused on him for a second before gliding to the other occupants.

His parents.

"Maya, welcome," his dad said, standing. He walked up to me and shook my hand kindly. I gave him a timid smile, before looking at his mom anxiously. She wasn't smiling, but she didn't look angry either.

"It's nice to see you again, Maya," she greeted, her voice cautious. I shook her hand stiffly, my nerves on edge. It was so obvious she was still pissed, why the hell did I let Noah bring me here?

"Same to you," I replied quietly. I looked away from her scrutinizing expression, already searching for a way out. Noah rubbed small circles on my back, sensing my anxiety, but for the first time, his touch did little to soothe me.

"So *you're* the notorious Maya everyone's been talking about lately," Noah's other brother interrupted. "I'm Lucas."

Lucas was *huge*. His biceps alone were the size of my leg.

"Hey," I said, ignoring how his muscular build resembled Mikhail's a little too much. "It's nice to meet you."

He walked up to me, completely oblivious to my uncomfortable aura, and leaned his head in close.

"Ana? You in there?" he whispered, tapping my chest lightly. Before I could even react, Noah quickly pushed him away from me.

"What the fuck is wrong with you?" he demanded harshly.

"Noah, *language*," his mother scolded.

Lucas immediately backed up and raised his hands in defense. "Sorry dude, I was just trying to break all the tension with a joke."

Noah narrowed his eyes at him, but to everyone's surprise, a small burst of laughter slipped through my lips. "Don't worry about it, Lucas. If she responds, I'll let you know."

His responding laughter echoed through the quiet house, with Noah and his father following along after. His mother gave a small smile and headed for the kitchen. "Noah, Lucas, Oliver—come help me with dinner."

"I'll be back in a sec, Maya, make yourself comfortable," Noah told me, kissing me on the forehead before meeting up with his family. I took a seat on the couch and looked around. This room made the house feel a lot homier, with all the colorful throw pillows, and the walls that were littered with family photos. Some with just Mark and Luisa, some with just Noah, Lucas, and Oliver, and some with—

Ana.

My breath caught at her smiling face and my fingers twitched, itching to grab the photo. I couldn't help it. I *needed* a closer look. I glanced toward the kitchen to make sure no one was watching me so I could examine her picture more closely but immediately froze at what I saw.

No one was paying any attention to me. They were all

huddled in the kitchen; Mr. Bennet was taste testing from the spoon in his wife's extended hand. Noah was chopping vegetables, laughing at something Lucas was telling him, while Oliver kept snatching bits and pieces from the bowl. I continued to openly gawk at them while they goofed around, suddenly feeling like I was intruding on a deeply intimate moment. I still couldn't bring myself to tear my eyes away from the beautiful scene playing out in front of me.

And there it was. That sharp twinge of jealousy I was so worried Noah would think I was going to feel, but it wasn't because of his money or the lavish lifestyle he got to be a part of . . . it was because of his family.

Everything I told him earlier was the truth. Struggling financially was incredibly stressful, but I never idealized living in a huge, fancy house, or driving an expensive car and wearing designer clothes. *This* was what I dreamed about. The way his family interacted with each other was what I always wished for. The way Noah and his brothers connected with each other was what I always craved and they weren't even fucking related. They had no blood obligation to love him, but they did. They loved each other so much.

This wasn't the first time I'd been persecuted with this inconceivable concept. I spent years watching my friends interact with their siblings in such a bizarre way. Once, Malak called her brother to ask him what sauce flavor she should get on her wings when we went out to dinner. They chatted on the phone for only a few minutes, a small smile on her face the entire time. It reminded me of when I phoned Mikhail in an emergency—my dad was getting taken away in the ambulance—and he called me a whiny bitch and told me to forget his number.

Bayan and her brother watched the same shows together every week; my brother had no clue what my preferred choice of entertainment was.

Dima travelled with her brothers; my brother couldn't sit beside me in a car for two seconds without trying to end my life.

Zara's brothers always picked up food for her on their way home from work; my brother would happily watch me starve to death.

Small things. Little moments and gestures they spoke about in passing and probably never noticed any significance in them.

I did, though. I always noticed. And it hurt. It hurt a lot.

That wasn't the sad part, though. The sad part was that even after all the years of torture Mikhail had put me through, there was still a part of me *waiting*. Waiting for him to change. Waiting for him to . . . be my brother. There was a hollow emptiness in my chest that was desperately waiting and longing to be filled with his love.

I was suddenly aware of something churning violently, deep inside my core, as I silently mourned the family I never got to have. I instinctively wrapped an arm around my abdomen to try and hold myself together, but I could feel the searing heartache spilling over the edge. I needed to *leave*. I didn't belong around these people. I was a needle standing on the sidelines, begging to stab through their bubble of pure joy and happiness.

"Maya, are you okay?" Noah whispered. I blinked back the tears that had appeared without my notice and saw him crouched down in front of me.

"Um, yeah," I muttered. "I can feel a migraine coming,

that's all. Can you point me to the bathroom so I can splash some water on my face?"

He didn't look convinced but took my hand anyway. We started into the hallway but his mom stopped us.

"Sorry, the bathroom on this floor isn't working right now. You can use the one upstairs—it's the first door on your left."

"I'll show her."

"Noah, I'm fine," I assured him. "Go be with your . . . family."

I couldn't even say the word like a normal person. It tumbled from my lips in a language that I would never be fluent in. He heard it too, in my voice, and his eyes saddened. "Maya . . ."

"I just need a minute. Please."

"Take two." He lifted my hand to his mouth and kissed my exposed fingertips softly before letting me go. I climbed the stairs one at a time, ignoring the pictures that continued to mock me everywhere I looked, and hastily grabbed the first door knob I saw.

It only took half a second for me to realize this wasn't the bathroom. I didn't know what clued me in first—the lavender-painted walls, the big plush bed with a generous amount of throw pillows and stuffed animals, or the three large ceramic letters hanging from the wall that spelled out her name.

I was in Ana's room.

I should have left the moment I realized, but instead, I stepped inside and shut the door quietly behind me. I stood completely still for a moment, too scared to move. Even though we had never actually *met*, I could feel her presence all around me. Her spirit still lingered in the fabric of her bedspread from the last time she lay there. Her aura was still deeply mingled into the fibers of her carpet from the last time her bare feet touched the floor. My nerves were buzzing with apprehension but my heart remained steady and silent in my chest. It was finally *home*.

I looked around the room greedily, drinking everything in. Ana was dead but her room was full of life. There were posters on the walls, and one of her drawers was still open from the last time she was rummaging for a shirt. There was an unzipped makeup bag on her vanity, and one of the bottles of nail polish that were neatly lined up was slightly crooked.

She died with periwinkle-colored nails.

My eyes flickered to the pictures covering every inch of the frame on her large mirror. I leaned in closer to examine them and traced her smiling face with my fingertip carefully. She was beautiful, which I already knew. There were pictures at three different proms, and in one of them, she was wearing a crown. There were pictures of her in a cheerleading outfit and some in a speedo and swimming cap with a gold medal around her neck. That same medal was hanging on a pin in her room, along with a dozen more. But the most recurring thing in all of her photos was Noah. Noah and Ana *smiling*. Noah and Ana *laughing*. Noah and Ana at the *beach*. Noah and Ana *canoeing* in a beautiful Canal. Noah and Ana *huddled* together under the same blanket around a campfire. Noah and Ana, Noah and Ana, *Noah and Ana*.

He always told me that I was oblivious to the way people looked at me, but the only oblivious person here was *him*. The way she stared at him in those pictures . . . the sparkle in her eyes when she smiled up at him . . . it was *painfully* clear how in love she was.

I snatched my hand away quickly, their pictures suddenly

burning my skin. *What a waste*, I thought bitterly. What a *fucking* waste. Ana did everything right. She took her broken childhood and used it as fuel to create an extraordinary and meaningful life for herself. She could've succumbed to the force of all her trauma and let it consume her. She could've let it take control of the reins of her future, but she didn't. I, however, *did*. How did she deserve to die and not me?

"Maya, what are you doing in here?" Luisa asked from behind me.

I spun around at the sound of her voice, terrified that I was caught, but she didn't look mad. Only peculiar.

"I'm sorry," I blurted.

"It's fine, but dinner's ready so we should——"

"No," I interrupted. "I'm *sorry*."

Understanding dawned on her and she looked away, but my gaze remained fixed on her face. On Ana's *mother's* face. I owed her more than some trivial, two-word apology. I owed her everything and before I could stop myself I was speaking the words I had never spoken out loud before.

"One hundred and thirty-three."

Her eyebrows shot up in confusion.

"One hundred and thirty-three people were on the transplant list the day Ana died. I looked it up after I found out what happened. Did you know they make that information public, for anyone to see?" She didn't answer. "One hundred and thirty-three mothers, and fathers, and *children*, people who meant something, people who were doing something—they were all waiting for years, *dying* for years—and when a heart finally became available they gave it to *me*?" A chuckle burst through my lips and suddenly I was laughing uncontrollably. "I mean; how does a person *live* with that?

How do *I* live with that? I am nothing! I *am* nothing, and I *mean* nothing, and I'm *doing* nothing, yet I got the heart. I won the prize. I *lived* and those one hundred and thirty-three people are probably dead right now."

"Maya . . ." she started.

"*Don't*," I demanded. "Don't try and comfort me. I know you hate me. I know you're mad, Mrs. Bennet, which is a good thing because I deserve it." My shoulders slumped as the truth finally tumbled out. "It should've been *me*. It should've been me who died in that accident, not Ana. I'm sorry the universe made an error and took her instead. I'm *so* sorry." I gestured around her room. "I mean look at this. She was *perfect*! She was perfect, and her life was perfect, and she was beautiful and happy and she should have *lived*!"

"Nobody's perfect," Luisa said softly.

"That's just it!" I explained. "She wasn't perfect, but she still *tried*. She woke up every day with a sense of purpose and drive, despite everything she went through. Ana was strong, Mrs. Bennet. Your daughter was so, so strong. They say God only gives the toughest battles to His strongest soldiers . . . *Ana* was a soldier. I am . . . a mistake. I took the Lord's second chance and laughed right in His *face*!" I stared at her intensely as my guilt turned into anger. "So don't you dare forgive me. Don't you dare stop being mad. If you stay mad at me, then that means *I* can stay mad at me."

"It's not your fault, Maya," she said slowly. "It's not your fault that Ana died. It's not your fault that those one hundred and thirty-three people didn't get her heart. None of this is your fault."

"I've been mad my whole life, Mrs. Bennet. It's all I know," I whispered. "If you stay mad then it will continue to justify my anger. Please don't take that away from me, Mrs. Bennet, please. It's all I have left."

"There is nothing for me to forgive," she repeated. "But you need to forgive *yourself*. Just because Ana's life stopped doesn't mean yours has to stop as well."

Grief was a strange emotion. Especially *this* grief. The grief you felt for someone you'd never met. The grief you felt for someone that gave you everything when you gave them nothing. The grief you felt when you loved someone that could never love you back. The grief you felt when you lost someone that was never yours to lose. And if that wasn't bad enough, that grief always branched off into a million other emotions. *Guilt*, because I survived and she didn't. *Anger*, because I survived and she didn't. *Sadness*, because I survived and she didn't. How was it humanly possible to feel so much for a stranger? I didn't know what to do with it all, where to put it, how to express it.

It was easier before when all I had was her name. Three letters carelessly strung together to create this idea of a person with whom I formed an irrevocable bond. But now I had more. Now I had *everything*. I had her story. I had her brother's love. I had her house, and her room, and her Sunday family dinners.

"Death hits survivors the hardest, but I can already tell you're stronger than you give yourself credit for. I look forward to knowing you, Maya. If you'll let me."

I didn't respond, but let her words live in my mind anyway, hoping one day I could resonate with them.

"I'll give you a few minutes," she said with a small smile, closing the door behind her. I walked over to Ana's bed and, after a second of hesitation, sat down. The springs quickly sprung to life beneath me. I ran my fingers over her blanket. I touched each stuffed animal. I laid my head back against her pillow. I stared at a spot on her ceiling directly above me. Directly above her.

And then I let myself cry.

~

"Oh my God, Noah, you were such a dork!" I snickered.

He groaned loudly from his childhood bed. "Can we leave please?"

"No way dude, I still haven't examined all your things," I said, flipping through his junior yearbook.

I heard him jump off the bed and felt his arms wrap around me from behind. "I can think of a million other things that we could be doing in my room," he whispered suggestively in my ear. "Things that I've *dreamed* about doing in here when I was a lonely and single teenage boy."

"You've been dreaming about me since you were a teenager?"

He kissed my neck. "Yes."

"But I'm three years younger than you, isn't that kind of creepy?"

"*Creepy*, but still perfectly legal," he chuckled. "I think we would've been friends if we went to the same high school."

"Yeah . . . definitely not," I disagreed. "I was a book nerd, Noah; you were a *computer* nerd. A geek. There's no way I would've associated with you."

"I thought you were into the whole . . . hot and geeky thing?"

"I am, but you blossomed *after* high school. Not during."

He tensed for a minute before laughing. "Now that's just *mean*, Maya," he said, taking the yearbook from my hands and throwing it across the room. I was about to protest but his arms were back around my waist, lifting me up and tossing me gently on the bed. He hovered over me slightly, pushing my hair out of my face.

"I'm sorry, did I hurt your feelings?" I asked innocently.

"Yes, my ego is *severely* bruised."

"Men shouldn't have egos. One little seed of self-esteem mixed in with all that testosterone is just a recipe for disaster."

He smiled cheekily. "I completely agree. Men *suck*."

His tone was mocking, but I knew he meant every word, which made me fall in love with him even more. His lips were suddenly on mine and my fingers were in his hair, and he was stroking my face, and every inch of his body was pressed against my body and I was on *fire*—

"Noah," I warned shakily, but not making a move to stop him, whimpering slightly as his lips continued on my collarbone. "We're in your *parents'* house. This isn't appropriate."

"Then let's be inappropriate," he taunted with a smirk before moving his mouth feverishly with mine again.

"*Noah*," I whispered against his lips. He released me immediately and rested his head against my chest. I looked at him lying on me, his hair tickling my nose, and burst out laughing.

He raised his head in confusion. "What could you possibly be laughing at right now?"

"I'm sorry," I said breathlessly. "I can't help it."

"Can't help *what*, weirdo?"

"You won't understand because you've been in relationships before," I sighed. "But this is all so unbelievable to me. I never imagined that I would be *making out* with

277

someone in their spaceship bed. I don't know, whenever I think of my current relationship status I have to laugh."

He leaned into me again, his lips at my ear. "If it's the spaceship bed that's stopping us, I can take you back to my *grown-up* bed and we can——"

"You're crazy," I interrupted before his words could send me into a frenzy again. "Since we're on *that* topic though, I should probably tell you . . . I'm saving myself for marriage."

"Okay," he said, not skipping a beat.

"*Okay?*"

"Okay . . . marry me?"

I wanted to laugh again, but the look on his face stopped me. He looked *serious*.

"You're crazy," I repeated.

"Crazy in love with you."

"Okay, settle down," I insisted, but I was melting.

His eyes darkened. "You know, every time you tell me to *settle down*, all I want to do is the opposite."

"Oh yeah? What's the opposite?"

"Act up." He brushed his lips against mine. "Misbehave."

"So you want to get married as an act of rebellion?"

"You don't have a soul that can be found twice, Maya. I want to spend the rest of my life with you, so yes, I would marry you right now."

"I love you too."

"But?"

"But nothing," I promised. "I just . . . I don't know, I honestly never really thought about getting married before. I never thought I would ever find someone that I would *want* to marry."

He scrutinized me thoughtfully. "What *do* you want?"

"What do you mean?"

"I mean, what do you *want* out of life? Where do you see yourself in five, ten, fifteen years?"

I looked away before he could see the first thing that popped into my head through my eyes. How could I explain that I never thought about my future because I never wanted to have one?

"Hey," he said softly. "I know things haven't been easy for you. You haven't had the luxury of thinking about *your* future, but I want you to try right now. Forget about money and forget about your family for a second, okay? If you could do *anything*, anything at all, what would you do?"

I was stumped. No one had ever asked me what I wanted.

"You talked about writing the MCAT before, is that something you still want to do? To be a doctor?" he probed after a moment of silence.

"I . . ." I trailed off, hating my answer.

"It's just us," he reminded me. "You keep trying to please everybody else's expectations for you, but I don't *care*. All I'll ever want for you is to be happy."

"Honestly, Noah," I sighed. "I don't think I ever wanted to be a doctor. I mean, I'm passionate about helping people and I always loved science and learning about the human body, but I was so consumed with this idea that I *had* to be a doctor in order to achieve success. That's why I kept putting off my MCAT. If I never wrote it, then I could never fail."

"Success isn't determined by the job you have, Maya. Success is determined by whether or not you find a job that you *love*. You know how rare it is for someone to find a career that brings them an income *and* brings them joy?"

"It wasn't just that. The main thing that fueled that career choice for me was to make a lot of money for my parents. To be able to give them everything they ever wanted, and could never provide for me."

"But what about everything *you* ever wanted?"

"That's just it, Noah. I never really wanted anything. Just peace and quiet. All I really dreamed about was being *alone*," I admitted. "Whenever my brother was acting out, or my dad was in a heated argument with him, I would always hide in my closet and . . . pretend. I would close my eyes and pretend that I was in a house in the middle of nowhere, surrounded by trees and acres of empty land. It wasn't a big house—just a simple, one-story home with an open concept. High ceilings so there could be large windows everywhere, filling the interior with natural light. I have a big farm out back— chickens, goats, horses—and a vegetable garden where I grow all my own produce. I have two indoor cats, and there are three rooms—a bedroom, a bathroom, and a library. I categorized the shelves by my moods, and I have a reading nook by the window. The kitchen cupboards are painted green, but the rest of the house is a clean, white color and I spend my days doing . . . nothing. Nothing but reading, and making my own jam."

I paused, thinking longingly. "I took a creative writing class for one of my electives in university. I loved it, and I was good at it. I don't know what I would even write about, but I think if I could do *anything*, I would be a writer. Create stories for people to fall in love with. Build a universe where people could completely lose themselves in. A place that felt like home and made you hope, and wish, and *dream* that something like that could happen to you too. A book for people who needed somewhere to escape to. A book for people like *me*."

I refocused my eyes on the present and looked at Noah, who was smiling warmly. "You know chickens are mini dinosaurs, right?"

"Yeah, but they can't fly which makes them not scary."

"Actually, some of them *can* fly——"

"Just let me have my chickens dude," I insisted, and he laughed.

"Well, I *love* chickens and jam," he told me seriously, stroking my cheek. "Do you think . . ." He hesitated, his voice suddenly shy. "Do you think you might have room for one more person in that perfect little dreamland of yours?"

"بشرط انو الشخص هذا هوا انت," I whispered.

He smiled but raised his eyebrows in confusion at my foreign speech.

"Only if that person is *you*, Noah."

He kissed me thoroughly. "Say something else to me in Arabic," he breathed into my mouth.

"أنت حمار."

He moaned and immediately fused his lips back with mine. "*Fuck*, that's so hot." He continued to trail his lips, tongue, and teeth along my jaw. "What did you say?"

"You're an ass."

"Oh, *mean*," he chuckled.

"And you love it."

His lips paused for a second before resuming their exploration of every inch of exposed skin. "I fucking *love* it."

THEN

Dear Ana,

She's back. Hiba is back.

I was doing my homework while my mom made dinner when someone knocked on the door. It was Hiba, standing on our welcome mat, with mascara running down her face.

"What's wrong?" I asked, sticking my head outside to see if Mikhail was there too. He wasn't. I looked at her again and noticed that she was shaking from head to toe.

"Hiba, what's wrong? Did something happen to Mikhail?"

She shook her head, instantly destroying that brief flicker of hope that erupted in my chest and replacing it with an acute wave of guilt. Was my soul so far gone that I would wish death upon my own family? If the answer was yes, then I deserved every ounce of destruction the universe chucked my way.

I think we both know that it was *a yes, Ana.*

I continued to stare at her, waiting for some explanation for why she was here but she didn't speak. She just stood there, quivering like a frail leaf caught in a tornado. Her eyes were frantically flickering around, before finally meeting my gaze and my stomach dropped to the floor.

"What did he do?" I already knew the answer, but I needed to hear her say it.

"He hit me," she said quietly, and those three little words broke me harder than anything Mikhail had ever done. They shook the ground

beneath my feet, threatening to crumble into the earth and drag me down with it. I wished it did. I wished it swallowed me up whole, and squashed me into a cloud of dust that was incapable of feeling anything. I didn't want to hear this, Ana. I didn't want to know this. I didn't want us to be the same. We were forever bound together in the same group. She was part of a statistic now . . . just like me.

"What's going on?" Mama asked from behind me. "What is she doing here?"

"Mikhail hit me," Hiba told her. I looked back at my mom, waiting for her to say something. Waiting for her to gasp in horror and disappointment. Waiting for her to maybe, finally, do something about him but she didn't.

"Did you hear what she said?" I demanded when she continued to stand there silently. "Mikhail hit her. Your precious son hit someone. He hit a girl."

"That's enough, Maya," she snapped. "Why should I believe her after all the lies she's told us in the past?"

"Are you . . . joking?" I scoffed in disbelief. "Are we still pretending that Mikhail is normal? Are you seriously so blinded by your motherly love that you can't accept the fact that he's dangerous? I mean, if you can't protect me fine, but she is innocent!" I shouted, pointing at Hiba. "She doesn't need to get dragged into this family's twisted drama!"

Silence, Ana. All she did was give me silence.

"Unbelievable," I muttered and fixed my gaze on Hiba seriously. "What do you want to do?"

"What do you mean?"

"I mean, what do you want to do?" I repeated. "Do you want to press charges?"

She looked taken back. "No way, I can't do that to him."

"Why not? Why did you come here then?"

"I came here because I thought you would understand."

"I do understand! That's why I'm telling you to press charges!" I shook my head in frustration. "Listen to me, Hiba. I don't like you. In fact, I really fucking hate you, but that doesn't mean you deserve to be treated like an animal. I know you think you can fix him, but you can't. You need to get out before he tries to suck you back into his arms, with all his manipulative charm and perfectly planned out tactics."

"We were arguing . . . it wasn't like that—"

"Don't," I snapped. "Don't make excuses for him. Don't try to decode his behavior when his intentions are clear as day. This is who he is!"

"You don't know him like I do, okay? You've never taken the time to get to know your brother—"

"I'm sorry I was too busy getting strangled and beaten to get to know him," I seethed sarcastically. I couldn't understand what was wrong with her. Was she so in love that she couldn't hear herself? She was even worse than my mother. "If you came here for comfort, or to bond over our shared trauma, you made a mistake. How can I comfort you when I can't even comfort myself?"

I stared at her, the memory of her and Mikhail interacting in the basement all those months ago flashing before my eyes. "I'm sorry you don't realize what he's done to you. I'm sorry I didn't fight harder for you. I'm sorry I didn't fight harder for you to believe me, but you and I are not the same, Hiba. Our experiences, while similar, are not the same. I got hurt by someone who was supposed to love me, and you got hurt by someone who supposedly does love you. You've had the privilege of meeting a side of Mikhail that I never got to." I crossed my arms over my chest, pushing back the painful jealousy. "I can help you get away from him, but I can't help you process what he did to you. I can't be your friend, Hiba."

She opened her mouth to respond but was interrupted by a car screeching to a halt in front of my house. Mikhail flung open his door and stormed toward us. I immediately stepped outside and stood in front of her.

"Stay away from her," I warned him as he approached closer. He obviously didn't listen to what I said and just glared at me. He wasn't that much taller than me anymore, but I immediately felt myself shrink three feet shorter under his dark stare. I forced myself to keep my stance, instead of cowering away like he wanted me to. This wasn't about me; it was about Hiba. I couldn't protect myself, Ana, but I could protect her. I had to. This was my fault. Mikhail was my fault.

But then his eyes flickered away and focused on the girl standing behind me. The girl I was trying to protect . . . except his demeanor suddenly transformed. His eyes, which were filled with disgust and hatred only seconds ago, were now brimming to the top with . . . love?

"Hiba, please come back to me," he whispered in a tone I had never heard before. "I love you, just let me explain."

"Don't," I breathed. "Don't fall for it, Hiba. This is all a part of his game."

"Shut up, Maya," he ordered menacingly. There he was, I thought in relief. There was the Mikhail that I knew and hated and didn't imagine. "Why can't you just let me be happy? Why are you always trying to ruin everything for me?" His eyes pivoted back to her, and once again he was a completely different person. "Don't listen to her, Hiba. I've told you all about her issues before. Let's just talk, okay?" His voice was soft and pleading and full of emotion. He extended his hand toward her . . . the same hand that had shoved me, choked me, slapped me . . . I closed my eyes against the image. There was no way, I reminded myself. There was no way he was capable of . . .

"Okay," I heard her mumble from behind me. I was sure that I was imagining it, but to my horror, I saw her push past me and take his hand. He pulled her into him, and my breath caught because I knew he was about to hurt her, but he was just hugging her. He placed his hand behind her head and stroked her hair, whispering softly in her ear. She nodded and pressed herself tighter into his chest.

"Hiba," I begged breathlessly. "Hiba, please. I can help you. I can go with you, please. Please don't . . ." My voice faltered away into the air, disappearing completely. It didn't matter, though. There was nothing I could say to convince her. She was already gone.

Mikhail lifted his head and looked at me again, all traces of calmness and love vanishing from his dark regard. "You will never know love, Maya. You will never be loved."

He didn't wait for a response. He just wrapped his arm around her shoulders and led her back to his car. I watched them, my feet glued to the porch, but she didn't give me a second glance.

I knew what happened next, Ana. I could see exactly how it played out in my mind. He took her out for dinner—somewhere fancy, but ultimately it was her choice. The weather was surprisingly nice today, so maybe afterwards he got her ice cream or frozen yogurt and they went for a romantic stroll. On the way, he'll stop at a floral stand and get her the biggest and prettiest bouquet. He'll shower her with tender words and soft touches and in a few days, he'll surprise her with a gift—jewellery, maybe? A new perfume?

The sick part of my brain I shared with Mikhail wished our relationship could be like that. The typical one where he hits you but then feels bad so he treats you super well for the next few days to make up for it. But that's the thing with Mikhail, Ana. He never felt guilty after he hurt me. There was no love involved. There was no love involved with them either, but she just couldn't see it.

I went back inside, still in shock. My mom was standing in the doorway, her face filled with pity. I turned away and headed toward the stairs, but her next words stopped me.

"Maya, honey, something came for you in the mail," she said quietly. "On the coffee table."

I was confused at first because nothing ever came for me in the mail, but then I remembered my university applications. I quickly went into the *living room, smiling when I saw two thick envelopes sitting on the table. The one on top was stamped from the University of Calgary, but I set it aside without opening it because that wasn't what I wanted. I picked up the second one, and I was immediately drenched in complete happiness when I saw the University of Toronto logo on the front. I flipped it over to rip it open but noticed that someone had already done the honors.*

I looked back at my mom standing silently behind me. "It's a felony to open someone else's mail," I told her.

"You got in," she replied. The envelope slipped out of my fingers at her words.

"Really?" I whispered, my voice filled with joy. "I got in?"

She nodded. "Congratulations."

She didn't sound excited though, she sounded crushed, *which instantly tainted my rare moment of delight.*

"Why didn't you tell me you were applying to go to Toronto?" she asked, her voice accusing.

I swallowed back the lump in my throat. "I didn't want to say anything in case I didn't get in."

"How could you possibly believe that? You're the smartest person I know."

"Fine. I didn't tell you because I knew you would say no."

"If you knew that we would say no, then why did you even apply in the first place?"

"Because I don't care," I snapped. "I don't care if you guys don't let me go, I'm going anyway."

"You would do that? You would leave against your parent's wishes?"

"That's not fair, Mama," I said, crossing my arms across my chest. "I'm not asking you guys for anything. I looked into it already, and I qualify for financial aid to cover everything—housing, books, tuition. I have some money saved up from tutoring, and I'll get a part-time job when I'm there. There's no reason to say no."

"Yes, there is. You know it's not okay for a single girl to live alone and away from her family."

"Oh my God," I groaned. "Don't use culture as a defense, Mama. You know that I'm responsible enough to live on my own, you're just trying to keep me trapped here."

She was quiet for a moment. "Do you want to get away from me that badly?"

"It's not about you. You know why I want to leave."

"So that's it then? I have no choice but to choose between my children?"

"That's not what I'm asking—"

"Yes, it is!" she snapped harshly. "This is what you've been waiting for. You want to use this as leverage so that I'll kick your brother out."

"What?"

"I may not be as smart as you, but I'm not stupid," she said, and then her shoulders slumped in defeat. "What do you want me to do? Do you want me to kick him out and onto the street? He has nowhere else to go. What will people say? He's my son, I can't do that to him."

"I know he's your son, Mama, but I am also your daughter," I pleaded, clinging to my dream as it slowly started to slip away. "You see how he treats me. I can't take it anymore, please. Please let me go."

"What about me? You're going to leave, and then what about me? I'm just going to stay here alone? Baba is only here during the summer, but what about the other nine months? You're not the only one that Mikhail treats badly, Maya."

Of course I knew how he treated them. Of course I heard the disrespectful and hurtful things he said to both of my parents when he was angry, despite all the things they did for him. As much as it hurt me to see him hurt them, it confused me just as much. I understood tolerating your kids when they were young, but he was a grown-up now. He should know the difference between right and wrong. It's not their responsibility to

288

parent him for the rest of his life.

"All the more reason to kick him out."

"I am his mother!" she said loudly, firmly, with finality. "Regardless of what he says or does, that fact will remain true. I am his mother and he is my son. He came out of my body. He is made of what I am made of. He is mine, Maya, and if you hate him . . . if you are so cruel to hate your own flesh and blood, then you must hate me too."

His *mother, Ana. Never* your *mother. Never mine.*

It was kind of beautiful to watch. She was the definition of what it meant to be a mother. Her love was selfless and unwavering. The sacrifices she would make and the devotion she had for Mikhail was immeasurable. She was the beaming source of strength and resilience during his difficult times. No matter what he did or said, her love for Mikhail would forever be constant and unbreakable.

It must be exhausting, I think. She must be exhausted. Too exhausted to stretch that beautiful kind of love to include me as well.

I wondered briefly if things might've turned out differently had I been born first? Had I been born a boy? Would Mikhail love me then? Would my mother?

I continued to look into her eyes, and I knew deep down that I couldn't do this to her. I couldn't leave her alone, and I would never forgive myself if something were to happen in my absence. Mikhail had never laid a finger on her, but there was no telling what he was capable of. I didn't need my mother anymore but she still needed me, so I grabbed the envelope . . . the thing I'd been desperately waiting for all this time . . . and with a heavy chest, I ripped my escape route in half.

I went to my room without another word, sitting in my closet and letting the tears fall. I had spent my whole life holding on to the dream that one day I would leave. I didn't let myself try to move on or deal with anything, because I told myself that I needed to wait until I left. I told myself that the key to my happiness was to just move away from my family.

I told myself to just keep pushing through all the bullshit because when I finally left my life would be perfect. Now it was too late. Now that I finally made it to what I'd been waiting for, the dream was shattered right before my eyes, and the ultimate truth was blossoming through the broken shards. I was never leaving. I was never going to escape. My home was in this prison, and it was about time I accepted it.

The only thing I had was my hope, Ana. My faith that things couldn't be bad forever, because I knew that with every rainstorm there came a rainbow. So despite all the attacks against my frail and thin shield, I continued to grasp onto the scraps and tatters that were left behind. I continued to gather the crumbs and specs that survived through all the destruction and desperately tried to fuse them back together only for them to get destroyed all over again. But I'm done. I have no more slivers of hope. I have no more fragments of trust left in the universe. The only thing I have is the darkness that's been flickering in the edges of my vision, patiently waiting for me to let it take over.

So I finally did the thing that I should have done all those years ago. I breathed it in completely and allowed it to swallow up my undivided existence. I let it seep into my veins and ooze into my bones, fusing all my cells together until my white skeleton turned pitch black. There was no dark cloud hovering over me anymore, but only because that darkness was now entirely and absolutely me.

NOW

Castaways
What time are we meeting? —Malak
Let's do 6 —Zara
I'm down for 6 too —Dima

That works for me, can't wait!! —Me

I smiled. I was *excited* to see my friends, which was rare. I loved them, and I knew once I got there I would enjoy myself, but it was the *after* part I always dreaded. The part when I went home and analyzed over every little thing I said and did until eventually, after hours of stress and torment, I would convince myself they all secretly hated me.

I swiped out of our group chat and hesitated before tapping on the conversation right below it. The only other person I texted besides my mom and Noah—*Bayan*. It looked exactly the same as it did the last time I checked.

Heyy —Me

Still on delivered. Still no response.

I tried not to let it bother me. I tried not to get offended because *this* was Bayan. She sucked at texting back. I still couldn't help and overthink it though . . . what if she *was* mad at me? How did things end the last time we hung out? Could I have said something rude or done something wrong without realizing it? But if I did, why hadn't she told me how she felt? Did she think I was the type of person who would get defensive and argue if she told me that I did something wrong? Did she not know that if I ever did something to hurt her, even if it was unintentional, I would apologize non-stop? That I would literally *grovel* on my knees until she forgave me? And even after that I still wouldn't forgive *myself* for ever making her feel anything less than amazing?

I quickly tossed my phone on my bed before I wasted any more time driving myself insane instead of getting ready. She was just busy. We didn't need to talk every day to remain close. That was the beauty of our friendship. I missed her, but I would see her soon.

I turned the water on cold and stepped in, instinctively drawing back at the temperature but forced myself to submerge under it. I squeezed a generous amount of shampoo into my palm and started to lather it into my hair, scrubbing my roots vehemently. My mind drifted to Noah as I washed my hair. I was already eager to see him and work on the bookstore after I saw my friends—

Knock, knock.

I paused my movements and faced the direction of the door, making sure not to open my eyes, but I didn't hear anything anymore—

Knock, knock.

"I'm in here, Mama!" I yelled loudly, hoping she heard me. I stepped under the shower head and started to wash the shampoo out—

"It's me, Maya."

My fingers froze in my hair.

Mikhail?

Did he not realize I was in the shower? It was silent, but I could sense he was still standing on the other side of the door.

Was he waiting for a response? I instantly cringed at the thought of talking to him, but what else could I do?

I swallowed back the awkwardness. "Okay, well, I'm taking a shower . . ."

"I need the bathroom."

What the fuck?

"I'm in here right now," I repeated, annoyed. He was so weird.

"I need to take a shower."

A wave of unease started to creep up at the tone he was using. He wasn't yelling, but his voice sounded off—

It wasn't a serene calm that he was exuding; it was an eerie calm—

I shoved the memory out of my head and started rinsing my hair quicker. I didn't bother answering, I mean, he didn't expect me to just get out mid-shower because he needed it? He could wait . . . but just to avoid any drama, I poured some conditioner into my hands and started to lather my hair before it was even completely free of shampoo. I just wanted to finish before—

"I said I need to take a *fucking* shower!" he screamed, smacking his fist roughly against the door.

—he *snapped*.

I immediately jumped back at the loud sound, feeling the force of his fist flow through the door and shove me violently against the wall of the shower. My eyes flung open as I looked toward the door, a sharp pain stinging through them as the chemicals dripped off my eyelashes. I still didn't close them. I needed to keep them open. I needed to *see*—

Another booming smack bounced off the bathroom walls. "I *told* you I needed the bathroom because I have a job interview—"

He never told me *anything*—

"*God*, you're always trying to sabotage everything for me!" he shouted through the door. "I told you I needed the fucking bathroom, Maya. For *fucks* sake get out! Get the fuck out!"

I cowered away from his voice and backed further into the corner of the shower. He continued to hit the door thunderously, the hinges rattling loudly in protest. Each deafening thud against the door hit my eardrums with a painful strike. I covered them with my hands but the sound just kept getting louder and *LOUDER*—

"Open the fucking door," he threatened darkly. "Open the fucking door and get the fuck out, or I swear to God I'll come in there—"

I shoved my fingers deep into my ear canals, drowning out his voice but proceeding to enhance the sound of my thrashing heartbeat. My harrowed breath was getting yanked out before it could properly circulate through my lungs, and then quickly getting sucked back in with a desperate gulp. I choked on water, soap, and *tears* as they swished together in my mouth while I tried to calm down.

He whacked the door again, but this time the loud thud was followed by a piercing crack through the air. I whipped my head toward the door, my vision blurry from soap and damaged corneas, but I didn't need my contacts to see the horror scene playing out in front of me. I watched as the bathroom door—my sole form of protection—slowly pushed open. Only a second passed before a tall, dark silhouette entered through the door and into the small space. For a moment I was filled with relief that there was still one more thing concealing me . . . until I remembered the drape hanging between us was clear and completely see-through.

My arms instantly flew down to cover myself, but I didn't have enough limbs to shield my entire body. I prayed that the cold water still managed to fog up the bathroom, but I could feel his intense stare on me through the plastic curtain. I slid to the floor of the shower and shrunk away from his gaze burning a hole in my skin. I was crying silently, fear blocking any noise from slipping through my trembling lips. He continued to stand there and leer at me, his menacing breaths coming out in pants of anger as I urgently tried to fall through the tub and into another dimension of this crucifying *hell*.

The bathroom tiles squeaked as he took a step closer, and my breath caught, feet scurrying to get away but there was nowhere to go. Nowhere for me to *escape*. My body continued to spasm, slipping and sliding in the wet tub. I heard the plastic crinkle as he grazed it gently, and suddenly I was a teenager again and three men stood over me with one of their hands inside my body. I was back in my bed and my brother was breathing down my neck as he watched me sleep with his fingers stroking the covers, my pajama bottoms soaked in urine. I was hiding in my cramped closet, resisting the urge to cover my ears against his screams so I could make sure my mother and father were okay. I was obsessively counting the steps from the curb to my front porch after school because I was too scared to go inside, but also because I was too scared I'd one day forget *why*.

The shower rings scraped against the metal rod above me and a hysterical plea forced its way through the blockade of emotions lodged in my throat, but I kept my eyes squeezed shut. If I didn't look, then it could never be *real*.

"Please," I whispered in a strangled cry. "Just leave me alone, Mikhail . . . I don't know what you want from me." I curled into a tight ball and banged my head against the wall, forcing myself to *wake up*.

I heard his fingers grip the edge tightly before completely tearing it off the rod and I was exposed. I clutched my body tighter, frantically wishing that I had the strength to snap all my bones into pieces so I could wash away with the water streaming into the drain.

You're imagining things again, Maya—

I heard him take one step into the tub.

Nothing is real, Maya—

But then my eyes flung open and through my blurry vision, I saw him, right there, standing over me, leaning down, and my entire existence shattered. Everything I'd spent the last months trying to rebuild . . . my spark that I was trying to reignite . . . my happiness, my *life* slowly fell apart, before completely deteriorating into thin air like it never even existed at all.

"*Please* Mikhail," I begged again.

My mom's voice suddenly flowed up the stairs and I heard the front door slam shut. I moved my head quickly, ready to scream for help. Ready to scream bloody fucking *murder—*

But he was gone.

I hesitated—what if my eyes were tricking me? I extended my hand slowly but all I felt was empty air, confirming with relief that he wasn't there. I quickly stood up, almost slipping in my haste, and turned the water off before sprinting to my room. I dropped to the floor after jamming my storage compartments under the handle, but I could still feel his dark, greedy eyes *raking* over me—

I leaned over as my morning coffee came hurling out of me and onto my rug. I watched the liquid start to quickly spread and darken the fabric of my carpet. The lingering stomach acid dribbled from my lips and onto my chin, leaving a wet trail of bile down my neck and the length of my body. I didn't bother wiping it off. It was only fair that I looked as *disgusting* as I felt inside.

I looked down at my hand and at the scabs that were *so* close to being healed. I could feel them burning for me to pick them. *Itching* for me to scratch them away, along with the images in my head. Who was I to deny them? I vigorously scraped and lacerated the delicate skin until it was raw, and my nails were chipped and covered with blood, and I began to wonder why I even bothered to stop picking in the first place.

Exhaustion and nausea swirled harshly behind my eyes and without warning my body tilted to the side and crumpled to the floor. It didn't stop there. The floor of my room suddenly transformed into liquid and I was *sinking* through. It was strange the way time suspended itself when you were falling. I should've been thinking about what was going to happen when I landed. I should've been fighting to swim back up for air. I should've been trying not to drown, but nothing mattered anymore. I didn't *exist* anymore—

"Did you hear me, Maya?"

I turned toward the sound of her voice, surprised to find myself in the passenger seat, and Malak was sitting beside me, driving.

How did I get here?

"No," I said automatically, my voice dull and scratchy. "Sorry, what were you saying?"

She continued talking about God knows what as I looked down, convinced that I would find myself sitting naked and covered in vomit. I wasn't. I was wearing the black jeans and blue sweater I'd picked out earlier, and my sneakers were laced up neatly on my feet. My hands were wrapped in cut-off cotton gloves, and Noah's jacket was around my shoulders. I looked in the side mirror and my face was clean of any . . . spit-up. My hair was brushed and my glasses were perched crookedly on my nose. I reached up and slowly adjusted them, surprised when I could *feel* them. I touched my body, and the seat, and my face . . . all very real. I was actually here.

But how?

"Anyway, that's pretty much it. Work has taken up most of my life, which sucks. But what about *you*, I feel like I haven't talked to you in ages. What's new?"

I opened my mouth to speak, not knowing what I was going to say, but we pulled into the sushi place we were eating at, saving me from having to respond. Zara and Dima were standing beside their car, waiting for us. I shut the door behind me and was quickly enveloped in a blur of hugs and a sea of *hellos, how are yous*, and *I miss yous*. We picked a booth by the window and ordered our food, while everyone started talking and updating each other on their lives.

I tried to pay attention but my mind was in a fuzzy haze. I couldn't remember how I got there. I couldn't remember getting dressed, or going downstairs, or if I even told my parents I was going out. I couldn't remember getting into Malak's car or her telling me that she was going to pick me up in the first place—did I ask for a ride? I pushed through the fog desperately—

I could still feel his dark, greedy eyes leering at me—

I choked on my food as the memories flooded back to me.

"Maya, are you okay?" Dima asked.

"Here, drink some water," Zara said, pushing my glass toward me.

"Thanks," I mumbled, taking a sip of the cold water—

I choked on water, soap, and tears as they swished together in my mouth while I tried to calm down—

I spit the water back into my cup as a strangled cough erupted through my throat. I felt like I was choking all over again but there was *nothing* there.

"I'm just going to go to the bathroom, excuse me." I pushed my chair back roughly and hurried to the bathroom. I barely closed the door behind me before the few bites of food I managed to scarf down, heaved back up through my mouth and into the toilet. I panted over the seat for a moment but nothing else came up. I flushed away the remnants of my vomit and walked to the sink to splash some water on my face, before placing my glasses back on and looking into the mirror to make sure my face was clean—

Mikhail glared back at me, his x-ray vision zeroing in on my body through my clothes—

I jumped back and immediately squeezed my eyes shut, but I still couldn't get him out of my head. I saw his face everywhere I looked. I couldn't get his *eyes* out of my mind, and I could feel his stare on every inch of my skin. Something rotten was boiling inside me. I was *dirty*. My clothes were dirty just from making contact with the rancid particles on my skin. I squirmed and twisted away from the feeling of my dirty and rotten clothes, but I couldn't get away. I needed to strip out of all the articles I was wearing. I needed to wash my body clean in the sink. I needed to scrub away all the dirt, and vomit, and *him* off my skin. I needed to—

I leaned against the wall as a whirlwind of emotions slowly

devoured my mind. I needed to get through this dinner. I needed to get through this dinner *first* and then I could figure out what do to next. I needed to suffer through just one more hour, and then I could let myself fall apart.

"Sorry about that guys," I apologized, taking my seat. I stared at them nervously, hoping they couldn't notice anything off about me.

"No, you're good," Dima replied. "Anyway, I have an update about the guy I'm talking to . . ."

I glanced down at my body frantically, feeling completely translucent. She was lying. I wasn't *good*. Nothing about me was good. How could they not *see*—?

Pay attention.

I looked back at Dima quickly, nodding my head as she spoke.

Stop active listening, Maya. It looks fake.

I halted my head mid-bob and focused on her mouth. They were moving but nothing she was saying registered in my ears. How did people read lips? Why weren't real-life subtitles a thing?

". . . I think I'm just going to wait until April when I graduate and see what happens because . . ."

You're still not listening.

She's talking about her graduation—

No, fuck, you're being so rude, Maya.

I smiled at her as she explained her plans. I couldn't wait to go to her graduation—

God, she can see right through you. This *is why they never ask you to hang out more often*—

Shut up.

Do you think they don't hang out without you? Do you think they don't have a separate group chat with just the three of them? Do you think—?

Shut *up*.

Everyone can see you, Maya. Everyone knows. Everyone can see your decomposing soul—

Shut up, shut up, *SHUT THE FUCK UP—*

"Do you want a to-go box for your food?"

I blinked at the waitress smiling down at me.

"Yes, please. Thank you."

"This was fun guys, let's plan something again soon," Malak said, gathering her stuff. "And Maya—" I froze "—we'll give you a pass today because you seem distracted, but you better contribute to the conversation next time."

I laughed breathlessly. "I've been out of it guys, my bad."

"It's okay, I feel you," Dima said as the waitress returned with my box. The wind whipped around us as soon as we stepped through the door, and I immediately welcomed the cold sensation on my face.

"Malak, you don't have to give me a ride home. My parents are going to pick me up," I lied. I couldn't sit in the small space of her car while she scrutinized me.

"Are you sure? I don't mind, really," she insisted.

"No it's fine, don't worry about it," I assured her, giving her a quick hug. I waved as she pulled out of the parking lot, my fake smile instantly disappearing as soon as her car was out of my view.

I stood still for a moment, the freezing weather nice on my skin. There was no way I was calling my parents to pick me up. There was no way I was going back to that house. I flinched just thinking about it. I needed Noah. He would make me feel seen. He would make me feel *clean*.

The restaurant we went to was also downtown, but it was

still a few blocks away from Noah's café. The temperature seemed to drop further with every step I took, but I didn't mind. Every time the cold wind hit my skin, my cells instantly woke up. I tensed against the frigid weather but didn't make a move to button up his jacket and make myself warmer. I needed this. I needed to stay *awake*. I needed to stay alert so I wouldn't slip back into the nightmare simmering in the edges of my memory, begging to barge through and consume me.

The cold could only last so long before the veil of numbness settled back over me and dulled my senses back to sleep. Everything after that was a blur. I remembered the sidewalk being empty—no one else was stupid enough to walk around in this bone-chilling climate. I vaguely heard footsteps getting closer, so I glanced up on instinct and saw a man walking in my direction. There was something familiar about his build and I was getting a strange feeling of déjà vu, so I squinted slightly through my glasses—

But the random stranger suddenly transformed into Mikhail before my eyes, and he was *charging* toward me—

And then I was gone.

Everything was gone. The sidewalk disappeared from under my feet, and the buildings around me vanished as the cold wind slapping my face was replaced with cold *water*. I blinked because obviously I was imagining things and when I opened my eyes again, my surroundings would have righted themselves back into reality.

But they didn't. I wasn't outside anymore; I was back in my bathroom. I was in my shower, *naked*, and standing on the other side of the curtain was Mikhail. He was staring at me mercilessly as I tried to shrink away from his relentless gaze and into the corner of the tub. I opened my mouth to scream but nothing came out. I tried to move my hands to protect myself, but they wouldn't move. They were shackled tightly behind my back with invisible binds. There was nothing I could do, nowhere to escape, I was *trapped*—

"Maya?"

I blinked. I was back outside. I was standing in front of *Espresso & Chill.*

"Why didn't you come inside, weirdo?" Noah teased. "Awe, did you bring me back some of your dinner? I'm starving."

He reached out to grab the box clenched in my fist but I recoiled away from him, dropping it.

He chuckled. "My bad, I forgot you *hate* sharing food . . ." He trailed off and I felt his eyes analyzing me carefully. "What's wrong?"

Finally, someone could *see* me.

"Maya, baby, what's wrong?" he whispered, concern lacing his voice.

I felt his hand touch my face and I jerked away again.

"Maya, you're *freezing*—" He broke off, looking around frantically. "Where's your car? Did you . . . *walk* here?" he asked in disbelief.

Yes.

"You need to come inside." I didn't budge. "I'm going to take your hand, okay?"

I moved away from him again instinctively.

"Hey, it's just me. I'm not going to hurt you," he assured me. "I promise I won't hurt you. I *love* you. Please, just let me take your hand. Let me take you inside."

He reached out slowly, testing my reaction, and brushed my hand slightly. When I didn't flinch, he added more pressure and then hesitantly interlocked his fingers with mine.

"Thank you, baby, you're doing so good. I'm going to walk you inside now, okay?"

Okay.

My legs moved without waiting for permission. He opened the door and led me inside, immediately surrounding us with all the chatter and noise of his café. He took me behind the counter and stopped outside the door that led to the upper level.

"Wait here. I'll be right back," he promised, squeezing my hand before letting go. It fell limply to my side, cold and *empty*. I watched as he whispered something into Ravi's ear, and then he walked to the front of the café.

"Hey everyone, I'm sorry for the inconvenience, but unfortunately we will be closing early today," he announced apologetically. "On your way out I'm going to give you a coupon for a free coffee and baked good on your next visit. Again, I apologize for the sudden disruption."

Me being the sudden disruption. I wanted to protest—he shouldn't have to close early—but my brain and my body were disconnected. My body was in the present, but my mind was stuck in the *past*.

"Don't worry buddy, you'll still get paid for the remainder of your shift," Noah told him as everyone filed out of the store. He locked the door and turned off all the machines before rushing back to me.

"Maya," he begged, his voice cracking. "Please, tell me what's wrong. Tell me what you need me to do, and I'll do it right now."

I'm dirty, I thought hopelessly.

"You're what?"

I didn't realize I had spoken out loud this time. I couldn't feel my lips moving.

"I'm dirty," I said louder.

"What do you . . . ?" His eyes examined my physique carefully. "You're not dirty, Maya."

"I'm dirty," I repeated. He looked at me, confusion and fear raging a war behind his eyes. What was wrong with him? Why couldn't he *see*?

"I'm *dirty*," I demanded again. "I thought you saw me? I thought you could *see* me? Why can't you see?!"

"Okay, okay," he soothed automatically. "You're right, Maya, you're . . . dirty." He had to force the word out. "What can I do to fix it?"

"I need to be clean," I pleaded. "Please, I just need to be *clean*."

"Okay, let's go upstairs. You can get clean upstairs," he agreed, and we walked up the stairs that led right into his apartment. He pushed open a door to the left. His *bathroom*.

"Wait here," he murmured, leaving the bathroom for a minute. He came back with a fresh towel and some articles of clothing. "There's shampoo and conditioner in the shower. The body wash is on the bottom ledge. If you need me to go get you anything specific from the store that you'd rather use, just tell me." He lifted his hands to my face, holding it gently between his warm palms. "Take your time. I'll be out here waiting for you." He pressed his lips against my forehead, breathing me in fiercely, before letting go and closing the door behind him.

I looked at his shower dreadfully. It helped that his bathroom looked nothing like mine, so the nightmare wasn't thrashing *too* hard against my mind, but it didn't matter in the end. As soon as I turned the nozzle on full blast and stepped under the water fully clothed, I was *back*. I couldn't see Mikhail this time but I could still *feel* him. He was all around me, swirling in the steam, vandalizing my presence piece by piece. The scorching water was starting to burn through all my layers, but nothing could harm me more than the constant feeling of his gaze pressing into me roughly from every angle. My fingers twitched urgently toward the shampoo bottle so I could scrub myself clean, but I couldn't move. I was frozen in the center of his incinerating stare. I couldn't even open my mouth to *breathe*. My chest was tight with suffocation, and my lungs were torn between gasping for too much air and letting out the deep sobs that were begging to escape.

It felt like I'd been standing in the shower for hours until eventually, I wasn't sure if I was even there anymore. How could I be sure that I wasn't in *my* house, trapped in *my* bathroom, with Mikhail breathing down *my* neck? I couldn't tell what was real. I kept running it over and over again in my head, that maybe Noah was nothing but a dream. A figment of my imagination that I invented to protect myself from all the pain I'd stored deep in my mind until today. His gaze tore through everything and now . . . I didn't know what was true. I didn't know how to make it *stop*. I had let myself fall for another one of hopes fatal snares, and now I was submerged into unabridged darkness.

"Maya?"

I blinked slowly, focusing through my obscured vision until I could faintly see his green and blue orbs lifting me out of my abyss.

"*Maya*," he repeated. He walked to the open shower, stepping through the water that had spilled out, and quickly adjusted the nozzle to a more reasonable setting. The water raining down on me instantly changed from hot to warm, relieving my skin. He carefully entered the tub and pushed my wet hair out of my face.

"Breathe."

My lips stayed glued together.

He gently massaged my neck and pressed his mouth against my ear. "Breathe, Maya," he whispered, taking a deep breath. He held it for three seconds and then let it out calmly. He repeated the action five more times before my lungs suddenly sprang back to life, gasping for air. He continued to breathe slowly and enunciated until my panting finally steadied and our breathing was synchronized.

"Did you know that whales don't die of old age?" I asked.

"They don't?"

"No. Eventually, they get tired of swimming back up for air, so they drown themselves," I said quietly. "I don't know how to swim, Noah. I don't know how to swim, and I'm tired of trying to struggle back up for air. I'm so fucking *tired*."

"What do you need, Maya? Let me help you, please."

"I need it to stop."

"You need what to stop?"

"I need everything to stop," I told him, a sob finally breaking through my clogged chest.

He wrapped his arms around me securely. "I know you're in pain and I know you're tired of fighting. I know you tried so many times but I need you to try again, okay?"

"I don't know *how*."

He was silent for a moment. "Was it your brother?"

I didn't answer, and I immediately felt his body tense against mine.

"You told me he stopped," Noah said, his voice accusing. He pulled back and looked at me with tortured eyes. "You told me it wasn't like that anymore, and a part of me didn't fucking *believe* you, but I let you leave anyway because I didn't want to make your decisions for you. I never should've let you go back there."

"This came out of nowhere, Noah, I don't know . . ."

"Can you tell me what happened?"

"I was taking a shower," I started slowly. "I was taking a shower and then he . . . he started knocking on the door."

Noah closed his eyes and leaned his forehead against mine. I could feel him trembling.

"He was calm at first. He knocked once and said he needed the bathroom. I didn't want to reply—I *hate* talking to him—but I didn't want to make him mad so I told him I was in there."

My heartbeat was accelerating and my words were coming out in desperate gasps as water filled into my mouth. "He started *banging* on the door after that, saying that he had told me he needed the shower and that I was trying to sabotage his job interview." I looked up at him intensely. "He never told me anything, Noah, I *swear*."

"I believe you, baby, I believe you," he assured me soothingly, stroking my face.

"He kept banging harder and screaming at me until—" I stopped, my stomach churning with disgust. "The lock broke and the door swung open."

"Fuck," Noah muttered, his fist clenching. "I'm going to kill that piece of shit."

"He didn't do anything," I said, suddenly feeling dramatic. "He just stood there in the bathroom, staring at me."

"Don't," he demanded. "Don't you *dare* belittle this, Maya. You're his *sister*! What kind of sick fuck just stands there and watches you while you're—?" He shook his head angrily.

"I curled up on the floor . . . covering myself." My tears started to slip in with the water pouring down on us. "I could *feel* his stare on my skin and everywhere around me, and—" I squirmed in his arms, desperate to get out of my clothes. "I feel dirty. I feel so fucking *dirty*, Noah. My core feels rotten, please, I need to get clean. I just want *out* of this body, please, I can't . . ."

"It's okay, baby, it's okay. Do you trust me?"

He was staring at me deeply, and I nodded. He rested his hands on my shoulders, never breaking my gaze, and gently slipped his jacket off my body. He tossed it and it landed with a loud *splat* on the bathroom floor.

"I'm going to take your sweater off, okay?" he asked, waiting.

I nodded again. I needed to be *clean*.

He slid his hands under the thick knit material and started tugging it upwards. It was heavy with the weight of so much water, but he eventually pulled it over my head and my arms fell limply back to my side. He kept his eyes locked with mine as he threw it to the side with my jacket, before doing the same with the thin turtleneck I had underneath.

"I'm going to take your jeans off now, okay?" he breathed softly. "If you want me to stop, just say so." He leaned down slightly, kissing my shoulder, before kneeling in front of me. He untied my destroyed sneakers, slipping them off my feet along with my socks. He glanced up at me, making sure I was okay, before unbuttoning my jeans.

"Lift your foot for me, Maya," he requested. I put my hand

309

on his shoulder for balance and did as he asked. After he successfully detangled both my feet from my jeans and disposed of them, he pressed his lips tenderly against my exposed abdomen and I shuddered. It didn't pass my notice that he never asked to remove my gloves.

He stood up and we faced each other quietly for a moment—one fully clothed, one partially bare, water raining down on us and Noah not looking anywhere but my eyes. This wasn't how this moment was supposed to go. The first time the love of your life saw you semi-naked was supposed to be special, beautiful, romantic. Not like *this*, me, standing in an old sports bra that wasn't doing my chest any favors and an underwear that was the complete opposite of tempting or desirable, and I was feeling . . . nothing. I was supposed to feel *something* other than dirty in this very special and beautiful and romantic moment because you only got one first. This first would never happen again, but as usual, with one look, Mikhail ruined it for me.

Noah moved, stroking my cheek softly before finally looking away. He grabbed his loofah, frothing some body wash on it before gently running it all over my body. I closed my eyes and focused on the rough bristles gliding across my skin, erasing all traces of Mikhail. Noah took his time scrubbing my shoulders, my chest, and my stomach to perfection. He got down on his knees and washed my legs, and then stepped around me in his spacious tub to work on my back.

He didn't flinch at the long scar running down my leg, or at the little one on my arm. He didn't flinch at the scar that stretched from my belly button down, disappearing behind my underwear, or the smaller one above my hip. I knew he *saw* them, but he just cleaned around them.

"I know you see them," I whispered. "You don't need to pretend they don't exist."

I felt his lips on my back as he dropped the sponge and wrapped his arms around me from behind, leaning his head on my shoulder. "Your scars aren't dirty, Maya. They don't need to be cleaned."

"Clean them," I pleaded.

"Scrubbing won't make them go away——"

"I said clean them," I repeated louder, kneeling down to grab the loofah.

"*Stop*," he demanded, grabbing my hands and turning me around to face him. His wet hair was slick to his face, and his clothes were drenched. "You're not dirty, Maya."

"Yes, I am," I protested weakly, still feeling remnants of my decaying soul lingering inside of me.

He stared at me intensely, a fierce fire raging in his bright eyes. Before I knew what he was doing, he let go of me and swiftly lifted his shirt off.

"Am *I* dirty?"

My sharp intake of breath replaced all the words I'd prepared to say. My eyes followed down his neck, and to his exposed abdomen which was covered in *tattoos*. All over his chest, and on his stomach and his arms . . . he was completely inked, stopping just where his t-shirt would end, which explained why I had never noticed them before. I examined them all in a wild frenzy, anxious to soak them all in. There were symbols and words, all intricately drawn and engraved into his skin permanently——

My name, right there, over his heart. It was small, and I could barely see it through the water and my blurry vision but it was *real*, inscribed between two interlocked pinkies. An infinite and irreversible promise.

No, he wasn't *dirty*. In fact, he had never looked more magnificent. I reached my hand out, mesmerized, and stroked my fingers against them . . . and that's when I felt it. I didn't know much about tattoos, but I was almost positive they were supposed to feel smooth. His chest felt like *my* chest.

All his tattoos were hiding scars.

I felt him shiver under my hand. "Tell me, Maya," he insisted. "Am *I* dirty? Am *I* rotten? Do *I* repulse you?"

"Who . . . ? What happened?" I whispered urgently. I was prepared to find them. I was prepared to hunt down the soulless *monster*—

"Am. I. Dirty?" he repeated louder.

"No," I said harshly. "You're not dirty, Noah, *these* don't make you dirty. They make you strong. They make you beautiful."

He cupped my face in his hands. "The same applies to you, Maya. *You* are strong and *you* are beautiful. Don't let him make you feel otherwise."

"I don't get it," I said, defeated. "How did you move on? How did you get over all the terrible things that happened to you? How are you . . . *okay*? I am wrecked through and *through*. I am completely ruined! What is wrong with me that I can't be okay too?"

"There is *nothing* wrong with you," he said vehemently, tightening his grip. "The difference between you and I is that I was *rescued*. I was plucked out of my miserable nightmare and placed into a new environment filled with warmth, and love, and *trust*. I was given all the resources I needed to heal. You weren't—*that's* how. How are you supposed to heal in the same place you got hurt? How are you supposed to recover from all the pain and torments of your past, when your past is *still* your present?"

He leaned closer, his lips just barely brushing against mine. "You were given a terrible beginning and an even more terrible middle, but . . . your middle is *unfinished*. Your middle is still going, Maya, and I'll be damned if I don't make sure the rest of it isn't amazing. I will give you the best middle, and the very best fucking end."

The force of his vow pushed away everything else on my mind. We were staring at each other, an intense bond molding between our gaze, and there were so many things I could say. So many things I *wanted* to say, but words were unnecessary. The blockade of my emotions had collapsed and all the passion and love came thrusting back through, consuming me entirely. It rose through my stomach and into my chest, knocking against my lungs and making it hard to breathe.

He leaned his head against mine, wiping away my tears until it was only water streaming down my face. "I don't know a lot of things, Maya," he whispered. "But I do know *one* thing, and it's that the universe will punish him for every single tear he's made you shed. If not in this life, then definitely in the next."

"I didn't know you were religious."

"I'm not," he replied. "I *wasn't*. But when I look at you . . . I can't help but feel like our souls somehow sprouted from the same seed. *You* are the sunshine that my roots need in order to grow. *You* are the water that my core needs in order to survive, Maya, and I'm not going to let anything or anyone take you away from me." He closed his eyes tightly and let out a shaky breath. "I was never a religious man but I swear, when I think

I.I.E

about you—" his voice cracked "—I get so extremely overwhelmed that you're real and that you're mine, and all I want to do is get onto my fucking knees and thank God for bringing you into my life."

I shut my eyes at his words, and let them sheave me in a shield of warmth. His lips were at my ear, murmuring gently. "Stay with me tonight. Let me hold you, Maya. Let me replace his gaze with my *touch*."

I nodded quickly. His presence was the only thing keeping me from crumbling to the ground.

"You need to get dry and change into some warm clothes before you get sick."

I shivered, only now realizing how cold I was. He turned off the shower and held my hand as I stepped out of the tub so I wouldn't slip on the river that had formed on the bathroom floor. He grabbed his towel and patted me dry, before wrapping it tightly around me. We stood in front of the steamy mirror, and I watched as Noah took his brush and started to gently comb it through my wet and tangled curls. Once it was free of knots, he sectioned it off with his fingers.

"You know how to French braid?" I asked, my eyes never leaving his through the mirror.

"Yes," he replied, securing it with a hair tie. "I used to do my mom's hair whenever she . . . couldn't."

I turned around to face him and pulled his head down to rest on my shoulder, running my fingers down his wet back. "My sweet boy."

He kissed my neck, letting his lips linger. "I'll give you a few minutes to get dressed. I need to clean up this water park of a disaster anyway," he said, chuckling at the mess. I smiled sheepishly and closed the door behind me.

314

I slipped into his clothes and walked over to the window where he had a chair and a telescope propped up, pointing at the sky. Noah loved space. He talked about it all the time—how beautiful and vast and unknown the universe was. I peered into the lens to see what he saw, but all I saw was myself, freshly twelve years old, standing in my big brother's room with tears in my eyes after he ruined the first and only birthday present I'd ever received, fingers pressed against my cheek which was warm and raw from his harsh strike. There was this voice in my ear—a powerful, confident voice—telling me to stand up for myself, to protect myself, to fight *back*. But there was another voice, too—quieter, softer, farther away—telling me to do nothing because I deserved it. Because it was *normal*. Every time I listened to the second voice, the louder she became, until one day that powerful and confident girl stopped speaking.

The consequences of that choice were littered in front of me now, shining like diamonds in the sky for anyone to look up and see. Every undiscovered comet, and meteoroid, and spec of fairy dust represented all the things I could've done, all the *people* I could've been had I just listened to that first voice.

I squinted hard, moving the telescope around the never-ending galaxy of hiding places, searching for her among the stars and the planets and the beautiful, vast, unknown universe, but she wasn't there. There was only me.

"I was right," Noah said from behind me. He was leaning against the doorframe with his arms crossed, watching me. "You *can* make the most basic articles of clothing look sexy."

I shook my head at him, smiling. "Do you have a washing machine?" I asked, clutching my undergarments in my palm.

"Yeah, I already put your other clothes in there," he told

me, walking to the door beside the bathroom. It was a small laundry room, with a shelf where he had all his clothes stored. I threw them in and Noah added some detergent pods, before turning it on.

"Are you hungry? I have a feeling you didn't eat much with your friends."

"I didn't, but I just want to sleep."

"Then let's go to sleep."

"You can, um—" I pointed to his shirt "—take that off while we sleep. If you want."

"Is that what *you* want, Maya?"

I nodded.

He took it off, once again exposing his pain that he turned into beauty.

"Do you want to talk about it?" I asked quietly, my voice breaking.

"I'm *okay*," he assured me softly. "We can talk about it another day. Let me take care of you tonight."

He turned off the lamp and slid in, pulling me against his body. His long legs intertwined with mine under the covers until every part of us was connected.

"I'm a cuddle person," he warned.

"The cuddliest." I snuggled deeper into his chest, my eyelids already closing with heavy exhaustion. "You know . . . there's another reason why I was always so hesitant to fall asleep."

"What is it?"

"It started a few weeks after I met you," I breathed. "You made me feel a certain way, so I would force myself not to sleep in fear that I'd wake up and it would all be a dream. That *you* would be a dream. I still fear that, Noah."

He tugged me closer and rubbed circles on my back under his baggy shirt. "You reignited everything that makes me real, Maya. As long as I have you, I can never cease to exist." I felt his lips continue to move on my forehead, but I had already slipped under the sweet blanket of unconsciousness.

THEN

Dear Ana,

It's been a while. I haven't felt the need to write. I haven't felt the need to do anything really. This world only gave me two options—feel pain or feel nothing.

I chose nothing.

On the last day we talked, after I found out that I couldn't leave, I went dark, Ana. Darker than I have ever been before. I couldn't even remember what it felt like to not *feel that way. It hurt at first until it didn't anymore, and I was desensitized. My pain didn't disappear, but it was dulled down. There was something incredibly satisfying about soaking up all my loneliness and sadness until it consumed me. The negative thoughts swirling around in my brain were oddly fulfilling, probably because I knew nothing bad could come from them. I could never get crushed with disappointment when disappointment was all I ever expected. I found that it was easier to pretend when I just drank up all my anguish and used it as fuel, instead of wasting my time and energy hoping for a happily ever after that I knew would never come.*

My only goal when I started university was to meet some new people to help pass the time, and I did. I made some friends on my very first day of school but somehow ended up losing them all by my last day. The cycle started again in my sophomore year when my friend Sahar started as a freshman and introduced me to her friends. It didn't take long to realize that I truly had nothing in common with them, which defeated the purpose of using them as a distraction, so I stopped trying. One day they stopped trying too.

I did stop for a moment after that and wonder what was wrong with me. I mean, besides the mess of absolute fuckery that made up my brain. What was wrong with me that made talking to people such a horrible experience? What was wrong with me that I couldn't seem to make friends, without being so excruciatingly awkward? What was wrong with me that I couldn't hold a single conversation without wanting to bolt halfway through? I used to think that I just wasn't meeting the right people, but how was it possible that I still *hadn't met the right people? I was always so preoccupied with what people thought about me and how people saw me, but I think my real fear was that they would see me the same way I saw me . . . which unfortunately was the* real *me.*

I wish I was more sociable and charismatic, Ana. I wish it didn't scare me to be perceived as an imperfect human, who had opinions and real experiences. I hated that being around others suffocated me, but I also hated how much I needed *them around, so I continued to match people's energy and morph myself into exactly what they wanted. I continued to cling to anyone that could tolerate me, even when I couldn't tolerate them.*

I eventually started a new job at this call center. I hated it. The only thing worse than talking to people was talking to people on the phone. People seemed to think basic human decency could get thrown out the window if they couldn't see the person they were speaking to, but I had no choice. My dad came back for good last summer, and I needed a job that paid better than my previous part-time gig. So I went to work every day and got yelled at for eight hours straight with a smile plastered on my face, while I rotted away internally.

Until something strange happened. It was on a Saturday and I worked from seven AM to three-thirty PM, as usual. The place was pretty empty at that time except for a handful of people, which included two girls. I didn't know them, but I always saw them on the days I worked so I assumed they were on a student schedule like me. I walked into work and headed straight for my usual cubicle that was alone in the corner, my eyes flickering to the girls who were chatting and laughing . . . then my feet turned direction, and I found myself pulling out the chair in the empty cubicle next to them. They immediately turned to see who it was, and I braced myself for the uncomfortable silence that was sure to follow, but they just smiled.

"Hey, I'm Dima," the one directly beside me said. "This is Zara."

"Hi, I'm Maya. Is this seat saved for anyone? Sorry that I just sat here," I replied awkwardly.

"No, you're good," she assured me. I nodded and logged into my computer while they continued their conversation. I tried not to eavesdrop and listen to what they were saying, but eventually, I glanced at Zara and that's when I noticed that she was looking at me while she talked. She was . . . including me in the conversation.

And that was the end of it. There was no official discussion or uncomfortable moment. I was already their friend, and it was great. They were exactly what I was looking for. They were nice and funny, and holding a conversation with them was so simple and easy. I started looking forward to going to work because I always had so much fun with them. Later that week, they introduced me to their other friend Hana.

Those first few months were probably the happiest I'd ever been—ordering pizza during our Friday night shifts and going to Starbucks on our breaks early in the morning. But as always, my happiness came with a price. A price whose name was Mikhail.

It happened today, Sunday, at around eleven AM. It's been about three months since I met the girls and I was sitting beside Hana, with Dima and Zara on her other side. I was in the middle of helping a customer add some channels to their TV package when I heard her gasp loudly.

"Guys, did you know that Mikhail's little sister works here?" she asked in shock, and my fingers froze on the keyboard.

"*No way,*" Zara said. "*How do you know?*"

"*I was looking for Jeffrey's name in the chat support so I could message him, and I saw her name on the list of people who work here. Maya Ibrahim.*"

It took them a second, but I eventually felt three pairs of eyes look at me. I rearranged my face into an acceptable expression before turning toward them. "*Yeah . . . that's me.*"

"*That's so funny, I had no idea you were his sister.*"

"*How do you know Mikhail?*"

"*He used to work here,*" she said, giving me a weird look. "*You didn't know that?*"

Of course I didn't know. If I did, I never would have stepped foot in that place.

"*I knew he worked at a call center, but I didn't realize it was this one,*" I lied. "*Did you . . . know him well?*"

"*Yeah, I did actually,*" she replied hesitantly. My nerves were frantic at that point, and I braced myself for what she was about to say because I knew it had to be terrible. How could I excuse his behavior? How could I convince them that his actions didn't define me? How was he capable of ruining my life at home and at work? I could never break free—

"*He's amazing,*" she continued, interrupting my panicked thoughts, and I inhaled sharply. "*See, I was engaged before, but it didn't work out. I was in a really bad place and Mikhail helped me through it. He let me vent and cry about my ex-fiancé for months, without complaining once. He was a huge comfort for me . . .*"

I wanted to cover my ears. I wanted to yell at her to shut up, to stop speaking, to stop lying to me, but I was frozen in my seat. As much as her words pained me and I was desperate for her talking to come to an end, I also craved more. I ached to hear everything and anything about the kind and loving stranger she was telling me about.

"*Anyway, I miss him. How is he doing?*"

Hana's words were still swirling around feverishly, constricting my airways in their path. I attempted to clear my throat anyway so I could answer.

"He's good," I told her, the words burning my mouth with their acidity on the way out. "He's doing really, really good."

"I'm happy to hear that," she said sincerely. "You're so lucky to have him, Maya. Tell him I said hi, okay?"

I nodded curtly and took myself out of available status so I wouldn't get a call. "I'll be back."

I made sure to keep my steps slow and casual as I walked to the bathroom. I made sure to close the door gently and lock it securely behind me. I made sure to turn the tap on full blast so that no one could hear me, but nothing could drown out the words ringing loudly in my ears.

Was this it, then? Could I never escape him? He was always with me, even when he wasn't. Everywhere I went, his shadow followed. Every thought, every word, every emotion *was tainted by his existence. Hana said I was lucky, but lucky how? Lucky because I had a brother who was capable of showing affection to everyone except for me?*

I didn't want to believe it. I always wondered how he had so many friends, and how he had a girlfriend that was so loyal she could seemingly forgive even the most terrible things. But then I'd remember all the disgusting and horrific stuff he'd done to me and I would force the thought out of my mind.

I couldn't force it out in that moment, though. It burst through my shield of numbness, and thoroughly intoxicated every corner and crevice in my body. The kind words they said about him carefully lacerated every fiber of my willpower into a puddle of goo on the bathroom floor. I hastily ripped a handful of napkins from the dispenser and shoved them into my mouth to keep from screaming, but they did nothing to block out the pain. I thought I knew pain, Ana. I thought I had felt pain. I thought I had experienced the worst pain this world had to offer, but this? *The pain of* not being good enough to be treated like a sister, or like a fucking human being? The pain of not being worthy of his kindness that I now knew existed? It was clawing at my chest and searing poison through my veins. For years, I convinced myself he was a monster through and through. I told myself he wasn't capable of loving anything or anyone, but I had it all wrong, Ana. He is capable of loving . . . he just isn't capable of loving me. He isn't even capable of liking me, and that knowledge was enough to pulverize me into dust.

I spit the napkins into the trash and splashed some water on my face, but the tears were still streaming full force, causing my blurry reflection to shift . . .

"Why do you hate me?" I asked his glaring face. "I didn't give you a chance to answer last time, but I'm giving you a chance now. Please, tell me what I'm doing wrong. What do they have that I don't?"

I wiped away the tears so I could read his moving lips, but Mikhail wasn't there anymore. I stared, eyes wide and determined, before redirecting my gnawing question at her instead.

"What did you do to him?"

She blinked but stayed quiet.

"What. Did. You. Do?" I repeated louder, leaning my head in closer. Still no response.

This was why I was so determined to keep surrounding myself with people, Ana. Even when we didn't have anything in common, or when it made me feel painfully uncomfortable. It wasn't because I wanted friends, or because I had suddenly switched over and became an extrovert overnight. It was because people proved that I existed. I had isolated myself for so long that all I had to keep me company was my mind, which was filled with sadness, self-hatred and doubt. Doubt that started as a small seed, and then gradually grew every time Mikhail watered it with his gaslighting words, and my parent's naivety to how dangerous he truly was. Now it was a full-grown tree, its thick roots coiled tightly around every *cell and membrane. I couldn't trust my own brain anymore. I couldn't trust my memories or my thoughts, and I couldn't decipher between what was real and what I had convinced myself was real. Until one day, I couldn't even tell if* I *was real anymore.*

But people changed that. When my friends looked at me, and talked to me, and hung out with me . . . that's when I knew I was real. So I forced myself to be a small blur in a big crowd. Not noticeable enough to be the center of attention, but just enough that once in a while people would glance my way and confirm that I was still there.

Mikhail broke my body, Ana, but the worst thing he ever did was break my mind. He always said that he was trying to make me better, *but all he did was ruin me.*

"Why can't you remember?" I demanded, pounding my fists against her head roughly. "Try harder, think *harder, why does he hate you?" Another tear slipped from one of her eyes and she flinched away from my harsh words. "Why does he hate us?"*

I counted to ten and waited but she just looked at me silently, her face clouded with shame and disgust. I guess I'll never know.

NOW

My eyes snapped open, confused with my surroundings before seeing a familiar set of hands resting on my stomach.

I shifted carefully in his arms and turned to face him. He was still sleeping, his whole body wrapped around me like a sloth. I lightly traced his closed eyelids, the slope of his nose, the outline of his lips. His mouth twitched into a smile under my touch.

"Hi," he whispered, eyes still closed.

"Hi."

"How did you sleep?" he breathed, pulling me closer, scattering kisses all over my face.

"Good. Best sleep I ever had."

"What did you dream about?"

"Who cares about dreaming when I have you in my reality?"

He gave me a lazy grin, and I tapped the small gap between his two front teeth. "I love this."

He bit the tip of my finger gently. "I love this." He released it and pressed his lips against my nose. "And this." Against my forehead. "And this, even though it's a menace." Against my mouth. "Mmm, especially *this*."

I pulled away. "Morning breath."

"But I *love* your morning breath," he insisted.

"Well, then you have a serious problem, Noah. You should

get that checked out by a professional."

He laughed and pulled us up into a seating position. "You have five seconds to swirl some Listerine around and then I want you and your mouth back here—" He stopped, his smile disappearing. I followed his gaze and froze.

My hand. The sleeves of Noah's sweater were so long . . . I didn't notice before I fell asleep . . .

"It's not what it looks like," I said quickly, snatching my hand away and under the covers.

"What is it then?" he asked, staring at me with concern.

I couldn't help myself. I *laughed*.

"Ugh, it's so gross and dumb," I chuckled, falling back on the bed. "I pick my skin."

He was silent for a minute. "You . . . what?"

"I *pick* my skin." He still looked confused. "You know when you get a pimple and you have this strong urge to pop it? Or when people always bite their nails?"

"Sure. . ."

"My bad habit is that I obsessively pick at my hands."

"So you pick at your skin until what? There's a mark?"

"Well, no," I sighed. "Okay, so it started three years ago. I was at my old job and I scratched my hand on a nail sticking out of my cubicle. No big deal, right? But for some reason I just couldn't stop touching it, and inspecting it, and rubbing it, and then eventually picking at it until it started to . . . bleed."

I scrutinized his face but he didn't show any reaction, so I continued. "Anyway, the scratch got bigger because of my incessant fingers, so I put a Band-Aid on it. I realized that as long as I couldn't see it or touch it, I wouldn't feel the need to pick at it. But then, after a few days, I peeled the Band-Aid off and the sticky parts ripped some of my skin, creating *more* marks on my hand."

He was still maintaining a poker face.

"When that didn't work I started keeping my nails short so I couldn't use them to pick . . . but I quickly found out that tweezers and nail clippers worked just as well."

His poker face was *too* fake now. He didn't want me to see his real reaction.

"The cycle just continued from there and somewhere along the line I started wearing gloves because they disguised the scabs, but wouldn't further damage my skin." I slowly lifted my hand from under the blanket, examining it. "It was getting better these last few weeks, but yesterday . . . anyway, what started as a silly bad habit somehow transformed into an obsession engraved deep into my brain. It's like an *itch* that can only be scratched when I pick away at every scab and mark until they're freshly new and open. It's *disgustingly* satisfying."

He flinched, and the poker face shattered. I finally broke him.

"Look, I know it's more than a bad habit—I'm not stupid. I just . . . I can only tackle one thing at a time." I glanced at him, embarrassment coloring my face. "I wasn't joking when I told you that I was an absolute mess."

I waited for him to say something. To tell me how concerning this was. To tell me how *crazy* I was, but he didn't. He just took my hand gently, the skin-on-skin contact more intense than any kiss or intimate moment we had ever shared. I watched as he lifted my hand gingerly to his lips and sprinkled kisses all over my damaged skin

"It's not gross and it's not stupid," he whispered. "Come, you barely ate yesterday. Let me make you a late lunch."

"Okay—wait." I looked around frantically. "What time is it?"

"Two thirty," he told me immediately. "What's wrong?"

"I'm late for work," I said, scrambling out of bed and tripping over his long pant legs.

"It's okay, Maya, I called in sick for you earlier."

I stopped. "You what?"

"I called in sick for you," he repeated slowly. "I also called in sick at Tysons for you, and I texted your mom and told her you spent the night at Bayan's house."

I groaned. "I totally forgot about my parents. I am *so* dead."

"I told her—"

"Yeah, and I told *you* I'm not allowed to sleep over at people's houses," I groaned into my hands again. "It's fine, I'll just go home right now and come up with something."

"What?" Noah demanded.

"I have to go back home—"

"You are *not* going back there."

"What do you mean?"

He looked at me in disbelief. "Am I . . . imagining things? Did your brother *not* completely violate every aspect of your existence yesterday?"

"Stop," I said quietly, cringing away from his words and the memory he made remerge into my brain.

"Your brother is an abusive *predator*, and your parents just sit there and enable his behavior."

"I said *stop*," I pleaded, covering my ears tightly with my hands.

"I'm not trying to hurt you," he said softly, walking toward me. "I'm just confused and I'm . . . scared. I'm always scared for you. I can't *think* when I'm not with you. I can't *breathe* properly until the next time I see you and can know for sure that you're okay. Every time you leave, I keep going through all these terrible scenarios in my head. Every time I say goodbye, I can't shake this feeling that it's going to be the *last* time I'm ever going to see you."

"I'm sorry," I said sincerely. "I'm sorry and I understand, but what did you think was going to happen? Where else am I supposed to go?"

"Here, Maya. You can stay *here*. Move in with me."

"What?"

"Move in with me," he repeated fiercely. "If you don't like this place then we can move somewhere else. If you don't want to live with *me*, then I'll get you your own damn place, just please, please, *please* tell me that you are not seriously thinking about going back to that toxic shit show of a house."

"Noah, my parents would *never* let me move in with you."

"I don't give a *fuck* about what your parents want. You're so obsessed and concerned with what they want and what they need when they don't deserve it. They had one job, and that was to take care of their child and they failed. They failed you, Maya, again and again, and I can't just sit on the sidelines and watch you suffer anymore—" His voice broke, and he shook his head in frustration. "I have *tried* to be respectful and let you do things your way, but I'm not making the mistake of letting you leave again. This isn't right. Nothing about this situation is *right*, how can you not see that?"

"Of course I can see that, Noah, I'm the one living in it!" I snapped. "Do you think I'm enjoying this? Do you think this is what I want? It's *not*, but I have no other choice."

"Yes, you do!" he said, pointing at himself. "Maybe you

didn't before, but you do *now*. I am giving you another choice. Move in with me. Move in with me and let me take care of *your* needs. Move in with me and move *on* from your family, and away from all the terrible things they put you through. Move in with me so you can finally *heal*."

"I don't need you to fix everything for me, okay? That's not why I'm here. *This* is me, Noah. *This* is my life. I thought you understood that. I thought you loved me just the way I am."

"I do love you just the way you are, but do *you*? I mean, isn't that why you stay there? Isn't that why you keep putting up with him? It's because you think one day he's just going to *stop*. You think one day he'll finally love you and in turn, you'll once and for all be able to love yourself. He has shown you who he is time and *time* again and, I hate to break it to you, Maya, but your brother doesn't love you and he *never* fucking will!"

His words slapped me harshly in the face. I looked away as my eyes started to sting, and a powerful rush of humiliation flooded through me.

"Maya . . ."

"No," I said sharply. "I'm leaving, and don't you *dare* try to stop me."

He stared at me regretfully for a moment before stepping out of my way. I walked passed him to his closet and grabbed my dry and clean clothes that were folded neatly next to his. I got changed in his bathroom, forcing the tears back into the miserable hole they came out of. My sneakers were in the corner looking cleaner than they did on the day I bought them, but I didn't let that sway me. Noah hadn't moved from his spot when I came out. I took my keys, wallet and phone without looking at him and stalked for the stairs.

"Maya, talk to me," he said, following behind me. I quickened my steps, shoving the door open and rushing into his empty café.

"Maya," he repeated. "Just stay here, okay? Stay here and yell at me, or cry, or break my fucking heart if you need to, but please don't leave. Please don't go back to that house."

He was pleading with me, but I was almost to the door. I was almost outside—

"*Maya.*"

I stopped. His *voice* stopped me. My name slipped out of his mouth in a pained appeal. I couldn't face him so I just stood there, waiting for him to speak. I could feel him behind me, desperately trying to lure me back into his arms, but I fought it.

"I love you."

I closed my eyes as the traitor tears finally spilled over. He knew I wasn't going to stay and he wasn't trying to apologize. He just didn't want me to leave without knowing *that*, and for the first time since laying eyes on him, I wished I had never stayed for that first cup of coffee. I wished I had never gone to Ana's grave. I wished I had never met him, and completely ruined his life.

I love you too, I thought sadly as I pushed open the door and left without looking back.

~

"Hi again," I said, taking a seat in front of Ana's grave. "Long-time, no talk."

I looked around to make sure no one was in my vicinity and could hear me conversing with a headstone. It was strange, though. The last time I was here I was so *envious* of

Ana, and all the other people who got to rest peacefully for the remainder of eternity. Who didn't have to suffer any more in this dreadfully long life. I desperately craved the quiet emptiness that revolved around this graveyard, but now? I was completely inebriated by the *suffocating* cloud of loneliness and isolation. The dark and gloomy void that had once captivated me, now made me want to run in the opposite direction. But I had nowhere else to go. These were the only people who couldn't complain or be pained by my presence. Even if they *were* affected by me, they couldn't say that to my face. They couldn't tell me to leave.

"I don't know why I'm here. The last time I came it was so intricately planned out," I said, chuckling humorlessly. "I created this entire detailed blueprint of what I was going to say to you and how I was going to do it. I was so fucking *dramatic*. I still am, clearly," I sighed, running my fingers through the grass, wondering if they were still here . . . and hating the small flicker of disappointment when they weren't.

"Why can't I stop?" I asked her. "Why can't I leave? Why do I feel so *obligated* to them? Like I owe them for something when what did they ever really do for me? *I* raised myself. *I* was there for myself—emotionally, mentally, and physically. I made myself small and invisible just so they didn't have anything extra to worry about. I went out of my way to never get into any trouble, or make any mistakes. I let them *take*, and *suck*, and *drain* everything I had until I was left with absolutely nothing. Or maybe I was just born with nothing. Maybe I was simply created as an empty cocoon with no caterpillar inside waiting to sprout its wings and evolve into a beautiful butterfly." I shook my head at the bleak parallel. "I mean, am I so damaged that I'm completely consumed with the idea of being needed by my parents because that's the only time I've ever received love from them? Am I so preoccupied with this incessant urge to *please* them, because I don't want them to hate me too? Am I so scared that one day they might realize I have nothing more to offer, and their love for me will dry up into dust and I'll have no one?"

"Did I ever really have them, though? Or did I just dump all my self-worth into the desires of my parents, and desperately cling to the twisted concept that I am meaningless without their validating stamp of approval?"

I heard soft steps in the grass behind me, and I immediately shivered at the acute buzz of pleasure that always rushed through me in his presence.

"He's right, you know," I told Ana, but also hoping he could hear me too. "Everything he said was the truth. Anything Noah ever says is the truth, which you would know I guess . . . thank you, by the way. Thank you for making sure he got adopted with you. Thank you for making sure he would get a better life. He deserved it. You *both* did."

"You deserve a better life too, Maya," Noah said from behind me, finally announcing himself. "If you want me to leave, I will."

"How did you know I was here?"

"You could say I know your mind *and* your heart very well."

I turned back and gave him a small smile at his attempt at humor.

"I'm so sorry," he said sincerely.

"Why? You were just being honest."

"It doesn't matter. I could see it on your face . . . how hurt you were by my words—" He broke off, ashamed.

"I *was* hurt by your words," I agreed. "But those wounds were already there, waiting to slice open. You just handed them the knife."

"I wasn't trying to hurt you. I'm so sorry."

"Thank you."

"Thank you?"

I looked into his pained eyes. "No one has ever apologized for hurting me. I was always the one bleeding, yet somehow I was still *always* made out to be the bad guy. So *thank* you for apologizing to me, Noah. I know you weren't trying to hurt me and I forgive you," I sighed, noticing the brown paper bag in his lap. "Is that for me?"

"Yes," he nodded, handing it to me but not moving any closer. "I couldn't let you starve because of my thoughtlessness."

"I don't mind your thoughtlessness. It automatically evens out our unconventional duo," I replied, my stomach growling at the thick bagel he brought me. I ate quietly, not saying anything more. Noah watched me, also not saying anything. It wasn't a comfortable silence. There were so many unsaid words swirling in the heavy air around us, and I was the only one who could release them.

"After my accident," I started in a low voice, "a psychiatrist came in to assess me because I had a . . . *meltdown* when I found out I was still alive. But she wasn't there to see if I was okay. She only came in to tell me that she knew there was nothing wrong with me. She came in and told me, while I was bound up to the bed like a rogue animal, that I had a *victim* complex." I squeezed my eyes shut at the memories. "'He's just *teasing* you, Maya', she said. 'Why are you *overreacting*, Maya?' 'That's how brothers *play*, Maya.'" I was crying now, my words drowning in my mouth. "She wouldn't release me until I said it. Until I repeated her words. Until I admitted it. And then, until I *apologized* to him."

Noah reached for my hand and I took it. "She needs her fucking license revoked."

"She was right, though—about one thing," I told him. "I couldn't see it at the time because I was so *angry*. Angry at Mikhail for lying about what happened. Angry at the universe for teasing me with death, only to shove me back into life. Angry at Ana for stealing my moment and saving me. And angry at *you*, for giving me the one thing I needed to survive when all I wanted was to be free."

"But after you . . . broke up with me, I guess," I said, laughing. "I was sitting in my car, thinking about what you said. You asked me to tell you why I lied, and I had come up completely blank. I couldn't think of how to answer, and I thought it was because I was so overwhelmed in the moment, but I realized later that it was because I had *no* answer. I mean yeah, at first I thought you would hate me, but I was just another transplant patient. Stuff like this happens all the time." I rubbed a strand of grass between my fingers. "And then once I got to know you and experienced how incredible you were . . . there was nothing about you that *proved* you would be angry or blame me for what happened. But I still chose to lie, which left me with only one answer."

"And what would that answer be?" he asked.

"The answer is that I wanted to sabotage myself," I said, meeting his gaze. "The answer is that, deep down, I wanted to be the one to ruin this before you could. All this time I was convinced that I was fighting against my family and the universe trying to drag me down when *I* was the one dragging myself down. My parents, while trying their best, didn't end up *doing* their best for me, and my brother is . . . terrible, but *I* am my own worst enemy, Noah. I'm not just the villain in *his* story, but in mine as well."

"So that's it? Victim or villain? There's no middle ground, it has to be either or?" He shook his head. "Her diagnosis was bullshit, Maya. You don't have a victim complex. You *were* the victim, over and over again, and when no one ever treated you like one you convinced yourself that you were the villain instead. But you don't have to be either of those things."

"They talked about you, you know—the nurses in my room. They thought I was sleeping, so they started talking about this guy who kept coming to the hospital looking for Ana. That's how I learned her name," I told him, the memory unfolding behind my eyes. "They felt bad for you. They couldn't understand why you kept coming back even after her funeral. They thought you were looking for *me*."

"I was," he said gently. "I searched for *months*, Maya. I wanted to find you and apologize. I *needed* to find you and make sure you were okay. I thought maybe my parents lied to spare my feelings when they told me you survived, especially when I never ended up finding you. I wish I looked harder. I wish I had found you *then*, but I'm so fucking grateful that I found you *now*. Now is better than never."

"That's because you were looking in the wrong place," I said, my breathing uneven. "I was immediately moved out of the ICU and onto the psychiatric ward because, according to my brother, *I* caused the accident."

"I'm so sorry he made you go through that. If I could take away all your pain and make it my own I would do it in a heartbeat, no questions asked."

"But you *can't*."

"No, I can't," he agreed regretfully. "I can't take away your pain but I can hold your hand while you face it head-on. You don't have to do this alone."

"That's easier said than done, Noah."

"I know, but it will *get* easier. You just have to do it every day. You just have to start somewhere."

"I always told myself that siblings fight," I whispered. "Every time he hit me, or screamed at me, or called me names, I would repeat that in my head over and over again until I wasn't even sure it had happened at all. I told myself that because *everyone* always talked about it, and laughed about it, and shared their experiences so I just assumed." I paused. "I eventually accepted that this wasn't . . . *normal*, but that just made me feel even worse because then I spent the rest of my life trying to figure out *why*. Why he treated me that way . . . why he couldn't love me . . . and when I couldn't come up with a reason that made sense, I just blamed myself. Because having an explanation was better than having no explanation at all."

"It's not your fault, Maya."

I didn't respond.

"It's not your fault," he repeated softly. "The way your brother treated you isn't your fault."

A small sob broke through my lips. "Then *why*?"

"He's sick—*that's* why. That is the only why."

"Sick people can't pick and choose when and who to be *sick* around."

"That doesn't need to be your problem anymore. *This* doesn't need to be your life anymore, Maya. You can move on from him."

"How, Noah? How do I move on—just like that—without getting anything positive from it? Something meaningful or valid that I can wear as a gold badge of honor to prove my heroic escape from the bad guy?"

"Why do you feel like you need to get something out of it to make it valid?"

"*Because*," I explained desperately. "Because if I just move on, then . . . none of it matters. None of my pain, or damage, or humiliation means anything. It'll be as if it never happened and I just spent all my years being miserable for *nothing*."

He grabbed my chin gently but firmly, forcing me to meet his fervent gaze.

"You," he said fiercely, "are not defined by the things that happened to you. You are defined by the things you made happen *despite* them."

"I didn't make anything happen—"

"*You* happened. This world has given you every reason to be vile and cruel, but instead, you are *kind*. You show love to everyone whether or not they deserve it. You are so good and selfless, and I am in awe of how strong and compassionate you are. *You* are the positive thing that came out of your pain. Your *heart* is your gold badge of honor, Maya."

"My heart?" I repeated. "My heart gave up on me ten years ago."

"I'm not talking about the heart in your chest," he replied. "The one that's only purpose is to pump blood through your veins. I'm talking about *this* one." He brushed my temple lightly. "The one that makes you who you are."

He dropped his hand from my face. "But you don't have to move on alone. I want to fill you up with so much love and joy that it heals all your wounds and replaces all your bad memories with wonderful ones, but I can't do that until you let me. I can't do that until you're *ready*."

I could feel him watching me intensely, waiting. Waiting for me to join him on the other side. Waiting for me to take his hand so I could lift myself from the cliff's edge. Waiting for me to take his hand, not as a life jacket this time, but so that I could finally pull myself out from the bottomless sea I'd spent all my years drowning in. *The cage is open*, I wanted to scream at myself. *Run, flee, leave, get out, get out, GET OUT!*

"Why is this so hard?"

"Because it's all you've ever known," he said softly.

How ridiculously unfair it was that the only thing harder than suffering was trying to move on.

"But that's the beautiful thing about being human, Maya," he continued. "We can always learn to know new things. Nothing is ever set in stone."

I stared at him for a very long time. The love of my life. The brightest spec of light in my labyrinth of darkness. My complete opposite but somehow also my perfect match.

"Okay," I said finally. "I'll move in with you, Noah."

He stood up quickly and grabbed my hand, pulling me up with him and crushing me to his chest. I willed my arms to wrap around him and break free from the restraints of affliction they were shackled in.

"I love you so much," he whispered into my hair. "I love you and I'm going to be with you every step of the way, okay? You will never be alone again."

I raised my arms slowly and wrapped them around him tightly. I wasn't choosing to float this time. I was choosing to learn how to swim.

"I guess I should get my stuff," I said eventually.

He pulled away slightly and brushed my hair out of my face. "Only when you're ready."

"I am, I just . . . my mom is going to be so upset."

"Maybe at first," he said softly. "But you've done *enough*, Maya. You've given enough. You've sacrificed enough. One day they'll understand."

Noah was right. I wasn't going to ask permission this time, only for her forgiveness. But I knew that I'd never truly forgive myself for ultimately breaking her heart.

He glanced at Ana's grave longingly for a few minutes before placing a kiss on his fingers and pressing them against her headstone. "Love you, A. Always."

A. His nickname for Ana. He looked back at me, wiping away the lone tear that had slid from the corner of my eye. I grabbed his hand as we walked out of the cemetery together, toward . . .

His car?

"You drove here?" I asked in shock, staring at the exact truck that hit me, except this one was my favorite shade of green.

"Yeah, it was just quicker and easier to get to you," he replied stiffly.

"What happened to your other car?"

"I got rid of it. I don't know why I insisted on holding on to it for so long."

"Are you . . . okay now? With driving?"

"Yes. No. I don't know."

"Those are all the options," I confirmed.

He let out a breathless chuckle. "I never made a concrete decision to drive, I just wanted to find you."

I brushed his cheek with my hand gently. If he could face

his fears, then so could I.

He was still staring at the car doubtfully without making a move. I slipped my hand into his pocket and pulled out the keys. "How about I drive? You don't know where I live anyway."

He smiled gratefully. "Thank you."

"Don't thank me yet," I warned him, unlocking the car. "I am a *terrible* driver."

~

I pulled up in front of my house and killed the engine.

"This is it," I announced awkwardly. I looked at my house sitting there, appearing so unimpressive in a row of identical duplexes, its coldness illuminated by the faint streetlamps. My stomach dropped when I saw Mikhail's car in the driveway.

"Maya, you know I don't care about—"

"Yeah I know," I interrupted quickly. "Let's just get this horror show over with."

I closed the door and waited for Noah to get out. He took my hand but didn't make a move to start walking. He was letting me lead, as always. I took a deep breath, pushing away all the panic and nerves starting to overpower me, and forced my foot forward.

"One," I whispered under my breath.

"Two," I whimpered, my heart thrashing against my ribcage violently.

"Three," I continued, shoving the memory aside. Noah didn't ask why I was counting. He just waited patiently beside me, only moving when I moved. Shockingly enough, it only took one try to make it to 52. Did my body know this was the last time?

I took my keys out of my pocket, but my hands were

shaking so much I couldn't get it in the hole. I couldn't do this. They were going to be so angry. They were going to be so mad at me—

"Maya," Noah said gently, taking my keys from me. I felt his hand under my chin, tilting my face upwards so he could see me. "I love you, okay? Whatever you decide to do, I love you."

"I want to get my stuff," I told him, my breathing erratic. "I want to get my things and I want to leave. I want to leave and I *never* want to come back."

He nodded and used my key to unlock the door and push it open. I stepped in first, my nerves easing slightly when I only saw my parents sitting in the living room.

"Salam Mama, Baba," I greeted them. "This is Noah, my . . . friend." I cringed at that word, but I was trying to lessen the blow of this situation. Announcing that I was moving out *and* that I had a boyfriend would send my parents into cardiac arrest.

"Oh . . . hi, it's nice to meet you," Mama said after a minute, but my dad stayed quiet, glaring at Noah. I needed to make this quick before they figured out I was lying.

"I'm just going to go upstairs for a minute," I said, slipping my shoes off and heading to the stairs.

"Do you want anything to drink, Noah?" I heard my mom ask. A twinge of agony stabbed through at her kind voice. She was going out of her way to make an effort for me, unlike my dad, and I was about to crush her feelings to the ground. I went into my room and grabbed my old backpack, hastily shoving stuff inside. Lucky for me, I didn't have that many things. I paused before leaving, taking one last look around my small room as my throat filled with sorrow. I looked at my closet regretfully—the place I went to cry. The place I went to scream. The place I went to *pretend*. I looked at the walls littered with scratches, cracks, and dents caused by various parts of my body getting shoved into them.

I used to fantasize about this moment. I would dream about the day when I would pack up my bag, and leave this house and my family forever. Now that my dreams were actually turning into reality, they didn't fill me with the sweet sensation of freedom like I thought they would. They squeezed me with a dire sense of *fear*. I could taste its acidic twang on my tongue as it threatened to devour me whole and force me to change my mind. But *this* wasn't who I wanted to be anymore.

Noah was still standing by the door, chatting with my mother. They both stopped as I walked up beside him.

"Maya?" she asked, looking at the bag in my hand. "What are you doing?"

I swallowed the ball of fear and uncertainty back down my throat. "I'm leaving."

She gasped. "Leaving where?"

"Don't you see, Fatma?" Baba said before I could answer. "She's leaving with *him*. They're dating."

"I'm not leaving *because* we're dating," I said, immediately hearing the insinuation in his voice. "I'm leaving because I need to leave this house."

My mom covered her mouth in shock, but my dad stood up and narrowed his eyes at me.

"What do you mean, you're leaving this house?" he demanded.

Anger flared through me at his tone. Growing up, I eventually learned that my father was the simplest, yet most

LIE

complex creature I would ever encounter. He was basically a large toddle—the way he threw a fit when things didn't go his way. His narrow-minded vision made it impossible for him to see things from anyone else's perspective. It used to make me mad and incredibly frustrated, but I soon discovered that if I just talked to him calmly instead of reacting to his anger with *my* anger, things usually ended smoother.

Usually . . . but not always.

"I mean I'm leaving. I don't want to live *here* anymore."

"Who do you think you are? This isn't how I raised you! I never taught you to disrespect your parents and go running off with some boy we've never seen before. You're going to behave this way for the first person to give you a *sprinkle* of attention?"

"Sir," Noah started, but I squeezed his hand to silence him.

"I don't want to fight, Baba. *Please*," I pleaded.

"Fine then, I'll make this easier for you," he said. "If you take one step out of this house, you are no longer my daughter. Done."

His sharp declaration of disowning me was like a strike across the face. I always bit my tongue, even when he was wrong, out of respect for my elders and his health. It was enough for me that *I* knew he was wrong, even if he never would. I wasn't going to hold back now, though. I wasn't going to stay composed for the sake of keeping the peace, or out of respect.

"I have *never* felt like your daughter. I have never once felt like I was a cherished member of this family."

"Oh give me a break," he said, rolling his eyes. "I put a roof over your head and food in your mouth. You have *nothing* to complain about."

"Yes, Baba, because that's the golden list of parenting and not the bare *minimum*," I snapped. "You were supposed to be my father, and instead you kept me locked up in the same house as that monster you call a son. But I guess it takes little to be a good son, and so much *less* to be a bad daughter, am I right?"

"I know that Mikhail has some issues, but he is your brother——"

"And yet he has never *once* treated me like a sister."

"That's life, Maya! It's filled with tests and hardships that should have made you strong, but instead, you're choosing to run away."

"That should've made me strong?" I repeated in disbelief. "Am I supposed to *thank* Mikhail for trying to make me strong? Am I supposed to be *grateful* for surviving him? I was a child; why did I need to be *strong*?" I asked with genuine curiosity. "I know he's your son and you were just trying to protect him and yourselves from getting sucked into the system, but what about me? Why didn't you notice how his behavior was affecting me? Why didn't you try to protect *me*?"

He sighed and looked away. "If you felt this strongly about your brother then how come you never said anything?"

I thought back to all the times I kept quiet about the things Mikhail had done. I thought back to all the things my *mom* had kept quiet about from my dad because the extra stress wasn't good for his health. But still, he should have *known*. They both should've known better.

"Was I not saying anything, or were you just not listening?"

"What's going on?" Mikhail demanded, appearing by the basement door. I felt Noah tense up beside me. "Who the hell is this guy?"

I glanced at Noah and he had his eyes shut tightly, breathing heavily. I held his hand tightly between mine in an attempt to soothe him, but it wasn't working. His face was pinched together as he tried to restrain himself, and he looked like he was in pain.

"Maya says she's leaving with her *boyfriend*," Baba told him.

"The hell she is," he said darkly, walking toward us. Noah instantly moved forward and stood in front of me. He didn't say anything, but the death glare he gave Mikhail stopped him in his tracks. I could tell it was difficult for him to stay silent. I could tell he wanted to hurt Mikhail for all the years of hurt he gave me, but he didn't.

He chose me over his anger.

Mikhail smirked at Noah and then turned to stare at me. I wasn't looking at him—I never looked directly at him—but I could feel his intense gaze on me, trying to tug me back into the darkness with him. I begged my mind to stay in the present. I willed with all my strength not to shrivel up under his evil stare.

"You're safe," I heard Noah whisper beside me, rubbing my arm. I basked in all his warmth, letting it shield me from Mikhail's foreboding aura.

"Oh my God," I heard Mikhail say. "It was *you*. You're the guy who punched me and then ran away," he laughed in disbelief. "You're going to disrespect your parents for *this* asshole?"

Noah continued to watch me carefully, not bothering to respond to Mikhail's rude remark about him . . . which only encouraged Mikhail to keep talking.

"Let me guess . . . Maya talked to you about me, right?" he laughed incredulously. "What lies did she tell this time?"

I finally looked at him in shock but continued to bite my tongue. I wasn't going to give in. He was *provoking* the part of me that we both shared.

Mikhail sighed dramatically like I was taking too much of his precious time. "Just sit down and let's talk about this like a family, Maya."

My hands instinctively twitched to cover my ears at the way he said my name instead of spitting it out like *vomit*, but it would've been a futile effort. Mikhail was a siren. His words were a manipulative song on the tip of his tongue, ready to bewitch anyone and anything into believing his innocence.

"Let's go, Maya," Noah said gently.

"Are you really falling for the act?" Mikhail asked. "You'll never stop, will you? You'll never stop pretending to be the victim. When will you admit that I *never*—"

"You never what, Mikhail?" I asked furiously, my anger finally giving in and simmering over the edge. "You never *what*? You never *abused* me? You never *terrorized* me? You never *violated* me? You never *manipulated* my doctors and our parents into believing that I was responsible for the accident *you* caused, just so they would lock me up? Tell them. Tell them what you did to me you fucking *coward*, tell them!"

My breath was coming out in frantic puffs of rage as all the years of pain poured out of me.

"You spent my whole life making me out to be this terrible person, just so you could justify the toxic way you treated me!" I shouted. "You will only ever choose to remember and recognize the version of myself that you held the most power over, and the worst part is that I let you. I *believed* you. I gave you the master key into my mind, and I let you convince me that I deserved it. That I wasn't worthy of love. That I wasn't destined for great things. That I was a mistake put on this earth, and my only purpose was to suffer under *your* hands!" I closed my eyes and fought against the torturing memories. "Because, if my own *brother* . . . my own blood and DNA couldn't find it within himself to love me . . . how could anyone else? You were supposed to be my protector, but instead, you were the person I needed protection *from*."

I looked away to collect myself before I broke down. He was *never* going to see me shed even a single tear over him ever again. "But I'm done. I'm done letting you have power over my life. I'm done blaming myself for the mess *you* created. I'm done waiting for you to own up to the things you've done, or for you to ask for my forgiveness because you know what, Mikhail? I. Don't. Forgive. You." I lifted my head and locked eyes with him, enunciating each word. "I *don't* forgive you and I never fucking will." I took an unsteady breath, glancing at my father. "I am *leaving*, and there is nothing you can do or say to stop me. I'm not going to let you keep me imprisoned in the center of all your twisted chaos anymore, and the only way for me to do that is to move out."

They continued to stare at me, stunned into silence. I'd spoken to them more in these last few minutes than I had in all my time living here. It was only temporary, though. Wrong or right, they always needed to have the final word, but this time I wasn't going to stay put long enough to listen.

I took my debit card out of my pocket and put it on the vanity facing the entrance, but before I could take a step through the door I heard a small sob. I whipped my head toward my mother who had been sitting quietly, watching as her family crumbled before her eyes. We had never truly been a family though, and it was time to stop pretending.

"Mama," I said. "*Please*."

She shook her head vigorously, knowing what I was asking without me having to say the words.

"*Mama*," I begged. "Mama, please, you have to let me go. I can't leave until you let me."

I felt something crack inside me as I looked into her eyes. My beautiful mother. My kind and *forgiving* mother. As much as Mikhail hurt me, he hurt her twice as much. She carried him in her womb for nine months and spent hours in agonizing labor, only for him to take her endless cycle of love and squash it into a pile of nothing. Mikhail broke her heart a million times, but she still loved him with every shattered piece. She wasn't perfect, but she did her best. She was placed in an impossible situation, with two impossible choices as a way out—protect her daughter and lose her son forever, or protect her son and lose her daughter forever. It didn't matter which option she chose, which road she crossed, left or right, up or down, sink or swim, red or yellow . . . she would lose either way. But while she was consciously *not* making a choice, she was also subconsciously *making* one too. Every time she turned a blind eye, or made excuses for him, the closer they became and the farther away I went.

I tried to stop it. I tried to force another option, another choice in her path—protect her son *and* keep her daughter forever. I tried to push this twisted and unhinged narrative where Mikhail and I could exist together long enough for her to open her eyes and clearly see which way to go, but we were only prolonging the inevitable. Something that was set in stone the moment my mother held her firstborn child in her hands.

It was always going to be him. She just couldn't bring herself to accept it.

So instead of making her suffer any longer, I made the choice for her. Instead of making her cut the invisible umbilical cord coiled between us, *I* did. Because no matter how many times my mother chose Mikhail, I would continue to choose her.

"It's okay, Mama, I understand. I forgive you," I promised. "But you have to let me go. You have to tell me to go, Mama, please."

She continued to stare at me, tears streaming down her tired and defeated face, but after a moment, I watched in relief as she slowly nodded. I placed my hand on my heart, where she would always live, and headed for the door.

"Do you really think he loves you?"

I froze. His voice . . . he was back. *My* Mikhail was back.

"I mean, maybe he *thinks* he does right now, but once he sees how truly fucked up you are—how fucked up *I* made you—he'll leave. I took everything from you, Maya. I made you *worthless*, so what the fuck could you possibly have left to make him stay?"

"Maya, let's *go*," Noah insisted stiffly, his hand going rigid in mine.

But I couldn't move. I was trapped in Mikhail's tight and suffocating grasp.

"Do you think you're different?" he asked. I could feel him beside me, whispering in my ear, lips barely grazing skin. "You think you're *better* than me, I know you do. I see the way you look at me . . . like I'm *beneath* you. I heard the way Mama and Baba always praised your good grades and your *perfect* behavior," he spat in disgust. "I tried to do you a favor and show you who you truly are, but you still managed to convince yourself you're better than me and now—" he chuckled in disbelief "——you've convinced yourself that someone actually *loves* you."

"Maya, don't listen to him," Noah pleaded. "Let's go."

"You've got it all wrong though, Maya," Mikhail said softly from behind me. "You and I are one in the same. We are *exactly* the same."

I didn't know why I was so shocked by his words when they were the same words I always thought to myself. That I was truly my brother's sister. But hearing them come out of his mouth . . . they sounded so foreign and unintelligible. Like gibberish.

I turned around and faced him. He was smirking at me like he *won*. "You know, I used to think the same thing. But . . . roses and thorns grow from the same roots, Mikhail. One of them lives to hurt people, while the other lives to be a symbol of love."

His smile disappeared from his face and he narrowed his eyes at me, but for once, he remained quiet.

"And for the record, I never thought I was better than you, but I am. I am *better* than you. You *huff* and you *puff* and you *flex* your muscles, but deep down you're just an angry, pathetic and insecure boy who uses violence against women—violence against your *sister*—to make up for everything you lack." I continued to stare him down fiercely, instead of shrinking under his gaze like a cloud making room for the sun. I was *thunder*. "You might be my brother and you might be my blood, but you will *never* be my family."

I turned away from him for the last time and left my house. Noah opened the passenger door for me and then headed for the driver's side no questions asked. I put my seatbelt on as he started the car, staring straight ahead, breathing hard.

"Maya?"

"I thought he was going to apologize," I whispered. "I thought after I said all of those things . . . after I said that I *wouldn't* forgive him . . . I still thought he might apologize to me." I laughed humorlessly. "He really *did* fuck me up."

"That doesn't make you fucked up, Maya," Noah disagreed gently. "That makes you *good*. It's a shame he never appreciated what a kindhearted and special sister he had."

"It doesn't even matter," I said, turning toward him. "He finally *acknowledged* it. He finally admitted it. He finally released me from the suffocating noose he had tied around my neck. The noose that was completely made up of my all-consuming doubt. He finally set me free."

"You are so strong," Noah said softly. "You will take back everything he stole from you. The next chapter of your life starts now, okay?"

I nodded shakily, still not comprehending . . .

"Maya?" he said again, waiting until I looked at him before he continued. "I'm so proud of you."

I gave him a small smile, hoping one day I could be proud of myself too.

"Wait." I placed my hand over his on the clutch before he could put it in drive, and turned to look at my house one more time. I looked at the porch—52 steps away—that I sat on for hours every day after school to avoid going inside. I looked at the driveway where it all started when Mikhail slashed my bike tires. I wondered briefly if my future would have turned out differently, had I just told my parents after he shoved me down the stairs. I pushed the thought away and searched my brain for a good memory. Just *one* happy memory from my time living in this house but I came up completely blank.

My fingers unclenched against the key in my hand, its shape indented red in my palm, and without another thought, I unhooked it from my lanyard and threw it out the window. It landed with a *clink* on the edge of the curb right before the grass began to sprout. The same place my trembling, anxious, frightened foot always took its first step. My number *one . . .* but never again. I would never complete that torturous path of 52 ever again.

"We can go now."

"Are you sure?" Noah asked and I nodded. "Okay then. Let's go home."

Home? Mikhail was a gas leak in my *home*. His poison odorless and colorless, but extremely deadly. And then thirteen years ago on my twelfth birthday, he took it a step further. He lit a fire in my eyesight, and I took the bait, letting my body—my *home*—completely burst up in flames.

When Noah told me he wanted to help me heal, I immediately assumed that he wanted to *save* me, so I rejected the idea in its entirety. That wasn't what he was saying at all. He wasn't trying to hand me the water I needed to extinguish the flames that were slowly licking my skin into charcoal. He was trying to open my eyes to the possibility that *I* was the one holding the match, not Mikhail, and all I had to do was stop lighting it.

No . . . Noah didn't save me. I saved *myself* when I carried on through all my heartache with weak and brittle bones. When I dragged my cold body off the shower floor instead of letting the water suck me through the drain and into oblivion. When I took care of myself as best as I could while the universe was trying so fucking hard to bleed me dry. Whether or not I wanted to, I still did it . . . and then I did it again, and again,

353

and *again*. It wasn't a valiant or thunderous effort, but it was enough. I was still *here*, stuck in the grey realm between surviving and living, and I just needed to push through to the other side.

I looked back at my house one more time before we turned the corner. I wasn't leaving my home, and I wasn't going to my new home either. It didn't matter where I went or where I lived, because it was time for me to start rebuilding the home within myself.

THEN

Dear Ana,

My parents kicked Mikhail out.

It wasn't without reason. He tried to kill me again—shocker, I know. I accidentally fell asleep and woke up with him on top of me. My mom saw him and . . . well, I'll save you the typical gory details. Leave it to Mikhail to exit with one final bang I'll never forget. She made excuses for him, begged me not to call the police, and then—after setting him up with an apartment and a monthly allowance like a fucking child—they kicked him out.

I didn't believe her, of course. I was convinced she only said that to keep me quiet, but then a few weeks later I came back from school and his room was empty. No goodbye. No apology. I was prepared to feel relieved, Ana. This is what I've been waiting for . . . but I'm not relieved. In fact, now that I think about it, the only time I've ever felt genuine relief was when I thought I was going to die.

It's not like I haven't thought about it before. Sometimes when I'm driving, I think about swerving into traffic . . . a truck would end things quickly, right? Or if I accidentally missed a step while walking down the concrete staircase at school . . . head injuries are the most common source of termination—at least, I would assume they are.

But regardless of how many times the thought has crossed my mind, I never do it. I push the image out of my head and keep driving according to the rules of the road. I take a deep breath and securely hold onto the railing until I've reached the bottom step unscathed. I don't do that because I want to live. I don't do that because I think I'll be missed, or because I care that all my thoughts and memories will become nonexistent. The reason I haven't taken myself out of the equation of life is because of . . . Him.

I wouldn't call myself a very religious person. I wouldn't call myself a religious person, period. *There are only a few things I truly resonated with—God only put you through what He knew you could handle, and suicide is a sin.*

I wasn't born thinking about taking my own life, so it wasn't something I ever had to worry about. But you could say my existence was rough from day one, and the only thing I had to fall back on was that God thought I was strong. God thought I was dedicated and brilliant, and I was so honored to be chosen out of all His creations to tackle these difficult hardships. It was a privilege, and I was determined to fulfill His trials with my head held high. I was filled with faith. Faith that if I just kept pushing through my pain and suffering, God would eventually reward me with ease in the end.

But then something happened, Ana. My faith slowly got chipped away with each test that got thrown my way, until it disappeared completely. Every time I got shoved to the ground, I was convinced it was the last time. I was convinced my life could only get better. I was convinced God was done, and He was going to show me the light . . . but He didn't, and instead hit me with His wrath again, and again, and again.

That's when I realized rock bottom doesn't exist. The limit to how much you can suffer doesn't exist. This world is just an endless game to see who can be the last one standing, but I want out. I don't want to win, Ana. I used to feel honored, but what if I'm reading it wrong? What if it wasn't an honor, but instead a punishment? Who's to say what's real? What if this never-ending cycle of torture was just my specifically curated version of hell? There was a moment when I woke up after my accident when I wondered if I was actually dead. What if I was right? What if I really did die that day? What if when I heard my heart stop beating, it had actually stopped *beating?*

It sounds ridiculous, and maybe my mind is too exhausted and wounded to think straight, but if I'm wrong then why hasn't He proved it yet? I did everything right, but He still turned His back on me. I tried so hard, Ana. I tried so hard to trust His plan, and believe that everything happens for a reason, but I think I'm done. I think it's time for me to give up. To make this more meaningful, I'll wait until the tenth anniversary of your death. I'll give Him five more years. Five more years to give me a sign, or a reason worth fighting for. After that though, I'll finally do the deed. I'll finally carve a new plan for myself like I should have just done from the start. It won't be gruesome, or painful. It won't be messy, or loud. I lived my entire life quietly . . . all I want is to die in the same way. The hospital prescribed me a bottle of opioids after my accident, but I never used them. I welcomed the pain from my physical injuries because it preoccupied me from feeling the agony raging on in my mind. I'm no doctor, but I'm pretty sure they'll do the trick.

People will think I'm selfish. People will judge my rotting corpse at my funeral and wonder how I could do that to my parents and all my loved ones. What they don't understand is that I am already dead. I am simply a hollow shell, with organs forcing me to stay alive while I deteriorate emotionally. I have nothing left to live for, Ana. My grades are slowly plummeting, and I have no urge to further my education after I graduate. I can't imagine living long enough to face the embarrassment of having no career and having to feel the judgment and disappointment from my parents. My aspirations in life have shifted entirely. How is it fair for me to deprive myself of what I truly need? My biggest problem is that I always put others first . . . well, I learned my lesson now. Besides, people might be sad for a little while, but they'll get over it. No one can dwell over a zombie, because they were never meant to be alive in the first place.

And hey, if I'm already dead, then killing myself shouldn't do anything, right? I should just wake up back in my room, right in the center of all my misfortune. If I'm really dead then nothing will happen, and if not, well, maybe I can finally meet my maker and get the answers I always needed.

With that being said, I think this will be my last letter. I'm sorry I didn't do your heart justice, Ana. I'm sorry I'm not going to continue your life through me, but . . . thank you. Thank you for being a source of comfort during the last five years, even though none of it was real. Thank you for being there for me when no one else was. In a sick and twisted way, you were kind of my best friend. I still hate you for saving me, but it helped a little, to feel heard and seen. But I have no more words to say to you. I have nothing left in me to give, so I guess this is goodbye. For now, at least. Maybe I'll see you on the other side, Ana. But if not, I promise to think about you for the rest of my miserable journey in hell.

NOW

I pulled into Bayan's driveway and killed the engine, waiting for her to come out.

She texted me back a few nights after I got settled in at Noah's apartment. Part of me wanted to be petty and not respond so she knew how it felt, but the bigger part of me knew that was immature. There was another part though—smaller than the others but somehow more powerful—that wondered if she would even notice if I didn't text her back.

"Hey," she greeted. "Did you get a new car? Congrats!"

"Um, no I didn't," I replied, backing out of her driveway. "It's Noah's car."

"Who's Noah?"

For a moment I completely forgot our phone conversation all those months ago was pretend.

"He's . . . my boyfriend, I guess. I met him when I visited Ana's grave back in December. He's her brother."

"*What?*"

"Yeah," I nodded.

"Does he know who you are?"

"He does *now*. I kind of . . . lied to him about it."

"How did he take it?"

The memory of me screaming outside his door flickered in my mind. "He was really, really mad."

"Wait, actually?"

"He had every reason to be. I lied to him every single day we were together. But he forgave me," I told her as we went through the Starbucks drive-through. "He's the one who hit me with his car that day. That's how Ana died."

"*What*?!" she screeched loudly. We were at the window now, so instead of responding I told the barista our orders and continued through the line. Once we got our drinks I parked in our usual spot and told her everything. Well, everything she *needed* to know.

"That's so crazy," she said when I was done. "Your parents probably freaked out."

"That's an understatement," I muttered.

She regarded me seriously for a moment. "Do you love him?"

"I do, yeah," I said with a chuckle. "It's still so strange feeling like this, but I've never been more sure of anything before. I am so completely in love with that dude."

"I knew there was something different about you when I came in the car," she said, smiling. "I can't believe you never told me about any of this."

You never asked, I thought, looking away. She stayed quiet, waiting for me to respond. Waiting for me to tell her why. I didn't want to lie, but I also didn't want to tell her the truth because I didn't know how she would react, and I didn't want to fight. We always talked about how we never argued, and how that made our friendship so special but maybe that was our problem. Maybe we *should* fight.

"You never asked," I said out loud this time.

"That's not fair," she replied, surprise lacing her voice.

"I know it's not fair of me to think like that, but . . ." I hesitated for a minute. "You never really seem interested anymore. I always ask you about everything, and you used to always ask *me* about everything too until you just stopped. I know it's not personal—or maybe it *is* personal—but either way, I noticed. And as much as I wish that it didn't, it hurt my feelings."

The car filled with a cloud of uncomfortable silence as she pondered my words. "I'm sorry," she said finally.

"I don't want an apology from you, Bayan, I just . . ." I finally looked at her, but I couldn't read her expression. "What happened to us? We used to tell each other everything. We used to hang out every day. You were my *person*."

"And now?" she asked, an edge to her voice.

"And now . . . I can't help but wonder that if I never reached out first, would we be hanging out right now? Would we ever speak again?"

"*Of course* we would. Where is this coming from?"

"Don't," I said with chagrin. "Don't act like this is all in my head. Things between us have been different for a long time and we just keep ignoring it. But then again, maybe things have always been one-sided and I'm only just now realizing it."

"What's that supposed to mean?"

"I'll be the first to admit that I came into this friendship pretty strong. I know that I can get a little . . . clingy," I admitted, cringing slightly. "But it's only because I love you so much. It's only because I was *excited*. I was so fucking excited that I finally found my best friend, and I had so much love to give. I guess I just assumed that one day you would eventually be at the same level as me, but you never did, and now we're just sitting awkwardly on this uneven see-saw."

"Maya, I don't understand . . . is this because I didn't text you back?" she asked, genuinely mystified.

"It's not weird to get offended when your best friend takes one to three business months to reply to your texts with a simple *hello*, if you even reply at all. But it's not about that."

"Then what is this about?"

"Why didn't you ever ask?"

"About the Noah thing?"

"No, why didn't you ever ask about *me*?" I snapped, harsher than I intended.

"I don't understand," she repeated.

I sighed, instantly regretting saying anything in the first place. "How is it that Noah—a total stranger at the time—took one look at me and knew I wasn't doing okay, but you never did?"

She averted her eyes away from mine and looked out the window instead of answering, but it didn't matter. I already knew the answer. I was almost positive that a part of me always knew, and I just never wanted to admit it to myself.

"That's not it though, is it? You *did* notice; you just didn't care."

"It's not that I didn't care," she disagreed. "I knew you were going through stuff . . . I just didn't know *how* to be there for you."

I closed my eyes against the sting of her words. "Listening would've sufficed. Merely *asking* would've been enough. I always listened to you when you needed to vent. I was always *there* for you. It was a privilege for me to be a source of comfort to you. It wasn't something I had to think about, it was simply second nature."

"I'm sorry," she said again, and I knew she meant it.

"I'm sorry, too. I'm sorry for taking what should've been a simple and fun friendship and turning it into something bigger and more complicated in my head," I told her quietly. "I guess I didn't realize I was subconsciously expecting things from you, and when you didn't deliver I would get hit with this extreme wave of disappointment, which quickly turned into guilt. I expected so much from you, Bayan, which was wrong of me, but . . . I never expected more than what I was willing to offer you. Which still isn't fair, but it doesn't make me a bad friend. It doesn't make *you* a bad friend either, and that just makes this so much harder."

"Makes *what* so much harder?"

"I have a lot going on right now. My life recently blew up, and I'm still trying to carve my way through all the destruction left behind. I don't want to have to keep putting up a charade of happiness to make people feel comfortable. I don't know, I guess I just need to be around people who *want* to be there for me."

"Maya, it's not that I *didn't* want to," she started again.

"I know, and I'm not mad. It was never your responsibility to be there for me, and that doesn't mean you didn't love me. It *hurt*, but if I'm being honest with myself, I think the real reason it hurt so much was that it made me internalize my own insecurities, and then come up with all these reasons why you never . . ."

I finally looked at her, all our memories and happiest moments lingering in the air between us. "I forgive you. I forgive you for not being there for me when I needed someone. I forgive you for not knowing *how* to be there for me when I needed someone, and I will never regret being that someone for you."

She gave me a small smile and clicked her seat belt into place as I started the car. Nothing more was said on the car ride back to her house, but I think we both knew what was happening anyway. What *needed* to happen. I stopped the car and waited, but she stayed put.

"So . . . are we just not going to be friends anymore?" she asked after a moment.

I swallowed down the lump in my throat. "You'll always be my best friend, but for the time being . . . I think we should stop forcing our paths to align and . . . go our separate ways."

She still didn't make a move to leave the car, and I didn't want her to either. But this wasn't about what I wanted.

"I don't want to be thinking about you," I whispered. "I don't want to be constantly wondering if you're waiting for me to ask you to hang out, and I don't want to be constantly wondering why you *aren't* asking me to hang out. I love you so much and I would drop everything for you in a second . . . but right now that's not what I need. Right now I need to focus on loving myself, instead of being consumed with my love for other people." She nodded before finally stepping out of my car and shutting the door behind her. I leaned back against my seat, waiting until she got inside before I left.

I loved her. God, I loved her *so* much and *so* hard that my love had grown into an extension of myself. A third arm, or a sixth toe. But that wasn't normal and it needed to get *removed*. Maybe not forever, but definitely for now.

She was my best friend. My twin flame, and unfortunately, over time, flames burned out. But sometimes they could get lit up again. If it was truly meant to be, sometimes the blackened end of the match can miraculously pick up a new spark and come back to life even brighter than before. But that wasn't important. I needed to stop running away and start dealing with all my shit. I needed to heal and figure out who I was outside of all my pain, and it wasn't fair for me to drag her along for the bumpy ride when that wasn't what she wanted. This didn't have to be goodbye. Maybe it could just be . . . a pause. Maybe we could meet again, once I was whole and new. Maybe we could make it work when I was finally in a place where I didn't need anything more than what she could offer.

"Noah?" I called out, looking around the empty café. I faintly saw some movement behind the white tarp and quickly walked toward the bookstore. I pushed it out of the way, and my eyes widened as I looked around the . . . *finished* bookstore? The last time we were here, we'd only completed about three-quarters of the paint job, but obviously, he had been working on it without me. The walls were done, and there were bookshelves stacked by each wall. There was a desk by the door, with a monitor and a register waiting to check out its first happy customer. And there, in the middle of the room, was Noah, smiling brightly. He was sitting on a blanket with a bunch of candles illuminating the room, and a covered dish with plates and utensils.

"What's all this?" I asked, taking a seat beside him.

"Well, you didn't get a proper welcome home party so we're celebrating today," he said, taking my hand in his.

"When did you finish the store?"

"A few days ago," he replied, tugging my glove off and placing his lips on the back of my hand. "Ravi helped me. I left the organizing and decorating part for you, though."

"Thank you," I said sincerely, lifting the top off of the steaming pan. "Lasagna?"

"Your favorite," he said, letting go of my hand and cutting me a piece. "How's Bayan? Did you have a nice time?"

I took my plate instead of answering him. It smelled delicious, almost as good as the one my mom used to always make for me. I wondered if I would ever get to taste it again, or if she was going to be out of my life forever too.

"Maya?" Noah said, noticing my shift in demeanor.

"Is it such a crime to want people to care about me just as much as I care about them?" I asked quietly. "Even if I care way too much?"

"No," he responded immediately. "But . . . just because they can't care about you the way you want them to, doesn't mean they don't care about you at all."

"So then I shouldn't have been upset that she never reached out to me? That she never *asked* if I was okay?"

"Of course you can be upset. We can't control how our emotions choose to react to things, but . . . not everyone is capable of comforting you in the way you need them to. It's not always personal, though."

I nodded slowly, the lump in my throat returning full force. "So me . . . pushing her away *wasn't* the right thing to do."

"If you did it because you know it'll benefit you, then it *was* the right thing. We're allowed to have boundaries, even if not everyone can understand them."

"I guess," I sighed, his words relieving me slightly. "It's just embarrassing; you know? I always felt like my love for her was almost . . . obsessive, or something. Like it wasn't normal to care about someone *that* much. In the end, it's my fault. My fault for constantly loving people so intensely that it literally *consumes* me, and then getting butt hurt when they can't do the same."

"Look at me," he said, taking my hand again and pulling me closer to him. He ran his fingers along my jaw softly, waiting until I met his gaze. "Don't ever apologize for caring. There's no such thing as caring *too* much, okay? The way you love is precious, and your heart is so pure. The selfless and unconditional way that you care about people is rare, baby. Never change."

He pressed his lips on my forehead. "Is that it then? You guys aren't friends anymore?"

I glanced back down at my plate. "I don't know. We didn't fight or anything, which I appreciated. I was honest with her, and she was honest with me. But . . . despite knowing that this was the right thing to do, there was still a part of me hoping that she *would* fight for me. Fight for our *friendship*. Now I'll never know if it's because she was respecting my space, or because I finally gave her the out she was waiting for." I took a deep breath and wiped away the solitary tear that appeared in the corner of my eye. "I never made this decision because I was starting to love her any less, but because I always loved *myself* less when she could never . . . anyway what's done is done. I'll always want her to be a part of my future, but if not . . . she'll still hold a permanent place in my heart," I chuckled, my face warming up. "That's not even what I wanted to talk to her about."

"What did you want to talk to her about?"

"*You.*" He looked at me quizzically. "I was so excited to finally tell someone about you . . . to talk about how I *felt* about you . . . to talk about how you made me feel . . ."

Noah blushed, and my heart skipped several beats at the sight. "You can always talk to *me* about me."

"You know how I feel about men and their egos."

He nodded, my favorite dimpled smile on his pink face, and we began eating in comfortable silence. His lasagna was delicious, of course, and I completely inhaled my plate before immediately getting seconds.

"How do you think you're going to organize the books?" he asked between bites.

"Well, I don't want to do the typical genre or author pattern. I feel like most readers choose books based on their moods, so I was thinking one shelf could be: books that ripped my heart out and broke it into a million pieces." He snorted. "Another one could be: books that transported me into a different dimension, and took me on a supernatural journey filled with magic and fictional creatures. And then the classic: books that made me lay in bed and contemplate my whole existence for days. Those are my favorite."

"This will definitely be the most unique bookstore that anyone will ever walk into," he concluded. "I have a big order of inventory coming in this week, so you'll be able to start soon."

"I don't even know when I'll have time," I groaned. "They scheduled me almost every night this week."

He was silent for a moment. "So quit."

"I can't quit, Noah, I'm still helping my parents out."

"The store should be ready within a few weeks, so you can just come work here. With me."

I moved the last few bites of food around my plate. I figured we were going to have this conversation sooner or later, but that didn't make it any less awkward for me. I knew he was just trying to help and I didn't want to be difficult, but . . .

"I'm not comfortable with you *paying* me. Especially now

that I'm living here rent-free, and using your car that somehow always has a full tank of gas."

"I pay all my employees," he disputed calmly. "And there is no rent to pay when I *own* this property, so I don't understand what the issue is."

I put my plate down, my appetite vanishing completely. He made a strong argument, almost like he'd prepared it beforehand. He'd gotten so good at understanding my face and hearing my unspoken words. How could I accept what he was offering, though? This wasn't how I imagined things would pan out. When I pictured my life after my family, I was still doing everything for myself, just like I had always done.

"This doesn't make you any less independent or capable, Maya," Noah said softly, reading my mind. He placed his warm hand on mine, halting my movements. I looked down, not realizing that I had absently started picking away at the skin around my fingernails. "Don't do that. Don't get sucked back into that toxic cycle of self-sabotage. It's whispering things into your ear because it doesn't want to let you go. I know it's hard, but you need to push it out. You need to tell it to get the fuck *out*."

I let his words swirl around in my brain, but something was blocking them from sinking in. Something that had its talons planted deep into my core and didn't want to let go. I didn't mind its presence before because it took up so much space in my head that there was barely any room for the pain. But that meant there was also no room for the happiness, either. I couldn't pick and choose what to let in, it had to be all or nothing.

"I don't know how to get to where you are, Noah."

"How did we learn to walk and talk? One step and syllable

at a time." He leaned in closer and gently tilted my chin toward him, forcing me to meet his gaze. "It's going to be really hard for a while, but one day you'll wake up and it'll suddenly be second nature. Do you remember what you said to me when we first met?"

"I said a lot of things, you're going to have to be more specific," I replied with a smirk.

He grinned. "You told me that healing is messy. And you were right."

"I'm pretty sure I stole that from somewhere."

"That's okay," he chuckled, before getting serious again. "You don't need to figure everything out right now, but let's settle on one thing, please? You can continue to take care of your family, but I am going to take care of you, *with* you. We'll take care of each other. You're mine."

I raised my eyebrows. "Yours?"

"Yes, *mine*," he repeated firmly, narrowing his eyes. "And I am *yours*. Do you have a problem with that?"

"I don't know; I've never really belonged to anyone before."

"Then I'll just have to be your first."

"And my *last*, Noah."

He leaned down and brushed his mouth on mine. "You have blessed me with the greatest honor, *habibti*."

I sighed. "I guess I'm quitting."

He smiled against my lips. "Wow, I didn't realize you were capable of being reasonable."

"Don't let this win get to your head," I warned him. "And I'm still keeping my other job at the hospital."

"Then I'll just have to get injured more often," he replied, kissing me again.

I laughed. "Obsessed much?"

"*Obsession* is an understatement," he whispered, his warm breath tickling my face. "My entire being *aches* for you in your absence. My heart beats your name against my chest with a heightened sense of desperation, and it can only be soothed by the tantalizing flavor of your presence in the air."

"Okay, settle down," I teased, but *I* was the one not settled. His words lit my frozen heart on fire, melting my entire existence into a pile of throbbing desire at his feet.

"What did I say about you telling me to settle down?" he asked, low and seductive. His lips were back on mine, all traces of gentle caresses disappearing. He pulled me into his lap, neither of us caring about the plates that clattered beside us, and demonstrated just how *obsessed* he was.

~

"I can't believe I fell for a skater . . . man," I stated, looking down at the skateboard. It was warm out today and he suggested we skateboard to Tysons so I could officially quit. I assumed he was joking, but he was being completely serious.

Noah chuckled. "Is that disappointment I detect?"

"No. The hair, the body, and now this? You are *exactly* my type."

"This is an electric one—does that still count as your type?"

"Oh, well, that's just cheating."

"I have a normal one too, but you'd probably fall off."

"I'm probably going to fall off *this* one."

"You'll be holding onto me the entire time," he assured me, placing the bulky helmet over my head.

"You seem a little *too* confident . . . have you done this before?" I asked, and then something occurred to me. "How

371

many other girls have you tried this with?"

He laughed. "None, silly."

"I'm curious now," I started slowly. "How many girls have you dated?"

He buckled the straps under my chin and tucked my hair behind my ears. "Why do you want to know?"

"I don't know, but tell me anyway."

He glanced down at me for a minute speculatively. "Six."

"Huh," I said surprised. "I never figured you to be a lady's man. How long was your longest relationship?"

"*Ours*," he said, kissing my nose. "No more stalling, Maya. I promise I won't let you fall."

"This thing was designed for one person though, not *two*. You're fighting with the laws of gravity at this point."

"True . . ." he agreed softly. "But I am not whole without you, so you could say that together we still make *one*."

"I just know that mister Newton is rolling around in his grave right now because someone is trying to dispute all his hard work with *love*." I blushed, smiling cheekily. I would never get used to hearing him say stuff like that. "But you did sway me," I sighed and carefully stepped onto the board, holding his hand for support. He placed his feet on both sides, making sure I was balanced properly. I wrapped my arms around his torso gently and watched the world pass by us in a blur. I hated to admit it, but it was actually fun.

"Are you okay?" Noah yelled over the wind whipping past us.

I nodded, tightening my grip on him. Before I knew it we rolled into the Tysons parking lot, and he slowed down. I looked at the doors anxiously, already wishing that I had just sent her an email instead of quitting in person.

"Don't be nervous," he assured me, taking my helmet off. "Do you know what you're going to say?"

"Yes. I'm going to tell Michelle that I enjoyed working for her, but I got another job. Then I'm going to walk into Sheila's office and I'm going to call her a bitch, and that for someone who only made like twenty cents more than me, she really let the power get to her head."

He laughed and smoothed my hair down. "Good luck. I'll be out here when you're done."

I nodded and walked into the store before I could chicken out. I waved at some of my coworkers on my way to the break room, feeling a little sad that I would probably never see them again. Working here sucked, but despite a select few, the people here were all great and I was going to miss them.

I knocked on her door and stepped inside after she told me to come in. "Hey, do you have a minute?"

"Yeah of course," she replied, pointing to the chair across from her. "What's up?"

"Um, I'm sorry to do this without any notice, but . . . I'm quitting."

Her face fell. "Awe, really? Did you get another job?"

"Yeah," I said smiling apologetically. "There's a new bookstore opening up downtown, and I'm going to be running it."

"You always were reading on your break," she said kindly. "I loved having you, Maya, so I'm sad you'll be leaving us. But that sounds like a fun experience and I'm proud of you. I hope you enjoy it."

"Thank you, Michelle. I enjoyed working with you."

"Hey Michelle," Sheila interrupted. "Oh, are you busy?"

Obviously, I thought. "It's fine, I was done anyway."

"Maya's leaving us," Michelle told Sheila before I could take another step.

"Oh no, really?" she said. I repressed the urge to roll my eyes at her fake tone. We both knew that she wasn't going to miss me. Actually, scratch that. She *would* miss having someone to bully in her free time. Hopefully, she didn't find a replacement after I was gone. "Well, it was certainly a pleasure working with you."

I looked at her and paused for a moment. My rehearsed statement was sitting on my tongue, eagerly waiting to slap her across the face. She was smiling at me and her expression reminded me of Mikhail. It was *goading*. She knew that *I* knew the way she treated me was unfair, and she wanted me to say something about it.

"It was a pleasure working with you too, Sheila," I said, smiling warmly back at her. "I wish you well." I gave her one last smile before stepping around her and leaving Michelle's office.

I knew she would think she'd won, but honestly, I didn't care. I wasn't going to dignify her unprofessional behavior with a response. Not everything needed a reaction. Being the bigger person didn't mean I was weak and couldn't defend myself, it just meant I was selective with what and who deserved my energy. And some bored, middle-aged assistant manager with raccoon eyeliner definitely did *not* make that list.

Noah was leaning against the wall when I came out. I admired the view for a minute—the way the setting sun illuminated his flawless skin, and how his water-colored eyes glowed under the sharp golden rays beaming down on him as he absently rolled his skateboard back and forth. My deep affection for him hit me forcefully as I kept watching, but it wasn't because of his beauty. It wasn't because he was kind, or because he offered me this new and amazing opportunity, or even because *he* loved *me*. I loved him because not once since the moment we met did he ever try to change me. Even when I was a little mean, or sad, or secretive . . . he continued to accept me. I spent all my years modifying my image into what others wanted to see, but I never had to do that with Noah. I was already the person he wanted, simply by being myself.

I stepped onto the board and kissed him, taking him by surprise.

"I'm guessing it went well," he whispered against my lips.

"I didn't do it."

"Didn't quit?" he asked in disbelief.

"No, I *quit*. But I didn't, you know, tell Sheila off."

"I knew you wouldn't," he said softly. "I love that about you."

"I don't know about *love* . . . but I think I'm starting to like that about me too."

"One day you're going to love every single part that makes you, *you*. But until then, I'll happily love you enough for the both of us. I'll love you enough to fill a billion hearts." He kissed me gently. "The parts you hate will always receive an *infinite* amount of love from me, Maya."

"What book did you crawl out of, and why haven't I read it?" I said, looking away as my face blushed.

"Probably because it hasn't been *written* yet."

"What do you mean?"

"I've been thinking about what you told me at my parents' house. About how you've always wanted to write a book."

"Yeah, I also talked about how I didn't have any *ideas* to

turn into a book."

"You don't need to come up with an idea when your whole life is basically the plotline of an epic novel."

It took a few minutes but eventually, his words sunk in and I was able to comprehend what he was saying. "You want me to write a book about my *life?*"

"Maya," he said seriously, taking my face in his hands. "Did you know that sibling abuse is a common type of abuse that occurs within families, yet it's rarely ever talked about? They call it the silent pandemic."

"Noah, I'm trying to move on from my past. How am I supposed to write a book about my life without reliving the entire thing?"

"Well, you've already written half of it . . . wouldn't you agree?" he said, referring to my journal. "Look, it's completely up to you, but I think . . . I think this might be good for you. Tell your story, Maya. Tell the world your story, and raise awareness about the things you went through. Maybe it will help someone that's going through the same thing. Maybe it will help *you* put your past to rest, so you can finally create a new story for yourself."

I didn't know what to say, so I just looked at the setting sun behind him, pondering his words.

"Like I said, it's completely up to you. But I think you could create something beautiful."

I leaned my head against his chest and wrapped my arms around his waist, his heart beating erratically in my ear as we skated back to the cafe. His words swirled around in my mind the whole way there . . . could I do that? Could I write a book about my life? It sounded crazy and way too embarrassing, especially if someone I knew read it. Why did I *care*, though?

Why was I still trying to hide away from my past, when I could just own it, accept it, and then hopefully move on?

I felt Noah's lips brush my cheek, pulling me out of my thoughts. "I'm sorry if I overstepped, it was just a thought."

"You didn't overstep. I was just surprised—that idea never occurred to me before."

"Alright, but there's no pressure here. You can do whatever you want, as long as you're happy doing it."

I smiled warmly at him as he unlocked the door. We walked through the café, but he stopped in the kitchen.

"I just have a few things left to do before we open tomorrow."

"Okay, I'll help."

"It will only take a minute," he assured me. "Go get ready for bed."

I nodded. "Noah?"

He looked back at me immediately. "Yeah, baby?"

"I love you."

His eyes widened slightly, surprised into momentary silence by the three little words spoken from my lips, despite him saying them to me at least a million times a day. It was no secret that expressing affection rendered on the side of awkward for me, given my past, but he never seemed to mind. The look on his face right now—pink, dimpled, *glowing*—made me want to change that forever.

"I love you too, pretty girl."

I left him in the kitchen while he did what he needed to do and got changed for bed. My eyes landed on my journal after I finished brushing my teeth and I hesitated. Avoiding things had been my coping mechanism for so long that it became this essential habit I couldn't live without. I turned away from anything and everything I thought might make me anxious, in the hopes that it would just take care of itself and disappear. I was always so terrified the outcome of things I wanted would end up being negative, that I just never even bothered to try. But I couldn't avoid reading my letters forever. I owed it to myself to at least try. I knew that the only way to truly heal from my past was to rip off the bandages that covered all my wounds and properly treat them this time.

Before I could overthink it, I flipped it open to the last empty page and started writing . . .

Dear Ana,

Hey, it's been a minute. Based on the last letter I wrote five years ago, you're probably surprised to be hearing from me again. Even though I could never actually kill myself, thinking about killing myself made things simpler. But it was a permanent solution to a temporary problem, and I know that now. I knew that then too, deep down, which was why I never did it.

I don't judge you, by the way, about the whole Noah thing. How could anyone not fall in love with him? I get that you didn't choose to fall in love with him because I didn't either. All I really wanted was to be his friend, I swear, but then I got to know him and that flutter of love started to creep up on me softly, until one day I thought I lost him forever, and that flutter transformed into an intense wave that completely consumed me. All I wanted was a drop of love, but he gave me an entire rainstorm. All I wanted was a single star to wish on, but he offered me the entire fucking galaxy and then helped me make each of them come true. I'm sorry he couldn't give you what you wanted, but he did give you the one thing you needed, *even though you didn't realize it at the time. The one thing I needed, but will never have. He gave you a brother, Ana.*

I thought about writing to you for a while now, but today seemed like the perfect time. Noah suggested I use these letters and all the horrible things I've gone through to write a book. It sounds silly, but I think I'm going to do it. Not because I've always dreamed of being an author, or because I think my life would make a good story—quite the opposite, actually. Noah thinks I can create something beautiful, but my life isn't beautiful, Ana . . . which is exactly what made up my mind. I don't want to write a story filled with sunshine and rainbows. I don't want to write a story about a girl in pieces who falls in love and gets magically put back together. Yes, Noah helped me. He has helped me in ways I never thought possible, and that's okay, I think. I'm still trying to wrap my head around the fact that I'm not alone anymore. But his love didn't heal *me. Only* I *can heal myself and after years of choosing to be numb, I have suddenly been overwhelmed with the wonderful urge to feel. I'm finally going to give your heart the future it deserves, Ana.*

I spent my entire life living quietly. I stayed pent up and repressed, always following the rules to avoid punishment and letting people down while keeping myself under the radar. Invisible. *But maybe that's my problem, Ana. Maybe I need to shine light on my pain, so others don't have to suffer in the shadows.*

My story is ugly and messy but it's also real. It counts, Ana, and I want to create something for all the invisibly broken people who want their stories to count too. This is my truth, and I'm finally ready to embrace it.

–Love, Maya

Suffering is hard, but healing is much harder.

You don't realize when you're living in it, but suffering is an addiction. The human body can only live in fight or flight mode for so long before that becomes your *default* mode. Our bodies are designed to keep us alive throughout any and all circumstances, so if you're trapped in a toxic environment, eventually your body will learn to adapt. All the organs and systems that work hard to make us function every day get so attuned to the chaos, that they'll ultimately start to use that pain as sustenance and ammunition to survive. So what happens when it all disappears? What happens when you take away your body's main source of fuel and energy? The answer is simple: it will start to decompose and subsequently go into withdrawal.

During the first wave, I slept. I slept all day and night. I couldn't *stop* sleeping. Noah had to call the hospital and get me a medical leave of absence because I simply could not stay awake. He helped me to and from the bathroom when I needed it because my body was too exhausted to stand up straight. He made me three meals a day in bed so I wouldn't die of malnourishment. When I could barely keep my eyes open, or move my lips, he would gently nudge the spoon into my mouth. When I was too drowsy to remember how to work my jaw, he would patiently walk me through it. It was humiliating, and truly terrible . . .

Or so I thought because then the second wave hit, and my body completely shut down. Once it realized it wasn't getting what it craved, it decided to just stop working. The connection between my brain and the rest of my organs seemed to get deactivated and I couldn't operate anymore. I couldn't walk. I couldn't eat. My temperature was too high, but then sometimes it was too low. My muscles were shaking, my bones were quivering and it *hurt*. My digestive system could no longer figure out how to absorb my food, so everything that went in came hurtling out within seconds. My nervous system was on the fritz—constantly sending my cells a whirlpool of contradicting signals. Everything hurt, everything ached, my essence was throbbing as it desperately tried to cling onto the fractured girl I was trying to let go of—

"Make it stop," I begged. "Please, make it stop. I need it to stop, Noah, I need everything to stop, *please*."

"Shh," he soothed. I couldn't see him and I couldn't feel him, but I knew he was there. "Your body is just trying to resurface everything you spent your whole life repressing. I know it hurts, but this is the *only* way. You have to let yourself feel your pain. You have to let yourself acknowledge how much it affected you. You have to validate all your experiences so your body can feel safe being *you*, instead of this person you conditioned yourself into believing you needed to be. Let it out, Maya. Grieve. Cry. *Scream*."

So I did. I opened up the latch and let the memories surge through my numbed mind, igniting all my senses on fire. I accepted each ripple with open arms and succumbed to every ounce of the wretched misery I was holding back.

Wave three was when the night terrors started. I kept having this recurring dream where I was tied to my bed, or glued to the floor of the shower, or trapped under the seatbelt in a car. I was always alone, but I could still feel *him* everywhere. He was mingled in the air surrounding me, trying to suffocate me with his invisible hands. But then I would have a moment where I knew I was dreaming, and I would feel relieved . . . until I remembered I had once lived through each of these nightmares, and I would wake up to the sound of my ear-splitting shrieks.

It was unbearable. The whole thing. Every second worse than the last. How could something that was supposed to be good for me, cause me so much distress? I was so, *so* tempted to call it on this attempt to heal . . . but I didn't, because throughout all the sleep, and pain, and terrorizing nightmares, there was one thing holding me back. There was one thing that I knew for sure was *real*, and it was the only thing keeping me together. It wasn't anything big or extravagant—strong arms wrapping around me tightly, and enveloping me in a blanket of warmth and safety . . . soft lips brushing against my shoulder or my collarbone . . . smooth fingers stroking my face and my neck gently . . . or even just the constant whispered *I love you's* in my ear . . . they were simple but so powerful.

Noah never tried to intervene. He never tried to tell me it was going to be okay. He was just *there*. He was always with me—giving me enough space to mend, but still near enough so I could reach out to him if I wanted to. And every time he could see in my eyes that I was silently struggling to hold on, he would lean in close and ask me one simple question.

"What do you need, Maya?"

And I would tell him, and then that was the end of it.

Eventually, the final wave hit, but it just happened to be the worst one. It was the wave when I suddenly woke up and realized how much time had passed. How many years I had wasted stuck in a bubble of despair and self-hatred, and then the sharp acceptance that I could never get those years *back*. I could never reclaim that time and do something worthwhile with it. I wasn't just waking up; I was getting reborn. And along with that rebirth, I was forced to mourn the girl I used to know and try to figure out who I wanted to grow into. I did myself dirty by convincing myself that the key to my happiness was to just move out of my house . . . because no matter how far I ran, I could never escape from the chaos that would forever be engraved in my mind until I finally decided to do something about it. I used to think fight or flight were my only two options, but there was a third *F* people failed to mention. You could choose to fight, and you could choose to flee, but you could also choose to *feel*.

It may have been the final wave of the tsunami, but the ocean never stops crashing against the shore. The sand just has to learn how to live with it.

four months later

"Hey, how was the meeting?" Noah asks as soon as I step through the door.

"It was fine." He gives me a look. "It was *good*. She liked my revisions, but she's still on me about the ending."

"Why doesn't she like it?"

"She thinks it's too . . . abrupt. Unfinished." I sigh and shake my head. "She wants it to be bigger and brighter—you know, the typical happily ever after bullshit."

"How dare she suggest such a *horrific* thing."

"I know, right? As if a girl falling for her heart donors brother isn't already a colossal fucking cliché in itself," I say with a chuckle.

He's quiet, so I glance at him. "What?"

"That's not how I see it. I mean, it's the truth—technically—but that's not how I see it."

"How do you see it then?"

He stares at me with soft eyes. "I am just a boy, and you are just a girl, and we fell in love over several cups of free coffee."

I laugh. "The free coffee was the only reason I kept coming back."

"Really? Because you never once left without fighting to pay."

"Yeah, but only because I like to be difficult."

"My favourite thing about you." He walks up to me, stroking my cheek gently. "It's *your* book, Maya. *Your* story. If you change something it's only because you want to change it, okay?" I nod and kiss him chastely. "I'm going to go help with the evening rush. Let me know if you need anything."

I take a look around for a moment and admire my handiwork over the last months. The second I came home from work or therapy or a book meeting, I would quickly change into sweats and spend the rest of my day in here. I didn't stress too much about having a huge selection of books and organizing them all into the perfect category. The most important thing for me is to create a comfortable and welcoming environment that feels like home. I don't want this to be a place where people just come in to pick out a book and leave. I have cozy chairs set up near the windows, and large pillows in the corner where people can lie down and read. I also put a hammock chair in the bookstore as well, swinging lightly from the ceiling, which is easily my favorite thing in here.

Anytime I'm not working on the bookstore, I'm writing. It was hard at first, getting sucked back into my past. I had pushed away so many terrible moments, and reading my letters was like getting dragged through hell. I forced myself to relive everything I fought so hard to forget, and somewhere between now and then, my heartache turned into ink on paper, my unspoken thoughts turned into chapters, and the girl I was always meant to become blossomed through the pages. When I look in the mirror these days, my perspective has shifted. Where I used to see weakness, I now see strength. Where I used to see damage, I now see resilience. Where I used to see cowardice, I now see bravery.

And whoever I used to be . . . that *before* girl I could never seem to remember . . . I know she's proud of who I'm slowly turning into. Keeping everything inside gave it power over me, but when I finally let it all out . . . when I finally gave my pain purpose . . . I was free.

Because this is the thing about pain—you can't run away from it, and you can't hide from it either. It will get felt whether you want it to or not, and time doesn't make it hurt any less, so would you rather feel it *now*, or would you rather have already felt it *then*? It seems impossible when you're in the middle of it, but if you just let it run its course, the pain will stop being the center of your universe and slowly fade into a distant memory.

Despite how it seems, my book deal *isn't* my consolation prize for everything I went through. I was so obsessed with this idea that in order to overcome my tribulations, I needed to get something out of it. I truly believed that success had to be loud, with some kind of physical trophy as proof of your triumph, and why would I have believed otherwise when that's what I was taught? When you succeeded at school, you were gifted a diploma and a graduation ceremony. When you succeeded at love, you were gifted a diamond ring and a wedding. When you succeeded at creating life, you were gifted a child and a family. And then, at the very end, when you succeeded at living a full existence, you were gifted a coffin and a funeral. But I think the successes that matter the most aren't celebrated with a medal or a roaring commemoration. I think the successes that are quiet and invisible to everyone but you are the most significant and one of a kind.

I spent my entire life wondering why Mikhail couldn't love me, but sometimes there is no reason why bad things happen to us. Sometimes things just *happen* without a heartfelt and meaningful lesson in the end to tie it all together. They can't be fixed or redeemed. They are terrible and heartbreaking and unfortunately, they are also life. I was so convinced that I needed closure to move on, but you don't get closure from the people who hurt you. You get closure from yourself when you finally realize and accept that you never deserved any of it. The last twenty-five years will always be a nightmare I will never forget, but a nightmare I eventually woke up from. And at the end of the day, it doesn't matter if he had a reason because there is *no* reason that can justify the way Mikhail treated me. I took that empty space in my heart waiting to be filled with his love and filled it with my own love instead.

Five years ago I was in so much pain that I decided to kill myself, but it wasn't because I wanted to die. If I truly wanted to die, then I wouldn't have waited for the anniversary of my accident—I would have just done it. No, I wanted that *feeling* to die. That crushing feeling of hopelessness I carried with me at all times. An extra limb that no one else could see except for me. But you can't kill feelings. It wasn't something I could hold in my hand and squeeze to death. It didn't have an extension cord that I could unplug and watch as it slowly lost its life. So I decided to kill its host instead. I decided to kill the thing that was providing my unwanted parasite residence and nourishment, which was . . . me. But just like so many things, I had it all wrong. I didn't need to kill that feeling. I just needed to *heal* it until it transformed into a new feeling.

Hope.

It's funny, though. God said that He would never put me through more than what I could handle, and I was so determined to prove Him wrong. But here I am, setting up my bookstore with the love of my life and I'm . . . fine. Not perfect. Not shiny, polished, or new. Just *fine*. Excellent, in fact. Maybe even top-notch and exceptionally fucking splendid.

The sound of the bell announcing someone's arrival pulls me out of my reverie, and I quickly turn to see who it is.

"Hey," a young girl greets me. "Are you open?"

"Um, not quite," I say apologetically. "It's okay, though. You can come in if you want. I'm pretty much done."

She hesitates for a moment before coming in. "Wow, it looks great in here."

"Thank you," I reply, my heart swelling. Until now, I'd never really felt proud of anything I had ever done. "Are you looking for something in particular?"

She shrugs. "Not really. I'm not a reader, but I'm kind of looking for a new hobby."

"Reading is definitely a trend right now," I chuckle. "I have a shelf dedicated to books that will hook you into reading by the very first line."

"What are these for?" she asks, pointing to the baskets of sticky notes I placed all around the store.

"They're for annotating. I couldn't always afford to buy new books, so I wanted to give people the option of checking them out instead of purchasing them. I was thinking each person that checked it out could leave some annotations before returning it, so everyone can read each other's thoughts and opinions. Kind of like a never-ending book club."

"That sound really cool," she agrees, taking one of the packs.

"My boyfriend inspired the idea," I say, smiling. "I was never one to annotate, but he let me pick out a bunch of books for him to read on our first date. One day he handed me a stack of books that were filled with little notes, and scribbles."

"That's so sweet."

"*He's* so sweet," I correct her.

"Maya?" Noah says from behind me.

"Speak of the devil," I say, turning to face him. "Noah, this is our very first customer."

He smiles at her before meeting my gaze again. "There's someone here for you. In the café."

"Who?"

"Why don't you just go and see. I'll finish up in here with her."

I stare at him for a moment, the tone of his voice worrying me. I head through the door without another word but freeze in my tracks when I see who he's talking about.

My mother.

We haven't spoken since the day I left. I keep wanting to text or call her, just to see how she's doing . . . but I assumed that she'd disowned me, just like my father had declared. Despite everything that happened, I never stop wondering how she is, or if she's okay. I still get hit with guilt whenever she crosses my mind—not because I made the wrong decision, but because the right decision for me hurt *her*. The only thing that gives me a sliver of reassurance is the money that gets withdrawn from my account every week. At least I know they're accepting my help, but . . . I still miss her. I always miss her.

I walk over to her table slowly and pull out a chair. I inspect her face carefully, checking for any signs of harm, but find nothing. She just looks tired. And sad.

"How did you know where I was?" I ask quietly. I never told her the name of Noah's café.

"He called me."

"*Noah* called you?" I ask, surprised.

She nods. "He said you missed me. He said you couldn't be happy until you knew that I was okay."

I look at the glass wall separating the café and the

bookstore and see Noah staring at us, his expression unreadable. I never talked about my mom since leaving, but he still knew how I was feeling anyway.

"How's Baba?"

"He's good. He wanted to come but——" I scoff, and she gives me a look. "He didn't mean what he said. You know how he is, he's ashamed. He feels bad that he couldn't do better for us. Do you think he likes that you had to put off school to help us pay the bills?"

"He has an interesting way of showing it," I mutter.

"He loves you, Maya, and one day he'll learn to be okay with your decision."

Her voice sounds broken, and her shoulders slump as she looks down at the table.

"I'm sorry, Mama," I whisper.

"It's okay," she says, taking my hand into both of hers. "I'm not upset with you."

Relief wells up in my eyes. "Really?"

She nods and stares at me regretfully. "Everything you said about Mikhail . . . was that true?"

I want to say no. I want to save her from the hurt I know will come with my answer.

"Don't lie to me."

"Yes. It's all true."

The crack through her heart snaps sharply against my ear drums.

"I'm sorry," I repeat, but she shakes her head.

"You have nothing to apologize for. I always knew he could get irrationally angry sometimes, but I never . . ."

"You saw what he did to me that day, before I called the police," I remind her. "And then again in my bedroom before you kicked him out. Did you really think *that* was the first time he ever laid his hands on me?"

"I didn't want to think about it," she says. "When I saw him strangling you—" her voice breaks—"it was terrifying. But then after you ran downstairs, he stared at me and he looked so confused and scared. It was like he didn't know what he was doing."

"He always was a good actor. And even if he *wasn't* acting, it's still not an excuse."

"Not an excuse," she agrees. "But Maya, you have to understand, he's my *son*. I didn't know what to do . . . of course I hated the way he treated you and the way he treated all of us, but it wasn't *all* the time. He wasn't bad all the time. It hurt me to see how much he affected you, but how could I send him away? How could I kick him onto the streets, when I knew he didn't have the means to take care of himself? I'm his *mother*—"

"You're my mother too," I reply, slipping my hand out from under hers. "You're my mother too, yet you chose *him*. You chose him every single time."

"Are you forgetting that I kicked him out anyway? I kicked out my *own* son—"

"And then you invited him back *in*. He has you guys wrapped around his finger, Mama. He hasn't changed at all, but you fell for it anyway."

"I'm sorry. I know I didn't do a good job with you," she admits. "You were just so . . . quiet. You never spoke up, and you never complained. I guess it was easy for me to sweep things under the rug because you never put up a fight."

"I only did that because I was trying to keep the peace. I saw how much you guys struggled with money and with *him*.

I didn't want to add anything more on top of that."

"I know," she sighs. "Baba and I . . . we tried our best."

And that's the end of it. There's nothing more to discuss because it all comes down to this truth. When you spend your whole life thinking one way, it gets to a certain point where you can't *un*-think it anymore. She raised me with the same rules and values that her parents raised her with it, and the cycle just continues from there.

As a child, you look at your parents like the masters of the universe. The *all*-knowing. The very *top* of the pedestal. You assume they hold the universal key to knowledge and can do no wrong. But the older you get, the more you start to realize that was never the case. You start to notice their mistakes— big *and* small—and you start to notice the mistakes they passed on to you. I can't fight what's normal for my parents, but I can create my own normal.

And even if they had decided to get help all those years ago, the type of mental assistance Mikhail needed just wasn't affordable. It just wasn't *accessible* to everyone, including us. And, knowing Mikhail, he never would have gone through with it anyway. You can't help someone who doesn't believe they need help. So no, I don't blame my mother. I don't blame my parents. They did their best with the knowledge they were given and that's that.

"It's okay, I forgive you. If not for you, then for *myself*. Holding all this inside was tearing me apart."

She gives me a small smile and turns her head away from me. I follow her gaze and see her staring at Noah, who is still staring at *us*. "So, tell me about him."

I can't help the huge smile that lights up my face. "He's my favorite person in the entire world."

"Do you love him?"

"I do," I reply softly. "I love him a *lot*."

"But he . . . he's the one who hit you. We realized as soon as you two left——"

"That accident was *not* his fault," I interrupt firmly.

She drops it. "You look different, Maya. You look . . . happy."

"It's been hard, but I'm going to be okay." I hesitate for a moment. "Do you want to meet him? *Officially*, I mean."

She nods, and I wave at him. He immediately stops what he's doing and comes over to us.

"Mama, this is Noah . . . my boyfriend," I say when he takes a seat beside me. He smiles at her and shakes her hand gently. I know how he feels about my parents, but he's willing to move past it, which I appreciate wholeheartedly. They spend the rest of the night getting to know each other, and I know things between us are going to be all right.

I hug my mother tightly in the doorway before she leaves, and hand her the plate of pastries Noah made for her.

"We're going on a trip this weekend, but maybe when I come back . . . we can have coffee again?"

She nods and smiles at me sadly. I know she's hoping I would have agreed to come home with her, but as much as I'd do anything for my mother, the best thing for our relationship is to love her from a distance.

I always believed our lives were split into two parts. Your life with your first family—the one you're born into—and your life with your second family—the family you *create* for yourself. The universe would then take the burdens written for you and spread them out equally within the two, to keep a balance between the pain and the ease. It was silly, and I had no proof to back up this belief, but it made me feel better to think that my second life might be easier.

For my mother's sake, I hope it's true. I hope her life before us was amazing. I hope she had a childhood filled with laughter, smiles, and *love*. I hope she was able to fulfill all her dreams before she got entirely consumed by the family she created. I hope her first life was filled with so much joy and happiness that maybe, just *maybe*, it could level out all the pain Mikhail and I had brought into her soul. But more than that, I hope my absence brings her some solitude. As much as it hurts to admit, it's clear that I was the source of all my brother's inexcusable anger. Now that I'm gone, maybe she can have the family dynamic she always wished for. Maybe she can finally try to find some peace in all the chaos, just like I am.

I wait until she safely drives away before locking the door, and I feel Noah wrap his arms around me from behind.

"Are you sure you're not mad?" he asks.

I turn around in his arms and look up at him. "I'm not," I assure him. "But why didn't you just *ask* me."

"I didn't think you would be able to call her yourself, but I knew you needed to see her."

I lean my head against his chest. "Thank you."

He nods and I feel his breath in my ear. "Anti *qalbi, waruhi, wahayati*."

I usually laugh whenever Noah tries to speak Arabic, but I'm not laughing right now. Right now I'm trying to keep myself from trembling into pieces.

"What did you just say?"

"You don't know?" he murmurs. I can feel the saliva from his lips wetting my skin.

"*I* know what you said," I reply shakily. "But do *you* know what you said?"

He chuckles and places a kiss on my temple. "You are my heart," he places a kiss on both of my closed eyelids, "soul," he places a kiss on the tip of my nose, "and life."

I hesitate for a second before speaking. "There's something else she wants me to add to my book."

"What?" He stares at me, waiting. "You're *blushing*, Maya. Why are you blushing?" He continues to stare before the realization hits. "*Oh*."

"Yeah."

"Well . . . are you? Going to add *that*?"

"I'm not sure yet. I've only ever written what I *know*, Noah."

His tongue is on my skin now and I can't feel my body anymore. All I can feel is heat as he continues to trail his lips along my jaw and down my neck.

"What are you doing?" I ask breathlessly, already getting intoxicated by his intimacy.

"Fueling your imagination," he whispers, biting my ear lobe gently.

I chuckle, my heartbeat erratic. "That's not the only reason. You know I'm not the biggest fan of *smut* in books."

"Really? Because . . . most of the ones you made me read were *filled*——"

"I mean *writing* it," I interrupt, my face heating up, and he laughs. "I'm not comfortable writing it."

"It's okay to get out of your comfort zone once in a while," he reminds me, sliding his fingers under my shirt and stroking my lower back. "Besides, you don't have to give them the whole slice of cake . . ." he mumbles against my neck. "Just some sprinkles here and there, to keep them satisfied." His lips are on my shoulder now, carefully grazing my skin with his teeth. "You can just, you know, insert fades into black . . ."

I can't comprehend what he's saying through the intense mush of lust that's overcome my brain. He continues to trail his lips lower, and my back arches into his body. I lift my fingers into his soft hair and scrape my nails against his scalp. He moans into my skin, and his lips move faster . . .

. . . insert fades into black.

~

"Are you ever going to tell me why you drove us to the middle of nowhere?"

"You'll see soon enough," he assures me.

"Are you sure you know where you're going?"

"Do you trust me?"

"With *directions*? No, not really."

He laughs, poking me playfully in my side. "I got us lost *one* time, Maya."

We continue down through the trees silently for a moment, our hands swinging between us. "I love the forest vibes. The only thing left is for a certain vampire to step out of the shadows, and then this will officially be the best day."

"If you told me ten months ago that I would be extremely jealous of a fictional character, I wouldn't have believed you."

"If you told me ten months ago that a real-life man would *replace* a fictional character for first place in my heart, I wouldn't have believed you."

He chuckles. "I still can't believe you never dated anyone before me."

"I wasn't looking," I reply. "I never . . . I always wanted to be *loved*, but I was never going to go looking for it. If it was meant to happen, then it would just . . . happen. I wasn't going to agonize over it, you know? I watched my friends fixate on finding someone, and then get heartbroken a million times so I told myself that I would stay single until it felt easy and simple . . . like breathing. I never wanted to be put in a position where I had to teach someone how to treat me, *especially* after Mikhail." I tighten my hand around his. "But at the same time, I didn't really want anyone. Not yet, anyway. Not until I had completely moved on from my past, which seemed impossible, so I guess I kind of just accepted it."

"So . . . you never wanted to fall in love with me?"

"Not at first," I answer truthfully. "Falling in love with you wasn't a choice I made. I didn't even notice it happening because it felt so soft, and safe, and *real* . . . just like you." I look up at him affectionately. "So no, I never wanted to fall in love with you, but I can never go back to a time without it. I don't *want* to go back. I can't imagine not knowing how it feels to be loved by you, Noah."

"And I, you," he whispers, letting go of my hand and wrapping his arm around my shoulders, pulling me against his body.

"We're here," he announces after a few minutes, pushing back some branches and moss and leading me into an empty clearing. It's cloudy out today, the mountains and trees shielding me from the sun. The wind is blowing calmly through the fields of green grass we've stepped into, and the trees thin out, leaving an opening at the very end that overlooks the water.

"The view is so pretty," I say quietly, not wanting my voice to disturb the calm bubble of serenity that encircles us.

"I'm glad you think so."

"How did you find this place?"

"I bought it."

I look at him in shock. "You . . . *bought* this land. Why?"

We reach the end of the clearing, so he stops and faces me, smiling tenderly. "I was thinking of building a house."

"Oh," I reply in surprise. "This would be a beautiful place for a house. Real estate is a great market to get into right now."

"Maya," he laughs. "I don't want to build a house so I can *sell* it."

"Okay . . . ?"

"I was actually thinking that a farm would look perfect right over there," he says, pointing to a spot in front of us.

A farm?

"And then over here," he says, walking toward the place he's referring to, "would be a great place for a garden, don't you think?"

I nod slowly, still not sure what he's getting at.

"Maybe you can start with planting strawberries," he suggests after a moment. "It's my favorite kind of *jam*."

I freeze.

"Nothing but reading, and making my own jam."

"Is this how you always imagined your happy place, Maya?" he whispers.

I meet his gaze, and he's staring at me intensely, waiting for me to understand. But he doesn't need to wait anymore because it's all clear now. He wants to build me the future I described to him. He wants to give me my happily ever after, but what he doesn't realize is that I already got it. My happily ever after was never the house, and the farm, and the garden, and the beautiful boy to share it with. That wasn't what would give me clarity and freedom. It was choosing to move on.

People think healing comes naturally. A papercut that closes up on its own after a few days—red, to white, to skin—without any effort from you. Emotions don't work like that. A wounded mind can't heal itself. It's a choice. You had to choose to heal. You had to choose to be better. You had to choose to be happy, and that choice, as difficult as it was, is my happily ever after that opened the doors to an infinite number of happily ever afters waiting to come.

"Not quite," I reply, and his smile falls. "I was always alone in my happy place . . . but I'd prefer *this* one, with you."

His smile quickly comes back to life, and he pulls me into his arms in a bone-crushing hug. "Thank you for saying yes. I thought I was going to have to beg on my knees for *hours*."

I chuckle into his chest. "I wouldn't mind seeing you beg on your knees."

He leans back slightly. "This house wasn't the only reason I was going to be on my knees today."

"What do you mean?"

He cradles my face in between his warm hands. "Maya?" he asks quietly.

"Yes?"

"*Habibti?*"

"Yes?" I laugh.

"What are you, right now? On a scale from one to ten?"

I think about his question for a second, vividly remembering the first time he asked me that. I snapped back at him instead of answering, but it was only because I was so extremely *low*. Now, though . . . it's crazy how a glimpse of your future can make up for a lifetime of your past. Everything that I had gone through, everything that I had to overcome, it all led up to this moment. My life suddenly makes sense.

401

"Ten, Noah. I've only ever felt true happiness when I'm with you."

"Good," he replies, releasing my face, and nervously crouches down on one knee.

"Noah?" I ask breathlessly. "What are you doing?"

He doesn't respond. Instead, he slides his hand into his pocket and pulls out a small black box.

"Maya Ibrahim," he starts, looking up at me, but then pauses. His lips are parted and the words are on his tongue, but he doesn't speak them. He just stares at me, pure love and devotion glistening tears in his eyes and I *know*. I know what he's saying even though he isn't talking and I hope my eyes are telling him the exact same things back.

"Sorry," he says, clearing his throat after many minutes. "I prepared a million different ways to express myself but it doesn't matter because they all mean the same thing . . . I love you, Maya. I sincerely and wholeheartedly *love* you, and I want to spend the rest of my life with you, right here, watching you read, write and make jam, in our peaceful and soft forever."

He flips open the box, revealing a ring. It's a thin gold band, encrusted with small diamonds. In the center, there's an oval-shaped sapphire that's a radiant spring green, with a hint of mint and chartreuse. It isn't loud, vibrant or extravagant, but instead, it's simple, dainty and *exactly* what I would have picked out for myself.

"Noah," I whisper, my heart feeling like it's about to burst with all of the overwhelming emotions building up inside me. "It's so pretty."

"Not prettier than you. Will you marry me, Maya?

I give him a watery smirk. "Are you sure you're not just

proposing so we can have sex?"

He shakes his head and laughs through his tears. "Maybe just a little bit."

"Okay, settle down," I tease, blushing.

"For you?" he vows. "For you, I'll do anything."

"Promise?"

"*Pinky* promise, Maya."

The flood of passion and sentiment is still crashing against my chest, leaving me speechless and breathless. I can't bring myself to open my mouth to speak, so I nod and extend my hand toward him with tears streaming down my face, and playfully tap his nose. He gives me that lopsided smile in response and slips off my glove before lifting the ring to my finger, but as soon as the cold gold touches my skin, something happens. It's like a bucket of ice water got dunked over me, and the explosive sensation in my heart suddenly turns into searing *pain*.

I gasp and yank my hand away, clutching at my chest. I'm expecting to find a knife or a gunshot wound, but there's nothing there.

"Maya?" Noah stands up immediately, losing the ring in the grass beneath our feet. "What's wrong?"

I meet his horrified gaze, but I still can't speak. All I can feel is pain—

"*Maya.*"

I can see it this time. Death. Its shadow is in front of me, arms wide and welcoming, and I can feel myself drifting to it effortlessly—

"*Maya, wake up.*"

I can hear Noah somewhere, his voice a million miles away, in another dimension.

"Baby, please. Please wake up. Please come back to me."

He sounds completely shattered. I want to comfort him, but I can't see him. I can't move. A sob cracks through the tunnel separating us and hits me full force.

"Please, Maya, I need more time. I need more time to love you. Please don't leave me, baby, please, please, please."

They say your life flashes before your eyes when you're dying, but the images I'm suddenly seeing aren't from my past. The blurry glimpses are ones I have never seen before—Noah slipping the ring on my finger, and me, Maya, smiling and laughing. He's lifting me up in the air, twirling us in circles before dropping to his knees, laying us back in the grass, lips moving urgently with mine, happy tears mingling together on our tongues—

"Just give me one more minute. Just let me look into your eyes for one more minute. Just come back to life for one more minute."

I'm in a white dress, a makeshift flower bouquet of all my favorite book quotes in my hands, and I'm walking toward Noah. There are other people there, but I can't tell for sure because all I can see is *him*, my favorite beautiful boy standing at the other end of the isle, one blue eye, one green eye, messy hair, black tux, high-top sneakers identical to the ones on my feet—

"Maya, please."

We're in a cabin. I don't know where, or how, or when. All I see is two moving bodies pressed together on a blanket in front of a roaring fire, surrounded by candles and light music that you can't hear over the sensual moans and heavy breaths of newlyweds making love for the first time—

"Maya."

The vast field of land is back except this time there's a

house with a green kitchen and a library with a reading nook and high windows. The sun is setting on the horizon, Noah is watering the plants, and I'm feeding the chickens while holding hands with a little, curly-haired girl with different colored eyes—

"It's okay, Maya."

I'm in a bookstore. *My* bookstore. Noah and I's bookstore, signing copies of my book, people lined up in the store, outside the store, all the way down the street—

"You can let go now."

I try to fight it. I try to cling on to the future that could've been. The future that will never happen. It seems cruel that when I so desperately wanted to die last December I couldn't bring myself to do it, and now when I so desperately want to live I can't bring myself to do it. I can't bring myself to stop that thing tearing through my heart. My borrowed, fractured, and imperfect *heart.* But if I learned anything in life, it's that it's cruel. So you need to take those brief flashes, and glimpses, and blurry images of joy and cherish them because one day, you'll be in the middle of something amazing and out of the blue, without any warning and without making any sense, you'll be gone and everything will become a memory. You can't guarantee a life filled with happiness—that's something you have to work for—but you can guarantee a life that will eventually come to an end—

"I love you, Maya."

This is my end.

EPILOGUE

Dear Maya,

Most people like to categorize their life into two stages: the before stage and the after stage. They usually do this when a life-changing event occurs. Something so groundbreaking and distinguished that it forces them to split their world in half. The problem for me was that too many earth-shattering things happened and I wasn't able to find a clear, and prominent line that separated my existence. What changed my life the most—before my mom died and after my mom died? Before I got adopted and after I got adopted? Before that car crash and after that car crash?

I couldn't decide . . . until I met you, and everything changed. I met you, and my decision was clear as day. I met you, Maya, and I fell in love with you so hard and so passionately that it shook the ground beneath my feet, and I couldn't go back even if I wanted to. I met you, and I knew in that moment that my life would forever be defined into before you, and after you.

And then you died.

I knew the moment it happened. I literally felt your heart, Ana's heart, the heart that lived in the two most important people I've ever had the pleasure of loving just stop beating.

I thought I knew death. I thought I understood death. I thought I experienced it enough times to be immune to the pain. I told you to let go because that's what you needed . . . but that's not what I needed, Maya.

They said you had severe cardiac allograft vasculopathy. They said it's the most common cause of death in heart transplant patients, especially within the first ten years. They said you were lucky. Most heart transplant patients, particularly in an emergency case like yours, don't live that long. Only I know that you weren't living for ten years, you were surviving. Your heart was too big and too pure for this world, but it just wasn't strong enough. I wish my love was enough to save you, but it wasn't. I failed you, baby, and I'm so sorry.

Your bookstore was a success. It's filled with people every day—some friends, some acquaintances, some strangers—and they all get together in the safe space you created and bond over books. But most importantly, your novel was a success. They love it, Maya. Everybody fucking loves it, most of all me. I read it every day. I whisper your words on my tongue and let them simmer around in my mind until they're engraved deep into my memory. I take all your pain, and all your love, and all your strength and I use it to reignite my heart so I can get through the days that are always so devastatingly long. It doesn't matter how many times I read it, because the ending is always the same. You were never too broken for me, Maya. No matter how many different endings you imagined for yourself, it will always end with me falling hopelessly and endlessly in love with you.

Every cent that your book makes goes to your parents. I know you well enough to know that even though you're up there, you're still worried about the people you left behind down here. You took care of your parents, and they're going to be okay. The only person you need to take care of now is you.

I finished building your house, just like I promised. I still wanted to create your happy place for you. I also did it for myself, so I could feel like I still had a piece of you left, but it doesn't feel like home without you in it. You were my favorite place, Maya. You were my home, and I still can't believe you're fucking gone.

I didn't realize how much you had changed me, until you were snatched away. Everything I was before you got tainted with your presence and the man who thought he knew how to exist without you is gone.

I.I.E

You liked iced coffee. I didn't, but for you, I love it. I love how the cold and artificially sweetened liquid feels in my body.

You liked to read. I didn't, but for you, I love it. I love every single cheesy and romantic word ever printed on paper.

You liked the snow. I liked the sun, but for you, I despise the rays of yellow light that burn my skin every day. For you, I cherish every single flurry that falls from the sky.

Seven billion people, Maya. Seven billion fucking people in this world, and I had to fall in love with the one heart that couldn't love me forever. Somehow I still see you everywhere. I hear your voice in my ear. I feel you in my arms when I go to sleep. My lips memorized the way your mouth felt against mine. Sometimes my body gets so entranced by your presence living within me, that it will start to sway back and forth in the empty streets when it snows, but then I blink and realize that I'm dancing with the wind, and not with you.

I miss touching you. I miss the way my body tingled the first time you brushed your finger against my skin. I miss the way my heart thumped excitedly in my chest the first time I saw your beautiful and sad face. I miss the way you used to look up at me through your long lashes, warm brown eyes shining brightly into mine. I miss the way my ears sang with delight the first time you said I love you. I miss the way it felt to trust you with everything that I was and to be trusted with everything that you were. I miss loving you, baby. I miss you, I miss you, I miss you.

We met by chance. Two darts getting thrown in opposite directions but somehow still landing at the same target. I think I always knew that I was going to lose you, Maya. I think I always knew that we wouldn't get forever. There was this voice in my head telling me that I needed to love you a little harder, and hug you a little tighter, and stare into your eyes a little longer. You told me once that I couldn't try to fix you without getting broken in the process, and you were right. But loving you for the short amount of time we had is worth every single second of pain. I hope you are at peace now, Maya, in a small house in paradise with chickens and two small cats.

You were my soulmate in this life, and you will be in every life that comes after. I'll meet you on the other side my love, but until then . . . I'll see you when I wake up at sunrise to say good morning, and then again as the sun sets when you say goodnight. Pinky Promise.

—Forever, your Noah

AUTHORS NOTE

to my readers,

thank you for taking the time to read my novel. i wrote this book for myself, but i also wrote it for you. the sister who grew up believing that family is only blood. the daughter who bases all her self-worth on her parent's approval. the girl who sincerely thinks she can't be loved.

if you relate to maya in any way, i'm sorry. i'm sorry they hurt you. i'm sorry you're in pain. i'm sorry no one believes you. i'm sorry you feel like your story doesn't count because it's not the *right* kind of trauma, but they're wrong. they, he, she, it, *society* is wrong. it does count. your pain is valid and it needs to be felt. stop waiting for their apology. stop waiting for them to love you in order for you to start loving yourself. stop waiting for tomorrow, next month, next year, after you move out, after you graduate, after you meet someone—do it *now*. life is short and tomorrow isn't promised, so take control and heal. let's heal together.

–love, i.i.e

p.s. noah has a story too . . . *before* he met maya, and *after* he met maya. stay tuned ;)

Made in the USA
Las Vegas, NV
05 June 2024

90662495R10243